PRAISE FOR JOSEPH

"Flynn is an excellent storyteller." — *Booklist*

"Flynn propels his plot with potent but flexible force."
— *Publishers Weekly*

Digger
"A mystery cloaked as cleverly as (and perhaps better than)
any John Grisham work." — *Denver Post*

"Surefooted, suspenseful and in its breathless final moments
unexpectedly heartbreaking." — *Booklist*

"An exciting, gritty, emotional page-turner."
— Robert K. Tannenbaum
New York Times Bestselling Author of *True Justice*

The Next President
"The Next President bears favorable comparison to such
classics as *The Best Man, Advise and Consent* and
The Manchurian Candidate."
— *Booklist*

"A thriller fast enough to read in one sitting."
— *Rocky Mountain News*

The President's Henchman
"Marvelously entertaining." — *ForeWord Magazine*

ALSO BY JOSEPH FLYNN

Watch for the fourth Jim McGill Novel
The Last Ballot Cast
Coming Summer 2012

The K Street Killer

A Jim McGill Novel
by
Joseph Flynn

Stray Dog Press, Inc.
Springfield, IL
2011

Published by Stray Dog Press, Inc.
Springfield, IL 62704, U.S.A.

Originally published as an eBook, November, 2011
First Stray Dog Press, Inc. Printing, December, 2011
Copyright © Stray Dog Press, Inc., 2011
All rights reserved

Visit the author's web site: *www.josephflynn.com*

Flynn, Joseph
    The K Street Killer / Joseph Flynn
    475 p.
    ISBN 978-0-9837975-3-1

Printed in the United States of America

PUBLISHER'S NOTE
This is a work of fiction. Names, characters, places, and incidents are either the
product of the author's imagination or are used fictitiously; any resemblance to
actual persons, living or dead, events, or locales is entirely coincidental.

Book design by Aha! Designs

DEDICATION

For Catherine

The K Street Killer
Major Characters

James J. (Jim) McGill, Second husband of President Patricia Darden Grant, aka The President's Henchman
Patricia Darden Grant, President of the United States, former Congresswoman, wife of James J. McGill, widow of Andrew Hudson Grant
Margaret "Sweetie" Sweeney, Jim McGill's investigative partner, former police partner
Galia Mindel, President Grant's chief of staff
Celsus Crogher, Secret Service Agent in charge of White House Security Detail
Donald (Deke) Ky, Jim McGill's personal Secret Service bodyguard
Leo Levy, McGill's personal (armed) driver, former NASCAR driver
Carolyn (McGill) Enquist, first wife of Jim McGill
Lars Enquist, Carolyn's second husband
Abbie McGill (18) daughter of Jim McGill and Carolyn Enquist
Kenny McGill (14) son of Jim McGill and Carolyn Enquist
Caitie McGill (12) daughter of Jim McGill and Carolyn Enquist
Andrew Hudson Grant, President Grant's late husband, billionaire philanthropist
Clare Tracy, Jim McGill's college sweetheart
Putnam Shady, Margaret Sweeney's beau and landlord, a lobbyist
Captain Welborn Yates, Air Force OSI, President Grant's (official) personal investigator

Kira Fahey, Welborn Yates' fiancée, White House staffer

Mather Wyman, Vice President of the United States, Kira Fahey's uncle

Edwina Byington, Personal secretary to the President

Artemus Nicolaides, White House physician

Dikran "Dikki" Missirian, Landlord of McGill Investigations, Inc.

Rep. Zachary Garner (D-VA), Member of the House of Representatives, Kenny McGill's new friend

Erna Godfrey, anti-abortion activist, incarcerated murderer of Andrew Hudson Grant, wife of Rev. Burke Godfrey

Rev. Burke Godfrey, Pastor of Salvation's Path Church, husband of Erna Godfrey

Derek Geiger, Republican Speaker of the House

Harlo Geiger, Derek Geiger's wife

Brad Attles, Derek Geiger's divorce lawyer

Rockelle Bullard, homicide lieutenant, Washington Metro PD

Marvin Meeker, Metro homicide detective

Big Mike Walker, aka Beemer, Metro homicide detective

Chana Lochlan, Former reporter for WorldWide News, Jim McGill's first client as a private investigator

Sir Edbert Bickford, CEO of WorldWide News global media empire

Hugh Collier, Sir Edbert's nephew, senior VP of WorldWide News

Ellie Booker, producer for WorldWide News

Elspeth Kendry, Secret Service Special Agent, McGill's threat assessment coordinator

Roger Michaelson, U.S senator (D-OR), the President's political nemesis

Bob Merriman, Senator Michaelson's former chief of staff, candidate for Senate

Anson Merriman, Robert Merriman's brother, a high-end lobbyist

Linley Boland, Car thief

The K Street Killer

A Jim McGill Novel

PROLOGUE

Federal Correctional Complex, Terre Haute, Indiana

Erna Godfrey, sinking into unconsciousness, felt her tongue slide back and obstruct her airway. She'd learned from her husband's doctor you couldn't actually swallow your tongue. It was held in place by a muscle called the frenulum. But many a fool had drunk himself into a stupor, lain down in exactly the wrong position and woken up in hell.

It was all a matter of the muscles of the throat and tongue relaxing from intoxication and the loss of consciousness. The tongue rolled back in the mouth and blocked the throat, making breathing impossible. Most times, the act of coughing and gasping for air would be enough to rouse a person, sit her up, restore the muscle tone of the tongue enough to thrust it forward and clear the obstruction.

But if a woman went lights out good and deep the struggle for air wouldn't rouse her. That was what happened to drunkards. Not that Erna drank alcohol. She considered doing so to be sinful. Also, her jailers wouldn't have offered her a small beer, had she wanted one.

They had been considerate enough, though, to provide her with mouthwash.

They should have gone with an alcohol-free rinse.

But the federal government was known to make mistakes.

Before Erna had set out to kill Andrew Hudson Grant, she had considered the possibility she might be caught. That notion hadn't particularly scared her. She felt the chances were good any jury would include at least one person who felt exactly as she did: The lives of the unborn were sacrosanct. It was the evil of those who had been given the gift of life and refused to extend the same consideration to the unborn that had to be stopped.

Congresswoman Patricia Darden Grant had been given the chance to vote in favor of the Support of Motherhood Act and she had rejected it. Even after she'd been warned that doing so would cost the life of her husband. Having made that choice, Erna had felt obliged to make Patricia Grant pay for it.

Erna had asked herself if she was ready to sacrifice her own life for her cause. Looking at things square-on like that had set her back on her heels a bit. It had been her intent to kill a very rich, well-connected man. People like him didn't get put down without somebody paying full price for it.

That was exactly what the judge had said after the jury had fooled Erna and come back with a guilty verdict: Her penalty would be death.

She'd had the last year in her cell to think about that. Had come to accept it. Had come to embrace it. Execution would be her badge of honor, proof positive she'd held fast to her beliefs. She would be remembered. Her example would inspire others.

But the moment Erna had made peace with the idea of dying the devil put an evil thought in her mind. What if her sentence was commuted? Not that she would ever be set free. She couldn't fool herself about that. But what if the death sentence got changed to life in prison with no chance of parole?

Erna knew she wasn't strong enough to handle that. Her mother had lived to be ninety-two. If she were to do the same, she'd have another forty years left. Might as well be a million if she had to spend all that time in a jail cell. She'd go crazy.

She was not about to have that.

She was all but sure that Patricia Grant, who had gone and got herself elected president, would demand that Erna be put to death for killing Andrew Hudson Grant. Ask the executioner to make it right painful while he was at it.

But the doubt the devil had sown wouldn't let Erna be.

What if the president took it to mind that Erna would suffer more rotting away in her cell, day after day, year after year? The very thought scared Erna silly.

So she made preparations to kill herself, just in case.

Not that it would be easy to commit suicide. A death row prisoner, even one like her at least a year away from execution, was closely watched. Still, she was determined to find a way. It helped that her demeanor with the prison staff, many of them small-town Christians, was always cooperative. She followed orders without hesitation or complaint. Her serene courage in the face of death earned the respect of even the toughest guards.

Everyone made a point of not disturbing Erna when she knelt in prayer.

Anna Lee, the nurse practitioner who took care of Erna's female complaints, had bonded so closely with Erna that she had once whispered to her, "I pray for you."

To which Erna had responded, "I pray for you, too."

She didn't need to go beyond that. It was enough for Anna Lee to know that Erna thought the nurse practitioner needed her prayers for playing a part in a system that was about to take a good woman's life.

After much thought and prayer, Erna came up with a plan, and the first thing she had to do to make it work was to go on a diet. Not starve herself. The warden would never stand for that. Still, she had to get her weight down and she cut way back on what she ate. When the prison doctor asked if anything was wrong, she told him she'd lost her appetite.

"A death sentence will do that to ya, Doc," she said.

After an examination showed nothing wrong with Erna, her

explanation had to be taken at face value. Next, she cut back on the hours she allowed herself to sleep.

Insomnia was common on death row, especially as an inmate's time grew short.

On Anna Lee's next monthly visit to check up on Erna's dysmenorrhea problem, the prisoner shared her new complaint.

"I'm having trouble sleeping," Erna said.

With dark circles under her eyes and her death row jumpsuit hanging on her shrinking frame, Erna cut an increasingly pathetic figure.

Anna Lee offered her the usual over-the-counter sleep remedy.

"Honey," Erna said, "that stuff might work in your neighborhood, but it don't do much good around here. What I'd really like is some hot cocoa."

That kind of treat wasn't on the prison menu and the warden wasn't about to get accused of coddling a killer. But Erna got the look of sympathy from Anna Lee that she wanted. She squeezed the nurse practitioner's hand and lay down on her bed.

"I'll just see what I can manage on my own," Erna said

She had to wait forty-eight hours for Anna Lee to return. Just stopping by to see how Erna was doing, she said. Having continued to limit herself to four hours of sleep a night, Erna didn't look good. In fact, if she were anywhere but on death row, she likely would have been rushed to a hospital. But short of a heart attack, a stroke or spontaneous combustion, condemned prisoners left their cells only to talk with their lawyers.

Erna told Anna Lee, "I think I might be losing the will to live."

The nurse practitioner didn't think that was funny.

"You've got to get more sleep," she said.

"I'm pretty sure that's what they have planned for me."

Erna's gallows humor brought Anna Lee to the verge of tears. She took Erna's hand, and transferred a tiny object to it. Erna made sure she didn't drop it.

"Bless you," Anna Lee said as she left.

Lying down that night, Erna took a guarded look at the

capsule she'd been slipped. It didn't look big enough to knock out a gnat, but she took the fact that it was bright red to be a good sign. The vivid color had to mean it was potent, didn't it?

She fervently hoped so.

She'd fasted herself to the point where she weighed less than she had in middle school. She'd been swallowing sips of mouthwash, forcing herself to get used to the awful harshness of it. She'd deprived herself of as much sleep as she could without collapsing.

It all might have been an exercise in folly. Chances were the federal government would be only too happy to kill her. No reason to go to all the trouble she had.

But Erna couldn't shake the devil's warning.

Then the next morning the warden came to her cell and proved Satan right.

"The president has commuted your sentence," he said. "You're not going to be executed. You'll do life with no chance of parole. We'll move you as soon as a space for you in another facility is found."

That was it. He walked off without making any personal comment.

Erna decided to take her life that night, but now that the time had arrived it wasn't so easy to do. Not that night or the next. It took her a week to work up the determination. In the meanwhile, Anna Lee came by and gave her two more red capsules.

As skinny and tired as she was by then, Erna thought the three capsules would be more than enough to kill her. But that morning they'd brought her a new bottle of mouthwash — twenty-one percent alcohol — so she washed the sedatives down with that.

She lay down, so exhausted she knew she wouldn't have to wait long for the alcohol and drugs to take effect.

She felt her tongue slide back and block her airway.

She was almost there now…

A glow appeared in the darkness, growing brighter as she drew near.

Then, in all his radiant glory, Erna saw her Lord and Savior. Only he wasn't smiling.

And standing at his side was Andrew Hudson Grant.

CHAPTER 1

Monday, August 15th, K Street, Washington, DC

Three a.m., a hell of an hour to get off work, Mark Benjamin thought.

There had been times, of course, when he'd worked through the night. But he'd been in his twenties then, single and full of purpose. The purpose had been twofold: to see that his client's special interests became the law of the land and to assure that his own net worth increased by leaps and bounds.

Mark Benjamin was a K Street lobbyist, and while not yet one of the giants of his trade he was well on his way ... except for the recent, unexpected and disturbing appearance of what looked to be a conscience. For that, he blamed his friend Putnam Shady.

Putnam had been a fellow plunderer of the public purse for as long they'd known each other. Even better, Putnam was still single and Mark had been able to enjoy, vicariously, tales of his friend's adventures with the ladies. Then a woman named Margaret had moved into Putnam's basement apartment. She was having the damnedest effect on him.

Mark looked up and down the street. Never a cab when you needed one.

His car occupied a preferred slot on the premium parking level of the building behind him. But he knew it was as risky to drive tired as it was to drive drunk. He could go back upstairs and sleep on his office couch. Tonight, though, he wanted to hold his wife, engage in some pillow talk, maybe even ask her advice.

Putnam had enlisted him to take part in a plan that was breathtaking in concept. Mark, disaffected by his work in ways he hadn't even realized, had jumped at the opportunity to take part. Inevitably, though, he'd started to have second thoughts. He had made plenty of money in his years of lobbying, but fortunes far greater than his had disappeared in the blink of an eye. What if his finances went south and so did Putnam's plan?

Then where would he be?

Cutting through his existential musing and the fog of his fatigue, Mark heard footsteps off to his left. Quite close to him. He hadn't noticed anyone approaching. Had heard no roar of a car engine, no screech of tires. Certainly no violin trills of impending doom. But there in front of him was a man with a gun.

Mark's eyes went wide and he said, "What do you —"

Want, he intended to ask.

But he never got the chance.

He was shot dead on the K Street sidewalk.

By the dawn's early light of a perfect summer day, homicide detective Marvin Meeker of the Metro Police Department regarded the crime scene and rendered his expert opinion.

"Looks like Porky Pig."

His partner, Big Mike Walker, a.k.a. Beemer, shook his head.

"Unh-uh, Porky wears a bow tie."

"Does not," Meeker said.

"Does so," Beemer insisted.

The detectives turned to the two uniformed cops, the crime scene technician and the M.E. for arbitration. None of them wanted to get involved.

Beemer said, "If he don't wear a tie, he wears a jacket or

somethin.'"

Meeker asked, "You sure?"

"'Course I'm sure. Them Disney critters might walk around with their asses hangin' out but they always got something on."

The crime scene tech spoke up. "Disney doesn't do Porky."

Both detectives looked at her.

She said, "The brothers do him."

"What brothers?" Meeker asked.

"Warner Brothers."

Both detectives chuckled. Beemer said, "It was any other brothers, ol' Porky'd be a plate of ribs."

Both detectives, the crime scene tech, the uniforms and even the M.E. laughed.

That was enough to make the good-looking African-American woman down on one knee beside the body of the victim look up.

"The minstrel show about over?" she asked the detectives. "You two ready to do some police work?"

The woman stood up. Six-one in her stocking feet, her shoes added another couple of inches. She looked down on both Meeker and Beemer. She outranked them, too.

"Sure, Lou," Meeker said.

Beemer nodded.

Homicide Lieutenant Rockelle Bullard said, "Good. Now that we remember we're all law enforcement professionals, what do you think we have here?"

Meeker was about to answer when a car pulled to a stop at the curb. Nice ride, too. A Porsche Boxster all shiny and black. A guy in a suit got out and looked at the body. Gawkers weren't unfamiliar at crime scenes but not many had the nerve to stare at a dead body with a bunch of cops standing right there wondering what his interest might be.

One of the uniforms was about to get the guy's story when Rockelle held up a hand. "Tell the gentleman I'll be right with him." She turned back to her detectives. "What do we have here?"

"Dead white man," said Meeker.

"Shot in the chest," added Beemer.

"Right here on K Street."

"Third one the last three weeks."

"Every one of 'em got a little pig pin stuck on his lapel and—"

All three homicide cops saw the gawker's head snap back when he heard mention of the pig. Now Meeker and Beemer wanted to go talk to him, too. But Rockelle hadn't released them yet.

"Anything else in common?" she asked.

"All of 'em wearin' Gucci 'n' Armani," Meeker said.

"Just like this one," Beemer said.

Looking over at the gawker, all three detectives thought: Just like that one.

Turning back to the victim, Meeker said, "Means he's likely some big shot lobbyist, too."

Rockelle flipped open the bloodstained billfold she'd taken off the body, paged through it with a gloved finger, stopped when she saw a family photo. The victim, a woman and two young children. She looked over at the guy in the suit.

"You care to step over here, sir?"

The gawker approached the cops and all of them saw tears forming in his eyes.

"You know this gentleman, sir?" Rockelle inclined her head at the body.

"I do. His name's Mark Benjamin."

Meeker asked, "That pig pin, it means something to you?"

"Mark wouldn't wear it."

Rockelle Bullard asked, "Why not?"

"He was Jewish. Used to keep kosher. Then he became a vegan."

Beemer said, "Maybe he just liked the cartoons."

The guy smiled; it only made him look sadder.

"He wasn't big on cartoons."

"Did you know Mr. Benjamin well?" Rockelle asked.

"In a certain way. We were both looking to improve ourselves; we played squash against one another. Mark is ... was in better shape than me, but I had a better feel for the game. I usually beat him, and he'd lie on the court after a game, just about like he is now, and ask God where was the justice."

Meeker said, "So you recognized the man from your car?"

"Yes."

He and Beemer both looked dubious.

Rockelle asked, "What's your name, sir?"

"Putnam Shady."

"Is there anyone who can confirm where you've been the past several hours."

"Yes. Margaret Sweeney."

Now, Rockelle reacted in surprise, recognizing the name. "Would that be—"

"Yes, that Margaret Sweeney. The one who works with James J. McGill."

Meeker asked, just to be sure, "You know the president's henchman?"

"We've never met," Putnam said, "but I've heard a lot about him."

Beemer returned to an earlier subject. "You think that pin looks like Porky Pig?"

Putnam said, "Only at a glance. If I remember right, Porky wears a bow tie. A jacket and white gloves, too."

Georgetown University

Jim McGill drove his ex-wife's Honda minivan onto the summer green, August hot campus of the Society of Jesus' outpost of learning in Washington, D.C. Close behind the minivan came McGill's armored, turbocharged Chevy, Leo Levy behind the wheel and Secret Service Special Agent Deke Ky riding shotgun.

Seated beside McGill in the minivan was his elder daughter, Abbie, who was trying hard to contain her anxiety as she took in the sights of the school where she would spend the next four years.

Seated behind McGill were his ex-wife, Carolyn, who was almost as nervous as Abbie, their son, Kenny, who was uncharacteristically quiet and their younger daughter, Caitie, who, completely in character, was measuring whether Georgetown lived up to her standards.

Glances in the rearview mirror showed McGill that Caitie, neck craning, approved of the soaring Gothic grandeur of Healy Hall but thought the pedestrian mid-rise right angles of Darnall Hall were no small comedown.

Darnall was a freshman residence hall. It also was the site of the student health center, campus counseling and psychiatric services and a restaurant called the Epicurean. A security analysis done by McGill, the Secret Service and the three Evanston PD cops — on detached duty — who would provide daily security for Abbie unanimously decided that Darnall was the best place on campus for Abbie.

If its architectural shortcomings made Caitie looked down her nose at it, tough.

McGill parked out front. They'd arrived two hours before the time any other freshman would be allowed to move in; getting Abbie situated wouldn't take long.

"You ready, honey?" McGill asked his daughter.

She bobbed her head.

The family exited the minivan. Each of them would carry a bundle of necessities that would see Abbie through her first semester of college. The three younger McGills shouldered the burdens their father pulled out of the back of the minivan for them and trooped off to the front entrance of Darnall where one of the university's Residence Life staffers held the door open.

Carolyn stopped at her ex-husband's side, and the two of them watched their children step inside the building. Carolyn's husband, Lars Enquist, had said his goodbye at the hotel. The president didn't want to turn a family moment into a circus; Patricia Darden Grant just couldn't go anywhere these days without a retinue of heavily armed men. So she had wished Abbie much success the night before.

With a catch in her voice, Carolyn said, "They're just so damn great, those kids of ours."

McGill took Carolyn's hand and smiled. "Each and every one of them."

"I'm glad you're going to be nearby for Abbie."

McGill's office on P Street was a ten-minute drive; the White House not much farther.

"Me, too." He paused, then asked, "What's up with Kenny? He's been awfully quiet."

Carolyn rolled her eyes. "Liesl Eberhardt."

"His girlfriend?"

"Ex-girlfriend."

McGill winced. "She dumped Kenny for another guy?"

"Worse. Decided that she just didn't like him, not the way he liked her."

Carolyn looked as if she might have a critical observation to make about young Ms. Eberhardt but she was pre-empted by the sound of a car horn.

McGill turned to look. They were supposed to have the place to themselves, but some eager beaver might have wanted to get a jump on —

No, it was Sweetie, arriving in a black Porsche.

Deke Ky had already interposed himself between the car and the president's henchman, and was reaching under his suit jacket where he kept his Uzi. But when he saw Sweetie get out of the passenger seat he waved to her. Then he went to the driver's side of the Porsche and shook hands with the guy behind the wheel.

McGill wondered if —

"Sorry I'm late," Sweetie said. "Where are the kids?"

She gave Carolyn a hug.

"They went inside just now," Carolyn said.

"Well, let's all grab something and join them." Sweetie picked up two boxes and headed for Darnall; Carolyn carried her daughter's stereo system; McGill took hold of two suitcases and closed the minivan's hatch.

He looked back at the Porsche. Deke saw he was ready to go inside and said goodbye to the guy in the driver's seat. He hustled to catch up with McGill.

"You know that guy?" McGill asked.

"He's Margaret's friend, her landlord."

"Putnam Shady?"

"Yeah, you never met him?"

"No."

McGill turned and saw Sweetie and Carolyn enter Darnall.

It was only natural for Sweetie to be present; she was Abbie's godmother.

But Putnam Shady? What was he doing there?

Two thoughts occurred to McGill: Had Sweetie finally met a man who had found a way into her heart? Or had Shady approached Sweetie on a professional basis, a client looking for a private investigator.

He passed through the door to Darnall that Deke held open for him.

And he realized: Might be both reasons.

The White House, the Oval Office

Galia Mindel, White House chief of staff, brought her signed letter of resignation to tender to the president — if that was the way her meeting with the president went. She got to her feet as Patricia Darden Grant entered the room. The president's pace slowed as she took notice of Galia's grim expression. Taking her seat, the president glanced at the schedule of her day's activities that lay on her desk. Then she turned her attention to Galia and gestured to her to be seated.

"Who screwed up, Galia, you, me or some third party who left us a mess?"

"I did, Madam President." Galia was never one to shift blame.

"Is it a matter of national, political or personal interest?"

"All of the above."

The president nodded. "I see. Shall I summon a firing squad?"

"Might be hard to get good help if you did that."

The president smiled. "Come on, Galia. It can't be that bad or you would have woken me up last night."

The chief of staff pursed her lips before saying, "I took my eye off the ball."

"The ball being?" Patti asked.

"Who your worst political enemy is. The person who most wants you to fail in your first term so you won't have a second term. The person who is working hardest to keep you from achieving your goals to get the country moving in the right direction."

Patti had to agree that would be a serious mistake, if Galia had actually made it.

Which she seriously doubted.

"Are you saying our principal political nemesis — yours and mine — is not Roger Michaelson, Democrat, the junior senator from the great state of Oregon?"

"Michaelson is your most obvious opponent. I've learned he intends to run for the Democratic nomination for president. He thinks he can win the primaries and then defeat you in the general election."

The president smiled once more but she also shook her head.

"Roger has never lacked for confidence, even when he should know better."

"Exactly, Madam President. You've beaten him before; you'd beat him again."

"But?"

"But you are going to face challengers in the Republican primary elections," Galia said.

Patti's first impulse was to say that was ridiculous, but she was too smart, and knew Galia too well, to let her emotions dictate her response. Even in the privacy of the Oval Office. The only person to whom she bared her soul was James J. McGill.

"Remind me, Galia, of what my standing is in the latest round of polls."

"Two-thirds of the American public view your performance in office favorably."

"And which members of my party might think they could do better?"

"The first to declare will be Senator Howard Hurlbert of Mississippi."

The president's eyes narrowed. Howard Hurlbert was a co-sponsor of the Support of Motherhood Act, the bill that Patti had refused to support even when threatened by militant anti-abortionists who would go on to take the life of her first husband, Andy.

Hurlbert was a handsome man, silver haired, possessing a honeyed Southern baritone. He'd gone on to win reelection in his state after Andy had died. He'd voted against every piece of legislation Patti had pushed. But...

Patti knew Hurlbert was a front man. Good at following a script. But she doubted he'd had an original idea in his entire life. Someone else was penning this scenario.

The president took a moment to consider who the author might be and then refocused on Galia. "Derek Geiger?"

Galia nodded. "Yes, Madam President, the Republican speaker of the House."

The man second in the line of succession to the presidency, and in the current Congress, the most powerful figure in the legislative branch of the federal government.

A shiver rippled through Patti. She looked back at her schedule.

"Vice President Wyman has an hour at the end of the day," she said.

Galia understood the implicit question: What does he want?

"I politely inquired why the vice president would like to see you; he politely told me to buzz off."

Try as she might, Patti couldn't see Mather Wyman conspiring with Derek Geiger against her. It wasn't in the man's nature. Still, she didn't like the coincidence of his wanting to see her today.

Galia waited patiently as the president weighed the situation. She decided that unless Patricia Grant came right out and asked for her resignation, she wasn't going to offer it. Now that Galia knew where the threat to the president lay she would be helpful in the upcoming fight. In fact, she was looking forward to the political bloodletting.

The president asked, "Is there anything else I should know, Galia?"

The chief of staff had one more bomb to throw.

"A matter just came to my attention, Madam President, after your schedule was printed. I received word that Erna Godfrey is on the mend with no obvious physical impairment."

Patti nodded, sensing another shoe was about to drop.

"And?" she asked.

Galia said, "Erna claims that during the time she was technically dead she saw Jesus."

"Jesus?"

"Yes ... and Mr. Grant was with him."

That sat Patti back in her chair. "Andy?"

"I'm afraid so. Erna says Jesus told her to mend her ways ... and now she'd like to see you."

The White House, West Wing

Captain Welborn Yates arrived at his White House office an hour before his workday officially began, as was his custom. Although he was only in his mid-twenties, he was having something of a career crisis. His first case as an investigator for the Air Force Office of Special Investigations had been to make inquiries into an allegation of adultery against Colonel Carina Linberg. That case had attracted the notice of the president, and she'd quickly made Welborn her personal in-house investigator. Well, her *official* investigator.

There was no question that James J. McGill was the president's first line of defense, but he worked *sub rosa.* Given Mr. McGill's spousal relationship to the president, Welborn could understand the need for discretion. He had no problem being the front man for the president's henchman. In two years on the job, he'd learned more from Jim McGill — and Margaret Sweeney — than he had at the Federal Law Enforcement Training Center.

The problem was, he'd recently revised his thinking on how he came to be in his present circumstances. He'd previously thought his being assigned to the Colonel Linberg investigation had been a random event, the luck of the draw, but as he gained experience, saw how things worked in the upper reaches of government and the military, he came to think otherwise.

He understood now that either General Warren Altman (ret.), the former Air Force chief of staff or, more likely, the general's former adjutant, Major Clarence Seymour (ret.), must have specifically ordered that the newest, greenest investigator on the OSI duty roster be assigned to the Colonel Linberg case.

One of them had specifically asked for him.

If not by name then by virtue of the wetness behind his ears.

He'd been meant to be the Pentagon's puppet. Only the president had intervened and made him a White House minion. Not that he could object to that. He worked for the most powerful person in the world, he'd been promoted in rank and most important his new job had led to meeting his fiancée, Kira Fahey.

Led to their meeting more intentionally than he had guessed at first. Either the president or James J. McGill had played matchmaker for him and Kira, Welborn was now sure. They hadn't wanted the president's handpicked investigator to fall prey to the considerable charms of Colonel Linberg. That just showed the lengths to which people in Washington would go to further their interests: They'd pair a young couple off for the rest of their lives.

Not that Welborn didn't love Kira. He was crazy about her. Their wedding day, postponed for almost a year after Kira's mother had required emergency heart surgery, was swiftly approaching and he hadn't experienced a moment of cold feet.

What bothered Welborn, though, was the growing feeling he was nothing more than a wind-up toy in games other people were playing. Older, wiser, more ruthless people pointed him in their desired direction and off he went. The thought chafed. He considered requesting a transfer out of the White House; he went so far as to think of leaving the Air Force entirely once his five-year obligation had been fulfilled.

But he was getting married. He and Kira both wanted children. He would need a reputable and substantial means of support — and there were few job opportunities that topped working for the president of the United States.

Though his cage was gilded, he felt trapped nonetheless, not even able to discuss his feelings with Kira. She'd think he was being foolish, and he'd have a hard time disagreeing.

Where else could he —

Welborn's phone rang. He answered the call, "Captain Yates."

The president had given him permission to bitly, i.e. abbreviate, his previous three-paragraph greeting.

"Welborn Yates?" a charming female voice asked.

"Possibly," Welborn said.

He wouldn't put it past Kira to play a trick on him.

"Who's calling please?" he asked.

"Chana Lochlan."

He knew the name: Chana Lochlan had been James J. McGill's first client as a private investigator; formerly the "most fabulous face on television," she was now the producer of a Peabody Award-winning news program.

"Captain Welborn Yates," he elaborated. "How may I be of service?"

"I'm trying to contact Jim McGill. He told me if I were unable to reach him, and he's not answering his phone, I should call Margaret Sweeney. She said if I were unable to reach her, and I got her voice mail, too, I should call you."

And that was how Ms. Lochlan got his White House phone

number.

"Good thing I get in early," Welborn said.

"A very good thing. I have a warning for Jim."

Welborn took down Chana Lochlan's message word for word.

Thinking all the while: Okay, he worked for the president, and now he got to be her henchman's henchman. Where else could he do that?

Washington, D.C., R Street NW

The speaker of the House of Representatives, Derek Geiger, Republican of Florida's 13th congressional district, and his divorce lawyer, Brad Attles, planned to seize control of the United States government. They called their plan Super-K. It was a rework of former majority leader Tom DeLay's K Street Project.

Geiger and Attles were putting the finishing touches on the plan at the Georgetown townhouse owned by the speaker's third wife, Harlo, the managing partner of HG Designs, a furniture design atelier with offices in Washington, New York and Sarasota.

Geiger had accurately assessed the public's tolerance for serial monogamy among politicians: three wives while in office. Despite having reached that limit and professing a love for Harlo unlike any he'd ever known, Geiger kept Attles on retainer. He had assured his third wife this was a mere formality.

Harlo had laughed and reminded him, "Honey, I'm the one who insisted on the pre-nup, and I'll be the one who brings the curtain down on this little road show."

Harlo's sass always made the Speaker's blood pressure spike.

That and a body that belonged on a pin-up calendar.

Geiger brought Brad Attles to Washington as soon as he got a seat on the Committee on Ways and Means, the place where tax bills and tax loopholes originated. His sponsorship was more than enough to land Attles a spot in the most important lobbying firm in town, Hetherington/Weems. New to lobbying, but possessing an intuitive understanding of human nature, Attles quickly mastered the arts of finding, grinding and minding.

Finding clients, grinding out a way to get language favoring their interests inserted into legislation, minding that the favorable wording stayed in place until the bill became law.

Attles' professional achievements were supplemented by the fact that he was, in his own words, "A very large Negro you can introduce to polite society."

Further adding, "It comes as a relief to people that someone like me would rather enrich them than rob them."

Despite his many sterling qualities, Brad Attles couldn't cook worth a damn.

The Speaker took six eggs and a pound of bacon off the griddle of the Viking range. He plated two meals and brought them to the kitchen table. Attles had already filled their coffee cups and two glasses with orange juice. They used the OJ to make a toast.

"To Super-K," the Speaker said.

"Super-K," Attles agreed.

Tom DeLay eventually wound up on trial in Texas and was sentenced to three years in prison. The judgment of the court was he had committed a felony by conspiring to launder corporate money and use it to make donations to preferred candidates running for seats in the state legislature.

DeLay had been released on bond pending appeal but it had been reported he'd had to raise — plead for — ten million dollars to pay his lawyers' fees. Fighting prosecutors and going about hat in hand was not the way Derek Geiger wanted to spend his golden years.

But then DeLay had made so many mistakes. He'd issued ultimatums. He'd divided the pie along strict party line: the pie for Republicans, the empty pie plate for Democrats. In his dealing with colleagues and the media, he'd had the *savoir faire* of Yosemite Sam.

Speaker Geiger had learned from DeLay. He never issued threats to anyone; Brad did that for him. He never took a nickel in donations or gifts from anyone. He flew commercial, coach in his early years, business class now. He extended his largesse to friendly, i.e. tame Democrats. He spoke publicly in measured tones.

With Attles' professional help, the speaker had managed to make lump sum settlements with his first two wives, holding on to his home in Sarasota and most of his stock portfolio. So he was able to make do with the $223,500 per year his day job paid.

He'd cash in big time after he left office.

By then he would be recognized as the man who had made the position of speaker of the House the most powerful in government. Super-K would see to that.

The plan called for organizing every lobbyist on K Street who mattered a tinker's damn. If the capital's lobbyists, the so-called fourth branch of government, wanted to advance any of their interests, they would have to see Brad Attles. He would talk to Geiger, and the speaker would tell the committee chairs whose interests would advance.

And whose would be ignored.

A flow chart of the plan would show money flowing in from corporate America and flowing out from the United States Treasury. At the confluence of these rivers of cash would be Geiger and Attles, but no prosecutor would ever be able to pry into their relationship. It was, and for many years had been, protected by attorney-client privilege.

There were limits and exceptions to the privilege, of course. It couldn't be used for the purpose of committing a crime or to perpetrate a fraud. But if Derek Geiger were ever to claim he was only consulting the attorney of record in his two prior divorces about ending his present marriage, who would be able to say otherwise?

It would be a shame to relinquish Harlo before he'd taken his full measure of her, but letting her go would certainly beat finding himself in a fix like Tom DeLay's.

Once they finished eating, Attles raised the subject of another woman who had to be taken into account, Patricia Darden Grant.

"You know," Attles said, "the biggest threat to this plan is sitting over there in the White House right now."

In an ideal world, the speaker thought, the president would have been just another politician on the hustle for campaign funds. But Patti Grant had made a small fortune from her modeling and acting careers and had been left billions by her late husband. She didn't need anyone else's money.

"She's not going to stand for being one-upped by you," Attles told the speaker.

The corporate money that would flood into Brad Attles' accounts would find its way to PACs supporting candidates for House and Senate seats who pledged their allegiance to the speaker. If some cuss with an ornery streak, someone who leaned too far right or too far left, didn't want to play ball, he would face a well-funded, well prepared, well behaved challenger in the next election cycle.

The same thing went for Patti Grant.

Howard Hurlbert wouldn't be the only challenger she would face.

Funding, running, electing and owning his own broad slate of candidates for both houses of Congress and the White House was how Derek Geiger planned to become the most powerful man in the country.

His guiding principle was: If you control the dough, you run the show.

He told his divorce lawyer, "I'll take care of the president."

Darnall Hall, Georgetown University

The finishing touches had been put in place in Abbie McGill's dorm room. Books filled shelves; posters adorned walls; a comforter, pillows and one stuffed animal from home dressed the bed; a rag-rug served as a yoga mat; the stereo was hooked up and ready to rock; two potted plants adorned a windowsill.

Even Caitie had to give a grudging nod of approval.

"It's not the Lincoln Bedroom, but it'll do," she said.

"I think it's charming," Putnam Shady said.

Sweetie had brought her friend in and introduced him to the family. He'd assumed the job of setting up Abbie's sound system and had proved deft at the task. Abbie and Caitie had both been taken with Putnam; Carolyn only slightly less so. Kenny had been content to shake Putnam's hand.

McGill thought Sweetie's landlord reminded him of some of the more slippery lawyers he'd known in Chicago, but if Sweetie gave the guy her stamp of approval, that was good enough for him.

Still, it did his heart good when Caitie, in saying goodbye, shook Putnam's hand and let him know in no uncertain terms, "Sweetie is very important to all of us."

Subtext: Don't trifle with her affections, Bub.

"She's important to me, too," Putnam said.

"Stop it," Sweetie said. "I might blush. Ruin my image altogether."

McGill said, "Can't have that. Let me walk the two of you out while there's still time."

He did just that, after Sweetie kissed all the McGill kids goodbye.

Outside the residence hall, the three of them stood next to Putnam's Boxster and Sweetie informed McGill, "Putnam says someone is going to try to kill him."

McGill played it straight. "Why would you think that?"

Sweetie's landlord told McGill about the Metro cops finding Mark Benjamin's body on K Street earlier that morning, and how Benjamin had been the third lobbyist to be killed in the past three weeks.

"I knew Mark, I knew Bobby Waller and I knew Erik Torkelson."

"Personally or professionally?" McGill asked.

"Both. The four of us were thinking of starting our own firm."

"Did you tell the Metro cops this?"

"I mentioned that Mark and I played squash."

McGill revisited his opinion about Putnam being slippery.

He shot a look at Sweetie.

"Why not tell them everything you know?" he asked Putnam.

"I don't deal well with authority."

"Sweetie?" McGill asked.

"It's true, he doesn't. Neither do you or I, particularly."

McGill couldn't deny that. If he tried, he'd hear Celsus Crogher laughing somewhere.

Putnam saw McGill and Sweetie were going to have to work things out. Something best done without a third party present to inhibit the flow of the debate. He extended his hand to McGill.

"Thank you for your time. It was a pleasure to meet you and your family."

McGill shook Putnam's hand, ignoring the look from Sweetie.

The one that said he could go along or stay behind, but she was in.

"One thing, though," Putnam told McGill.

"What's that?" he asked.

"I hope I'm wrong, but your son, the way he looks reminds of someone else I knew. I think you should have a doctor look at him."

The suggestion blindsided both McGill and Sweetie.

Giving Putnam time to get in his car and drive off.

United States Penitentiary, Hazelton, West Virginia

Reverend Burke Godfrey needed every ounce of self-control he possessed not to bristle as he was frisked — felt up, damnit — by the correctional officer. He had tried explaining to the warden who stood nearby, a deadpan expression on his bulldog face, that he was a man of God. He had come to the prison that morning, after not seeing his wife for almost a year, only to minister to her spiritual and emotional needs.

Godfrey thought they wouldn't be treating him like one of the animals in the adjoining men's prison — or even the harlots there in the secure female housing unit — if he'd had his lawyer with him. But visitors weren't allowed to bring lawyers with them; legal counsel was presumed to be necessary only for those presently incarcerated.

Not for those who might become future inmates.

That was the way Godfrey read the warden's eyes.

The correctional officer stood up, having made sure the minister didn't possess a gun strapped to either of his ankles, and nodded to his superior.

Godfrey asked the warden, "Do you enjoy humiliating people, sir?"

A splinter of a grin lanced the man's face.

"Reverend, what you experienced was a routine security procedure, done for the safety of all involved. You didn't expect special treatment, did you?"

Burke Godfrey *always* expected special treatment.

It was an indignity when he even needed to mention it.

It was an affront when he didn't get it.

And when a man laid a hand on his privates ... he didn't yet have the words for that.

But he would soon enough.

"May I please see my wife now?" he asked.

"Yes, you may. For the next thirty minutes."

Burke Godfrey turned red. "That's all?"

"That's all the inmate — your wife — asked for."

Erna looked far better than Burke Godfrey had ever expected. Being in prison, she'd had no choice but to let her hair go gray, but somehow she looked younger than the last time he'd seen her. Her brow was smooth, her eyes were clear, her face was a slender oval. Except for the gray, she looked remarkably like the girl with whom he'd fallen in love.

He wanted to take her in his arms — not in the gentle way a man already past his middle years might do, but with the passion of the brash young fellow he'd been the first time he'd seen her. He wanted to have her here and now. But the best he could do was place a hand on the slab of clear plastic separating them.

Erna put her hand opposite his.

"They could have let us sit across a table from each," Godfrey said. "I was told they do that here."

"Not for me, not after I hoodwinked a nurse. That poor woman in Terre Haute lost her job for giving me those sleeping pills."

Godfrey had wanted Anna Lee put in a cell after it came out that she had smuggled sedatives to Erna. He still felt that way. But he wasn't about to argue the matter now.

"Oh, Erna," he said. "I almost died when I thought I lost you."

Tears made Erna's eyes glisten. "I'm sorry. I'm so sorry for so many things."

"Why did you try to … do what you did to yourself? I had Benton Williams ready to appeal your case. I still do. We can —"

Erna dropped her hand and shook her head.

"No," she said. "I don't want an appeal. What I thought I wanted was to become a martyr. After my sentence was commuted, I tried to kill myself because I couldn't face being in prison for so many years. Now, I've accepted this is where I'm meant to be."

Godfrey pulled back, trying to understand Erna.

He looked for a sign she wasn't in her right mind or that she'd been coerced. Maybe even brainwashed. There was no way he could comprehend what he'd just heard.

Instead of explaining her own words, she repeated what Godfrey had said a moment ago. "You said you almost died when you thought you'd lost me."

"I did. I thought my heart was going to stop beating."

Erna nodded. "I believe you. I also know Patricia Grant felt a lot like that when I took her husband from her."

Now, Burke Godfrey pushed his chair back, not from lack of understanding, but having perceived a threat.

"She married again soon enough," he said.

"I'm glad for that, but the hurt I caused her still hasn't healed."

"She told you that?"

"Andy Grant told me."

Godfrey bounded to his feet. He stepped behind the chair, as if the plastic barrier between him and Erna was insufficient protection. He was unmoved by the tear he saw slide down his wife's cheek.

Erna said in a quiet voice, "Burke, I'm trying to do what's right. I'm trying to save my soul. You have to do the same. You have to do what's right."

Godfrey turned his back on Erna and banged on the door for the guard.

He wanted out, now.

Erna had been optimistic limiting the visit to thirty minutes. They'd been together for fewer than ten.

It took only slightly longer for Galia Mindel to hear that the visit between Reverend Burke Godfrey and his wife had not gone well. But she'd save that information for later. The president had a busy day ahead and didn't need any distractions.

Arlington, Virginia

"How you doing, pal?" Jim McGill asked his son Kenny.

He and Sweetie had taken Kenny to the California Pizza Kitchen restaurant just outside the capital. Caitie, Carolyn and Lars had opted for Chinese in Georgetown. Abbie's roommate, and former Evanston schoolmate, Jane Haley, had arrived and the two young college women were lunching on campus, taking their first steps in independent living.

Kenny looked up from his pasta, dabbed tomato sauce from his mouth.

"I'm okay, why?" He saw Sweetie paying close attention to him. "Don't I look okay? Did I spill some food on myself?"

Sweetie shook her head. "You're neat as a pin."

"I've been working on my table manners."

"Doing a good job, too," McGill said. "That have something to do with Liesl Eberhardt?"

Kenny returned his attention to his pasta bowl.

"I don't want to talk about her."

"Happens to all of us," Sweetie told the younger McGill.

She hadn't heard the news from Jim yet, but it wasn't hard to figure out what was bothering Kenny.

Kenny shot her a look. "Someone broke your heart?"

He clearly didn't believe that was possible.

"Not intentionally, but yes. Happened a long time ago."

"What happened?" Kenny asked.

Sweetie looked at McGill. He held up a hand and answered for her.

The two of them knew each other's life stories, better than anyone else did.

"Kenny," McGill said, "the boy Sweetie loved died in a boating accident."

Laying his fork down and taking Sweetie's hand, Kenny said, "That's awful."

"Yes, it was," Sweetie told him.

"Did it hurt for a long time?"

Sweetie nodded.

"Is that why you never got married?" Kenny asked.

"One of the reasons, anyway."

Kenny released Sweetie's hand.

"I wonder if I'll ever find anyone else," he said.

McGill and Sweetie were careful not to laugh or even smile.

"A good-looking guy like you," McGill said, "it's a sure thing."

Kenny looked at his father and said, "But Sweetie's beautiful and —"

"I think I've found someone," she said.

Both McGills looked at her: Kenny with a smile, Jim with raised eyebrows.

"That Putnam guy you were with this morning?" Kenny asked.

"Yeah, him."

"He looks kind of cool," Kenny said.

"He is, kind of," Sweetie agreed.

McGill looked to see if Sweetie was just playing with Kenny, trying to help him out of his funk, but she shook her head. She was telling the truth.

Slippery Putnam Shady was the man for Sweetie?

McGill found it hard to imagine.

But he knew he'd have to accept it.

For the moment, though, he asked Kenny, "Other than a heavy heart, how are you doing?"

"I'm okay, Dad, really."

But Kenny had finished less than half his lunch, an irregularity impossible to miss.

McGill said, "How about if I get you a quick once over from a doctor I know?"

Kenny shook his head. "I don't need anything like that."

"Did I mention that this doctor works at the White House? Usually sees no one but the president. Treated Patti last year after she took that nasty fall in England."

That perked Kenny up. He no doubt was remembering Caitie getting to have an adventure in Washington with their father while he and Abbie were stuck at Camp David.

"Does this doctor work out of the residence?"

Kenny had already enjoyed Thanksgiving dinner in that part of the Executive Mansion.

"No, he has his own examining room, a place few have ever seen."

Relatively speaking, McGill thought.

That was good enough for Kenny. He smiled broadly. Made McGill think that he and Sweetie had been worrying about nothing.

Until Kenny said, "I have been getting tired a lot lately. More than usual, you know?"

The president was too busy to be bothered with Welborn's inquiry as to where James J. McGill might be. Edwina Byington, the president's personal secretary, gave him a clue: Georgetown University. The McGills, mother and father, were dropping off Abigail for her first day at college, but that had been earlier.

"I would imagine that once Ms. McGill is ensconced," Edwina

said, "the family might go out for a meal together. But I don't have any information as to where that might be. If it were a spontaneous choice, the president wouldn't even know."

For a heartbeat, Welborn thought it strange that the president wouldn't know where her husband was at any given moment. But then the First Couple was a generation older than he was, each was in a second marriage and … maybe that's how he and Kira would do things, too, when they got to that point.

Welborn thanked Edwina and returned to his office.

The information Chana Lochlan had given him — her warning — was hardly life-threatening but it was certainly something Jim McGill would want to know. Welborn had Deke Ky's personal cell phone number, and if anyone would know where the president's henchman was, his personal Secret Service agent would.

Thing was, Welborn couldn't decide if the situation rose to —

"My, my, the thrill is gone."

Welborn dispelled his reverie and took notice of his fiancée, Kira Fahey, standing in his office doorway. She told him, "There was a time when you could feel my very approach. Now, I'm invisible."

With a smile, Welborn said, "You used to wear more perfume."

"You're horrible. Why I'm marrying you is a mystery to me."

"I'll find out; I'm a trained investigator. And I'd be happy to feel your approach or anything else you might care to offer."

Kira blushed and smiled simultaneously. She looked down the hallway, in the direction of the Oval Office.

Turning back to Welborn, she asked, "How can you talk like that in the White House? What if the president overheard you?"

"I imagine she'd be pleased; she and her husband brought us together."

Kira nodded. "I was wondering if you'd figured that out, too."

"We'll tell our children," Welborn said, "but they'll never believe it. Is there anything I might do for you, Ms. Fahey?"

Kira looked as if she might say something risqué, but she liked to talk dirty only behind closed doors.

She told Welborn, "A Lieutenant Rockelle Bullard of the Metro

Police, an acquaintance of yours, I believe, called while you were out of your office. She'd like to speak with you."

"You got her phone number, of course."

"Of course."

"I'll call her, see if she'd care to drop by."

"Impress her with your fancy digs?" Kira asked.

"Introduce her to my beloved."

Kira beamed, before asking, "What's the real reason?"

"I'm looking for James Jackson McGill. If he shows up here, I don't want to miss him."

"I'll advise the boys in blue." The uniformed Secret Service. "Have them let you know if they see him. I'll escort Lieutenant Bullard in, too."

"You're too kind to me," Welborn said.

"Just remember, flyboy, my services come at a cost."

Welborn said, "I'll pay any price, gladly."

Special Agent Elspeth unmoved presented herself at SAC Celsus Crogher's White House office. Kendry was new to the White House Security Detail. The daughter of an army officer and an Iranian mother, she spoke both Farsi and Arabic. Her most recent assignment had been in Amman, Jordan, working with a strike force to break up a counterfeiting ring.

The bad guys were threefold: Iranian Revolutionary Guards, Jordanian middlemen, and Mexican coyotes. The IRG weren't printing funny money, they were forging U.S. Treasury checks payable to ghost Social Security recipients. The Jordanians bought the checks from the Iranians for ten cents on the dollar. They couriered them to Mexico and sold them to the coyotes for an additional twenty-five percent. The coyotes put them in the hands of illegals they'd brought into the U.S., let the illegals take one percent of the value of each check they cashed as a credit against their border-crossing fee.

All of the major players involved were making piles of money. The Iranians had the additional pleasures of bleeding the U.S.

Treasury at a time when it was already hemorrhaging red ink, and placing added stress on a critical security agency of the Great Satan's government, the Secret Service.

The raid just outside the Jordanian capital that took down the ring's operational leadership turned into a firefight. Elspeth Kendry killed the top IRG man present and the Jordanian second in command. If she hadn't needed to change clips, she said, she might have gotten a Mexican, too.

In any case, there were too many people in the Middle East who now wanted to get her, and with a commendation from the director she was shipped off to the White House. Elspeth thought she'd give the assignment a year without complaining before she asked to be returned to the field.

She stood at parade rest as SAC Crogher reviewed her file.

He looked up and said, "Have a seat, Kendry."

She sat, every bit as erect as Crogher. When dealing with male superiors, she made sure her body language conveyed nothing but professionalism. The guy in front of her looked like someone who might actually appreciate that.

Crogher asked, "Do you know who James J. McGill is?"

"The president's husband."

"Do you know anything about his background?"

"Only what's available in the public media."

Elspeth wondered if she was about to be warned this McGill guy was a philanderer or a shoplifter or something else the public must never know.

"He's a private eye," Crogher said.

"I think I read that. He has his own firm."

"He works cases."

"Really?"

"Yeah, really. He has a concealed carry license. He allows us to provide him with only one special agent for personal security. At the president's insistence, he also has an armed driver. But McGill has been known to go off on his own without any protection at all. One time he had a taxi pick him up at the White House and disappeared."

Elspeth repressed a smile.

She said, "Mr. McGill must be a handful, sir."

"He's a pain in the ass is what he is."

Kendry thought SAC Crogher was either someone who trusted his people to keep their lips zipped or he was close to burning out.

Crogher said, "He's also smart, occasionally helpful and has the fastest weapon draw I've ever seen."

"That's interesting, sir."

The SAC leaned forward, not like he was scoping her out, despite her exotic good looks, more like he was about to share a deep, dark secret.

"He's also a charming bastard. Not that I'd know anything about that sort of thing, but that's what I hear. What you have to remember, Kendry, is that you work for me not him."

Had to be personal hard feelings at work here, Kendry decided.

"Of course, sir. But what is it exactly you want me to do?"

"I want you to watch the whole world for hostile Arabs, Iranians or any other sort of asshole who might want to do James J. McGill in. You're his distant early warning line."

"Yes, sir."

"That's the easy part, Kendry."

Elspeth picked up on her cue. "What's the hard part, sir?"

"If you do learn of a threat, you have to convince that sonofabitch McGill he isn't Superman."

How about that, Special Agent Elspeth Kendry thought.

Her new job might be fun after all.

McGill introduced his son, Kenny, to the White House physician, Artemus Nicolaides. The two McGills were in the anteroom of Nicolaides' suite. Leo dropped Sweetie off at the North Portico Entrance of the White House.

Before exiting the Chevy, she told McGill, "I'm going to keep an eye on Putnam."

"Is he in trouble?" Kenny asked.

"You're taking the case?" McGill wanted to know.

Answering the questions in order, Sweetie said, "Not with me around and yes."

"What's the case?" Kenny asked.

Sweetie looked at Jim. He gave a minimalist nod. Answer honestly but not at length.

"Some unknown bad guy might want to hurt him," Sweetie told Kenny.

Kenny turned to his father. "Why wouldn't Sweetie take the case, keep her friend from getting hurt?

"No reason at all," McGill said, not wanting to complicate matters with either his son or his friend.

Simplicity, however, would not suffice.

"Dad, you're not going to let Sweetie do this alone, are you? Caitie was being corny this morning when she told Putnam that Sweetie is important to all of us, but she was telling the truth, too."

McGill remembered how proud he'd been of Caitie when she'd voiced that sentiment. Now, his son was calling on him to be true not just to Sweetie but himself, too. Darn kid.

"Margaret," he said, "I will be happy to assist you in any way I can."

Kenny's effort on Sweetie's behalf had earned him a kiss on the cheek.

He'd walked into the White House with his head in the clouds.

Now, Nick was bringing him gently down to earth.

"So, young man," he asked, "why are you here to see me? Are you no longer the strongest, fastest, smartest boy in your school?"

"I was never any of those things," Kenny said.

"I will take your word on that, though you must allow me a moment of doubt. But I can see your resemblance to your father, so certainly you must be among the most handsome."

"I used to think so," Kenny allowed.

A man of affairs, Nick diagnosed the situation immediately.

"A young lady has led you to believe otherwise?"

Kenny hung his head and nodded.

The was enough for Nick to put an arm around Kenny's shoulders. "Come on, Kenny, step into my examining room. Anything you care to tell me in there is protected by doctor-patient confidentiality.

Nick looked back at McGill and gave him a wink.

"Kenny says he's been getting tired more than usual," McGill told Nick.

Seeing the examining room door close behind his son, he felt a chill in his heart.

Fell's Point, Baltimore, Maryland

There were plenty of neighborhoods in Baltimore where a car could get boosted in broad daylight. Grabbing a car in Fell's Point while the sun was shining, though, was a risky proposition. In the gentrified, harborside neighborhood, packed with bars, restaurants and tourists, the cops kept a close watch on things. So did the residents, for that matter. And the cars were the kind that had all the latest alarms, immobilizers and recovery systems.

They were also some of the sweetest rides in town with the highest cash value for an enterprising car thief.

Achilles Mitchell was way beyond enterprising. He was educated, a graduate of the Automotive Institute of America, had manufacturer specific training in high-end wheels. He knew exactly what he needed to do to steal the Bentley Continental Flying Spur he'd spotted on his first pass down the one block length of Lisbon Street.

The car retailed for one-seventy K or so. He could deliver it to a shipper and pocket twenty large for thirty minutes work, get back to the luxury car dealership that employed him without being a minute late on his lunch hour.

The only possible hitch Achilles saw was a guy sitting on the stoop of a townhouse across the street from where the Bentley was parked. White guy wearing shades, a polo shirt and khakis. Looked like he might live in the place where he was perched. Just waiting for his girlfriend, maybe, to stop by for a quick rhumba under the covers.

Sonofabitch was still there when Achilles reappeared to make his move.

The car thief weighed the risk. Couldn't really tell how tall the white guy was, him sitting down and all. But he looked kinda skinny, and past the age where dudes thought they could get physical out on the street.

Achilles had sunglasses on, too. He was six-three and figured he had forty pounds on the white guy. If the sonofabitch stayed where he was, he probably wouldn't be able to give the cops a good description.

"Hey, officer, the fucker was black. Short, kinky hair and all that. No, I didn't get a good look at him. Wouldn't do any good, my looking at mug shots."

Achilles made his move, got into the Bentley like he had a key. Overrode the software that ran the security system in the time it'd take most people to adjust their seat and mirrors. A glance to his right even showed the dude across the street had taken off. Wearing the smile of a craftsman completing a job well done, Achilles turned the engine on.

The only flaw in the entire exercise was not closing the driver's door behind him; he always left the door open until he got the engine cranked, in case he had to make a quick exit. Be damn foolish to get caught inside a car that wasn't yours. Without looking, he grabbed the arm rest to pull the door closed and was surprised when it met resistance.

That gave him a chill: a sign something might have gone wrong.

When he felt a gun barrel pressed against the back of his head, he knew it had.

The skinny white guy?

Achilles never got an answer to his unspoken question. A .22 caliber round entered his brain and overrode its operating system. Didn't even come out the other side of his head and leave a mess in the car.

It was the skinny white guy. He pulled Achilles out of the Bentley, left him lying on the sidewalk, looking more like a passed-out drunk than a homicide victim, and was gone within seconds. Proving you didn't need a fancy technical education to steal a Bentley.

To be fair, the white guy had been stealing cars longer than Achilles had been alive.

For most of his grand-theft-auto career, he'd done no physical violence.

But after a job in Las Vegas — goddamn Vegas — everything changed.

Making his getaway, he'd crashed his boosted ride into a car filled with young guys.

Three of 'em, all Air Force pilots he'd found out later, had died.

A fourth guy, another pilot, had survived.

That was the guy who scared the thief.

He was sure that bastard would come for him someday.

So now he didn't leave anyone alive behind him.

The White House, the West Wing

Kira, true to her word, delivered Rockelle Bullard to Welborn's office. The Metro homicide lieutenant looked around and shook her head in wonder. Welborn rose to greet her.

"Good to see you again, Lieutenant Bullard," he said, extending his hand. "Kira's introduced herself? Told you our good news?"

She smiled and said, "Yes, she has."

Kira told Welborn, "Let me know if there's anything else I can do."

Rockelle turned to Kira and said, "A pleasure meeting you, Ms. Fahey. I hope you and the captain here have a fine life together."

"Thank you." Kira gave Welborn a wave and departed.

Welborn gestured Rockelle to a guest chair and took his seat behind his desk.

"You're a *real* lucky man," Rockelle told him.

"I know. Just show up for work one day and wind up meeting the president of the United States and the woman you're going to marry. Get a promotion for doing a so-so job on your first case."

"Yeah, how does that work?" Rockelle wanted to know.

"I told the president my mother voted for her. She seemed to have a soft spot for me after that."

"It's all politics then?"

"What else could it be in this town?"

"Too damn true," Rockelle said.

"So, how may I help Metro homicide?" Welborn asked.

Rockelle told him all about the three dead lobbyists wearing pins that may or may not resemble Porky Pig. Then she told him about the fourth lobbyist, this one still breathing, whom she met that morning. Asked Welborn did he know the man.

Welborn nodded. "Sure, I know Putnam."

The homicide lieutenant made a sour face. "You do? Damn, I was hoping he was just blowing smoke, trying to keep us from breathing too heavy on him."

"You'd do that, Rockelle, make people sweat?"

She smiled. "Like an August night in Alabama."

That being the case, Welborn thought it worth mentioning to say, "He actually is Margaret Sweeney's boyfriend. Or close to it."

"Puts him right next to the president's henchman then, doesn't it? And we all know who that man's close to." Rockelle looked out Welborn's open door. "She ever stop by here?"

"It's been known to happen."

"That'd be something, me meeting the president."

"She's a lot like you."

Rockelle rolled her eyes.

"What I mean is, you both make a powerful impression."

The homicide lieutenant laughed. "Now I know how you get ahead; you're just a natural sweet-talker."

"There are those who might disagree." He thought Calanthe Bao, now residing in federal custody, certainly would.

"We won't talk about them. Let me just explain things a little more and maybe if I get to solve this case, I'll make captain, too."

Rockelle told Welborn it was her considered opinion that Mr. Putnam Shady was holding out on her. He knew more than he'd let on. Most times, that'd call for him being sweated for a good long time. Except everybody knew if a person of interest had money and/or connections the questioning couldn't be quite as forthright or lengthy.

"You think you might help me?" Rockelle asked. "If you know Mr. Shady well enough for him to cooperate with you, that is."

"I actually know Margaret Sweeney better," Welborn said. "I could ask her to ask him."

"She'd be willing to help?"

Welborn gave it a moment's thought. "Yes, I think she would."

"Then I'd owe the both of you favors."

"Sure," Welborn said, "but then you'll have *two* friends in high places."

The Oval Office

The president welcomed the vice president into her office. Being a considerate hostess, she inquired if he'd like a cup of coffee or a soft drink.

"Madam President," Vice President Mather Wyman said, "if it's all the same to you, I'd like a scotch on the rocks. Maybe a bowl of peanuts, too."

All right, Patricia Darden Grant thought, something was up, but whatever it was she would roll with it. She asked Edwina to have a bottle of Laphroaig, a bucket of ice, two glasses and a large bowl of shelled peanuts sent to her office."

"Any cigars, Madam President?" the secretary asked dryly.

"We'll let you know, Edwina."

The two top elected officials in the land contented themselves discussing the upcoming wedding of the vice president's niece, Kira Fahey, to Captain Welborn Yates. Both of them were enthusiastic about the chances for the young couple having a wonderful life together.

Within minutes, Edwina led a young Navy Culinary Specialist pushing a linen draped liquor cart into the Oval Office. The specialist built drinks to order and placed the bowl of peanuts within easy reach of both the president and vice president. He was about to withdraw when Edwina cleared her throat. He'd forgotten to set out the napkins. The omission was quickly corrected, the specialist blushing.

"Very nicely done," the president told the young man.

"Never had better service," the vice president agreed.

"I'll see you're not disturbed, Madam President," Edwina said, shepherding the specialist out with a motherly pat on the back.

Mather Wyman shook his head as the door closed. He was in his sixties, and he said to the president, "Young people keep looking younger to me every day, Madam President, and they still keep turning out to serve our country, here and in places far more dangerous."

"We must be doing something right, Mather." She raised her glass. "To the United States and all who love it."

The vice president touched his glass to hers and they sipped their drinks.

Hoping to put the vice president at ease, Patti Grant picked up a few nuts and popped them into her mouth. She chewed for a moment and asked, "So how serious is it, Mather, whatever you have to tell me?"

The vice president put his drink down and clasped his hands, looked Patti in the eye.

"Not terribly, Madam President. It's just that I've decided to retire at the end of our term. I won't be running for office with you again."

Park Reservation Number One

The government didn't believe in simplicity, but it revered

pecking orders. For those reasons, the National Park Service designated the exterior walls and the grounds of the White House as Park Reservation Number One. McGill thought he really shouldn't kvetch, not even to himself, about the bureaucratic mentality. The grounds were immaculately kept and offered all sorts of outdoor amenities.

At the moment, he was shooting hoops on the basketball court. Nick had poked his head out of the examining room and told him he'd like to run a few tests on Kenny and there was no reason why McGill should have to linger in a stuffy waiting room. As a father, however, Jim McGill felt it was his obligation to stay close to his son; he'd been tempted to go into the examining room and see what Nick was doing. Only the fear that he might embarrass Kenny kept him from barging in.

Perceptive fellow that Nick was, he recognized McGill's recalcitrance, and opened the door wider. McGill saw Kenny sitting on the examining table with his shirt off and a smile on his face. He gave his dad a smile and a wave. Nick arched his eyebrows.

McGill shrugged and got up to go, holding up his cell phone: Call me.

He went to the residence and got his personal basketball. Out on the court he started knocking down shots. He told himself it was a good sign that his touch with the ball was so accurate. That bit of wishful thinking carried him only so far. What he really wanted was another game of one-on-one with Senator Roger Michaelson.

He wanted somebody to bash if it turned out Kenny wasn't all right.

The basketball court was shielded from public view by stands of closely planted trees, but the uniformed Secret Service officers who patrolled the grounds took immediate note of McGill's presence, and following instructions they'd received earlier, made two phone calls to report their sighting.

McGill saw them and assumed they were only following orders from Celsus Crogher — or Galia Mindel — to report his whereabouts. Both of them liked to keep tabs on him.

But a few minutes later McGill saw Welborn Yates approach. He was disappointed the young Air Force investigator wasn't dressed for playing ball. The longer Nick kept McGill waiting, the more anxious he got. A game, even against an opponent he didn't intend to maul, might have dispersed some of his nervous energy.

He considered calling out to Welborn to go get dressed for a game. He usually was loath to throw his weight around with any of the White House staffers, but he honestly couldn't remember the last time he'd been so worried. If this was the kind of stress Carolyn had to deal with all the years he was a cop, he owed her an apology.

To hell with it, McGill thought. He was about to step out of character and tell Welborn to suit up when he saw a trim, dark-haired woman appear and follow Welborn, heading McGill's way. She stopped for a moment to exchange a few words with a uniformed Secret Service officer who was passing by, so she wasn't a gate crasher. No, the way she carried herself, the gray tailored suit she wore, she was Secret Service too, a special agent.

Welborn was close enough now to raise his voice in greeting.

"Good afternoon, Mr. McGill. Sorry to interrupt, but—"

McGill held up a hand, nodded in the direction of the special agent walking their way.

"Do you know that woman, Welborn?"

He turned to look and said, "No, sir, I don't."

Welborn's posture became defensive, touching McGill with his concern.

The woman saw she was about to confront two men on edge.

"Whoa, guys." She stopped and raised her hands. "I'm on your side."

"Who are you?" McGill asked.

"Secret Service Special Agent Elspeth Kendry." Using two fingers she fished out her ID. She told McGill, "SAC Crogher told me to see you at my first opportunity."

"Why?"

"I'm your new threat assessment coordinator."

McGill remembered his promise to Patti to permit Crogher

to have one of his minions brief McGill on just how many people wished him ill on any given day. He turned to Welborn.

"And why are you here?"

"To bring you a warning," Welborn said.

That got Elspeth Kendry's attention.

But before matters could be discussed further, McGill's cell phone played the first two bars of "Take Me Out to the Ballgame."

Washington, DC, Northwest

Sweetie and Putnam each ordered a chicken salad sandwich at Camille's Cafe on F Street. They had arrived during a lull and chose a table in the shade. Putnam's trust in Sweetie was such that he took the seat with his back to the street. There was also a practical aspect to his choice. If someone appeared on the sidewalk who needed shooting, he didn't want Margaret to have to waste time turning around.

As they were currently seated, he was confident she could shoot past him and do no unintended damage.

Sweetie took a sip of ice tea, a step down from the stuff they served at the White House but entirely respectable for a commercial place. She scanned the nearby environs and then turned her attention to Putnam.

"So how serious is this threat to you?" she asked.

"Serious enough to put you in my will."

Very little surprised Sweetie, but that did.

"What?"

"Really. My first thought was just to leave you your basement apartment, but then I thought that might make it hard for the estate to sell the rest of the building. And what if they did find a buyer and you didn't like your new upstairs neighbor? So if I go, you get the whole place."

Sweetie didn't see any sign that Putnam was BS-ing her.

But he could be a sneaky tease.

"That's very nice of you," she said, "but a whole townhouse

would be far too grand for me. I'd have to sell it, give the money to charity and find new, suitably modest quarters."

Now, Putnam was taken aback; he didn't see any sign Sweetie was joking either.

"You'd do that? Sell a bequest?"

"I'd make sure the money went to a worthy cause."

Putnam said, "That's all very well, but it's not in keeping with the spirit of my intent."

Sweetie shrugged. "What can I say? I'm not someone who lives extravagantly."

"What if I asked you to move upstairs with me right now, while I'm still alive?"

That gave Sweetie pause. "Are you asking that?"

Putnam firmed his jaw. "I would, if I knew you'd say yes."

"I think, maybe, you've figured out by now I'm not the kind of girl to live in sin."

"More's the pity but, yes, I know that."

Sweetie took a deep breath. "So, what we're talking here, all of a sudden, is —"

"Sure sounds like it," Putnam said. "Funny how something like that can sneak up on you. I didn't even think to get you a ring or anything."

"If you ever do, make it something simple. Understated."

Having made her implicit acceptance to an unvoiced proposal, Sweetie turned to look for the approach of any assassin who might spoil their unspoken plans. She jumped when Putnam took her hand. Pulled it back, as it was her gun hand.

"Margaret, we're very close to doing something here, but when we do it for real, I promise I'll do it right. Not over chicken salad sandwiches."

Sweetie smiled at him. "I like chicken salad, but okay." Turning her attention back to the threat horizon, she added, "Now, tell me what's going on."

Putnam looked around, too. Not for a gunman but for any signs of a snoop.

Finding none, he told Sweetie, "This situation is this: Two groups of lobbyists and politicians, one of which includes me, are doing battle to decide who's going to run the federal government."

Sweetie turned her attention back to Putnam.

Again, she saw no indication he was pulling her leg.

"Yeah, I know," he said, "the things I get myself into, but it was bound to come to this sooner or later. Only thing is, I never thought it would turn into an actual shooting war."

The White House, the Oval Office

Patti freshened her drink and the one in front of the vice president.

She hadn't given the least consideration to the idea that Mather Wyman wouldn't be her running mate again. But she would bet Galia had, if for no other reason than a good many men in their sixties never lived to see their seventies.

"Are you well, Mather?" Patti asked.

He grinned. "As sound as the dollar used to be."

"Will be again, if I get my way," the president said.

The vice president's expression turned rueful. "And there, Madam President, is the rub. I fear for our ability to govern. Not just yours and mine, but the country's collectively. We're beset by such divisive partisanship that gridlock is the norm in Washington. The rest of the world is racing into the future and we're still debating the theory of evolution. Robber barons and their useful fools decide too many elections. Our party used to be criticized for being country club elitists, but I think we were far more egalitarian then than we are now. I'm just sorry that I did not come to you with my decision sooner."

Mather Wyman's bluntness left Patti almost speechless.

But she managed to say, "Why didn't you come to me sooner, Mather?"

"Two reasons. I believe that you're an exceptional woman and possibly will be a great president. I'd hoped that your election would be the start of a new, more reasoned era in government. Regrettably, it seems to me that hope has died."

Patti sighed inwardly. She thought she'd given Mather Wyman a portfolio of duties important enough to keep him busy and make him feel valued. He was her administration's lead voice on education, energy and immigration. Of course, if he'd felt all his best ideas in those areas had been stymied by Congress …

"Perhaps if we'd talked more, you would feel more hopeful," Patti said.

They had two scheduled lunch meetings per month. Mather had told her he wasn't someone who needed a lot of handholding, but now the president felt as if she hadn't been sufficiently attentive. The problem was, so many people needed her time.

"What was your other reason, Mather? You said you had two."

"I had to decide what I would do with myself."

"Get as far away from Washington as you can?"

Mather Wyman laughed. He held the bowl of peanuts up to the president. She took a handful. He put the bowl down and filled his hand and then his mouth with goobers. He kept smiling as he chewed and his mischievous look gave Patti reason to think something good was coming.

After he swallowed and took a sip of scotch, the vice president said, "There was a Republican president my dad took me to see when I was a boy. He was a war hero, but he warned against the military-industrial complex; he believed in the right of workers to bargain collectively; he appointed the chief justice of the Supreme Court that decided school segregation was illegal, and once that decision was handed down he sent federal troops in to enforce it."

"Eisenhower," Patti said. "So you're going to enlist in the army?"

Mather Wyman laughed again. "No, Madam President, I'm going home to Ohio to run for a seat in the House of Representatives as an independent. But I'm going to wear a button on my lapel that says, 'I'm like Ike.' I'll explain the similarities between my ideas and his. I'm not sure how that will sell these days, but the fellow holding the seat at the moment is a dolt. So I just might win, and if I do, I'm going to come back here and give all sorts of people heartburn."

The president nodded, thinking that was a fine idea.

"Are you going to borrow from Lincoln as well?" she asked.

The vice president shook his head. "That's too much of a reach for me. On the other hand, the first woman to reach the White House, someone who is a historical figure in her own right, she might wear Lincoln's mantle more comfortably."

Patti laughed at that and finished her drink.

And wrote the first check to the Wyman for Congress campaign fund.

Then she sent for Galia.

White House Physician's Suite

Welborn Yates and Elspeth Kendry stood in the outer office getting acquainted through the vehicle of polite debate while McGill, Kenny and Nick gathered in the examining room.

"Come on, Captain Yates," Elspeth said. "You can tell me about the nature of the warning you received. I'm supposed to know these things. It's my job."

A moment after receiving the phone call on the basketball court, Jim McGill had sprinted for the White House, alarming several of the uniformed Secret Service officers patrolling the grounds. Nothing made those guys freak out like the thought that a threat had somehow slipped past them.

Elspeth held up a hand to calm them down before the situation became an exercise in Keystone Kops burlesque. The uniforms slowed their pace, but they continued to follow at a trot. Elspeth and Welborn, meanwhile, dogged McGill's heels. They were both sure they could overtake the president's henchman, but even in the event of a mad dash across the South Lawn protocol was to be observed.

You didn't upstage the senior person.

They both saw McGill gather his son into his arms as a sober-faced Artemus Nicolaides closed the door to the examining room.

Neither Welborn nor Elspeth cared to speculate as to the news that was being delivered to the senior McGill.

So they turned to a discussion of their respective responsibilities.

Welborn said, "If it were a matter of physical safety, I'd tell you, but it's not."

"How do you know?" Elspeth asked. "Does your training include such analysis?"

Welborn's mother had long ago instructed him that a woman might know things he didn't, and he'd often found that to be true. He took a seat, glanced at the door to the examining room and then at Elspeth Kendry.

He was still trying to decide if talking to her would be a betrayal of a personal confidence when Deke Ky burst into the room.

"Holmes," Deke said in a loud voice, "is he —"

Welborn held an index finger to his lips: Shush.

Deke knew how to pick up on a cue, but he continued in a quiet voice, "I heard he was running like his life depended on it."

"Maybe not his," Elspeth said softly. She nodded her head at the door to the examining room.

"Kenny," Welborn said.

Deke winced. He took the seat next to Welborn.

The Air Force officer told the Secret Service special agent, "This lady would like me to tell her something I learned relevant to Mr. McGill."

Deke got back on his feet and asked, "Who are you?"

"A colleague," Elspeth said.

She couldn't believe the number of tightly wound guys around this place. Maybe it was something in the bottled water at the White House. She explained to Deke who she was, what her duties included, and how Captain Yates was holding back on something maybe she should know.

Deke looked at Welborn. "Tell her. She'll know better than you if it's something that could be a threat. If it's not, don't worry. She didn't get to where she is by being a gossip."

Elspeth smiled. "Why thank you, Special Agent. That's the nicest compliment I've had all day."

Welborn said, "He's a silver-tongued devil, our Deke is."

The Secret Service agents turned to him. Their looks said the same thing: *Give.*

Welborn gave: "WorldWide News has decided James J. McGill has enjoyed his privacy long enough. With or without his cooperation, they intend to have a TV crew follow him through his workday for an unspecified length of time to show the American people how he can be both the president's husband and a private investigator. They hope, my source says, to watch as he works a juicy case. Juicy is their word not mine. In short, they intend to put his life under a microscope."

Before either Deke or Elspeth could sort through the security ramifications of all that, the door to the examining room opened. Kenny McGill and Doctor Nicolaides appeared to have put on what they considered to be brave faces. So had the president's henchman … only he couldn't hide the fear in his eyes.

White House Examining Room

As soon as McGill had rushed into the room, the first thing Kenny McGill had said to his father was, "Dad, I'm going to be all right. Nick's going to see to it; he said so."

Not wanting to make a bad situation worse, McGill had only asked, "What else did he tell you?"

Kenny had taken one of the two chairs in the room; Nick had taken the other.

A sign of solidarity, McGill realized, his heart sinking.

Kenny said, "Well, first he asked me how I'm doing. Was the way I went about my day any different lately from what it usually was."

"Went about your day?" McGill asked.

That was Nick speaking; those weren't Kenny's words.

"Yeah. You know, the things I do every day. Were they any different?"

McGill went down on one knee in front of his son. "Were they?"

Kenny nodded.

"How?"

"I told you about getting more tired than usual, and maybe you noticed I don't eat quite the same way I usually do."

"You mean like a buzz saw."

"Yeah. I like to eat like that, but nothing tastes good to me now."

"What else, Kenny?"

His son looked down, avoiding McGill's eyes.

"There are some things I didn't tell Mom." He looked up, a plea for understanding on his face. "I didn't want to worry her; I didn't want to scare myself."

Kenny was doing a bang-up job of scaring him, McGill thought.

In a soft voice, he asked, "What other things, Kenny?"

"My nose bleeds almost any time I sneeze ... and I get bruises when I don't even remember bumping into anything." Tears started to run from Kenny's eyes. "Dad, I'd be scared if I didn't have Nick."

McGill shifted his gaze in the direction of the White House physician.

"We're going to do some blood tests," he said. Then, not waiting for lab results, Nick silently mouthed the one-word reason for the tests: *Leukemia.*

McGill didn't have any trouble doing the lip-reading, and the word couldn't have hit him any harder if it had been shouted. But he did his level best not to show his fear.

Kenny asked his father, "I couldn't have a better doctor than the guy who takes care of Patti, could I?"

"No way," McGill said. "He's the best."

Kenny nodded, taking comfort in that reassurance. He firmed his jaw, making McGill proud. Scaring him all the more. Kenny got to his feet and so did McGill.

"Nick says we've got some work to do," Kenny told his father, "but if it's okay, I want to see Mom now."

"Absolutely," McGill said.

He knew if they were going to get Kenny through this everyone would have to help.

White House, Chief of Staff's Office

Galia Mindel picked up her notepad and her favorite pen to take with her into the Oval Office. She was burning with curiosity as to what Mather Wyman had on his mind. She didn't doubt for a minute that would be the subject of her discussion with the president.

Maybe she couldn't strong-arm Wyman into telling her why he wanted to see the president but she could take comfort in knowing she'd get the word before anyone else. In fact, there was only one man in the building who could keep secrets from her and —

He entered her office at that very moment.

Without a knock or a by your leave.

James J. McGill all but collapsed into one of her guest chairs. She would have bristled at his lack of manners under most circumstance, but the man looked nothing like his usual confident, energetic, wise-cracking self. He looked almost lost, as if he'd chosen her office at random because he had to get off his feet before he fell.

Galia glanced up, saw Captain Yates standing in the hallway. He looked stricken, too, but what really scared Galia was when Yates pressed his palms together in a prayerful manner and then closed her door.

Good God, Galia thought, what was going on? If divine intercession was needed, what could the problem be? She put down her pad and pen and picked up the phone to do something she'd never done before.

"Madam President," Galia said, "I'll be with you shortly. Something unexpected has come up … yes, of course. I'll let you know if I need more time."

The woman was extraordinary, Galia thought, a chief executive secure enough to know there were moments when even she was not at the top of everyone's to-do list. Galia sat on a corner of her desk and tried to engage McGill's eyes.

"What can I do for you, sir?"

Rare was the day that she called McGill sir, but it seemed appropriate at the moment. He looked up at her and seemed to remember why he was there.

McGill asked, "Does the president have anyone coming to stay at Blair House soon?"

Blair House was just across Pennsylvania Avenue from the White House. It was where VIP guests of the president were welcome to stay when they came to town.

Galia shook her head. "It's open for the next several weeks."

McGill wondered if that would be long enough.

He said, "And it's the president's prerogative to decide who may stay there?"

"Yes, it is. Would you care to tell me what—"

McGill told her about Kenny, how his son was relying on Nick to see him through his treatment, how his ex-wife and his daughters, their step-father, too, maybe, would need a place to stay.

Galia Mindel and James J. McGill had had their differences, many of them, but Galia was the mother of two grown sons and if one of them … she had to repress a shudder. She stood and put a hand on McGill's shoulder.

"I'll see to it that Blair House is yours as long as you need it. We'll get the best people in the country to take care of Kenny."

McGill got to his feet. "Thank you, Galia. I'm sure the president is as busy as ever. I'll let her know what … what the situation is when I see her. It's probably best not to distract her before then." And then McGill was gone.

He was right about not distracting the president, Galia thought. But what reason could she give Patricia Darden Grant for keeping her waiting?

WorldWide News, Washington Bureau

Hugh Collier was having trouble paying attention to the Yank producer they'd assigned to him. Hell, he was having trouble keeping his eyes open. He'd gotten in from Sydney little more than an hour ago, and before boarding the plane he'd played two hours of football and had drunk beer for three hours after that. Doing all that should have helped him sleep, what with the luxury afforded by one of his uncle's Boeing 777-VIPs, except the flight seemed turbulent for every one of its bloody 9,758 statute miles.

He'd never been afraid to fly, not even halfway around the world, but that bloody flight was enough to make a bloke stay within a longneck of the ground. More jolts than he'd ever got playing footy. He doubted he'd slept more than —

He felt a gentle hand on his arm: the producer. "Mr. Collier, would you like to get some sleep and try this again in the morning?"

It was the Yank producer, telling him he'd nodded off once more. She was a thin bird, a bit severe in her appearance, but he could tell already she was smart, and she had a pleasant voice. Soft and sweet, almost intimate. Soothing to the ear.

If he'd cared for women, he might have given her a tumble. But he was a man's man, and that was one of the reasons he'd been dragged so far away from home. Dear old uncle, Sir Edbert Bickford, master of the global media empire known as World-Wide News, wanted to know if James J. McGill was queer and his marriage to the president a masquerade.

His lordship had put it to Hugh: "Imagine what a brilliant ruse it would be, President Grant marrying this fellow, giving him all the protection of both marriage and the presidency when for all we know he's nothing more than her personal assassin, waiting to be dispatched against her worst enemy. Kill one, terrorize all and get away with it."

Hugh thought Uncle Edbert should retire to one of his collection of tropical islands and write thrillers under a suitably butch pen-name and publish them through one of his many conservative imprints. With his imagination, he'd be a smash success.

Uncle, of course, had seen through Hugh's impassive demeanor and knew he was thinking subversive thoughts.

"What about that Roger Michaelson fellow?" he asked. "He's a United States senator and this McGill brute almost beat him to death … and got away with it."

"It was a rough game of basketball, Uncle, that's all," Hugh responded.

A damn rough game, Hugh thought. If McGill could run a bit, he might make a decent footy player.

Uncle was not to be dissuaded. The truth was, with another American presidential election in the offing, Edbert Bickford was going to do his best to determine who the next occupant of the Oval Office would be. He had absolutely no use for Patti Grant, but before he went after her hammer and tong, he wanted reassurance James J. McGill wouldn't take his head off for being impertinent.

A reasonable precaution, Hugh agreed. McGill certainly didn't mind a bit of brawling. The story about him and his three friends taking on that great ugly brute under a bridge in Paris was certainly enough to occupy a chap's imagination.

Uncle, of course, also wanted to know if McGill was gay because he always wanted to know that about his potential enemies. Confirmation of a sexual orientation other than one's own made adversaries easier to despise, gave one license to pursue any means to vanquish them. And who better to ferret out one nance than another?

Hugh might have taken offense at such bigotry, except Uncle paid him so bloody much money. Had educated him to a fare-thee-well: Oxford, Columbia and UCLA. Degrees in literature, business administration and law. Made him the highest paid, most well rounded chap on his football side, and sponsored the team to boot.

Most important, the crusty old bugger had taken him under his wing after his own father had turned him out for being gay. There was precious little Hugh wouldn't do for Uncle Edbert. If this berk McGill were to take a crack at Uncle, he'd put a quick end to that.

A quick end to McGill, if need be.

If he could get past the Secret Service, of course.

He realized he'd closed his eyes again, and forced them open.

He smiled at the producer.

"What's your name, dear?"

"Ellie Booker."

"Lovely. Would you have a car brought 'round to take me to my digs, Ellie? You're spot on about my needing rest. But I'll be right as rain in the morning."

Blair House

Carolyn took the news the hardest. McGill was sure she had to bite her tongue to keep from screaming. The results of the lab tests were in: Kenny's white cell count left no doubt that Nick had the diagnosis right. Kenny was upstairs sleeping now, with Nick watching over him, and would be admitted to George Washington University Hospital in the morning. Johns Hopkins, up in Baltimore, was generally thought to have a somewhat better reputation, but Galia and Nick were already lining up an all-star team of cancer specialists to consult with their colleagues in Washington, who would have the hands-on responsibilities.

McGill explained all that to Carolyn, Abbie, Caitie and Lars. Kenny really would have the best doctors in the country lending their knowledge and skills to help make him well. Reason, however, did little to dispel fear. Carolyn sobbed into Lars' shoulder, keeping her anxiety quiet enough not to disturb Kenny's sleep. Abbie took her cue from Mom and rushed to McGill, crying against his chest as he held her.

Only Caitie refused to yield to fear as a first resort. She stood apart from her father, looking at him, fists clenched at her sides, clearly wanting to strike out at someone or something. She turned her gaze on everyone present.

Almost vibrating with rage, she said, "We won't let Kenny die, we won't."

McGill could tell she was about to repeat her oath at a shout. He shook his head. That was when Caitie ran to him and cried, but hers were tears of frustration. She was ready to do anything to help her brother, but she had no idea of how to help him.

Pray, McGill thought. No atheists in the cancer ward.

He told the others, "We need to call Sweetie. She should be here."

Caitie stepped away from her father. Now she had something she could do.

She pulled out her cell phone. She had Sweetie on speed-dial.

The White House, the Residence

Blessing, the White House's head butler, brought McGill a glass of ice tea. They were in the room the president called McGill's Hideaway. Sensitive to the moods and needs of the First Couple, Blessing had no trouble seeing something was seriously amiss with McGill. He looked … not defeated but sorely wounded.

Only Blessing's professionalism kept him from overstepping his boundaries.

"Will there be anything else, sir?" he asked.

McGill shook his head.

"The president has been notified I'm on the premises?" he asked.

"The moment the Secret Service saw you, sir, at her request."

McGill nodded. "We'll need some time to ourselves."

"Of course, sir. No interruptions."

"Unless it's my family or Margaret Sweeney."

"Very well, sir."

Patti arrived just as Blessing was leaving. She exchanged a few whispered words with the head butler. He gave a small bow and closed the door behind him.

The president crossed the room to her husband and embraced

him, holding him wordlessly as his tears fell on her shoulder. She led him to the room's large leather sofa and they sat next to each other holding hands. McGill was trying to find the words to tell her what had happened when Patti spoke first.

"Which one?" she asked.

Galia hadn't let on as to the nature of the crisis, but had said Jim would be speaking to her later. Understanding that her chief of staff was deferring to her husband out of respect for his wishes and seeing Jim more distraught than … than any time since Andy had died, she knew something life changing had happened to one of the people he held most dear. It wasn't her; she had the gut feeling it wasn't Sweetie and it probably wasn't Carolyn, either.

So, one of the children. But which one?

"Kenny," he said.

McGill gave Patti the bad news.

She squeezed his hands, but sat back and looked him in the eye. Comforting her husband would have to take second place to helping his son. Kenny was a charmer, and he'd long ago captured her heart. The president was not about to let —

McGill saw where Patti was about to go and told her Nick had already gotten the ball rolling on Kenny's course of treatment.

Patti nodded in approval. "Nick's very good, but Harlan Mallory knows every top medical specialist around the world."

Mallory was the Surgeon General. The only reason McGill was aware of him was because his confirmation hearing had made news. Mallory was an outspoken advocate of doing anything and everything to maintain and advance public health. At the hearings, members of the president's own party had given the man a hard time when he refused to budge from his insistence that public schools must provide comprehensive sex education starting in the eighth grade.

Going farther, Mallory said that parents should be given remedial sex education so that they could initiate meaningful instruction on reproduction and other facts of life with their children at home as soon as the onset of puberty.

That caused an uproar, until Mallory leaned forward and told his Congressional inquisitors, "Implement this plan and you'll cut the number of unwanted pregnancies in this country by half. Fail to implement it and the responsibility for an unguessable number of abortions will be yours."

McGill liked the idea of a fighter like Harlan Mallory being on Kenny's team.

"Yeah, that's good," he said. "Please call him."

"He's on the line right now."

"Galia told —"

"No. She didn't. I just told Blessing to have all of my cabinet secretaries and senior advisers called. I figured I'd cover the bases. For whomever you needed."

McGill's heart swelled. Patti kissed him.

She said, "Let me go talk to the Surgeon General. We'll do everything we can for Kenny."

Putnam Shady's townhouse, Florida Avenue

Putnam stood in his living room, looking out the window at the street. He waved to Sweetie as she drove away in her Malibu. Cool old car, he thought. Would have been better, though, if it were a convertible and she had waved to him as she left, her hair blowing in the breeze. But she hadn't waved or even looked back.

She had kissed him before she was out the door.

Not just a peck on the cheek or a sisterly closed-lip buss.

An honest to God kiss, full of passion.

Almost took the starch right out of him.

She had told him about Kenny McGill, and that was awful. Probably, it was sympathy for the kid that got Margaret worked up, provided a little transference of deep feelings to him. That was okay. He'd take a kiss like that from Margaret any way he could get it.

He sat down on the sofa adjacent to the picture window. There was a gun on the end table next to the sofa, a Walther PPK. It was a recent gift from a friend. Putnam thought he vaguely remembered the Walther being the gun James Bond used, but the friend who'd given him the weapon said a single round from it didn't have much stopping power. His advice had been to keep right on shooting once you acquired a target.

Sweetie had told him pretty much the same thing when he'd shown the weapon to her. It had surprised him that she hadn't chastised him for having the gun. Then she shared with him the story that James J. McGill's first wife, Carolyn, whom Sweetie described as a peacenik, had felt the necessity to acquire a handgun when she thought there were people threatening her children.

True, Margaret had shaken her head while telling that story, as if to silently regret what the world was coming to, but she went on to tell Putnam that she'd given Carolyn instruction in how to fire her weapon effectively. She said she would take him to the shooting range, too.

In the meantime, she'd shown him how to hold the weapon in a two-hand grip, how to sight a target, how to squeeze not jerk the trigger.

Hardly the stuff of romance, but an intimate experience nonetheless.

Then the call came from Caitie McGill and Margaret was off.

But not before he got his kiss — and a warning to make sure all his doors were locked and the security system was armed. Putnam thought he'd go up to bed, see if he could fall asleep and make it an early night. Remember the feeling of Margaret's lips on his.

See if he could remember a prayer for Kenny McGill, too.

He turned off the lamp on the end table, darkening the room, picked up the Walther and got to his feet. That was when the first shots crashed through his living room window. Putnam, holding on to his gun, dived for the floor.

Another volley shattered more glass, flinging shards on him.

Putnam wanted to shoot back — without exposing himself. He could have just fired out into the sky, but Margaret had warned him of the possibility of hitting an innocent bystander, one who might be blocks away, with an errant round. Spilling the blood of anyone he shot would be a moral burden, she'd told him, but shooting an innocent person would be a crushing weight on his soul.

All that was well and good, but as a third volley entered his home and crashed into the wall behind him, Putnam knew he'd better do something fast before the sonofabitch with the gun poked his nose in the now empty window frame and saw him cowering on the floor.

He rolled onto his back, looked up at his ceiling and fired off round after round, figuring the projectiles would lose most if not all of their lethal power by crashing into the ceiling above him and the second floor roof.

But the shooter outside would only see the muzzle flashes, hear the percussion of shots being fired. He would learn that Putnam was armed and the jeopardy of being shot was now his, too. He wouldn't know, Putnam hoped, that the gunfire wasn't being directed at him.

He also hoped that at least one of his neighbors had called the cops by now.

He knew the response time was pretty good in his neighborhood.

If he could just hold out until — he felt the gun click empty.

Margaret hadn't showed him how to reload yet.

All he could do now was hope and — he thought he heard someone running off.

He remembered a prayer he could say. One for blessings received.

CHAPTER 2

Tuesday, August 16th, Blair House

Kenny McGill awoke a changed fourteen year old. He had always been a better than average student but never a great one. He was pretty much that way with most things: better than run of the mill but nothing special. He knew he could shine in at least a few subjects, but he just didn't push himself. Couldn't see any reason to go all out.

In that way, he was unlike both of his sisters. Abbie was ridiculously smart and approached everything she did like it was a work of art: Every detail had to be perfect. Caitie was maybe half-a-notch below Abbie for brains, but Caitie would run right over you to get what she wanted. When Caitie had told him she was going to be president someday, just like Patti, he didn't doubt it for a moment.

Not that he'd let her know, of course. She was still his kid sister.

He was going to hold on to the upper hand as long as he could.

What Kenny was good at was sizing up people, and what he'd seen yesterday was that everyone in his family had been scared silly by whatever was wrong with him. Even Dad, and that gave Kenny a shiver. Normally, he'd have let himself be scared, too.

He had been getting scared until Sweetie arrived. She came

into his room, sat on the edge of his bed and held his hand. He could see that she might have been worried a little, too, but she wasn't going to let herself be scared. Heck, Sweetie had stepped in front of a bullet to save Dad, and she hadn't let that stop her. She got well and went back to being a cop, went back to being herself.

As Kenny was talking to her, he decided that's what he was going to do, too.

Get better and be himself.

No, he was going to be *better* than he used to be.

You got real sick, who knew what could happen to you? Maybe the reason to go all out was you had to do it while you still could. You never knew when it might be too late. He was going to give it everything he had to get well.

Then he'd think about what to do with the rest of his life.

He looked to his right and saw Nick dozing in a chair in the near corner of the room. The White House physician looked to Kenny like he was going to wake up with a stiff neck, if he'd been sleeping in that position long.

Before he said anything, he thought about how he felt. Not great, but not too bad. Nothing really hurt. He hoped he wouldn't get to hurting. What he felt like, he needed to be recharged. Plug him into an electrical outlet.

Kenny called out to the White House physician.

"Hey, Nick."

Blinking, Nick looked over at his young patient.

"I was resting my eyes."

Why did old people always say that, Kenny wondered.

"Me, too. I think they call that sleeping."

A wide smile brightened Nick's stubbly face.

"You are your father's son."

Kenny nodded. "Yeah. How about we get this show on the road?"

Washington, D.C., Lafayette Square

More than one early rising tourist did a double-take. In reply, the president of the United States smiled and said good morning. Yes, it was really her. Out for a stroll. Celsus Crogher strode at the point of a diamond formation surrounding the president with other Secret Service agents following aft and on both sides. There were emergency vehicles on all four sides of the square and air cover, too. But the president was out walking among her fellow Americans.

A round of spontaneous applause put extra bounce in her step.

A young father plucked his child out of the stroller his wife was pushing and raised the toddler high, the better to see Patti. The little girl, if an outfit with pink stripes still meant anything, seemed to catch the spirit of the moment and smiled broadly at Patti before sticking her hand in her mouth. The president stopped briefly to speak with the family.

She waved and said hello to everyone who called out to her.

Entering the lobby of the Hay-Adams Hotel, she felt much better than she had leaving the White House.

Hay-Adams Hotel, Presidential Suite

"Madam President," Reynard Dix said, "thank you so much for sparing me a few minutes of your time."

Reynard Dix was the chairman of the Republican National Committee. The president was meeting with him in the grand old hotel because the Hatch Act forbade elected and appointed officials from engaging in political activity while on duty or in a federal workplace, e.g. the White House.

As president, Patricia Darden Grant was the titular head of the Republican Party. Truth be told, she and Galia had both devoted themselves to the affairs of state and had not tended much to the nuts and bolts of party politics. She'd never been one of the boys.

As a woman running for the Republican presidential nomination, Patti had entered the field as an outsider, a dark horse. There had been support for her in some quarters because of the pain she'd suffered in losing her first husband, Andy Grant, to an assassin. Some of the savvier political consultants in the party went so far as to suggest she would make the best vice presidential nominee the GOP could have on the ticket.

Not only was she a sympathetic figure, she was glamorous and well spoken.

She could be the Stepford veep.

Other wiseguys in the consulting class said it wouldn't work. Have Patti Grant as the number two and the president, whoever he was, would spend all his time trying to nail her.

Patti had put an end to all the schoolboy leering by passing the word through Galia that she would be nobody's vice president — and she would have none of the party stalwarts running against her as her vice president.

Hard feelings about this hard line position abounded, especially with Galia Mindel running Patti's campaign.

The idea of *two* women at the top of the party was more than many of its members could abide. Who the hell did these broads think they were, Democrats?

They might as well have been, Patti thought, because after the election she and Galia kept right on, filling many White House staff positions and cabinet posts with independents and Democrats while giving only pro forma attention to the suggestions and pleadings of the party apparatchiks.

One of whom was Reynard Dix, now offering her a chair and refreshments.

Patti took the seat and declined coffee.

"What can I do for you, Mr. Dix?" the president asked.

The chairman had helped himself to coffee and put his cup and saucer on his lap.

"Looking at the calendar, Madam President, I thought it would be a good idea for us to touch base."

Patti had never liked Dix. She thought of him as a phony's

phony.

"Touch base regarding what?"

"Well, there is an election coming up."

"Yes?"

"Unless, I've overlooked something, Madam President, you've yet to announce your intentions about seeking another term."

Patti smiled. "Are some of my would-be successors getting restless?"

"There's never a shortage of ambition in this town, Madam President."

Patti had to laugh at that.

"No doubt, Mr. Dix." Patti thought as long as she'd had to see the chairman, she might as well sow a seed or two of mischief. "Have you heard about Roger Michaelson?"

"What about him, Madam President?"

"I have it on good authority he's going to run for the Democratic nomination."

"To be president?" the chairman asked.

"He's already a United States senator, Mr. Dix. Do you think he would seek a lesser office?"

"No, no, of course not. You just caught me by surprise. Pardon my asking, but are you sure of this?"

Patti nodded. "Let me ask you, as party chairman, who among us in the Party of Lincoln do you think might be best positioned to defeat Senator Michaelson?"

Not possessing the keenest of intellects, Dix still knew the immediate reply to offer, "Why, you've already beaten him, Madam President."

"So I have. Who else in our party would do as well?"

Dix was impolitic enough not to deny anyone would run against the president in the party primaries. He gave her question serious consideration, mentally ticking off how Patti's would-be challengers would stack up against the junior senator from Oregon.

By the expression on his face, not well.

He needed a jolt of caffeine to bolster himself.

Patti stood up and clarified matters for the chairman.

"I intend to run for another term, Mr. Dix. I'll make the announcement at a time and place of my choosing. Please let any potential primary challenger know that I'll make him or her look worse than Roger Michaelson ever could."

The president left the room before the chairman could get to his feet.

Celsus Crogher fell into step ahead of her.

He spoke into the microphone at his wrist, "Holly G. is moving."

Miss Shirley's Cafe, Baltimore

"You make quite a first impression," Teddy Spaneas said.

He'd never met the thin man sitting across from him. The guy had let Teddy order breakfast for him and still hadn't said a word five minutes after they had walked into the restaurant.

"You don't have a voice, my friend? Perhaps you're not the man I was expecting, just some lucky fellow who is letting me buy his breakfast."

The thin man smiled. That said enough. He was the man Teddy wanted.

"Perhaps you think I am not a man of good character," Teddy suggested. "You think I would betray a potential business partner?"

The waitress came with their orders.

The two men ate in silence.

When they finished, the thin man said, "Let's talk in the conditional tense."

Teddy was a natural businessman, but he had never gone past the eighth grade.

"What does this mean?" he asked.

"Could, would, might, may. Like that."

Teddy understood perfectly. "If you could help me, I might be interested."

The thin man nodded.

Teddy added, "If you might have done me a favor, I might have shown some appreciation."

The thin man had dropped the Bentley Continental Flying Spur he'd stolen from the guy he'd popped in Fell's Point at the waterfront gate of Spaneas Import-Export — with the motor still running. The word he'd been given was they would know what to do with it, and they paid a fair price, too.

He'd walked away from the car without saying a word to anyone, leaving only a plain white business card placed in the driver's sun visor. The card had two sequences of numbers printed on it. The first sequence was for an offshore bank account; the second was for a disposable mobile phone.

When the thin man found an appropriate deposit had been made to his account, he turned the phone on. The call came within ten minutes. He gave the time and location for the meet and threw the phone in the bay.

Now the two men were talking, after a fashion.

Teddy said, "I might be interested in working with you again if you are able to specialize."

Steal cars to order, the thin man knew.

"That might work," he said.

"Might be steady work," Teddy said. Then he smiled. "Or you might like something more challenging and rewarding."

The thin man had always liked the idea of a big score.

"I might," he said.

"Good. I'll pick up the check."

As Teddy got up, he took a copy of *The Baltimore Sun* out of his coat pocket and left it on the table. Thing was, the paper was over two years old. It was open to a story about the new president's husband. There was a picture of the guy, James J. McGill, getting into a Chevy sedan. The car had been detailed to a mirror finish, but cars didn't get stolen for their wax jobs.

Without laying a finger on the paper, the thin man read the story. It said the president's husband got ferried around in the Chevy by a guy who was a former NASCAR driver, and when the driver, Leo Levy, had been asked how fast the car could go, he'd said, "Really fast. Other than that, I'm not supposed to say."

So there it was. Somebody famous — McGill — had a tricked out Chevy that was so hot a pro driver called it really fast. Now, somebody else with money wanted that Chevy stolen for him.

Might be some rich SOB in another country. Might be a good ol' boy right here at home who'd have a new paint job put on the Chevy and laugh his ass off every time he got behind the wheel. Either way the price tag would be as high as what a super-exotic fetched. Over a million bucks easy.

Given the risk of stealing the car, his cut would be higher than usual.

It would be a big score and ...

He just might be interested.

Washington, D.C.

Thing One, the president's preferred limo, formerly known as The Beast, was waiting at the curb outside the Hay-Adams when Patti stepped out of the hotel. Celsus Crogher opened the door for the president and saw her safely inside. He took the shotgun seat and Thing One moved ahead by a distance only slightly greater than its own length before coming to a stop. It sat idling, the driver awaiting further orders.

Galia had been waiting in the back seat for Patti. She was there not only to hear how the meeting with Reynard Dix had gone but to bear witness to the next obligation on the president's schedule.

"The video link is ready, Galia?" the president asked.

"Yes, ma'am. The link is secure, she's waiting and and once you're connected we'll be recording."

Patti nodded. "Let's get it over with. No wait. I want to be able to shut this down the moment I feel ... the moment I want to."

Galia handed a remote control to the president and indicated a red button to press if she felt the desire to end the conversation.

Patti gave a nod and Galia reached over and pressed another button.

Erna Godfrey's face appeared on a video screen mounted on the divider separating the president and Galia from Celsus Crogher and the limo's driver. A red light in the top margin of the screen indicated that the president's image was being seen in the secure female housing unit of the United States Penitentiary in Hazelton, West Virginia.

It was the first time the two women had seen each other since Erna Godfrey had been sentenced to death. Seated behind Erna and to her right was the prison's warden.

Erna got right to the point.

"I don't have any right to ask you to forgive me, and I won't. But I will say I'm as sorry as I can be, as sorry as anyone might be, for taking the life of your husband. It will hurt me every day I live thinking about what I did, and that's no less than I deserve."

Patti had expected an expression of remorse. She thought it would inevitably be a prelude to a plea for a further reduction in Erna Godfrey's sentence, a reason to hope that she might someday be a free woman. The president was determined that Erna Godfrey would spend whatever time she had left behind bars.

Even so, there seemed to be a ring of honesty to her words.

Galia put her right hand over Patti's left hand.

Out of the corner of her eye, the president saw her chief of staff give a small shake of her head. The meaning was clear. Don't say anything Erna Godfrey's lawyer might use as rationale for a judicial appeal.

Erna continued, "I don't blame you if you can't bring yourself to talk with me. You might even think I'm trying to trick you somehow. But I'm not. I just want you to know that my repentance is sincere. I hope to study for the ministry, and the ministry I hope to pursue is to bring the Lord's mercy to other women in prison who have sinned as grievously as I have. To do that, I'll have to spend the rest of my life in this prison or another one. I've made peace with that." A sad smile formed on Erna's face. "In a way, accepting that has brought me comfort. I won't ever again be tempted to do anything so stupid, anything so horrible. Mrs. Grant, I really am sorry. I hope that someday you'll be able to believe that."

Erna Godfrey's plea for credibility gave Galia such a startling idea she almost began to vibrate. In fact, she may have squirmed in her seat because the president held up her hand to caution Galia, let the chief of staff know she shouldn't say a word.

Erna went on, "There's only one more thing I have to say. In case you're thinking all of this was some way for me to ask for something from you, it's not. But I am trying to do something for someone else. I'm trying to save my husband's soul."

Then, on her own, Erna Godfrey did what Galia had hoped to pressure her to do.

She confessed Burke Godfrey's participation in the plot to kill Andrew Hudson Grant.

She did that and said she would testify against him in court.

Galia was stunned.

The president had another concern in mind.

She spoke to Erna for the first time. "You said you saw Jesus?"

"Yes, ma'am, I did."

"And you said you saw my husband, Andy, too."

"I did."

Patti took a deep breath and asked, "How did Andy look?"

Erna told the president, "He was at peace."

The president hit the red button before Erna Godfrey could see her cry.

Blair House

With Nick's approval, it was decided that Leo Levy would have the honor of driving Kenny McGill to the hospital. The Chevy assigned to the president's henchman came equipped with flashing lights and a siren, in the event a need for urgency arose, and it could travel faster than any ambulance on the planet, with a driver behind the wheel who was uniquely experienced at high-speed urban driving.

Kenny was thrilled by the idea.

He would have liked to ride shotgun, just him and Leo in the car.

Turning on the lights and sound effects would be cool, too.

But life was such that even in his current condition Kenny had to make concessions. Nick had to come along, and Mom, too. Carolyn had said they would ride in the back seat and she would pray that there'd be no need for either flashing lights or a siren.

With a smirk, Caitie added, "You know if you did get the kind of ride you wanted, I'd come along, too."

His sister would certainly want to, Kenny knew. He'd have to work out a secret agreement with Leo to give him a thrill ride another time. But Caitie's comment brought to mind a point to which Kenny had been addressing serious thought that morning.

"Caitie," he said, "school's going to start soon. If you want to stay in Washington, you'll need a tutor or something."

Kenny's words made Caitie whirl like a dervish in her parents' direction.

"I'm not going home, not until we know Kenny will be okay."

McGill held up a calming hand. "We'll work something out."

He wasn't simply placating Caitie; he agreed with her completely. The family would do better by staying together, at least for the near term.

But Kenny wasn't done. "Abbie, you've got to get a good start on college. I don't want you to fall behind because of me."

Abbie repressed her sadness and nodded. Then she gave her brother a hug and held on to the point that Kenny told her she was getting mushy. Abbie laughed and defiantly gave her brother a kiss on the cheek.

"Lars," Kenny told his step-father, "if you need to go home to run your stores, that's cool." Carolyn nodded in agreement. Kenny added, "You might want to come back on the weekends, if you can. Don't want Mom getting lonely."

Carolyn blushed, and everyone laughed at that.

Then Kenny turned to his father.

"Dad, you've got to help Sweetie with her case. You know she'd be there for you."

The kid was right, McGill knew. He said, "I will, but I won't be far away if you need me or you just want to talk."

"I know," Kenny said. "Where is Sweetie anyway?"

McGill was wondering the same thing.

Then Kenny had another question. "Dad, you think Patti might stop by and see —"

Celsus Crogher knocked on the open door to the room.

He said, "The president would like to know —"

Kenny was way ahead of the SAC. He darted past Crogher and disappeared around the corner, almost giving heart attacks to several special agents following Holly G. as they saw an un-identified figure rush the president. Adrenaline surged and hands reached for weapons. It was only after the president embraced the boy and kissed the top of his head that they collectively exhaled.

Crogher, who'd almost had to call off the troops, shook his head.

Another McGill male giving him fits.

Kenny led Patti by the hand into the room where the family had gathered.

Passing Crogher, Kenny gave the SAC a sidelong glance.

Hardly in the mood to play along with a gag, Crogher remem-bered what Holly G. had told him about the boy's problem, and he made a good guess what the kid wanted.

So he intoned, "Ladies and gentlemen, the President of the United States."

Kenny shot Crogher another quick look.

The SAC added, "And Mister Kenneth McGill."

To which Patti added, "Did somebody forget the flourish of trumpets?"

That got a laugh, but for a heartbeat Carolyn felt a deep green pang of jealousy, seeing Kenny hand in hand with Patti, his affection for her obvious.

How could an everyday suburban mom like her compete with

Patricia Darden Grant?

Before she could tell herself that would be impossible, her jealousy was overtaken by a moment of grace. If Patti Grant could make Kenny happy, especially now, she would welcome her and be grateful.

Carolyn stepped forward and hugged the president. She introduced Patti to Lars. There was a moment of small talk before Nick cleared his throat.

"We should be going," the White House physician said. "A number of very busy people will be waiting for us."

Patti asked, "Can I give anyone a lift?"

She took everyone who hadn't already booked passage with Leo.

Washington, D.C., Florida Avenue

Rockelle Bullard watched as Putnam Shady stood outside his townhouse with Margaret Sweeney and Welborn Yates. Except for the uniformed cops keeping the crime scene perimeter secure and the techs doing their thing, Rockelle was the lone representative of the Metropolitan Police Force in attendance. In the event that she had to swallow either her pride or a large helping of BS from someone who outranked a mere homicide lieutenant, she'd sent her detectives off to work actual murders.

If they were on hand and saw Rockelle humbled, her authority wouldn't be undermined, it would be gone. And things were going to be hard enough as it was.

She'd been out on the street all night, and went right after Mr. Putnam Shady the moment he stepped out of his house. Margaret Sweeney had asked her to wait until then. Ticked Rockelle off, but she decided it would be smart to play along.

She said to Putnam, "Tell me something you forgot the last time we talked."

There was no question in her mind the guy whose house got shot up knew a lot more about the three dead lobbyists — and maybe the pig pins — than he'd told her before. He played squash with Mark Benjamin? He knew a lot more than that, and she told him so.

To her surprise, the man didn't argue.

He said, "You're right, I do."

"Well?" Rockelle said.

"If I told you, you'd never believe me."

Getting right up in his face, Rockelle said, "I'll be the judge of that."

So he told her, and she didn't believe him.

Not one little bit. But as crazy as life in Washington could be … Rockelle called Welborn Yates. Maybe he could get the guy to talk straight. She was pleased that Captain Yates was on the scene with her within twenty minutes. It really did chap her backside, though, that a man fifteen years her junior, with little more than two years on the job, already held a superior rank.

It was only because Welborn was so polite, honest and co-operative that she liked him at all. Oh, hell, she liked him a lot. Didn't mean, though, there weren't times she wished she could get mad at him. Like right after he showed up and Putnam Shady gave him the same cock-and-bull story he'd given her.

Only thing was, being a fed and hearing a story of what would be a gigantic federal crime if it wasn't pure craziness, he hadn't dismissed it out of hand. No, what Captain Yates had done was discuss the matter with Margaret Sweeney.

Shady swore to Ms. Sweeney and Welborn Yates he'd been truthful. Now, the three of them, in the light of morning, were looking at Mr. Shady's residence. Adding to Rockelle's headache, she'd been told Ms. Sweeney lived in the basement apartment in the building. Several rounds of gunfire had gone through her front windows. Had she been home at the time …

It was going to be a heavy lift, to put it mildly, to persuade Ms. Sweeney that she should be content to let the police handle the chore of finding the shooter. Rockelle could even sympathize with her. The woman had spent twenty years as a cop in Chicago;

she'd told Rockelle that when she was polite enough to introduce herself.

Hearing Putnam Shady's story again, Margaret Sweeney hadn't thought the thing to do was scoff at it. No, she had made a phone call of her own.

And look at who was coming right now.

The man himself: James J. McGill, husband of the president of the United States. He was nice enough to explain himself to the cops at the perimeter. Showed them his ID like he was no big deal, all the while the Asian guy standing next to him — had to be Secret Service — looked like he'd reach for his Uzi if the Metro cops so much as gave the man any lip.

Things worked out with no blood being shed and McGill joined his friends.

Rockelle stood close enough to hear Putnam Shady say yet again: "What we plan to do is seize control of the United States government."

Mr. McGill didn't seem to find the idea fanciful. Not even when Mr. Shady added as he had before: "In a perfectly legal way, of course."

The president's henchman took a minute to digest that. He whispered something to Ms. Sweeney. She turned to Rockelle and said, "Lieutenant Bullard, why don't you join us?"

Rockelle headed their way.

Knowing McGill and friends wouldn't be asking her permission to work the case.

Wondering if they'd be nice enough to leave something for her to do.

Q Street NW, Washington, DC

Hugh Collier woke up hungry. It reassured him when his appetite traveled with him. There were times when he seemed to leaved the damned thing back home in Oz. Oh, he'd feed himself on a more or less regular schedule, but he didn't enjoy one meal in ten, and the food he consumed seemed to supply inadequate nutrition. Left him listless, not up to form.

It was at such times that he was susceptible to making one of his rare mistakes.

That morning the mere thought of food had him salivating. Breakfast would be just the thing if his biological clock had reset itself, but he was still on Sydney time, fifteen hours ahead of the Eastern U.S. He wanted a thick steak, grilled just enough to brown the outside. Fries and a green salad. And a beer or two.

He rushed through his morning scrub and shave and appeared in the kitchen with his hair still damp. It brought him up short to see … what was her name again, the Yank producer? Ellen? No, Ellie. Ellie … Booker. Yes, that was it.

She was sitting at the kitchen table with a cup of coffee and a notebook.

Jotting notes to herself, it seemed.

Had she spent the night? He assumed she knew his preference in bedroom companions, but that didn't mean she couldn't have kipped in a room down the hall. There were four bedrooms in the townhouse.

She looked at him standing there, his hair still damp, trying to suss things out, and she knew just what he was thinking. She held up a ring of keys. Now he remembered: She'd let him into the townhouse last night. He hoped she'd laid in his grocery order as well.

"Filet mignon's in the fridge, ready to broil," she said. "Salad's ready to be dressed. If you really want fries this early in the morning, that's doable. If you want to be a little more sensible, you can nuke an Idaho in the microwave."

Hugh thought that was a sensible idea. His taste buds might think it was dinner time but he didn't want to be weighted down through a full day's work. He was beginning to like Ms. Booker. She'd studied his preference and … probably made notes what they were.

"Might we have any beer in the house, Ellie?" he asked.

Just one wouldn't hurt.

She told him, "Epic Armageddon, Wild Thing and Little Creatures."

He pulled the fridge door open and saw she wasn't having him on. Two pale ales and a stout. Kiwi, Aussie and Yank. All of them among the best money could buy. Restraint would not be easy. He shifted his gaze to the filet mignon and the salad. Think food first, cobber, he told himself.

He put the steaks on to broil and dressed the salad with spices and a sprinkle of brown rice vinegar, no oil. He sat across from Ellie, thinking she would make a wonderful catch for a bloke inclined to sheilas. He looked at her jottings as he took his first forkful of salad. He couldn't make out what she'd written, but he clearly saw her nose wrinkle.

"Too much garlic?" he asked.

"Or too little salad."

He smiled, glad she wasn't a suckup. He moved to the chair on his right, giving her more breathing room. He said, "What sort of hieroglyphs are you using there?"

She smiled at him, showing a beautiful arrangement of sparkling Yank teeth.

If his younger brother weren't such a miserable sod, just like their old man, he might have arranged an introduction.

Ellie told him, "It's a variation on Pitman shorthand my aunt taught me. She worked at the Pentagon. Doing some sort of secret stuff."

Hugh seized on the most interesting part of what he'd heard.

"How many people know this variation?"

"Well, there's my aunt and me, and she's dead."

Hugh got up to turn the steaks with a broad smile on his face.

He wondered if an experiment in bisexuality might be in order.

"How many people might suss out your secret writing?"

"Some, but they'd have to be code specialists with a secretarial background."

"How much is Uncle Edbert paying?"

She told him. He awarded her a fifty percent increase, saying he could do such things.

"So, this McGill bloke, this president's henchman, is he an odd fellow like me?"

"You mean gay?"

"I do."

"No."

"You're sure?"

"He's forty-eight years old. Absolutely nothing I've found on him, and I've looked everywhere, indicates he's anything but heterosexual."

Hugh took the filets off the broiler pan and put them on a plate. They were browned and sizzling outside now, but would be a cool red in the center. Just the way he liked his beef. He grabbed an Epic Armageddon from the fridge, didn't need a glass.

"That'd be a bloody long time to stay in the closet without even poking your nose out," he told Ellie. "So we'll have to find some other way to embarrass James J. McGill — and his wife, the president."

Ellie said, "McGill has an ex-wife, but they get along better than most married people I know."

Hugh cut into the first filet: perfect. He didn't like to speak while eating, but he didn't mind listening. So he prompted his new colleague.

"You have found something else, though, haven't you, Ellie?"

She smiled. "There is this one old girlfriend."

Washington, D.C., GWU Hospital

Kenny McGill may have been a VIP patient, but he had to cough up health insurance information like anyone else. Fortunately for him, his mother handled the chore and she arrived at the billing department well armed. The primary carrier was McGill's policy. After kissing Kenny goodbye at the hospital door, McGill had given Carolyn his insurance card. He had coverage for himself and all three of their children.

Secondary coverage was provided for Kenny by the policy Lars provided for his wife, his step-children, and the employees of his drug stores.

In case there were any gaps left by the primary and secondary policies, the president had taken out a tertiary policy on Abbie, Kenny and Caitie. After all, they were her step-children, too.

The lady at the billing department smiled when she learned how swaddled in health insurance young Kenneth McGill was.

"Everyone should be so well covered," the woman told Carolyn.

"I'll take it up with the president," Carolyn told her.

She rejoined her children, Lars and Nick.

The president had kissed Kenny goodbye, too.

He had insisted that she, like everyone else, had to keep up with her work.

There had been a discussion on the way to the hospital whether Kenny should be treated on the pediatric or adult oncology floor. Nick said it was a judgment call best left to the patient. Kenny chose the adult floor. Unspoken but understood by all, Kenny was determined to face his treatment and his fate like a man.

Nonetheless, he took his mother's hand when he saw how many medical professionals were waiting for him. There were a dozen doctors and an equal number of nurses.

Washington, D.C., Offices of McGill Investigations, Inc. P Street, N.W.

McGill made room for Lieutenant Rockelle Bullard. In fact, when the building's owner, Dikki Missirian, brought refreshments, McGill saw to it that she got the first bottle of sparkling water.

The man definitely had a way about him, Rockelle thought.

Charmed people without half trying.

Rockelle saw that Margaret Sweeney was the most important person in the room to McGill, but Welborn Yates, Deke Ky, Putnam Shady and even her own sweet self were made to feel valued. She almost felt as if she'd been inducted into some secret society. No application necessary. No spooky initiation ceremony required.

McGill asked Putnam to tell his story one more time.

The lobbyist said, "Congress is for sale, has been forever, but since the Supreme Court did away with limits on political spending things have gotten a lot worse or better, depending on your point of view. However you look at it, the amount of money spent on political campaigns has exploded. Naturally, everybody who makes a substantial contribution to a successful candidate expects a return on his investment, and for the most part the rate of return beats anything you can buy on the stock market."

McGill, a Chicagoan born and bred, knew all about pay-to-play politics.

He asked, "So what are you saying, Putnam, the sheer amount of money has changed the game?"

"Money plus organization," Putnam said. "Right now, Speaker of the House Derek Geiger is about to put a plan into effect that he calls Super-K. He's laid down the law to the heads of all the big K Street lobbying firms. Hire Republicans, fire Democrats. Make contributions to preferred candidates in the amount specified or your pet legislation will go precisely nowhere."

Welborn said, "Wasn't that tried before? And didn't the idea bomb?"

"Yes and yes," Putnam said. "But an Air Force guy like you has to remember that quite a few early airplane designs flopped before the Wright brothers got their flyer off the ground. Learn, improve and implement, that's the idea. From what I've seen, Geiger's refinements could work … if they were left undisturbed."

"How do you know all this?" Rockelle Bullard asked. "How is it you've got all this information?"

Good cop, McGill thought. He'd been about to ask the same thing.

Putnam Shady took a deep breath and let it out audibly.

"Mark Benjamin, Bobby Waller, Erik Torkelson and I were all rising stars in our respective firms. Each of us was on his way to becoming his shop's biggest rainmaker."

"Money maker," Rockelle clarified.

"Yeah. We were all on our way to becoming big rich."

"You had a problem with that?" Welborn inquired.

"Left to our own devices, probably not."

McGill made the right call. "Someone close said the personal cost was too high."

Putnam nodded. "My friends all married well. The kind of women who made them better men. I've even met someone who's … undertaken a heck of a reclamation project."

Sweetie wasn't given to blushing, especially not when she was in cop mode.

She said, "You know about Geiger's plan because you were told about it, taken into the big boys' confidence."

Rockelle nodded. The shape of things was becoming clear.

"We were told," Putnam said. "We were trusted and proved untrustworthy."

McGill said, "Because you came up with your own plan. One that would sit better with the women in your lives."

"We did. We saw the flaw in Geiger's plan and figured out how to exploit it."

Deke spoke for the first time. "But you didn't cover your tracks and look what happened."

Putnam nodded again, the pain of losing his friends clear in his eyes.

"Yeah, just look."

McGill wanted to keep things moving. He had worries of his own, and now he could see more coming.

"So what's your plan," he asked Putnam, never doubting that Sweetie's landlord would do his best to make the plan work, if only to honor his lost colleagues. "How are you going to seize control of the United States government?"

Putnam asked him, "You know how Mutual of Omaha works?"

Putnam's explanation was so simple, so elegant and so compelling that everyone in the room sat or stood in stunned silence. The implications of his plan for the future of the country were profound.

It gave the old G.W. Bush notion of an ownership society a whole new meaning.

Deke, given his duties and his discipline, was the first to come back to the here and now. He looked out a window. Turning to McGill, he said, "TV van just pulled up outside; people getting out. Man with a camera, another with a microphone."

From his tone, the Secret Service agent might be describing a coming armed assault. Metaphorically, he was absolutely right. Deke had relayed to McGill the warning Chana Lochlan had passed to Welborn.

McGill told Deke, "Go downstairs, find out who the talking head is, let him or her up alone, no camera, no microphone. Have your colleague ..."

"Elspeth Kendry," Deke said.

"Yes, please have Special Agent Kendry set up a security perimeter to keep the rest of these people far away." Deke started for the door, but McGill held up a hand. "Them or any other media people attempting to do an unscheduled interview."

Deke gave McGill a look. McGill read it accurately.

"I know, keeping the paparazzi at bay isn't your usual chore, but think about it. Someone wanted to pop me or, say, Putnam, it'd be pretty good cover."

Deke said, "The Secret Service has thought of that."

"I hadn't," Putnam said.

"How far away do you want Special Agent Kendry to keep these people?" Deke asked.

McGill said, "For WorldWide News, the other side of the Continental Divide. Anyone else, West Virginia will do."

Climbing footsteps sounded on the staircase. Deke moved quickly out the door to turn them around. Air Force Captain Welborn Yates followed, providing close support.

Washington, D.C., R Street NW

Harlo Geiger gave her husband a shove, not hard enough to be mean but forceful enough to remove his spare, gray-haired, per-matanned frame from atop her. He flopped onto the satin sheet next to her. He reached over and put a hand on her arm.

"Give me a minute," he said. "We'll try again."

She reached a hand over to him, found what she was looking for and shook her head.

"Honey, a minute's not gonna be near enough time." She let go of him. "Maybe next week, if you get yourself some of those pecker-upper pills."

That was mean, she knew. Derek prided himself on his ability in bed. But she knew the dawn always came when the cock just refused to crow. She was surprised, though, that the day had come with her in the bed.

It was almost enough to make a woman think she'd lost her allure.

Harlo had returned early from a sales trip to Europe. Her latest furniture designs had been well received in Amsterdam, Helsinki and Berlin. Less so in Milan and London. After those chilly receptions, she'd canceled her stop in Paris. She'd decided to come home early and surprise Mr. Speaker.

She hadn't worried that she might catch him carrying on with some floozy, someone younger and less accomplished but with a backside that perched just a half-inch higher than her own. Like any other man, like *every* politician, Derek Geiger wasn't beyond being tempted. Unlike most of his colleagues in government, though, he had a more adult sense of restraint. That was, ambition came before rutting.

Harlo had taken a room at the Mandarin upon her return. Not merely to spend the night but to have a pleasant place to shower, to have the opportunity to buy some new clothes, perfume and inti-mate apparel that Derek had yet to see her model. She would sneak in on her husband before dawn. Launch her own commando raid.

He was still sleeping — alone, smart boy — when she sneaked into their bedroom. She stripped down to her cut-out halter teddy and stood next to where he lay. Let him inhale the scent of Clive

Christian No. 1 she'd applied a bit heavier than usual. Took him less than a minute to catch hold of the fragrance and flutter his eyelids open.

That was the moment of truth.

Would he get her name right or think she was someone else?

"Baby," he said with a sleepy smile.

Leave it to a politician to fudge things.

She slid under the top sheet with him and started doing things to him that had always made him stand to attention in the past. But that morning nothing she tried produced results, and she went at him like a hooker working on commission.

Mr. Speaker leaned over and kissed her in a fairly sweet way.

He hadn't taken offense at her gibe.

He told her again, "Just give me a minute."

But he was asleep a heartbeat later, his breath coming in a buzz too soft to be called snoring. Sounded more like a muted guiro. The man was sleeping peacefully. Almost as if he'd been hauling some harlot's ashes most of the night and had sent her packing shortly before his dear wife had come home.

Traveling inside the veil of her own perfume and adding the smell of her perspiration to the bedding, Harlo was unable to detect another woman's odor. But her suspicions had been aroused all the same. Because Mr. Speaker was justified in taking pride in his bedroom prowess.

Maybe she'd just caught him after he'd been tapped dry.

That could explain why he hadn't take offense at her insult.

He knew he didn't need to spray starch his thing.

Harlo got out of bed and took a shower. She put on a pair of Plain Jane panties and a T-shirt from her alma mater: SCAD, the Savannah College of Art and Design. She stepped barefoot past her sleeping husband and went to search the rest of *her* residence: the title to the townhouse was in her name; she'd bought it with her own money. Maybe she'd find a wine glass in the kitchen sink with lipstick on it.

She didn't. The place was as neat as the proverbial pin. With one exception.

In Derek's office, a faxed message lay on the machine's reception tray.

It was from Brad Attles, her husband's personal lawyer.

The caption on Attles' message was Re: Divorcing Harlo.

The *sonofabitch*. She'd told Derek she would be the one to make that call.

She picked up the phone to call her D.C. lawyer.

The White House, the West Wing

Following Deke Ky's direction, Welborn Yates made contact with Elspeth Kendry and asked her to enforce McGill's wish to keep the media, especially WorldWide News, at a far remove. He'd slipped past Deke and the crew from WWN that the Secret Service special agent had bottled up on the stairway leading to McGill's offices.

Welborn had waved to Deke and said, "Reinforcements will be here soon."

Deke gave a minimal nod but said nothing. He was busy staring down a burly guy at the head of the interview/ambush team. The guy was handsome enough to be a talking head, but he looked as if, under other circumstances, he might be willing to dance a few rounds wearing sixteen-ounce gloves.

Trying to push your way past a working Secret Service agent, though, that was just plain crazy. It made the departing Welborn recall Mr. T's signature caveat. "Pity the fool!" Welborn called out, giving the caution as much bass rasp as he could muster. Looking back, Welborn saw the camera operator, the sound guy and a thin woman look his way and appear to take his warning to heart. The woman followed him out the door to the street.

Welborn stopped before getting into McGill's Chevy.

"Would you care to introduce yourself?" he asked the woman.

"Ellie Booker, producer, WorldWide News," she said.

"A pleasure," Welborn said, "but I must be going."

"I don't get to know your name?" Ellie asked.

"Not at the moment, but I can tell you I'm a federal officer. So is the fellow blocking your friend's way, who, if he doesn't take a step back and mind his manners, is closing in fast on a very unpleasant experience."

Welborn opened the Chevy's door. Leo turned the engine over.

"What kind of reinforcements are you going for?" Ellie asked.

"The kind with very little patience."

Elspeth Kendry's face had lit up when Welborn told her what McGill wanted.

Screwing with the media was every cop's dream job.

Now, Welborn sat in his office wondering what new turn his work would take.

No doubt something he never would have dreamed of when he'd entered the Air Force Academy with the goal of flying fighter jets. His reverie led him to the times he'd actually lived his dream, flying high and oh so fast. Until the car crash in Vegas had taken that away from him. Had taken the lives of his friends Keith Quinn, Joe Eddy and Tommy Bauer.

"Why are you looking so sad?"

Welborn blinked and saw Kira standing in the doorway to his office.

"Thinking about the guys," he said.

Kira knew which guys Welborn meant. She nodded in sympathy.

"I had an idea," she said. "Wanted to ask your opinion first."

"Tell me."

"You know how we had to postpone our wedding?"

"I have some memory of that, yes," Welborn said.

Kira cut him some slack; a moment ago, he'd been mourning a loss.

"I don't want to postpone it again. I want to be your wife soon. Though I will concede there are moments when I wonder what the hurry is."

Welborn grinned. "Let's do it right now. Go to city hall, get married on our lunch hour."

"I was thinking of something with just a bit more charm."

"Do you really think we'll be unlucky again? Have to set another date?"

"You've heard what's happened to Kenny McGill?"

He had, but he didn't know how Kira had come by the news.

But then the White House tom-toms might have sounded while he was elsewhere.

"And my uncle told me something in confidence," Kira said.

Her uncle the vice president, Welborn knew.

"I won't ask you to break that confidence," Welborn said. "But I'll take it to be a matter of significance."

"It is, and thank you for not asking."

"You're sensing that storm clouds might be gathering?"

"I am."

"Can we allow enough time to have your mother and my parents join us at the river?" he asked. "Nuptials along the Potomac might be nice."

Kira liked the idea. She told Welborn, "I did call Father Nguyen. His schedule is fairly open this week."

Francis Nguyen, they'd agreed, would be the celebrant at their wedding ceremony.

"That's a good sign. Ms. Fahey, I will marry you any time of day or night, any day of the week. Whenever you will have me."

"I've always suspected as much," she said with a smile.

Welborn laughed and added, "And if I'm busy doing derring-do, I'll get it done."

The Missirian Building, Georgetown, P Street

Hugh Collier never did get past Deke Ky. The Secret Service special agent backed him down the stairs and onto the sidewalk outside Dikki Missirian's first investment in American real estate. By the time Collier stepped outside, Ellie, the camera operator and the sound guy had already vanished.

The whole thing was like something out of a movie, Collier thought. One of those films where everything looked normal, but people behaved in ways you'd never expect. He had to remind himself this was Patricia Darden Grant's Washington not Vladimir Putin's Moscow. Journalists didn't fear for their lives in the United States, and they didn't disappear.

Even so, he was dead sure the slant-eyed bastard with his right hand under his suit coat would have shot him dead, had he tried to bull past him. Collier was a quick bloke, had moves on the football field that left defenders grabbing at air. But that was his game. The game on the stairs was one he'd never played, there was far more at stake and he knew in his bones he'd come out second best.

But where the hell had Ellie and the words-and-pictures men gone?

Whisked off to the gulag, all of them?

Replaced by an exotic bird — looked a bit Persian — with her own concealed weapon and a glint in her eye every bit as predatory as the Asian bastard. The two of them exchanged a glance. The bastard gestured to the woman, pointing down. Collier knew he wasn't free to go. Custody had just been passed.

The woman pulled a chair out from one of the two café tables outside the building.

"Have a seat," she told Collier.

"And if that's not what I care to do?" he asked.

"Then I'll arrest you."

"On what charge?"

"Refusing to obey a lawful order from a federal agent," Deke said.

A newsman being pushed around by feds would have been brilliant theater for WorldWide News, if only there had been a camera to capture it. Uncle Edbert would have soiled himself in his excitement. But Hugh Collier didn't see so much as a curious onlooker with his cell phone out.

He sat down. Not liking being bullied at all.

That was normally his prerogative.

***

Jim McGill appeared a moment later, followed by Sweetie and Rockelle Bullard. Right behind them came Dikki Missirian carrying a tray holding bottles of Perrier, glasses and a bowl of mixed nuts. He waited for McGill and the ladies to be seated and served the refreshments. He nodded to everyone and went inside.

McGill sat opposite Collier, with Sweetie to his right and Rockelle to his left.

He extended his hand to Collier. "I'm Jim McGill."

Collier took McGill's hand. Each of them was strong; neither was adolescent. The handshake was just that, not a test of the other guy's pain threshold.

"Hugh Collier."

"Of WorldWide News."

"You'd been alerted to my approach," Collier said.

McGill wasn't about to give away anything.

Collier told him, "Might have been your people saw us coming. Or perhaps someone inside my organization gave you a call."

McGill's response was indirect. "What do you want, Mr. Collier?"

Sir Edbert Bickford's nephew sipped Perrier from the bottle and looked at McGill.

"If not a public figure, Mr. McGill, you're a figure of public interest. You're married to the president of the United States, you work as a private investigator after a long career as a policeman. Your exploits both in uniform and in a private capacity are becoming legendary."

McGill smiled. He looked at Sweetie.

"Legends in our own time," he said.

"I'm almost impressed," Sweetie said. She had her eyes on Collier, not pushing it, just keeping up a light pressure.

"Don't underestimate yourself, Ms. Sweeney. You've cut quite a swath yourself."

"Pride is a sin, Mr. Collier. A deadly one."

"So it is, but we'll all expire from something. Might as well make life interesting."

Collier turned to Rockelle.

"I'm sorry, I wasn't briefed on you."

"My publicist got laid off," she told him.

"Some sort of police, though," he guessed.

"The touchy sort."

Turning back to McGill, Collier said, "My brief is to do an in depth study of the life and times of James J. McGill, how he manages his roles as the president's henchman, a private investigator and who knows what else." Collier turned to look at Sweetie, just long enough to suggest he thought she might be more than a friend to McGill. "How do you do all that and manage to keep such a low profile?"

McGill knew he'd better wrap things up before Sweetie took an active dislike to Collier. "I'd tell you, except I signed an exclusive deal with Ken Burns, effective as soon as the president leaves office."

"So you'll be of no help to me?" Collier said.

"None at all."

Collier raised a name from the past. "All because Monty Kipp made an unfortunate joke about putting President Grant on page three?"

Page three was where Sir Edbert ran photos of incompletely dressed women in the foreign editions of his tabloid newspapers. Kipp, the former Washington bureau chief of WorldWide News, had, in an inebriated moment, confessed his ambition to put the president on page three. McGill had discouraged him.

Chana Lochlan had told him of Kip's scheme, too.

At the moment, Collier was fishing for confirmation of that fact.

And trying to see just how simple a mark McGill might be.

McGill stood up. "I have a lot to do, Mr. Collier. I'm a private citizen, despite being married to the president. As for the inquiring minds who might like to know me better, tough. Special Agent Kendry will tell you how much elbow room you'll need to give me."

Collier got to his feet. "That could be a story in itself."

"Run with it," McGill told him. He turned to leave.

Deke and Elspeth moved in on Collier.

"One last thing, Mr. McGill."

McGill looked back. "What's that?"

Collier told him, "Clare Tracy says hello."

McGill smiled. "Nice to hear from her again."

He turned and went back into Dikki's building.

Wondering how the hell Collier had learned about Clare.

GWU Hospital

Carolyn Enquist had never heard of HLA. Not many people had. Hearing that the acronym stood for human leukocyte antigen didn't clear matters up any. In fact, being brought face to face with her ignorance of Kenny's disease only served to scare her.

Nick and the squadron of doctors and nurses he'd enlisted had taken Kenny off to begin his … the word that came first to Carolyn's mind was ordeal, but she amended that to treatment. Then, accompanied by a silent prayer, she changed treatment to cure.

One nurse had stayed behind, a mature woman whose pretty face made her seem younger than her years. Her name tag read Barbara Marcos. She had questions for the family, starting with whether they knew what HLA was.

She wasn't surprised at Carolyn's inability to answer.

But she'd learned from the intake report that Lars Enquist was a pharmacist.

"Mr. Enquist, do you know about HLA?"

Lars said, "They're proteins, markers. Most of the body's cells have them. "

Caitie piped up. "Why's that important?"

Lars looked at the nurse. She gestured to him to continue.

He told Carolyn, Caitie and Abbie. "The markers are like your personal brand. Your immune system recognizes your brand, knows it's not something foreign that has to be attacked."

Lars glanced at Barbara Marcos to make sure he had it right. She nodded, and Lars continued.

"The donor bone marrow cells are what help a patient recover, but that can't happen if the patient's own body attacks those cells."

"How do you know who's a good match?" Abbie said.

"We're family," Caitie said, "we should all match, right?"

Barbara shook her head. "Full siblings, same mother and father, have a twenty-five percent chance of matching. To find whether any of you match or not, we'll need a sample of your blood to test."

Carolyn said, "But with the girls and me and my former husband, we should have a match among the four of us, shouldn't we?"

It became clear why Barbara Marcos had been chosen to talk with the family. She knew the facts and she wouldn't shy away from them, but the depth of her caring was clear on her face. She said, "It would be great if the math worked that way, but it doesn't."

"Why not?" Caitie asked indignantly. "Twenty-five percent times four equals a hundred percent. One of us has to be a match."

"I wish that were so, but in this case you can't add individual percentages or multiply them. I'm afraid the number you have to keep in mind is this: Approximately seventy percent of patients who need a bone marrow donor have to go outside the family."

"Oh my God," Carolyn said.

Lars put an arm around her. "I'll be tested, of course."

"Thank you, Mr. Enquist," Barbara said.

Abbie and Caitie put their arms around their stepfather.

Then Caitie looked at Barbara and beamed.

"Sweetie!" she said.

"I beg your pardon." Barbara didn't understand.

The others did and bobbed their heads.

Carolyn said, "Margaret Sweeney, a dear friend."

"She would consider donation?"

"If not one of us here or my former husband, she'd be our first choice," Carolyn told Barbara. "I have no doubt she would help Kenny."

"That's good. Think of as many people as you can, ones who would be willing to donate. The wider the net you can cast, the better."

Then Caitie asked, "How do you get bone marrow from someone anyway?"

Barbara Marcos turned to Lars to see if he might be of help again.

He was. "What they do, Caitie, is something called a bone marrow harvest. They take the stuff they need from your pelvic bone."

Caitie tried to imagine that. "But how do they get *into* your pelvic bone?"

"With a needle."

Caitie grimaced, as did Abbie and Carolyn.

Barbara said, "There's also another way. It's called peripheral blood stem cell donation, PBSC for short. Cells are taken from circulating blood, then the blood is returned to the donor. No surgical involvement at all."

"Why don't they just do it that way all the time?" Abbie asked.

Barbara told her, "The doctors have to decide which way would work best for each patient." Then she added, "You'll ask Mr. McGill to come by and give a blood sample?"

"Of course," Carolyn said. "Jim wouldn't have it any other way."

As they headed off to have their blood drawn, Carolyn whispered to Barbara Marcos, "What if none of us is a match? Neither family nor friends."

"Then we go to the registry and look for a donor."

"Does that work?"

"Sometimes." Barbara said.

That was always the hardest answer she had to share.

The Oval Office

Attorney General Michael Jaworsky arrived punctually and paid close attention to the video recording of the president's conversation with Erna Godfrey. Every so often he made a note on the pad of paper resting on his lap. Each note occasioned a small nod of his head.

The president watched the recording sitting perfectly still.

This time she did not cry when she heard that the soul of Andy Grant was at peace.

Galia Mindel kept one eye on the video and the other on the president and the attorney general. She deeply hoped each of them would want to proceed with an immediate indictment of the Reverend Burke Godfrey as a co-conspirator in the murder of the president's first husband. Doing so, however, would not be without consequences.

The political ramifications would be huge. The religious right of the president's own party would explode in rage. Loud protest would also issue from conservative Democrats. Fundamentalist religious figures would cry that one of their own was being persecuted. Political enemies large and small would accuse the president of subverting the very institution of matrimony, saying that Patricia Darden Grant had purchased Erna Godfrey's testimony against her husband by commuting her death sentence. The most vicious among the opposition voices would assert that a further reduction of Erna's sentence would be granted once Burke Godfrey was convicted and, no doubt, sentenced to death.

Burke Godfrey's trial would be exactly the kind of three-ring political circus no incumbent president needed as she geared up for reelection. Barring the start of a major war or a complete economic collapse, *U.S. v. Godfrey* would be the wall-to-wall story of every news outlet in the country.

Despite the brass-knuckle battles that would ensue, Galia couldn't wait to get started. Her sense of justice was biblical in nature, and specifically Old Testament. She saw no way in the world she wouldn't want the head of any man who had killed her husband, and she expected no less of Patti Grant, but ...

Before Patricia Darden Grant's election, Galia remembered, she had pointedly limited her role in Erna Godfrey's trial to sworn testimony. She'd given no interviews on the subject. Once in office, she'd stayed well clear of making any effort to expedite the damn woman's execution. She'd even decided to commute Erna's death sentence without any counsel from Galia.

No one had advised her on that matter but her current husband — Galia being unaware of the president's discussion of the matter with the Queen of England.

Galia wondered what James J. McGill would have the president do with Burke Godfrey. He'd said, at one time, everyone involved in the death of Andrew Hudson Grant should be strapped to a gurney.

Had he experienced any change of heart about that?

"Galia?" the president said.

The chief of staff snapped to attention, straightening in her chair.

"Yes, Madam President?"

"The video's over, but you're still staring at the television."

Before Galia could say anything, the attorney general intervened.

"It is a thought provoking piece, Madam President. Ms. Mindel is obviously looking at it from many angles."

Michael Jaworsky had been the smartest, toughest, most effective U.S. attorney in the country before the president had nominated him to his current post. He'd put away mobsters, terrorists and investment bankers. That last class of ne'erdowells had their defenders in Congress, but Michael Jaworsky, a lifelong bachelor, had been confirmed by a vote of ninety-three to five.

"Thank you, Michael," Galia said. "You'd make a good defense lawyer."

Jaworsky laughed. "Perish the thought."

The president refocused her subordinates on the matter at hand.

"What would you advise, Michael?"

The attorney general glanced at his notes. "The first thing we do is put Lindell Ricker and Walter, Penny and Winston Delk into protective housing. If you'll permit me, Madam President, I'd like to do that right now."

"By all means," the president said.

Jaworsky made the call, cupping his hand around the phone's mouthpiece. Neither woman was more than a few feet from him, but neither heard a word he said as he gave the order that the four active accomplices to Erna Godfrey's murder of Andy Grant be sheltered in ways that would protect them from any violence, planned or coincidental, that might befall them in their respective federal prisons.

The attorney general put the phone down.

"We'll let Ricker and the Welks wonder what's happening for the time being; nobody tells them anything. Let their consciences conjure what they will. In the meantime, I'll be leaving for Hazelton, West Virginia within a matter of hours to speak with Mrs. Godfrey."

"You, personally?" Galia asked.

"Me," Jaworsky said.

Galia had no desire to complicate matters by raising the subject of an independent counsel, but she wondered if the direct involvement of the nation's top law enforcement official might look like the administration was greasing the rails for Burke Godfrey.

"Madam President?" Galia asked.

"Do it, Michael," she said. "Let's see how sincere Mrs. Godfrey is."

"We'll also need to have FBI agents keep track of Burke Godfrey's movements, and we'll need to search his offices and homes to make sure no documentary evidence suddenly goes missing. I'll need to take care of that quickly, too."

"Use Galia's office as soon as we're done."

"It will look better if I use my own office," the AG said.

"You're right, of course." Patti shook her head at her misjudgment.

"Don't be hard on yourself, Madam President. I can't begin to imagine the heartache all this has rekindled in you. You handled yourself very well in your conversation with Erna Godfrey. Nothing you said could in any way be viewed as either coercive or vengeful. That's very important."

Patti only nodded. Small comfort, but she'd take what she could get.

The attorney general said, "What we have to do is get any and all evidence we can to buttress Erna Godfrey's statement that her husband was involved in this crime. Documentary evidence will be important; corroborating testimony from at least two of Mrs. Godfrey's co-defendants will be essential. We get those things and we'll be able to build not just a strong case but one that will convince a majority of the American people."

Galia was pleased the attorney general understood the politics involved, and intended to win the minds of a far greater number of people than just the members of the jury.

Getting better than half the voting public was what Galia wanted.

Now, all they needed to move forward was —

The president said, "Don't let us keep you, Michael. Make this work."

With that the prosecution of the Reverend Burke Godfrey was set in motion.

Galia started to make her plans accordingly.

Washington, D.C., National Portrait Gallery

The Merriman brothers, Robert and Anson, were idly glancing at the paintings hung in the Twentieth-Century Americans exhibit. The theme of the paintings was the never-ending struggle to attain the American goal of justice for all. Images of those who had struggled to that end included reformers from Teddy Roosevelt to Martin Luther King, Jr.

Neither of the Merrimans kidded himself about possessing a similarly noble character; their interest wasn't art — it was conversing in a place where their words were unlikely to be recorded and where their adversaries would be easy to spot. Appropriate to the setting, though, they kept their voices down.

"So, you're out now, right?" Anson asked his older brother.

"Roger Michaelson comes back to the Senate after the August recess, and he's got a new chief of staff."

"I'm available for the occasional phone call," Bob said. "On the cuff."

Anson repressed a chuckle. "You charged Mom for doing the dishes. Don't tell me you're giving freebies to Michaelson."

"Okay, I won't tell you."

"So who are you hiring to run your campaign?"

Robert Merriman would soon announce his campaign to run as a Democrat for the Senate seat from Oregon that his former boss, Roger Michaelson, would be leaving to run for president.

"Haven't decided yet," Bob said.

"Bullshit. You know who you want. If you're not telling me, it's because you're still negotiating money and authority."

Robert Merriman stopped in front of a portrait of John F. Kennedy.

His brother stood next to him. They looked at the image of the assassinated president.

Kennedy had died younger than either of them was now.

"You think he had any idea what was going to happen to him?" Anson asked.

"You mean a premonition?" Bob shook his head. "No. If he had, he would have sent Lyndon Johnson to Dallas alone."

"Bobby Kennedy would have liked that."

"Better than what happened, that's for sure."

"If Johnson had taken the bullet, Bobby might've pushed himself for VP."

Robert Merriman looked at his brother and grinned.

"You saying the Kennedys were closer than we are?"

"I'm not the one keeping secrets," Anson said.

"Chickenshit stuff. You want to hear something big, I'll tell you — under pain of death for talking, of course."

Anson nodded. "Death, sure. What's the secret?"

"I'm working on getting Patti Grant's endorsement for my Senate run."

Anson smiled. "Nice parlay: getting a Republican president to endorse a Democratic candidate for the Senate, thinking you can not only do it, but you can make it work to your advantage. That takes imagination."

Then Bob told Anson exactly how he would make everything work.

The younger Merriman's eyes went wide in wonder.

"Jesus, wouldn't that be something?"

"Yes, it would."

"That's worth a tidbit in return. One of the guys in my shop is an in-law to Gerald Mishkin. You know who he is, of course."

Robert Merriman had never married. He thought a wife would be a vulnerability, children a distraction. He dated single women no younger than ten years his junior. What he and the ladies did was strictly their business and they kept the curtains drawn as they went about that business. Voters said they preferred married candidates, but the way things had gone with straying political spouses the past twenty years, Merriman was betting people would find his approach refreshing.

Nonetheless, he knew Gerald Mishkin was the capital's top divorce lawyer.

"Who's untying the knot?" he asked.

Anson told him, "That would be Mrs. Speaker of the House, Harlo Geiger."

Robert Merriman chuckled gleefully. "Strike three, he's out."

The White House, South Portico Gate

Leo Levy drove McGill and Deke up to the South Portico entrance to the White House. The back door, as McGill thought of it. Leo stopped right where he was supposed to and waved at the uniformed Secret Service officers. Every man and woman in the uniformed service, a number approaching five hundred, knew McGill and his car, knew Leo and Deke.

Once the uniforms got to know that McGill was a regular guy

who just happened to be married to the president, they would respond in a friendly manner when he chatted with them. Some had even joked with him. Dan Cuyler, an Irish-American with a dry sense of humor, approaching McGill's car at that moment, had even started a running gag of doing a sign-countersign bit with the president's husband, like the two of them were spies.

It started one day when Cuyler had looked at McGill with a straight face and said, "The wind is in the willows."

To which McGill had replied, without missing a beat, "And there's dandruff on the pillows."

Leo and Deke rolled their eyes at the routine, but the uniforms appreciated it.

Cuyler always concluded the act with, "Pass, friend."

But today Cuyler's appearance was serious. In fact, the uniformed officer stood to attention opposite McGill and snapped off a perfect salute. Uneasy now, McGill returned the gesture from the back of the car.

"Everything okay, Dan?" he asked.

"May I speak personally, sir?"

"That's the way I like it," McGill said.

"We've heard about Kenny."

McGill shouldn't have been surprised, but he was. There were over three thousand people who worked full time at the White House. Part-timers and volunteers added hundreds more. But the guys on the gate already knew about Kenny.

"He's getting the best of care," McGill said.

"Yes, sir. But we understand he might need a bone marrow donor. I hope you don't mind, sir, but we've started compiling a list of potential volunteer donors, in the event no one in your family is a good match."

McGill was stunned. He'd heard from Carolyn less than an hour ago about going down to the hospital to give a blood sample … and the Secret Service was already thinking about helping his son. Their kindness brought a lump to his throat.

"Thank you, Dan. You're talking about your uniformed

colleagues?"

"Us and the presidential detail and the vice presidential detail. Wouldn't be surprised if the Marines got in on the act. Probably the Navy guys in the Mess, too. And the National Park people."

McGill had to blink away tears.

"Thank you." He extended his hand to Dan Cuyler. The officer shook it and saluted once more.

As Leo drove onto the White House grounds, McGill asked Deke, "You have anything to do with this?"

Deke's voice was impassive. "Might have."

Leo told McGill, "Count me in, too, boss."

McGill nodded. "Thank you, both of you."

Then a thought of the purest irony struck McGill: What if the one person who could save his son turned out to be Celsus Crogher?

GWU Hospital

Kenny McGill sat alone in a space that somebody had tried to make look like a living room in a really nice house. There was a sofa and two arm chairs. There were shelves filled with all sorts of books and magazines. There was a flat-screen television. There were Wii and PlayStation consoles.

A nurse had even given him an iPad and showed him how to use it.

Thing was, he didn't want to do any of that stuff. He couldn't stop thinking about what was happening to him. He was sick and getting sicker. Nobody came right out and said so, but they didn't have to. He'd had physicals before — you had to, to play sports at school —but they hadn't been anything like what he'd just gone through. It had been like getting tackled by a football team of doctors and nurses, and some of those doctors and most of those nurses were women. If he'd had the time to think, he'd have turned red all over.

Good thing he hadn't done that; they'd probably have thought he was sicker than he was. Which had to be bad enough, because when they'd finished taking his blood, his pee, his spit and even — *yeesh* — some of his poop, and had stopped looking at him every which way except inside out, he'd asked to see his family.

He could have used a hug right about then. But he'd been told everyone was busy. With what, he'd wanted to know. When they told him the truth, they were all giving blood samples to see if they might help him out, he was sorry he asked.

Jeez, were they going to put someone else's blood in him? He'd heard about transfusions, of course, but the way he'd been gone over, he didn't think it would be as simple as just topping off his tank.

If he had to take in anyone's blood, though, he wanted it to be his dad's blood. In fact, it'd be kind of cool having Dad's blood in him. Maybe it'd give him an edge over other guys. Look at what his dad did for a living. Look at who he was married to.

Even Lars' blood would be okay. He was a good guy. He made Mom happy. His stores had to be making money because they had a nice house and got new cars every other year. Except for the old Volvo Lars had been given by his grandfather. Lars loved working on that car, kept it looking great and it never failed to start no matter how cold the weather got.

Dad or Lars, that was whose blood he wanted, if he needed any. He loved his mother and his sisters, but —

An old guy walked into the room, stopped short when he saw Kenny.

Like he was surprised to see someone else there.

Kenny said, "I'm not in the wrong place, am I? Is this your room?"

The guy smiled, and Kenny was glad to see it. Otherwise, he would have been kind of scary. He was huge, had wide shoulders and the biggest hands Kenny had ever seen. He looked like he might have been even bigger once, but then he must've got kind of skinny because his clothes hung loose on him. What was left of his hair was white, but neatly combed. His eyes were light blue with lots of red veins.

Kenny had heard that guys who drank too much got eyes like that, but he didn't smell any alcohol on the old man. He actually smelled kind of good, like that aftershave Dad used when he was going somewhere fancy.

The old man told Kenny, "No, this isn't my room, but they do reserve it for certain people."

The guy had a cool voice. Deep but friendly. Like somebody on the radio or TV. Somebody whose voice was a big part of his job, somebody who got paid because other people wanted to hear him talk. He sat in an easy chair opposite Kenny, and the boy was glad when the old man didn't pick up a book or a magazine.

"What kind of certain people?" Kenny asked.

"Sick people," the old man said with a shrug.

A trill of fear rippled through Kenny, but then he realized the old man was talking about himself. He immediately wanted to know —

"I'm pretty bad off," the old man said.

"I'm sorry," Kenny told him.

The old man shrugged again. "I really don't have room to complain, being two hundred years old."

For just a second, Kenny bought the line.

Then the old guy smiled once more and there was a twinkle in his eye.

"You are not," Kenny said.

"No, I'm not. I just feel like it."

"Can't they do anything for you?"

"Well, I am here for my meds. After I take them, why I feel a hundred years younger."

Kenny knew he was being kidded again, but he didn't mind.

He stuck out his hand. "I'm Kenny McGill."

The old man took Kenny's hand, engulfing it. Taking it easy. Being gentle.

"My friends call me Zack," the old man told the boy.

The Oval Office

Edwina Byington, the president's personal secretary, age seventy-something, told McGill to add her name to the list of potential donors. She even tried not to act annoyed as McGill paced back and forth in front of her desk. She asked if he'd like some White House ice tea, one of his favorite treats.

When McGill said no, she knew how worried he was.

Edwina then made an executive decision.

"The president is with her chief of staff, but the attorney general left some time ago, so maybe it wouldn't be too serious a breach if I buzz her to see how long she'll be busy."

McGill was about to tell her not to bother, but Edwina had already acted.

"Madam President, Mr. McGill is here. Shall I —"

"Send him in, please," the president said. "I'll need some time alone with my husband, Edwina."

"As you wish, Madam President." Edwina told McGill, "She'll see you now."

McGill nodded and entered the Oval Office. Galia was just getting to her feet.

Patti came around her desk to greet her husband. She took his hands and kissed him on both cheeks. A gesture of affection the two of them had acquired during their vacation last year in Paris.

Galia asked, "Does Dr. Nicolaides need help with anything at the hospital?"

McGill shook his head. "Not that I know."

The chief of staff turned to the president. "If it's all right with you, I'll send one of my people to the hospital to report hourly to me on Kenneth's condition. If there's any significant development, I'll let you know."

McGill knew that Galia was doing more than being kind. She was trying to keep the president from being distracted from matters that would not wait. That was just the way things worked.

Even so, he said, "Thank you, Galia."

She nodded and left.

The door had no sooner closed behind her than the First Couple embraced and drew comfort and strength from one another. They broke the hug with a kiss and sat next to each other on one of the sofas placed in front of the president's desk.

"Things aren't critical with Kenny, are they?" the president asked.

"I haven't heard that they are. I'm going over to the hospital soon to see what's what, but I wanted to talk with you first. So I barged in on Edwina, hoping you weren't in the middle of something big."

Patti took McGill's hand. "We just finished something big."

"With the attorney general."

"Yes." Patti told McGill about Erna Godfrey's video confession and promise to testify against Burke Godfrey. She also informed her husband how the government would start to build its case against the reverend. McGill, however, focused on the part of Patti's narrative that struck him hardest.

"She said she saw Andy, and he was at peace?" McGill asked.

Patti's eyes filled and she nodded.

She understood that Jim not only felt happy for her; he felt relief for himself. He held himself to blame, at least in part, for Andy's death. More than that, though, with Kenny's life in jeopardy, the hope for salvation and eternal life in the company of the Lord was one devoutly to be cherished.

Devotion, of necessity, had to yield to practical considerations.

"You'll be buying yourself a world of confrontation," McGill told Patti.

"I know, but I came to understand something today that made me feel peaceful."

McGill asked, "What's that?"

"That I won't mind being a one-and-done president as long as I can complete my term the way I want. You don't have any trouble with that, do you?"

"The sooner I can get you away from the circus the better."

"Don't get your hopes too high. I might wind up getting reelected, but at the very least I'm going to turn the national conversation upside down. I'm going to kick over apple carts at every opportunity. Give the whole system a massive jolt of shock therapy."

McGill nodded. He not only approved, he also appreciated the opening his wife had just given him. He told her of the murders of the K Street lobbyists, the pig pins attached to their bodies and Putnam Shady's plan to seize control of the government.

The president listened closely to her husband's words, sorted through the ideas they carried and probed for weaknesses. Given the current political realities, she couldn't find any flaws in Putnam's plan. Which meant she had far more work to do than she thought.

The workings of the Congress of the United States would have to be rebooted.

She told her husband, "I know you've steered clear of involvement in political matters up until now, Jim, but with this case, with this situation, that has to change."

"I know. I might be the one to get you kicked out of office."

"Good thing we have a nest-egg," the president said.

"Yeah, I have two pensions and Andy left you a little money."

"We'll scrape by. But before then I'll want to see Mr. Putnam Shady."

"Tell me when and I'll have Sweetie bring him by." He kissed Patti. "I have to get over to the hospital. If you get a free moment, let's see Kenny together."

"I'll make the time," the president said.

She kissed McGill.

He asked, "Have you heard —"

"Of course. The volunteer effort to find a donor for Kenny."

"Yeah, it just …" McGill had to collect himself.

"Scares the hell out of you and makes you feel great all at the same time."

McGill nodded. Then he asked, "Did Celsus volunteer?"

"Yes, he did. So did Galia."

"Oh, man." He hadn't thought Galia might be the one.

"Jim," Patti said, "put my name on the list, too."

Georgetown

Derek Geiger, the speaker of the House of Representatives, the man second in line of succession to the presidency, returned home and found his suitcases on the doorstep of the townhouse he'd long considered to be his home in Washington, D.C. It hadn't been that long, actually. Geiger and Harlo had been married for only four years; he had anticipated the union would last between six and ten years, a personal record.

That was before he'd had lunch with Brad Attles an hour earlier.

Geiger's attorney had asked him, in the moments after he'd paid the check for their meals, if he'd read and approved the recent revisions Attles had made in their strategy to handle the divorce proceedings that would eventually occur between him and Harlo. Attles had somehow come by Harlo's corporate tax returns — Geiger didn't want to know how. The lawyer was tracking the annual income figures of Harlo's furniture design business.

Attles could show a direct correlation between the revenue growth of HG Designs and Harlo's marriage to the speaker. Further, those revenues increased in direct proportion to the speaker's growing prominence in his party. Therefore, the lawyer reasoned, any claim for compensation in a divorce between the two parties should be offset by the monetary gain Harlo's enterprise had enjoyed from her becoming the speaker's spouse.

In normal circumstances, Geiger would not only have agreed with Attles' argument, he would have cheered for it. He would have toasted it, had it turned out that Harlo would owe him money, should she want a divorce. As it was, however, he felt a chill and had a question.

"When and how did you send your revisions? Because I never

saw them."

Now, Attles felt a fright, too. "I faxed one sheet to your house late last night."

The speaker winced. Harlo, dressed like a million-dollar courtesan, had slipped into their bed last night ... and he'd been unable to satisfy her. It hadn't worried him. Maybe once a year, he just wasn't ready to go. Give him twenty-four hours, he'd be as good as ever. Which was good for a young man and fantastic for a guy his age. He'd rolled over and went back to sleep as deeply as if he'd just acquitted himself heroically.

After he'd wakened, cleaned up and headed to his home office, he'd checked for messages, including faxes. The tray had been empty.

Harlo was already up and gone by then.

A grim Attles intuited what had happened. "Harlo came home early? Please don't tell me that."

Hoping against hope, Geiger said, "Priscilla came to clean the place this morning. If your fax fell onto the floor, she might have thrown it away ... unread."

Attles said he'd return to his office and figure out if there was anyone he could bill while he was busy praying things had worked out as the speaker had said.

As speaker, Geiger was provided with a car and driver. When he felt the need, or wanted to show off, he could summon a detail of Capitol Hill Police officers to act as his bodyguards. But when he met with Brad Attles he dispensed with all the perks and traveled alone by taxi. He saw his bags waiting for him while he was still inside the cab.

He asked the driver to wait, giving him enough money for the man to comply.

Maybe, please God, Harlo had only meant to scare him.

He hurried up the stairs, hoping his wife had set his suitcases out empty, a threat ... but the bags weren't empty and neither was her threat. Worse, he could now see a new lock had been put on the front door.

He picked up his suitcases and turned to head down the steps.

That was when he saw the camera crew facing him.

Harlo had set a trap for him.

The red light was on; they were shooting his moment of humiliation.

A blonde with a microphone was leading the charge toward him.

Luckily, the cab driver had spotted the media ambush before it had started to move. He had the passenger door open for him. Geiger threw his bags in the rear seat and dove in after them. The driver hit the gas before the speaker had the door closed. The man stopped at the corner of the block to make sure his fare didn't fall out.

As Geiger closed the door, the driver asked, "The Hay-Adams?"

The speaker nodded. The RNC had its suite there.

It was a short drive, leaving the speaker with but one thought to occupy his mind.

Goddamn woman.

WorldWide News, Washington Bureau

Sir Edbert Bickford's media empire spanned the globe to an extent that even Queen Victoria's imperial reach couldn't match. Being a man who always expected the worst from both his enemies and his minions, he felt compelled to be in constant motion to oversee his holdings, destroy his enemies and flog his workers on to ever greater efforts.

Verbally flog, though he wished he could get away with actual lashes.

The Boeing 777-VIP he'd dispatched to carry his nephew, Hugh, was but one of three that normally served Sir Edbert exclusively. He liked to have two backup jets so he'd never be caught short in case man or nature conspired against him. Having but one spare aircraft left him on edge. Anxiety always depleted his thin reservoir of patience.

Arriving in Washington, he'd been in a foul mood even for him.

Having been stuck in evening rush hour traffic, after being denied the use of a helicopter to carry him above the mob, for reasons the aviation bureaucrats wouldn't disclose, only deepened his distaste for his fellow man.

All of them.

Even his nephew, who told him moments after his arrival at his Washington bureau that James J. McGill had met with Hugh and had told the lad to sod off. Worse, the bugger had the nerve to use his Secret Service thugs to keep Hugh and his cameraman so far away even a telescopic lens couldn't shoot him.

Sir Edbert had displaced his bureau chief from his office and sat behind the man's desk, looking as if thunder clouds would soon gather about his frowning visage and start throwing bolts of lightning.

Hugh sat in a visitor's chair as impassive as if he'd been chiseled from granite.

The young woman sitting next to him, his American producer, Sir Edbert had been told upon their introduction, seemed equally unfazed by his vile mood.

"I had been informed," Sir Edbert began, "that this blighter McGill went about his business with but one Secret Service agent and a driver."

"Things change, Uncle, in ways that are not always to our liking."

Hugh wasn't apologizing, simply explaining. The worst thing you could do, he'd learned from the start, was not stand up to the old bastard. He'd tear into you whatever you did, but afterward he'd think more of you if you fought back.

Sir Edbert leaned forward. "The point of power is to *make* conditions change to suit your whim."

"I'm afraid I'm not as close to God as you are, Uncle, in terms of my ability to work wonders."

The American woman tried but couldn't quite restrain a smile.

He turned on her.

"You think my nephew is funny, Ms. Booker? My nephew mocking his employer and yours. I noticed he's recently augmented your salary." Sir Edbert Bickford always learned quickly about any unusual increase in employee compensation. He had people whose sole responsibility was to keep staff costs in line. "I could make your salary disappear altogether, and blackball you from the business."

Ellie Booker glanced at Hugh Collier.

He sat quiet, curious to see how she'd respond.

Ellie told Sir Edbert, "I'm sure you could do that, sir, but all I'd have to do is change my name, dye my hair blonde and get a boob job. You'd hire me back to read the news for you at twice my new salary."

Hugh rocked with laughter.

If he weren't a man's man, he'd have asked Ellie to marry him.

Sir Edbert saw the affection between the two of them. It made him wish young Hugh weren't a nance. Couldn't he see that woman was ever so much more ... no, of course he couldn't. Who a man fancied wasn't a matter of choice. Only fools like the boy's father thought rubbish like that was true.

Still, these two were valuable resources to him.

He wouldn't squander them.

A sour smile formed on his face.

"Very well. I'll torture a peasant or two on my way out of town. In the meantime, tell me something that will give me a sadistic little tingle," he said.

Hugh gestured to Ellie, letting her have the stage.

"The speaker of the House was thrown out of his house by his young wife."

Sir Edbert's smile turned gleeful.

"How do you know?"

"We have video. We were tipped off."

"By the wife?"

"By an anonymous male voice."

"No doubt someone in the wife's employ," Sir Edbert said. "Did the speaker comment?"

Hugh said, "He dived into the back of a taxi that took off with the door still open. We have video of that, too. But, Uncle, this chap is one of the people you champion."

Glee departed from Sir Edbert's expression to make way for simple wickedness.

"Of course, he is. But capturing an important man in an embarrassing moment is the brightest coin you can have in your pocket. The poor fellow will never want you to take it out and spend it."

A fancy way to dress up a blackmail threat, Ellie thought.

"You're off to a good start," Sir Edbert said. "What's next?"

"Uncle, don't you think there's a good story in Mr. McGill's use of armed government agents to keep the news media out of his way?"

"I do not," he snapped at Hugh. "Think, boy. If word got about that brute force was a legitimate strategy to keep the press at bay everyone with a full purse would employ it. Then where would we be? And this fellow McGill, from all I've read, is a popular chap. He might be just the one to start the trend. What I want is to bring him down. That would be a start on diminishing the president. You're sure he's not like you?"

Hugh smiled. "He's quite a bit like me, a proper tough bastard. But he's not gay."

Sir Edbert turned to Ellie Booker to get a woman's confirmation.

"He's not gay, but he is human."

"Meaning what?"

"I've been looking into his family."

"One of them is gay?"

Hugh sighed, drawing a dirty look but no comment.

Ellie said, "One of them is sick. McGill's son, Kenneth. He was admitted to George Washington University Hospital."

Certain news organizations, WorldWide News among them, had people who kept watch on hospitals that celebrities used. If someone newsworthy tried to slink in unnoticed, well, they really should know better than to think they had a right to any privacy at all.

"A sick child," Sir Edbert said, "that might bring the bastard more sympathy."

Hugh said, "Unless the child brought the condition on himself."

Sir Edbert brightened. "Drugs? We can only hope. Yes, keep an eye on that situation. Do you have anything else?"

Ellie said, "With McGill's increased level of Secret Service protection, we have to accept that we're not going to get close to him. But Mr. McGill has a business partner, a former colleague in both the Chicago and Winnetka, Illinois police departments. She has no such protection. She might be the way in."

Both Sir Edbert and Hugh smiled in genuine appreciation.

"A *female* business partner, that's very good," Sir Edbert said.

"What's her name?" Hugh asked.

Ellie said, "Her name is Margaret "Sweetie" Sweeney. She's blonde and stunning."

Uncle and nephew spoke as one: "Sweetie."

They laughed deeply.

Ellie didn't mention that Margaret Sweeney had the reputation in the American media of being so tough she didn't need any bodyguards and that she didn't suffer fools lightly. Of course, that might have been a useful public relations ploy to avoid unwanted attention.

They'd have to see.

Washington, D.C., Northwest

Despite Brad Attles' imposing size, there were people in the nation's capital who might think to confront him physically. Especially at night. Walking home alone because he was too distracted to drive. Needing to be alone with his thoughts.

Holding a gun made even twerps think they were giants. The thing about guns, though, you had to be able to actually hit someone in a place that mattered if you wanted to put him down for good, not just piss him off.

Attles always remembered the story he'd read about the first death the Japanese military had suffered at the hands of an American after the attack on Pearl Harbor. One of the emperor's pilots crash-landed on the Hawaiian island of Niihau. He confronted a local and shot the man three times, in the chest, hip and groin. The Hawaiian responded by grabbing the pilot and smashing his skull against a stone wall, killing him.

The lesson of that encounter was recorded in Island lore: Never shoot a Hawaiian three times — it makes him mad!

Attles had been shot once himself, on the inside of his left thigh. If he'd been hanging the other way that night, he'd never have known the pleasure of loving a woman. It took only the one shot to raise Attles' hackles. He knocked the pistol from his assailant's grip with one hand and broke his neck with the other. Just grabbed and squeezed. The dumb bastard's spine cracked like an old, dry stick and the life went right out of him.

All because the stupid white boy had accused Brad Attles of looking at his ugly little girlfriend with the wrong thoughts in mind. Attles wouldn't have … well never mind that, it hadn't been the girl's fault. It was the white boy's mistake.

Same error in judgment that Japanese pilot had made.

The Hawaiian who killed that pilot got medals.

Attles would have gotten the electric chair.

A black man killed a white man in Louisiana that was the way it went.

So he went to stay with his aunt in Florida. He lived the straight and narrow, did his best in school, kept right on to become a lawyer. He met Derek Geiger when the two of them were buying Jaguars from the same dealership one afternoon. They became friends and Brad saved him from getting skinned by his first ex-wife. After that, his place in the world was set. Set nice and high once Geiger went off to Congress and became speaker.

Now, Brad Attles was sure he was about to be brought low. Derek Geiger had called with the news: Harlo had found the fax he'd sent to the speaker. Had locked the man out of the townhouse she owned. Had left his bags out on the stoop. Had called a news crew to shoot video of the man's humiliation.

Harlo had even gone so far as to cut all of Derek Geiger's clothes into pieces before she packed his bags. Left him nothing to wear but what he had on. Wanted to let him know just how mad she was at him. Give him a taste of what was coming, too.

Despite all the cause the speaker had to be angry, he still wanted Brad Attles to be his divorce lawyer in the upcoming battle with Harlo. But Geiger warned Attles that he had better come up with a good excuse for how he knew the details of Harlo's business income. If anybody could prove Attles had bribed someone at the IRS into providing the information or he'd had some techie hack a federal database, he'd be in deep shit.

That, of course, was exactly what Attles had done.

Paid off an IRS techie to get what he wanted.

Shit, if Harlo's lawyer was any good, he'd already alerted the feds about Attles' illegal possession of Harlo's tax data. The little computer dweeb Attles had paid ten K, and who suddenly re-minded him a great deal of that broken-necked white boy back home, would fall all over himself to make a deal, get himself a reduced sentence.

The feds would come for him next, and they'd ask him one simple question: Had Speaker Derek Geiger been involved in this criminal act?

Geiger hadn't been involved ... but it was tempting for Attles to think how his life would be a lot easier if he lied and said, sure enough, it was all the speaker's idea.

Brad Attles had never thought of himself as a Judas, but when you're facing —

Somebody cleared his throat, sounded like he was about to bring up a lung.

Pulled Attles right out of his reverie. He saw a guy with a gun.

A great big gun. Not a peashooter like that cracker in Louisiana had.

Attles would have been worried if —

He never got to complete the thought. He was shot twice in the chest.

When the cops found him, there was a pig pin on his lapel.

Detectives Meeker and Beemer of the Metro Police had concluded by now the pin was a knockoff of Porky Pig.

CHAPTER 3

Wednesday, August 17th , GWU Hospital

As with anything else of consequence, there were always new lessons to be learned about donating bone marrow. Research showed that matching a small number of human leukocyte antigen (HLA) markers was the most important factor to a positive transplant outcome. Matching six specific markers was the goal for any would-be donor: two A markers, two B markers and two DRB1 markers.

A prospective adult donor had to match a minimum of five of the six markers to be acceptable. Matching all six was ideal.

McGill and Sweetie came the closest to qualifying with four matching markers each. Carolyn, Abbie and Caitie had three apiece; Lars had only two. Everyone in the family was disappointed that none of them would be able to donate to Kenny. With Nick and Dr. Divya Sahir Jones, the acting chief oncologist on Kenny's team, for company, McGill and Carolyn went to Kenny's room to break the news.

And to encourage him with the further news that dozens and possibly hundreds of volunteers would be lining up to be potential donors.

When they arrived at Kenny's room, however, they were forced to wait.

Kenny was on the phone. He held a hand up to everyone, asking a moment's indulgence. Both McGill and Carolyn thought their son looked unnaturally pale, but they were encouraged to see a smile on his face.

"Yeah, I think it should be okay," Kenny said. "I know Caitie said she would donate, and she's younger than we are. Huh? No, I don't know that. Mom and Dad and Lars take care of that stuff. Right now, they're staying at this cool place right across the street from the White House. What? Oh, sure, I can do that. Hold on."

Kenny put his hand over the phone and asked the room nurse for the hospital's address. He relayed it to the person on the other end of the conversation. He smiled again and said, "Thanks. Yeah, I look forward to — What?" The boy's expression became serious. "Sure, of course. Don't worry about that ... well, try not to. I'll be here, promise. Yeah, bye."

Kenny put the phone down. Took a deep breath and sighed.

He told his parents, "That was Liesl Eberhardt."

Carolyn said, "How nice of her to call. Is she going to send you a card?"

McGill read his son's eyes and knew it was more than that.

"She might bring one, I suppose," Kenny said.

"Liesl's coming here?" his mother asked.

Kenny nodded. "Her mom's going to find a hotel close by."

McGill said, "She asked about donating?"

His son bobbed his head, trying to hold back tears.

"In case one of you guys don't match. She said she's organizing other kids from school, too. You know, make the number as big as possible in case ... So what did they tell you? Can one of you be my donor?"

Carolyn and McGill stood next to Kenny's bed, told him what the blood tests showed. Told him that the Secret Service, the Marines and lots of other people at the White House would be coming in to be tested, too.

"Patti will be coming as well," McGill said.

"To visit?" Kenny asked.

"Sure, that too. But she'll have her blood tested like everyone else."

That took Carolyn by surprise, but she kept it to herself.

Dr. Jones and Nick outlined to Kenny what his immediate course of treatment would be. He listened closely as they began, but his attention began to drift. He said he was getting tired and would like to sleep.

His parents kissed him goodbye.

Everyone but the room nurse left.

Kenny thanked her for allowing the call from Liesl to reach him.

"Anyone else outside your family you want to hear from, other than Ms. Sweeney?"

Kenny thought about it for a minute. He yawned. He was so tired.

But he had one name to offer. "There's this old guy with white hair who comes in for his meds. His name's Zack."

The nurse nodded. She knew just who Kenny meant.

Washington, D.C., *The National Mall*

Sweetie and Putnam had been running the Mall when the call came. Sweetie had moderated her pace to allow Putnam to keep up, but his fitness level was increasing and she was approaching the pace she used when running alone. She took his near arm as she plucked her phone from the waistband of her shorts. The two of them moved into the shade of a tree that bordered the running path. Sweetie did a three-hundred-and-sixty degree scan before she answered.

No villains in sight.

She saw the call was from Jim McGill and answered by saying, "You, me or Carolyn, who gets to donate?"

"None of us," McGill told her.

Sweetie's jaw clenched. This was one of the rare times when she wished she allowed herself to use profanities. Putnam understood her need and filled the gap.

"Damn," he said.

"So we get the volunteers lined up?" Sweetie asked.

"Yeah. Patti, lots of people at the White House, Kenny even has a classmate flying in."

Putnam overheard and tapped his chest.

"Putnam says put him on the list, too."

McGill said, "Please give him our thanks."

Putnam waved his hand: no big deal.

"He says he's glad to do it."

"We still appreciate it. Did you tell him Patti wants to talk with him?"

Sweetie hadn't. Putnam's eyebrows rose. He mimed, "The president?"

Sweetie nodded. "He'll be happy to do that, too."

Putnam looked like he'd rather have a needle inserted into his spine.

"Give Edwina a call," McGill said. "She'll set up a time."

"Right."

Putnam pointed at Sweetie.

"My friend would like to know if I can accompany him?"

"I thought of that, and Patti is always happy to see you, Margaret."

Putnam looked somewhat relieved.

McGill asked, "Any new developments?"

Sweetie said, "If it hasn't gone public yet, it will soon. We got a call from Lieutenant Bullard early this morning."

"Another shooting victim?" McGill asked.

Sweetie said, "Yes. A man by the name of Brad Attles."

The name was unfamiliar to McGill and he said so.

"Putnam says this one is going to make headlines. Mr. Attles was not only a prominent lobbyist but was also Speaker Derek Geiger's personal divorce lawyer. Extricated him from two prior marriages without serious financial damage."

There was more to the story than that, Sweetie had been told, but she wasn't about to share that news via cell phone. There were too many people with scanners who might be listening in. She wondered how soon it would be before smart phones encrypted their calls.

"We'll deal with the media," McGill said. "There have been no further threats against Mr. Shady?"

Now that Putnam had volunteered to step up for Kenny, there was, in McGill's opinion, another good reasons to keep him upright and breathing.

"It was a quiet night," Sweetie said. "Now, we're jogging at the Mall."

"Okay. I'll sit in on the meeting with Patti, too."

Sweetie thought that was smart. It would be good for all of them to have something to take their minds off Kenny's situation.

"Good," she said. "See you then."

Ending the call with McGill, she took another look around.

And saw a thin woman with a camera crew pointing at them.

She had to have some fine eyesight to spot them standing there in the shade.

Sweetie didn't know who they were or what they wanted but she asked Putnam, "You think you can outrun a bunch of TV snoops?"

Putnam nodded and they took off, staying off the running path, dodging between the trees. Making it tougher for the guy lugging the videocam. But the thin woman was wearing sensible shoes and if not catching up she was at least matching their pace.

As they ran, Putnam's phone sounded.

He let voicemail answer.

Missing, for the moment, the call from Speaker Derek Geiger.

Washington, D.C. 24th Street, NW

The car thief used a credit card bearing the name Stephen

Tully to rent a gray Ford mid-size sedan from Hertz. The only time he drove a stolen ride were the minutes — never more than thirty — between the instant he grabbed it and the moment he dropped it off with the buyer. He did everything he could to limit his exposure to the cops.

That was why the only job he screwed up, the one in Vegas, still bothered him years later. Those Air Force guys in the other car either had to be in mad hurry to get back to base or they were just complete assholes. Sure, they'd been in the right — had the green — but so the fuck what? They had to see him coming. Had to see he wasn't slowing down.

Anybody with the brainpower of a bedbug would have known he wasn't going to stop. Goddamnit, the light going his way hadn't turned red more than a second before. But the Air Force hotshot behind the wheel jumped the green like a drag racer. He must've thought he could clear the thief's car. Expected he'd give his buddies a scare and himself a giggle.

Leave them all with a good story to tell when they got old.

Shithead. Three of 'em never would get old, and the fourth …

He was the one who haunted the thief every day of his life.

"You see that, mister?"

The kid in the passenger seat had spoken to him. He said he was fifteen, looked maybe ten. Tully was paying the kid's dad for his time. The dad had been another car thief. Now, he *consulted,* read tech manuals by day and at night told dudes who still boosted what they'd need to do to get away with high end cars.

The consultant also had a guy who hacked into manufacturers' computer systems and got all the latest factory specs. Tully had gone to him to see if he had any information on McGill's special Chevy. He didn't, but he said he might know someone who could get it.

The price would be high, of course.

The thief told him to get the price and he'd see if his buyer wanted to pay it.

In the meantime, he'd try to get a look at the Chevy and the guy who drove it, because as he'd shown in Baltimore there was more than one way to steal a high-end ride. Sometimes it was as simple as dusting the guy behind the wheel.

He'd kept that option to himself.

As it was, he'd had to talk in front of the consultant's kid.

"The boy's the next generation of the business," the guy had said.

"I'm good with math," the kid explained.

"Genius with electronics," the proud father added.

"How the hell old are you?" the thief asked the kid.

He claimed to be fifteen … but the thief thought the little bastard could pose as his son if he did the tourist bit, walk around the White House, eyeball the grounds, see if he could spot the Chevy, get a better idea of what was what. He'd look a lot less suspicious if he had a kid with him.

Turned out the little shit's time billed out at five hundred a day.

But they'd not only spotted the Chevy, they'd seen the driver get in and turn the engine over. They were even able to follow the Chevy to an outdoor parking area on 24th Street.

The lot was monitored by cameras. The thief saw a guy get out of the Chevy's back seat. He looked like he might be carrying a gun. An Asian guy got out of the shotgun seat and he definitely was packing. But now the kid was asking if he'd seen something.

"See what?" the thief asked, driving past the lot.

"The two black sedans following us. Saw 'em in the sideview. Was just the one at first, then another pulled in behind it. First one has guys in it, guys like us don't want to know."

The thief stopped for a red light. A black sedan pulled up on his right. He looked over. Casual, no big deal. Saw two guys in the front seat. Cut from the same mold as the Asian guy. The thief put his eyes back on the road. But out of the corner of his eye he saw the kid give them a wave.

Being cute, the little asshole.

The light turned green and the thief checked for cross-traffic.

He made it through the intersection without accident or arrest.

"Guy in the Chevy has some protection, huh?" the kid asked.

Sure the hell did. Maybe too much. Of course, if the thief wanted to retire ...

Knocking off that Chevy could be the score of a lifetime.

Salvation's Path Church, Richmond, Virginia

The Reverend Burke Godfrey sat in the front pew of his chapel, the original church he and Erna had purchased. His head was bowed, his eyes closed. He beseeched the Almighty to visit his grace upon Erna that she might see the error of her thinking. Turning him in to the feds, landing him in prison, that would put an end to the ministry he'd worked his whole life to build.

If Erna refused to see the light, he begged the Lord to bring him home right now. Let his last moments on earth be right where he sat. He would pass with a smile on his lips, and the word would spread. He'd died at peace in the place that meant the most to him. Thousands would attend his memorial service. He'd become even larger in death than he had been in life.

Though Godfrey had spoken publicly many times of hearing directly from the Lord, no heavenly voice reached him when he needed it most. The only thing he heard was the steady beat of his heart. He'd never been one to exercise. The only way he worked up a sweat was preaching to his flock. And if he had any weakness of the flesh, it was eating. He loved home cooking, had always had at least one helping too many, and once Erna had been sent away the extra food rose to two helpings. But his heart kept beating good and strong, like it might go on forever.

Lord, where was the fairness, he asked.

Seated halfway back in the church was the reverend's lawyer, Benton Williams. He'd been summoned by Godfrey and could have waited for the him in his office, but he wanted to observe the man, determine what his state of mind might be. Knowing that would be helpful in planning a strategy for Godfrey's upcoming trial. The lawyer was sure the preacher's judgment day was coming, at least in the legal sense.

Godfrey hadn't told Williams why he wanted to see him when he'd called, but the lawyer had long ago charmed Willa Bramleigh, the televangelist's personal secretary, and she had felt it within the bounds of propriety to tell Williams that Reverend Godfrey had recently returned from Hazelton, West Virginia: the residence now and for the foreseeable future of Mrs. Godfrey.

As far as Williams knew, it was the first time the reverend's wife had allowed him to visit her. That might have been a good sign, if the meeting hadn't necessitated a call to a criminal defense attorney. Drawing the inference wasn't hard. Mrs. Godfrey had told her husband to set his affairs in order because his circumstances were about to change.

Simply put, she was going to implicate the reverend as a participant in the crime for which she was already being punished.

Put more simply still, she was going to rat him out.

Benton Williams thought a lifetime of monogamy deserved better than that.

He wondered if Godfrey would allow him to destroy Erna's credibility by destroying her. He'd been on the clock since the preacher had called him and asked him to come to Richmond. Now, sitting silently in a church, the lawyer was shifting into high gear.

Ellie Booker sat at the back of the church, looking at the place with a TV producer's eye. She thought the architect had done a terrific job restoring the old church. At first glance, the place had the look of a traditional place of worship. But there were no seats with obstructed views. The placement of the platforms for television cameras were both strategic and inconspicuous. The lighting, even dialed down now that the cameras were off, was gorgeous; she'd bet it was positively celestial when the lumens were cranked up. She was also sure the sound system and acoustics would be first rate, too. Mike up the reverend and she was sure even a whisper would reach the back row.

The place, she estimated, would hold five hundred, but the feeling was still cozy, churchy. Ellie wasn't particularly religious, but she appreciated good stagecraft. A place like this created an atmosphere where messages would be easily received and accepted.

The only reason she was there, however, was because Benton Williams had asked her to come along. Having chased but failed to catch Margaret Sweeney and the guy she was with earlier that morning had left Ellie Booker gasping for breath and more than a little pissed off. She was sure a jock like Hugh Collier could have caught them, but he was off pursuing another lead. Leaving her to literally chase the story in D.C.

Aussie prick.

Ellie wasn't one to let anger distract her for long, though. If McGill was inaccessible and Margaret Sweeney had run off to parts unknown, she'd do what any good TV snoop in her situation would do: find her target's enemies and see what they had to say about him. Foremost among McGill's adversaries, as she saw things, was Reverend Burke Godfrey. When she had called the man's church, the woman answering the phone referred her to the reverend's attorney.

That sent a chill down Ellie's spine. The presence of an attorney in any situation involving a prominent person suggested that a scandal or even a crime was about to go public. In other words, great TV was in the offing. When Benton Williams had asked if she'd like to accompany him on the drive to Richmond, she'd felt like a little girl about to be given a pony for her birthday.

She hadn't been allowed to bring a video crew with her, but if she played things right, she was sure she could get something good on camera later. In the meantime, she'd be patient and mind her manners.

The thought of being civil had no sooner crossed her mind than she saw Reverend Godfrey stand and notice his lawyer sitting behind him. He waved Williams forward. The lawyer got to his feet and glanced Ellie's way. He held up a thumb and index finger.

Give him just a moment, she understood.

Ellie nodded. No problem.

There was a story here and she was going to get it.

With any luck, it would involve James J. McGill.

In a satisfyingly nasty way.

New York City, Midtown Manhattan

The entity known as Mother's Milk, located in a high rise building on Park Avenue, was neither the headquarters of a dairy nor the offices of a lactation consultancy. It's name came from a widely known piece of political wisdom attributed to the late Jesse M. Unruh, the 54th Speaker of the California State Assembly.

In words that had echoed through the years, Unruh had said, "Money is the mother's milk of politics."

Money was what Mother's Milk was all about. The organization had offices in ten major American cities, and would be going international within a year. Em's Em, as it was colloquially known, raised money to back legislation at all levels of government in the United States to promote the welfare of women and children and the formation of cohesive family units, both traditional and innovative.

The founder, CEO and head of the New York office of Em's Em was Clare Tracy.

She was willing to see almost anyone who cared to visit her office. The only conditions were that visitors come unarmed, recently bathed and in possession of a civil tongue.

Other than that, Clare's philosophy was, "Let's see what the cat dragged in."

That morning the feline had produced a strapping fellow from Down Under. Clare's sister had moved to Australia ten years earlier to work as a marine biologist. Clare had visited Brianne often enough to recognize the way a certain class of men from the Lucky Country held themselves. They evinced a sense of restrained bravado. Cocky but charming.

As soon as Clare's secretary, Gorgeous George, introduced Hugh Collier, the head of Em's Em said, "Ozzie, Ozzie, Ozzie. Sydneyside?"

Hugh smiled and said, "Aces. You've visited, more than once."

Clare nodded and waved her visitor into a guest chair.

George took their drink orders and left.

Clare got straight to the point, as she always did. "We're in the business of taking money from people, Mr. Collier."

"Proper bushrangers." Bandits. Hugh made his comment with a grin.

Clare smiled right back.

"In a sense. But we take our swag by appeals to people's better nature not their sense of self-preservation. How much would you care to donate?"

Hugh Collier was more than just a handsome face. He'd come prepared. He placed two checks on Clare Tracy's desk, one atop the other. The uppermost negotiable instrument was made out to Mother's Milk in the sum of ten thousand dollars. Clare picked it up and looked at Collier's signature, the name of the bank, the account and routing numbers.

Clare had seen many a check and this one looked as good as any.

She tucked it into a desk drawer and said, "Thank you very much, Mr. Collier. I assure you your money will be put to good use."

"I have no doubt," he replied.

George came back with their drinks. A sparkling Poland Spring for Clare, a Cascade Premium for Hugh. Donors were welcome to drink beer, in moderation, if they chose. George gave Clare a look as he poured for her. He'd run a quick check on their benefactor and the odds were good he'd more than covered the cost of his beer.

George retired to the outer office.

"Cheers," Clare said, raising her glass.

"Cheers," Hugh said.

After a pro forma sip, Clare got right back to business.

"This second check of yours, Mr. Collier, it's from the same account and bank as the first one, but it's unsigned, lacks the name of a payee and a dollar amount. Was it torn from your checkbook by mistake?"

Hugh said, "Possibly. It depends on whether you mind me asking you a few personal questions. If you do, I'll put it back in my pocket. If you don't mind, I'll be making more money available to you."

Clare smiled. She loved situations like this. She was a counter-puncher.

"If I'm not interested, will you stop payment on the first check?"

"No, that's for your organization. It will be honored in full."

"The second check would also have to be made out to Em's Em. The only remuneration I accept is my salary."

"As you like."

Clare said, "I've led a busy life, Mr. Collier, but hardly one of titillation."

Hugh said, "I believe you were once acquainted with James J. McGill."

Clare's eyelids closed momentarily. When they reopened her eyes were sapphire bright and diamond hard. It wouldn't have surprised Hugh Collier if she tried to run him through with her letter opener.

Instead, she plucked a pen from a holder on the desk and extended it to him.

"Sign your name to the check, Mr. Collier."

Hugh knew he had to comply or leave. He signed.

Clare took the pen back and inscribed Mother's Milk as the payee. Then she wrote the figure 100 in the dollar box. She showed what she'd done to her guest.

"The answer to your first question is a bargain, Mr. Collier. One hundred dollars. For each successive answer on the subject of Jim McGill, I'll add a zero. That way, we'll find out quickly how interested you are and how much money you have to spend."

George reentered the room. He was half again as big as Hugh. His knuckles looked liked they'd known the impact of fist to jaw, but his face was unmarked. No scars, no thickening of soft tissue. He watched impassively.

Hugh asked, "Where did you meet James J. McGill?"

"At DePaul University in Chicago, freshman English composition class."

Hugh moved on to the obvious question. "Was he your boyfriend?"

Clare added a zero. "Yes, for a time."

Given the multiplication factor involved in the dialogue, Hugh cut to the chase. "Were the two of you sexually intimate?"

The tab reached ten thousand. "Yes."

Hugh considered whether to take things further. Ms. Tracy was exacting a serious toll for her answers, but the next question was too important to omit.

"Did you become pregnant by James J. McGill?"

George started to move toward Hugh but Clare held up a hand.

The total was now one hundred thousand dollars. "Yes."

Next stop was a million dollars. Hugh wondered if Uncle Edbert would reward him for asking another question or fire him. It wasn't necessary for him to ask whether Clare Tracy had been married to McGill at the time she became pregnant. Ellie Booker's research had already shown McGill had been married only two times: to Carolyn Roberts and to Patricia Darden Grant. So there was no question that young Ms. Tracy and Mr. McGill had done the naughty while still single.

But it would be oh so interesting to know what had happened to their child.

And the woman in front of him seemed cold-bloodedly willing to tell him.

He was just about to ask the question when his business school training kicked in. The cost of his question would be nine hundred thousand dollars. Was there a less expensive way to get the answer?

Hugh felt sure there must be.

If there wasn't, he'd blame Ellie Booker for the failure.

He got to his feet, but didn't bother to extend his hand.

"Thank you for your time, Ms. Tracy. Both checks will be honored."

He gave her a small bow and made his way out past Gorgeous George.

Five minutes later, after enduring all the painful old memories she could bear, Clare picked up the phone and called Jim McGill for the first time in almost thirty years. She didn't have his number, but she reasoned that if she called the White House and left her name and number he would get back to her.

The West Wing, Captain Welborn Yates' office

Kira Fahey sat in a guest chair, opposite her fiancé, and made a face at him.

"Getting cold feet?" Welborn asked.

She'd just told him everything was set for their scaled down wedding. A simple ceremony was set for that Saturday, three days hence. It would take place at Vice President Wyman Mather's official residence at Number One Observatory Circle. Francis Nguyen would be on hand to bless the union. The District of Columbia marriage license had been obtained at a price of forty-five dollars. Welborn had paid for that; Kira bought lunch.

The guest list, at a minimum, would be Kira's mother and Uncle Mather and Welborn's mother and father. If the president and Mr. McGill were available to attend and so inclined, they would be welcome.

"My feet are as warm as my heart," Kira said.

Welborn wasn't going anywhere near that one.

Instead, he said, "You're worried we might offend someone who won't be there."

"Yes, I'm concerned, considering the original guest list."

Welborn had dozens of names on that list; Kira had hundreds.

"It would be impractical," he said, "to ask people to drop things at the last moment and rush to Washington. Most of them are probably off on vacation and not easily reached."

"Thank you, Mr. Practical."

"Insufficiently supportive?" Welborn asked. "We could always do a webcast."

Kira asked, "Who would we get to play the groom?"

Casual sniping was a character trait they shared, but Kira relented.

"We're terrible aren't we?" she asked. "There are so many people with real problems and we go on about inconveniences."

Welborn nodded. Their troubles were nothing compared to having a seriously sick child like James J. McGill or losing a husband and father like the families of the lobbyists who had been gunned down. Still, a marriage, if you hoped to have it last a lifetime, was nothing to take lightly.

"How about this?" he asked. "We'll come out and be honest. Confess to everyone on the original guest list what irregular lives we lead. Admit our plans oft go awry and our impulses have been known to get the better of us. So we'll beg everyone's pardon, via the Web, and ask anyone who's free to drop by this Saturday."

Kira said, "You're right, only a few people will be able to make it on such short notice."

"But everyone will appreciate that we extended them as much courtesy as possible. Given the circumstances and our deep character flaws, they'll probably forgive us."

Kira smiled and said, "Forgive me, anyway. But sending wedding invitations by e-mail. How tacky is that?"

Welborn said, "Wedding planners everywhere would certainly let us know, but we can jazz things up. In each e-mail, we'll include a secret password. Can't get in without it."

Kira liked the idea. It gave things a note of exclusivity.

Before she could comment, though, Welborn's phone rang. He came to attention while still seated and said, "Yes, ma'am. Right away."

He replaced the receiver and got to his feet.

"The president," Kira said. "Summoned you chop-chop, did she?"

"Always time for a brief but memorable kiss."

He gave Kira a touch-and-go buss.

"Be still my heart," she said.

Already out of sight, he called back, "Think of something good for the secret password."

The Oval Office

Senator John Wexford (D-Michigan), the majority leader of the Senate and Congresswoman Marlene Berman (D-New York), the minority leader of the House of Representatives shook hands with the president and looked around. They had thought they'd been invited to the White House for an impromptu meeting of the chief executive and the Congressional leadership, but their counterparts from the Republican side were absent.

Only Galia Mindel was there with them.

"Coffee, Mr. Majority Leader?" she asked. "Tea, Madam Minority Leader?"

Their preferred beverages were ready and waiting for them.

"Please, Marlene and John," the president said, "make yourselves comfortable."

Wexford took the cup Galia extended to him.

"Will the Senate minority leader and Speaker Geiger be arriving soon?" he asked.

Patti said, "No, I have not asked them to be present."

For just a second Marlene Berman looked as if she might return her cup of tea to Galia.

Patti smiled. "It's okay. I haven't brought you here to sandbag you, honest."

The president took her own cup of tea and sat on the near sofa. The two Democrats, still wary, sat opposite her. Galia took a seat to Patti's right, but she wasn't partaking of either coffee or tea. She'd have liked to hold a pen and notepad, but the president had vetoed that idea. She didn't want to put her visitors any more on edge than they already were.

Wexford put his cup and saucer down on an end table.

Berman kept hers on her lap.

Patti opened the discussion. "The chairman of the RNC, Reynard Dix, spoke with me yesterday. He asked me if I intend to run for another term."

Both Democrats laughed involuntarily.

The president smiled. "I was a bit surprised myself. I pointed out that my poll numbers suggested it might be a worthwhile idea. That was when Mr. Dix informed me that I could expect to be challenged in the Republican primary elections."

That revelation caused the two Democrats to look at one another.

"I promised Mr. Dix that I would beat any challenger badly."

Marlene Berman nodded. "I believe you would, Madam President."

Wexford kept his own counsel on the matter.

Patti continued, "I did wonder, though, if Mr. Dix's message wasn't a clumsy attempt to try to rein me in, bind me more tightly to the party orthodoxy. Present me with a group of challengers who would hew to a strict conservative dogma and show me as being ... unlike them."

The majority leader picked up his coffee cup and smiled.

"That's what I'd do in their place," he said.

"And what would you do in my place, John?" the president asked.

"Please allow for my political bias, Madam President, but your best move would be to show the country you're nothing like your competitors. You're *better* than them."

Wexford took a sip from his cup, put it down with a smile.

Now, Marlene Berman looked at Galia.

Saw John Wexford had given exactly the answer the president had wanted.

She asked, "Are you asking us to help you secure your party's nomination, Madam President?"

Patti laughed. "That would be highly bipartisan of you."

"It would be political suicide for Marlene and me," Wexford said.

"Well, I certainly couldn't ask that of you. No, the reason I asked you here today is to let you know that I'm going to announce some new policies soon. Some I'll be able to implement on my own and others ... well, that's where I'll need some help in Congress."

"And you're coming to us for help with that?" Marlene asked.

"Let me tell you what I have in mind," Patti said. "See how much of it you can support."

The president told them what she had in mind for the remainder of her term, and the two Democratic leaders loved all of it. They promised to do everything they could to muster support.

Wexford closed the meeting by asking, "Madam President, are you sure you're in the right party?"

"John, I've been asking myself that very question."

After Wexford and Berman left, the president went to the residence where Jim, Sweetie, Putnam Shady and Rockelle Bullard were waiting for her. Sensing a need for one more person, she summoned Captain Welborn Yates.

White House Roof

At least once a day, when the president was in residence, SAC Celsus Crogher went to the top of the building and surveyed the grounds and the surrounding city streets. He also checked the two-story basement. He worried less about an underground attack, saw it as far less likely. To make up for that deficiency in imagination, he had tasked a special agent who came from a coal-mining family to worry about nothing but an underground assault. The man monitored sensing devices that would detect any burrower larger than a mole.

The insectivore variety.

Keeping pace with Crogher as he walked the roof's perimeter was his new subordinate, Elspeth Kendry.

"So Holmes has you stiff-arming the press for him?" Crogher asked.

"Yes. At the moment, it's only the crew from WorldWide News."

Crogher grimaced and shook his head.

"Leave it to that guy to subvert his security detail."

"There's no serious threat on the radar, sir. There's always the possibility of a lone wolf attack, but ..."

"But what, Kendry?"

"Special Agent Ky confirmed your observation about Holmes' quickness. Said he's never seen a faster gun draw, and Holmes, I hear, knows how to take care of himself in close quarters combat."

Crogher gave his subordinate a baleful look.

"So you think everything's peachy the way Holmes wants it?"

"Permission to speak frankly, sir?"

Crogher nodded.

"In your position, I'd be unhappy if I couldn't lock Holmes in a secure room for as long as Holly G. is president."

Kendry's imagery made Crogher smile. Fleetingly.

"And in your position, Special Agent?"

"I don't think there's a lone wolf in the world that could get past both Special Agent Ky and Holmes, and from what I've learned Leo Levy is probably the best driver in the entire federal government."

"So everything is peachy."

"Well, it's always fun to frustrate pushy reporters."

Crogher had to agree with that.

"But to show you how sharp Leo Levy is, he called me to say he thought he saw someone checking out Holmes' car outside GWU Hospital this morning."

Crogher stopped his rooftop patrol and looked at his subordinate.

"Someone made an approach to the vehicle?"

"No, sir. Just eyeballed it a beat too long. Like he might know it's more than your average Chevy sedan."

"You're checking on that."

"We are."

"Why didn't Levy report through Special Agent Ky?"

"He called us first because the special agent was with Holmes. I'm sure he's passed the word by now."

Crogher nodded and resumed his patrol, for all of two steps.

Then something caught his eye and he looked north to Lafayette Square. Instead of the usual smattering of tourists moving in random ways, a large number of people was entering the park, seeming to march several abreast. Crogher asked, "What the hell is going on over there?"

Kendry saw large, charter buses, at least a dozen.

People were pouring out of them.

It was a public park but both the SAC and the special agent got the feeling an organized assault was about to be launched on the White House. Not with weapons. With electronic media. Both saw TV cameras being set up in the square.

Kendry said, "Permission to —"

"Go," Crogher told her, "go."

White House, The Residence

Edwina Byington gave the president a note as she exited the Oval Office.

"For Mr. McGill," Edwina said. "The switchboard verified the caller's identity. She was a former college classmate of your husband in Chicago. I was asked to route the message through you, Madam President."

The White House phone operators fielded four thousand calls a day on average, Monday through Friday, and a smaller number on weekends. One of their duties was to screen crank callers. If a message was deemed legitimate the chances were extremely small it was some adolescent-minded radio personality playing a prank.

"Thank you, Edwina," Patti said, "I'll see Jim gets it."

"Yes, ma'am."

Patricia Darden Grant placed great value on a right to personal privacy, especially where her husband was involved. But there were times when she, like anyone else, could get just a bit curious. A female former classmate? Someone raising funds from DePaul alumni? Or was it a personal message? The president might actually have peeked at the note had Galia not been accompanying her to the residence.

As it was, she stuck it in a pocket and gave it to Jim unread as soon as she saw him.

She'd trust him to tell her what it was about, if she needed to know.

The other four people waiting in the room, McGill's Hideaway as it had been dubbed, had risen when she'd entered. She nodded politely to Captain Yates, who knew enough by now not to snap to attention in an informal setting. She gave Margaret Sweeney a brief hug. She shook hands with Lieutenant Rockelle Bullard of Metro Homicide when they were introduced.

When Sweetie presented Mr. Putnam Shady to the president, she looked him right in the eye and said, "I understand you intend to seize control of the government, Mr. Shady."

Putnam looked from Patti to Galia and back.

Neither of them seemed amused.

Putnam didn't wilt. He told Patti, "It's either me or Derek Geiger."

GWU Hospital

Kenny McGill had been drifting in and out of sleep all morning. Each time he woke up, it seemed harder to do. Like he was getting too weak to open his eyelids. He wondered if that was part of dying. He knew by now what his diagnosis was: acute myelogenous leukemia. Dr. Jones had told him he was in a serious fight and he had to be absolutely determined to win it. Kenny'd had the feeling that if Mom hadn't been standing right next to the doctor she would have told him he was fighting for his life.

Thing was, he was so darn tired. He didn't see how he could fight at all.

At least he wasn't hurting. He'd been warned that might happen. His bones and his joints might start aching. But so far that hadn't been a problem. Dr. Jones said she'd give him medicine for the pain, if he needed it.

He'd also been informed the medical team was considering a treatment called chemotherapy for him. Dr. Jones said this treatment was really strong, because it had to be. It would be hard on him. But it was a possible way to get his blood and bone marrow back to normal. The thing that scared Kenny most about the chemotherapy was that it must be so awful just the thought of it had made Mom turn away so he wouldn't see her cry.

But he'd heard her sob all the same.

That was when he'd wished Dad had been there ... but he'd told everyone they had to keep busy with their own lives. He didn't want his problem spoiling things for everybody else. He still felt that way, but maybe he could have someone call Dad, ask him to come by.

Calling for his father was what Kenny had in mind when he woke up this time.

At first, he thought he was alone, and that scared him. All the other times someone had been in the room with him, his nurse at least. Usually, there were doctors, too, some of them he didn't remember seeing before. Mom was there most times. Abbie and Caitie had been there once. Abbie was trying hard not to cry; Caitie looked so angry Kenny thought she might try to shake the leukemia out of him.

But now he didn't see —

"How are you feeling, young man?"

The voice came not from the side of his bed near the door where people usually stood or sat. It came from the other side, where the room's windows were. Kenny turned his head and saw the big old guy with the white hair.

Kenny tried to answer him, but all he could get out was a short croak.

The old guy — Zack, that was what he'd said his name was — brought Kenny a glass of water and held it to his lips. The water was cool and as it trickled down Kenny's throat he couldn't remember anything ever feeling better. He bobbed his head when he had enough.

Zack told him, "Don't worry, no one has forgotten you. There's a whole gaggle of doctors and nurses standing just down the hall talking with a lady I guess might be your mother. They let me in because you were kind enough to put me on your visitors list."

Kenny had met Zack only the one time before, but he was very glad to see him now.

He said, "I'm scared."

Zack extended a large hand and Kenny grabbed it with both of his. For someone so old and who had said he was sick himself, Kenny was surprised how strong and warm Zack's hand felt. Just holding it made him feel better.

"Being scared is the first step toward fighting back," Zack said.

"It is?"

"Sure. The doctors told you they need your help, I bet."

Kenny nodded.

"Well, they weren't kidding. Fighters survive a lot more often than people who just go along for the ride."

"Are you still fighting?" Kenny asked.

Zack smiled and it seemed to Kenny as if his big hand grew warmer.

"I've got a round or two left in me."

"How old are you, really?"

"I'm seventy-eight." Zack seemed to think about that. "There was a time I thought that was pretty old. Now, I wonder how I got here so fast."

Kenny said, "It does seem old to me. Right now, eighteen seems old."

Zack put his other hand around both of Kenny's.

For the first time since he'd been in the hospital the boy felt safe.

"Here's what you do, young man. You think of all the things you want to do with your life. Think of big things. Grand things. You fix your mind on them. Hold them bright and clear where you see them. Tell yourself that neither this disease nor anything else will stop you from achieving your goals. Do that and your chances will be much better."

Kenny smiled and within minutes fell asleep again.

The next time he awoke Dr. Jones was back.

She told Kenny people were lined up down the hall to see if they could donate to him.

But if they didn't find a donor soon, they'd have to begin the chemotherapy.

McGill's Hideaway

Putnam Shady told the president, "Plain and simple, just about everyone in Congress is for sale, and they sell themselves for pennies on the dollar. You might have to donate tens or hundreds of thousands of dollars, maybe even millions if you're trying to move a bloc of votes, but you get back hundreds of millions or billions in government contracts or custom-tailored tax breaks. That's the reality and everyone in this room knows it."

Patti bided her time, but Galia shook her head.

She said, "Everyone knows that's the way it's been for a long time, but nobody has ever seized control of the government."

Putnam smiled. "Not individually, not yet, but the lobbying community is justifiably called the fourth branch of government. But who the hell elected us? No one. When do our terms of office expire? Never. Can we be expelled or impeached? No."

McGill said, "You can be indicted, tried and locked up."

"That's true. But we're better at reproduction than Hydras. Cut off one head, you won't have two grow back, you'll have ten."

Patti said, "Please explain how Derek Geiger and you plan to consolidate the power of the lobbying community."

Good at detail, Putnam explained in the order the president had requested.

He outlined for her Geiger's Super-K plan.

Rockelle Bullard leaned forward to listen closely.

When Putnam finished, the president asked, "So Speaker Geiger intends to use Mr. Attles as his firewall?"

Putnam looked over to Rockelle Bullard. She knew what he wanted and nodded.

"He intended that, yes," Putnam said. "But Lieutenant Bullard informed me earlier today that Mr. Attles was shot to death late last night or early this morning."

McGill had heard the news earlier, but he listened with all the others as Rockelle provided an outline of what the police had learned thus far, not that it was much.

"I almost feel silly asking all of you to keep this confidential, but please do," she said.

Patti reassured her, "We will all respect your request, Lieutenant."

The president's tone of voice made everyone understand an executive order had been issued.

Putnam continued, "Geiger and Attles were two of three pivotal figures. You're the other, Madam President. You don't need Geiger to raise money for you. You can do that yourself or spend your own money. Your independence, your power and your variance from party orthodoxy make you a threat to Super-K. You can count on your party running a number of challengers against you in the primary elections."

Both Patti and Galia sat up straighter, hearing that.

Everyone saw the reaction, but Putnam understood it.

"You've already heard that from someone," he said. "But maybe you don't know quite all of it. Having you knocked out in the primaries would be the preferred outcome, but Geiger isn't counting on that. What he wants his straw men to do is to poison the base against you so badly that even if you are nominated, large numbers of Republican voters will stay home or vote for a third party candidate. Geiger's plan is to try to make the electoral hill you have to climb so high that even you won't be able to do it."

Galia said, "You want us to believe that the Republican speaker of the House would prefer to see a Democrat elected president?"

Putnam told her, "Not just any Democrat, a get-along-and-go-along guy. The speaker, through ... whoever he finds to replace Attles, will be investing millions to support his preferred Democratic candidates. You know, the conservative members. Guys who are closer to him ideologically than you are, Madam President."

Galia thought Putnam's information sounded plausible, but she had one key question.

"How do you know all this?" she asked.

Putnam sighed. "I've already explained this to Margaret, Mr. McGill, Captain Yates and Lieutenant Bullard, but the long and short of it is I was taken into the confidence of the senior partner of my firm. So were Mark Benjamin, Bobby Waller and Erik Torkelson."

Patti and Galia were unfamiliar with the names Putnam had mentioned.

Rockelle filled them in. "Madam President, those three men were also found shot to death on K Street. They were all lobbyists. Metro homicide is working their cases." Turning to Putnam, she added, "It would have been helpful to know all this sooner."

"Sorry," Putnam said. "After Erik died — he was the first — Mark, Bobby and I decided we had to keep on at all costs. I'm trying to do that, and not get shot myself."

Galia said, "You have your own agenda, Mr. Shady."

"We call it Share America. It's modeled after mutual insurance companies in which the policy holders are also the company owners. It shifts lobbying from a corporate basis to a populist basis. We're going to work for pocketbook issues that better the lot of the middle class and those striving to become middle class. We ... I plan a rollout of ten million stakeholders paying an annual membership fee of one hundred dollars."

"Nets you a billion dollar startup," McGill said.

"Yeah," Putnam said, "A modest amount for a commercial endeavor but more than enough to buy majorities in both houses of Congress."

Galia said, "What's to stop the special interests, those *multibillion* dollar businesses you alluded to, from outspending you or even buying a majority of shares in Share America?"

Putnam appreciated the chief of staff's cynical turn of mind. He decided he'd like to get to know her better. Maybe offer her a job someday.

"We thought of both those things," he said. "Nobody can buy more than one share of Share America. Nobody can contribute more than a hundred bucks per year. That way nobody gets to be the eight-hundred-pound gorilla. As for being outspent, I'm counting on the fact that Share America will be outspent initially. I'll use that to expand our base."

McGill thought he started to grasp the true genius of Putnam's plan.

"You get to the point where both sides are throwing so much money at politicians, people are going to gag and say enough's enough. There'll have to be reform."

Putnam didn't agree, not entirely.

He said, "Well, maybe, if you get a couple of new justices on the Supreme Court. But what my friends and I had in mind was more like having masses of people say to the pols, 'What's the matter, our money's not good enough for you?' Any pol who kept taking donations from Geiger's side will be spotlighted and knocked out of the box by someone the people paid for."

The president looked as grim as anyone could recall seeing her.

"Why should the American people have to buy any officeholder?" she asked.

Putnam said, "Because, Madam President, that's the only way we'll get a government of, by and for the people again."

That left everyone silent long enough for Rockelle Bullard to raise her hand like a schoolgirl with a question. At first, no one knew whose attention she wanted. But when Putnam pointed a finger at his chest, she nodded.

"You said Mr. Bradley Attles was what, pivotal, to Speaker Geiger's plan?"

"Yes, because he was both a major power in the lobbying community and he was Geiger's personal lawyer. If any investigator were to accuse the two of them of doing something illegal, they would have used attorney-client privilege as a shield against the investigation."

Rockelle asked, "So what happens now that Mr. Attles is gone?"

Putnam smiled. "My guess is the speaker is trying to fight off a heart attack while looking for the best possible replacement."

"You have any idea of who that might be?" Galia asked.

Putnam was about to offer a handful of names when he remembered that he hadn't been returning his phone calls. He took his phone out of his pocket, and brought up the list of the calls he'd missed, and right there was …

Derek Geiger's name and number.

Putnam extended the phone so everyone could see who had called him.

It took only a moment for all present to figure out the reason for the call.

Putnam said, "Guy must be nuts, if he thinks I'm taking Attles' job."

Lafayette Park

A platoon of uniformed Metro cops was waiting for orders about what to do with the unexpected influx of hundreds of people off a dozen chartered buses. The seven-acre park was a public space, open day and night to anyone who cared to use it. The Peace Vigil people had been camped out there continuously since 1981, but they were exactly what their name suggested, peaceful, and after thirty years were more of a local institution than a protest movement.

The newcomers were unknown to the police captain who had to decide what to tell his troops: maintain order or disperse the gathering. If dispersal were to be his choice, he would need a lot more cops. But the last thing he wanted was to have a riot on his hands, tear gas clouding the sky, skulls being cracked. There was no way that would look good on his personnel record.

The Metro captain was greatly relieved when a dark-haired woman in a good business suit came up to him and showed her Secret Service ID.

"Captain," she said with a smile, "if it's all right with you, why don't we take a listen to what these people have to say?"

A microphone stand had just been placed on a small platform.

The Metro captain asked, "Are you taking personal responsibility for whatever happens, Special Agent?"

Elspeth Kendry said, "Sure. My boss sent me to check things out. He's on the roof across the street watching us right now."

The captain looked at the White House, saw several figures on the roof.

He also saw a large number of uniformed Secret Service officers gathered on the grounds across the street. Celsus Crogher was not one to take chances. Elspeth would bet the SAC had uniforms surrounding the entire White House Complex, in case the mob in Lafayette Square was just a fake-out.

"Your people will back up my people, if it comes to that?" the Metro captain asked.

"I'll give a whistle," Elspeth told him.

Then she whispered something into the microphone at her wrist the captain couldn't hear. But he wasn't worried now. The feds had assumed responsibility. Anything went wrong, the egg was on their faces. The order went out to the Metro uniforms: Maintain order, politely.

Elspeth made her way to the front row of the crowd.

Flashing only her smile not her badge.

Law Offices of Gerald Mishkin

The anonymous male voice that had alerted WorldWide News to Speaker Derek Geiger's ignominious ejection from his marital abode belonged to Harlo Geiger's divorce lawyer, Gerald Mishkin — one of three she kept on retainer. She had them positioned in all the places she did business: Washington, New York and Sarasota. She believed in being prepared for moments that must inevitably come.

Despite taking her own precautions, it ticked her off that Derek had made his own preparations for the dissolution of their love match. Doing her due diligence before she married the speaker, Harlo had investigated each of the two previous Mrs. Geigers, and there was no question in Harlo's mind that she was by far the hottest babe that sneaking political bastard had ever married.

It bruised her ego that Derek had been able to see past his lust for her and make plans to safeguard his future, both politically and financially. That and the creep not being able to put up a tent pole for her the last time they would ever share a bed. It was enough to make a girl start to doubt her sexual magnetism.

Her choice of having WorldWide News shoot the video of her husband was based on canny calculation. She knew Sir Edbert Bickford had made his enormous fortune by catering to the insatiable appetite of the drooling class to see rich gasbags shot out of the sky. Catching one of the most powerful men in American government in a soap opera moment must have made Bickford quiver in delight.

The only thing that would have made it better was if Derek had been accompanied by a bimbo. Maybe, technology being what it was, they could drop one in after the fact.

The worst thing would be if Sir Edbert decided to sit on the video.

Do a favor for Derek Geiger in expectation of a far greater return.

Say a tax law written to benefit him and no one else.

Harlo couldn't have that so before coming to see her lawyer she'd visited her publicist who was busy right now spreading the news of the Geigers' impending day in divorce court. Once media competition came out with the story, WorldWide News would have to scoop them with the video.

As grounds for the divorce, Harlo was going with mental cruelty. The sonofabitch Derek had been living under her roof — eating on her dime, too — and was scheming all the while to dump her. Made him a gigolo. A welfare freeloader. A real prick.

Once again, Harlo's thoughts turned to the possibility that her husband had found a new girlfriend. Could he really be that reckless? Of course, he could. It came with the job description for a politician. Send Dr. Jekyll to Washington and Mr. Hyde was bound to start making cathouse calls.

Harlo said to her lawyer, "Jerry, do you have a good investigator on call?"

Gerald Mishkin, J.D. Harvard Law, said, "Sure."

"Let's have him find out who Derek's sleeping with when I'm out of town."

"You have reason to suspect he is? We wouldn't want to make that charge lightly. When the respondent is the speaker of the House of Representatives, you don't want to allege anything you can't prove."

"You're happily married, aren't you, Jerry?"

Caution entering his voice, the lawyer said, "Yes."

"I won't snoop into your personal life any farther than that," Harlo said. "But I'll say hypothetically that if a happily married man was set upon by his wife, and she was wearing nothing but a smile and the sexiest lingerie she could find, why, that man might be expected to behave predictably."

Mishkin nodded. Couldn't help but think of his client in the scenario she'd conjured.

Felt a response that made him glad he had a desk to shield his modesty.

Harlo could still see his face, knew he got the idea.

"Now if that happily married man failed to respond predictably despite his wife's most earnest efforts, what would a poor girl be left to think? That she'd suddenly become Whistler's Mother? That wasn't what she saw in the mirror when she put on her teddy."

Mishkin's mind coupled the image of Harlo in a teddy with earnest efforts and he got the point. He said, "Your suspicions bear investigating."

Harlo said, "I'm glad you think so."

She could see beads of sweat on his brow. Reassuring if not endearing.

But then the lawyer rose in her esteem.

He said, "Maybe, given the respondent's prominent status, we should go a step beyond my usual investigator."

"And where would that extra step take us?" Harlo asked.

"Well, I know this fellow Putnam Shady."

Harlo grinned. "What a wonderful name for a private eye."

"He's a lawyer, actually. But he has a tenant in his basement apartment. Her name is Margaret Sweeney and she's the investigator."

"One who can stand up to Derek?"

"Maybe, but her partner certainly can. He's James J. McGill."

Harlo Geiger clapped in delight.

"The president's henchman," she said. "That's marvelous."

So good, in fact, she chided herself for not being the one to think of it.

"Shall I call Putnam?" Mishkin asked.

"Right this minute," Harlo told him.

Lafayette Park

Reverend Burke Godfrey waited on one of the chartered buses. He hated being back at the scene of his greatest embarrassment, his humiliation at the hands of Margaret Sweeney. He thought it was a big mistake. But the TV producer, Ellie Booker, and his lawyer, Benton Williams, had insisted it would be a brilliant stroke. It would carry the fight directly to the White House, and he shouldn't worry about last time because that could be spun as a win for him. History was rewritten all the time, he was assured.

Maybe. He thought it was possible for an organization as powerful as WorldWide News to distort perception in his favor. What he was certain of, though, was that he wouldn't fare well if Margaret Sweeney were in the audience, looking once more like an avenging angel come to smite the charlatans, hypocrites and fools.

He'd told both Benton and Booker he wouldn't be going out to speak if Sweeney were present. Benton had assured him that the woman would be escorted from the gathering if she had the nerve to show up. Ellie Booker grinned when she heard that. The televangelist knew just what the producer was thinking: a tussle with that beautiful demon being hurled from the throng would make great television.

He'd like to see that himself, once he was sure the earth didn't open and swallow anyone who tried to lay a hand on Sweeney. If God were on her side — and now Erna's — Burke Godfrey really was in trouble.

The door to the bus was open and he could hear the sound people getting their levels right. You wanted everybody to be able to hear you, but you didn't want the volume so loud you bowled people over. You wanted to avoid screeching feedback, too.

Preaching in the modern age took preparation. Godfrey heard an audio technician with a pleasant voice ask, "Everybody hear me okay?"

The crowd roared in response, and their voices raised Godfrey's spirit.

These were his people and they were still with him.

No, these were but a few of his people. His congregation numbered in the millions and could be found clear across the country. He could visit any state in the nation, even Alaska and Hawaii, and find good souls who would offer him shelter and a meal, never asking for any recompense except a kind word and a blessing.

Remembering the extent of his flock bolstered Godfrey further.

He heard his lawyer begin to speak. "Good afternoon, everyone. My name is Benton Williams and I have the distinct honor, privilege and responsibility of representing a great man, the Reverend Burke Godfrey."

The crowd applauded and cheered.

Waiting for a lull, Williams continued, "That is, I'm his lawyer, but I hope you won't hold that against me."

A wave of laughter reached Burke Godfrey. It made him feel warm on two counts. His people still loved him and his lawyer would certainly know how to charm a jury, if it came to that. And all it would take would be one juror — say a middle-aged woman who worked at WalMart — to keep him from ever being convicted of anything. Benton would find that juror and —

"As you know," Williams said, "we gathered here today on the spur of the moment, and the good men and women of the Metro Police Department — and the Secret Service across the street — have the responsibility of seeing that this exercise of our first amendment rights proceeds peacefully. We owe it to them to be cooperative."

There wasn't even a murmur from the crowd now.

They understood they'd just been warned.

But so had the cops. Freedom of speech and the right peaceably to assemble were not to be denied to any American.

Satisfied that a reasonable accommodation had been implicitly agreed upon by the two camps, the lawyer concluded by saying, "I think it's time we all heard from Reverend Burke Godfrey."

There it was, the all's clear sign.

Margaret Sweeney was nowhere to be seen.

The reverend stepped off the bus, his emotions balanced on a tightrope between fear and exultation. He stopped in his tracks for just a moment, a knot in his guts telling him to turn and run for all he was worth. But he'd been spotted already and a cheer went up from the congregation. It seized him like a riptide, drew him toward all the smiling people waiting to bob their heads at his every word.

This was what I was born to do, Burke Godfrey thought.

For better or worse, there would be no turning back for him now.

The crowd parted before him like the Red Sea before Moses.

He hopped onto the platform with Benton Williams. The lawyer raised Godfrey's hand and the throng cheered louder. It was wonderful to loved by so many. Burke Godfrey felt young and powerful again.

Until he saw the dark-haired woman standing right in front of him.

She wasn't cheering, wasn't clapping. She just stood there watching.

She wasn't Margaret Sweeney.

But she might as well have been.

Thing One — moving

Every time McGill got into Patti's presidential limo he felt as if he was entering a bank vault, the doors to the vehicle were that thick. Leo had whispered the specs to him: each door was clad in eight inches of military grade armor. The windows were five inches of ballistic glass. Each door was said to weigh as much as the cabin door on a Boeing 747.

The limousine's cabin included a sealed air recirculation system.

Thing One weighed in at eight tons.

McGill would bet it took a special hoist to change the oil.

He never could have abided having a limo like Thing One as his regular ride, but he felt warm all over knowing that Patti moved about in the equivalent of Fort Knox on wheels. Not that she had to worry about fender benders. Cops up front cleared the way for her; cops behind made sure nobody tailgated.

The presidential limo had departed from the South Portico entrance of the White House so the first couple didn't see the gathering in Lafayette Park, but SAC Crogher had advised them that the featured speaker at the impromptu gathering was Burke Godfrey.

McGill asked his wife, "Want me to have Sweetie drop by and throw a scare into him?"

Patti shook her head. "We have to be very careful."

She told McGill that the attorney general's investigation of Godfrey had already begun.

"So everything gets done by the book," McGill said. "It won't just be the court that will have to approve of what you do, it'll be the history books, too."

"The books that aren't written and published by the opposition."

"Sir Edbert Bickford and friends." McGill said. "You do have someone over in the park looking after your interests?"

"Celsus sent your new Secret Service liaison, Special Agent Kendry."

"She's good," McGill said. "I think she'll be a help."

"Celsus told me you had her chase away Sir Edbert's nephew."

"Is that who the guy was? Yeah, I did. Anything wrong with that?"

"I'll leave it to the two of you to work that out."

"Celsus and me?"

"You and Special Agent Kendry."

"Thanks." McGill appreciated how Patti did her best to allow him to live as normal a life as possible. "Remind me to give you a foot rub tonight."

The president laughed.

The motorcade pulled up to the entrance to George Washington University Hospital. Celsus got out of the front seat of Thing One to check with the agents who'd been sent on ahead of the president to make sure all was well. An agent stood in front of each door of the passenger compartment and would not allow either half of the First Couple to exit until the all clear sign was given.

McGill abided the security protocol without demurral.

He always did when Patti's safety was involved.

She asked him, "What should I do first, see Kenny or have my blood drawn?"

"Ask the guys if Kenny's awake." The Secret Service would know. By now, they'd have checked to see if any ne'erdowell was lurking under Kenny's bed. "If he's awake, we'll go right up. If not, you'll get the blood test done."

Patti was showing extraordinary compassion and generosity to Kenny by taking time out of the middle of her day. Even so, making the most efficient use of her time was a necessity.

The agent putting himself between the president and the rest of the world flashed a hand gesture: less than a minute before the doors would open.

A thought occurred to Patti. "Did you ever look at that note I gave you?"

"No." McGill fished around in his pocket. "Didn't you look at it?"

"I did not."

McGill rolled his eyes. "I don't have any state secrets."

"Edwina said it was from a female acquaintance at DePaul."

McGill's hand stopped moving. "Really?"

Patti noticed how her husband went still. "Is that significant?"

"I told you about —" He took the note out and looked at the name on it. "Clare Tracy."

The president's eyes widened. "You know Clare Tracy?"

"I'm sure I told you. She was my college girlfriend. How do you know her?"

The Secret Service agents opened both passenger doors of Thing One.

The president and her husband didn't carry on a conversation across the roof of a limousine. They tabled the matter until they had their next moment of privacy. Each of them wondering about the other's relationship with Clare Tracy.

McGill wondering why Clare had called him after all the intervening years.

Putnam Shady's Residence

Sweetie and Putnam sat in the kitchen of his townhouse sipping drinks: ice tea for her, Slim-Fast for him. Putnam would have preferred something with a little moral ambiguity — alcohol — to it but he was slimming down and it was amazing how many calories even a little booze added to the waistline. His impetus to lose weight was the fact that Sweetie was increasingly willing to be seen in public with him. On one sojourn he'd caught their side-by-side reflections in a store window and that had been enough.

He didn't want to be the schlumpfy guy with the buff woman.

He doubted that he'd ever look as fit as Margaret but he wanted to get close.

Get close to her in as many ways as he could. But now he thought he'd suffered a big setback. Instead of agreeing immediately to Jim McGill's plan to talk with Derek Geiger and go along with whatever scheme the speaker had in mind — become the president's spy, in effect — he'd said he had to think about it. He would have turned the suggestion down flat and not worried a bit whether the president or McGill liked it, if he didn't worry that such a rejection would put him on the outs with Margaret.

Worse, such faint-heartedness might have caused her to move out.

He didn't think Margaret was the kind to allow for do-overs.

"Are you mad at me?" he asked.

She hadn't said a word to him all the way home.

"No," she said.

There was no shading of sarcasm in her reply.

She was being quiet not angry.

Still uncertain of his standing, though, Putnam pushed the issue. "Why aren't you ticked off? I wasn't exactly helpful back there at the White House. Jim McGill and the president are your friends."

Sweetie looked at him. "They are. You are, too."

"But not in the same way."

"Now, you're beginning to annoy me."

"Sorry." But the flicker of displeasure actually made Putnam feel better. "You know I have trouble with authority, right?"

"I've noticed."

"I tried to be as restrained as possible with the president. I actually voted for her."

Sweetie grinned. "You're really something. If you thought I was mad at you because I wasn't saying anything, you're wrong. I was considering the moral dimensions of what Jim wanted you to do."

"What, take advantage of a guy trying to destroy his wife's presidency? Seems pretty moral to me. Just not terribly safe. I screw up with Geiger and I could be finished in this town. You consider what happened to three of my friends, and ..." Putnam nodded at the sheets of plywood covering the spaces where his living room windows had been. "I might be finished everywhere."

"You have reason to be concerned," Sweetie agreed.

Putnam laughed. "You say that like I might be late feeding a parking meter."

Sweetie could see the bullet holes in the ceiling of Putnam's living room.

"You handled being shot at very well," she said. "You got out of harm's way; you gave your assailant reason to think you were returning fire; you took care not to hit any innocent third party. All in all, you're tougher than you want anyone to think."

Putnam smiled, genuinely warmed.

"Stop it, you'll turn my head." Of course, that might have been exactly what she wanted. Make him think he was dashing, heroic, James Bond with a pot belly. Send him into harm's way to foil Derek Geiger's evil designs. It almost worked. But he was true enough to himself to ask, "What moral dimensions were you thinking of?"

Sweetie said, "The most basic one, really. Is there ever any justification for doing the wrong thing to achieve the right end?"

Putnam turned Sweetie's question on its head. "Wouldn't it be immoral to fail to do anything you could to prevent the triumph of evil?"

"That's how you see your Share America plan? A means to prevent the rich and powerful from taking over the country? More than they have already."

Putnam nodded, serious now.

"What's going on here is a twenty-first century American revolution. It's just getting started. I thought it could be fought with ideas, money and cunning, but apparently any kind of warfare calls for blood to be spilled."

"I see," Sweetie said. "I think you're right about war and blood. But wouldn't you be acting immorally, by your own reckoning, if you failed to do all you could to prevent what you see as the triumph of evil?"

In the quiet that followed Sweetie's question, Putnam heard her trap clang shut.

She hadn't really conned him. She'd just let him paint himself into an ethical corner. By his own reasoning, as she'd just said, he would be derelict if he failed to do everything he could to stop Derek Geiger's Super-K plan. Including spying on him for the president.

He had to shake his head in admiration.

"You are really good, Margaret" he said. "I'd hoped to live to see the good guys win this fight, but now I've got to risk my precious pink backside by snooping on the enemy."

Sweetie reached out and patted Putnam's cheek.

"You'll be fine ... but you better call Geiger back before he finds somebody else."

White House, Chief of Staff's Office

Galia was reviewing what she was coming to see as Patricia Darden Grant's bucket list — the policies she wanted to put into place and the issues she wanted to introduce into the national dialogue before she left office — when her phone rang.

The caller ID brought up the name Robert Merriman.

Merriman was the former chief of staff to Senator Roger Michaelson, and the current candidate to take his old boss's seat in the Senate. Michaelson was taking the big jump, running for the Democratic nomination to be president, with the knowledge that if he didn't win he'd be out of office.

Galia took the call.

"Good afternoon, Bob. Are you calling to ask for the name of a good criminal defense lawyer?"

Merriman's laugh seemed genuine.

"Sure, Galia. Why don't you give me the name of the guy you keep on retainer?"

"Sorry, *she* defends only innocent clients. Is there anything else I can do for you?"

"Yes, I'd like fifteen minutes with the president."

Bob Merriman's younger brother, Anson, was a lobbyist. Galia didn't have Anson's client list at the top of consciousness, but it wouldn't surprise her if the big billygoat Merriman was trying to gain favor for his junior sibling in return for, say, a large donation to his campaign fund.

"Oh, gee, Bob, there are so many people who need a favor."

"No doubt, but I'm one of those rare types looking to do a favor."

"Really? What kind of a good Democrat would do that?"

"Oh, the kind like Majority Leader Wexford and Minority Leader Berman."

Merriman was plugged in to the chiefs of staff of every significant senator and member of the House. He knew about Wexford and Berman meeting with the president before it happened ... and he didn't mind showing off to Galia. In fact, he liked it.

It went a long way toward providing credibility for what he was about to claim.

"Okay, Bob, you know a few things."

Merriman said, "One of them is something you've already figured out, too, Galia. Namely that the president isn't going to win reelection as a Republican."

"She isn't?"

"No, she's not. The sympathy bounce she got from standing on principle and losing Andy Grant is long gone. The hardcases on the right are reasserting themselves. They'd rather see our side win than let Patricia Grant have a second term."

Galia said, "And you don't want to see your side win?"

"Of course, I do. But there's only one candidate we could put up who'd be a mortal lock."

Galia had had the same thought herself, but hearing someone else about to voice it came as a shock.

"You're not suggesting —"

Merriman said, "Sure, I am, and don't pretend to be so surprised. The only way Patti Grant wins a second term as president is on the Democratic ticket."

"Even if that were true," Galia said, "why would she need you?"

"I'm going to be her Sherpa," Merriman told Galia, "in return for her endorsement."

Captain Welborn Yates' Office

"How come we always meet on your turf?" Rockelle Bullard asked.

Welborn pointed out. "We were already in the building. It was closer."

The answer, though undeniable, didn't keep the homicide lieutenant from frowning.

"You weren't looking for a logical response?" Welborn asked. "You'd have preferred a wisecrack or something else to give you a conversational leg up?"

"You talk to your girlfriend like that?" Rockelle asked.

"My fiancée? All the time."

"And she puts up with it?"

"She does the same to me."

Rockelle shook her head in disgust. "Great, we get a suspect to interview, the two of you can tag-team him. He'll beg for mercy in no time."

"Come on, Rockelle, play nice. We've worked well together before."

The Metro cop leaned forward, narrowing the distance between them to the width of Welborn's desk.

"You know and I know this case should be my jurisdiction. I should be the one running it. I shouldn't have the president and half the federal government looking over my shoulder."

Welborn leaned over his desk, narrowing the gap between them to inches.

"I have the greatest respect for your ability as a cop but be honest: Would you really want to arrest Speaker Geiger, if it comes to that, or have me do it?"

The two of them looked at each other without blinking.

Until Welborn added, "Because if that is what you want, I'll step aside and let you make the arrest. No matter who the perp turns out to be."

Rockelle still didn't blink, but she sat back.

Welborn said, "I know, it's tough. You're wondering just how far your bosses will back you, and how much weight they'll be able to carry if they do. My boss on the other hand will back me and who's going to give her a hard time?"

Rockelle had to nod at Welborn's appraisal of things.

"You got it pretty damn sweet."

"I'm willing to share. Besides stepping aside, I'll also step in. If you find someone you're sure did these killings but think he's got too much pull for you to risk an arrest, call me, I'll put the cuffs on him."

"No matter who?" she asked.

"I'd probably have a hard time locking up James J. McGill."

"How about Mr. Putnam Shady?"

"Margaret's guy? Why would he kill his friends?"

"Not them. Brad Attles, the speaker's man, Mr. Pivotal. Putnam Shady's enemy."

Welborn frowned. He didn't see that either, but if you looked at it logically ...

Rockelle said, "Makes sense, doesn't it? Evening things up a little for his side."

"I just don't see it," Welborn said. "He's never struck me as the homicidal type."

"Lots of folks in this town could win a best actor award."

There was that, Welborn thought.

"And now the speaker wants Mr. Shady to come work for him? Shady can't lose, can he? He keeps the faith, he'll sabotage Geiger's plan. He gets greedy, he'll make it work."

"But he couldn't know ahead of time the speaker would call on him to replace Attles."

"Why not?" Rockelle asked. "He and his late friends were the next big things, weren't they? His friends get killed, who's left?"

"Now, you're thinking Putnam did kill his friends?"

"Sometimes I figure things out right while I'm saying them."

"No," Welborn said, "he wouldn't have killed his friends."

"But with Attles it's a maybe?"

It was Welborn's turn to frown. He did entertain a sliver of doubt, but ...

"I don't think so."

Rockelle folded her arms. "So maybe we better each work our own leads."

"Yeah, maybe."

"But you'll still be willing to step in if I bring you proof?"

The answer was a long moment in coming.

Then Welborn sighed and said, "Yes, I will."

And then he added, "Assuming you share everything you've found out so far."

GWU Hospital

Patti had her blood tested before she and McGill went up to Kenny's room. They had been informed McGill's son was sleeping when they entered the hospital, and he was still asleep when the president finished having her blood drawn. Patti said she wanted to see Kenny anyway, just stop in and take a look, say hello even if the greeting went unheard, if that was all right with McGill.

He nodded. His chest was too constricted with fear to speak. He took his wife's hand and they went upstairs. The Secret Service had the elevator car waiting. Celsus rode up with them. More agents were waiting when they exited.

Even on such a personally trying errand, the president was obliged to smile and nod at the hospital staffers who directed the same gestures to her. One woman, a senior nurse, McGill thought, caught his eye. She steepled her hands in a prayerful manner and brought them to a bowed head. He could only hope the Almighty would hear and act on any entreaties made on Kenny's behalf.

"Dad!" Kenny called out the moment McGill appeared in the doorway to his room. His voice was only a fraction of its normal booming volume, but his son's joy at seeing him was as great as any time McGill could remember. Kenny smiled even wider when he saw the president. "Patti!"

Both visitors had to mask their feelings at seeing how pallid the boy looked. McGill went straight to his son's side, placed one hand behind his head and the other under his back, clasped him and kissed his forehead, which McGill thought felt warm.

"Hey, c'mon, Dad," Kenny protested. "Even Mom doesn't get that mushy, and you're blocking my view of Patti."

McGill stepped back, feeling it was safe to reveal his face now that his son had put a smile on it. He gestured to Patti to step forward. "Madam President."

Patti briefly took Kenny's right hand in both of hers and kissed his cheek.

The boy smiled at his father. "See, that's how you do it."

McGill asked his son, "How are you feeling, Kenny?"

The younger McGill peered past his two visitors, saw no one else.

"Just between us," Kenny began. He paused to look at Patti.

She told him, "It's okay. Your dad swears like a sailor when we're alone."

Kenny giggled. "You're just saying that."

"I am, but please tell us what's on your mind. Most people won't say boo around me."

"Okay," Kenny said. "I was going to say I feel like shit. I'm tired. My bones are starting to ache. Dr. Jones says they're going to start me on some medicine soon that's going to make all my hair fall out."

McGill said, "You know, I've sometimes wondered how I'd look with my head shaved."

Kenny made his eyes cross. "Don't even think about it. Patti might find someone new." Before the president could object, Kenny went on, "Hey, did you hear Liesl Eberhardt is coming to see me tomorrow. She and her mom are both going to see if they can be donors."

"That's great, Kenny. Someone else you know just had some blood drawn."

Kenny turned his face to Patti. "You did?"

"I did," the president said.

"But you're so busy. How could you take the time, I mean if you're the one."

Patti took Kenny's hand again. "I have good people working for me; they'll keep the lights on, and I set my own schedule."

Kenny grinned. "Must be cool being president."

"The job has its moments."

Kenny turned to his father. "How's the case with Sweetie going?"

"We have some work to do," McGill said.

"But you'll get it done, right?" Kenny asked. "Because the important part of the way I feel, the only good part really, is that I'm not scared anymore."

Just hearing that made McGill anxious.

"No, why not?"

"Because, Dad, I'm going to beat this junk, it's not going to beat me. I've got too many things to do. I know what I want to be when I get older."

"What's that?" McGill had heard Kenny speak of any number of ambitions. Most of them involved law enforcement or the military with the occasional mention of motor cycle racing and professional surfing.

But his son fooled him. "I want to be a doctor. Not just for some sick kids but for all of them. Dr. Jones told me the way I can do that is to become a medical research doctor. I can't think of anything better than not only getting well but coming back and kicking this disease's ass for everybody."

McGill told his son, "You'll have my full support."

"And mine," Patti said.

SAC Crogher stepped into the doorway and said, "Ma'am."

He'd been waiting just out of sight, had overheard every word. The president said, "Yes?"

"The medical team and Mrs. Enquist are down the hall. It's time for the chemo." A heartbeat later, Crogher added. "Mr. McGill, may I have just a moment with your son?"

McGill remembered that the SAC had volunteered to be Kenny's donor, if he was compatible. So maybe he had some other way to be helpful.

"Sure, Celsus."

McGill gave his son another kiss, this one brief.

The president did the same.

Both said they'd be back to see him again.

They stepped toward the door as Crogher moved past them. Neither McGill nor the president turned to look directly at Kenny and the SAC but both watched from the corners of their eyes. Crogher bent over the boy and spoke directly into his ear, far too quietly to be overheard. Kenny nodded, and Crogher said another word or two.

Then the visit was over and it was time for the chemo.

Q Street, N.W.

Returning to Washington, Hugh Collier called Ellie Booker and told her to come to his D.C. townhouse. It wasn't a power play,

and she knew that he was gay so there was no worry about un-
wanted sexual attention. But Ellie told him she was at a rally in
Lafayette Park, just across Pennsylvania Avenue from the White
House.

He was about to insist she heed his demand when she clicked
off on him, saying Burke Godfrey was about to start speaking.

Hugh looked at the wireless phone in his hand. He was sure
that if he called back he'd only get voice mail. The bloody nerve
of that sheila. He'd had her pay bumped by half and this was the
way she treated him. He fumed for ten seconds and then laughed
at himself.

Ms. Booker stood her ground with Uncle Edbert; she wouldn't
let some boy wonder from Down Under intimidate her.

Hugh would have to trust that, in her efficient way, she'd call
him back as soon as she was able. He'd wanted to see Ellie at his
digs because it had finally penetrated his thick footballer's skull
that James J. McGill must have an ally inside Uncle Edbert's local
offices.

McGill heretofore had been buffered from the world at large by
light security, one Secret Service agent and one armed driver. But
by the time Hugh had arrived McGill had security reinforcements
in place that put him beyond the reach of any pesky chaps with
microphones, videocams and annoying questions. Coincidence?
Not bloody likely.

Some quisling had betrayed Sir Edbert Bickford. Worse, it
was likely a matter of principle not greed. Somebody was protecting McGill, a.k.a. the president's henchman. And the president
in question, Patricia Darden Grant, was a heretic to her party's
faithful. She didn't bow to Wall Street money; she didn't genuflect
to the American mullahs.

Had she done both, Uncle Edbert would have been her champion not her nemesis.

There was only one conclusion to draw: WorldWide News had
been infiltrated by an undercover *liberal*. From the dossiers Hugh
had read, this was just the sort of political espionage that might

be expected from Galia Mindel. Had Hugh made his suspicions plain to his uncle, the purges would have begun immediately. The bloodletting would have been of a scope and intensity to set old Joe Stalin's ghost to cheering.

The madness might even engulf Hugh, but he was a man whose own father had thrown him into the street. He knew enough to hedge his bets against any decline of fortune. He lived modestly when he couldn't charge his indulgences to a company account. The lion's share of his salary had been placed in numbered accounts in tax havens around the world.

Being shown the door once more might sting but he'd be able to salve his wounds in a beachfront villa somewhere. Maybe he'd even organize his own football league. One strictly for blokes like himself.

In the meantime, he turned his TV on to Uncle Edbert's local station.

The better to see just what Ellie Booker thought was so important.

Lafayette Park

It was the thought of being undone by yet another woman that braced Burke Godfrey's spine. He took the microphone from Benton Williams and spoke to the dark-haired woman standing directly in front of him. "Are you a member of my flock, sister?"

His tone said clearly she was not.

Elspeth was surprised by being publicly singled out.

She knew immediately that retreat would be a mistake.

Her best response would be to advance.

She stepped up onto the speaker's platform, catching Burke Godfrey off guard, backing him up a step and making several people gasp. The crowd's tension was eased as Elspeth moved past Godfrey and whispered something to Benton Williams. The lawyer, by contrast, looked as if he'd been struck by lightning.

He bobbed his head several times. He took the microphone

from Burke Godfrey and the man by the arm for a quick conference. Elspeth stepped down from the platform and returned to her former place in the crowd, people making room for her. A couple of onlookers thought to question her, but she placed a shushing finger to her lips and nodded to the stage.

Benton Williams addressed the gathering; Burke Godfrey stood behind him.

"Reverend Godfrey will speak in just a moment, but first I want to remind all of you that this is a peaceful gathering and it is in everyone's best interest that it remain so. What you are about to hear might upset you but, please, remain calm and orderly."

The lawyer's words of caution alerted the Metro cops to be on guard. From his perch on the platform Williams could see they were readying themselves to take action. The uniformed Secret Service agents across the street were moving to reinforce their Metro brethren.

"Please," Williams beseeched, "everyone remain calm."

He'd misjudged the situation and his client badly. He had never thought things might come to grief, but the potential for a bad end to things had just become painfully clear.

The lawyer glanced at the woman who'd spoken to him. She'd identified herself as a Secret Service special agent, had given him a glimpse of the automatic weapon under her coat. She'd warned him that Godfrey had better choose his words carefully, not incite the crowd to riot. If he singled her out for criticism and anyone laid hands on her she would use her weapon and any deaths that resulted would be on Godfrey's head — and his.

Williams took a deep breath and said, "Please welcome the pastor of the Salvation's Path Church, the Reverend Burke Godfrey."

The lawyer had told the pastor just whom the woman he'd called sister was and what she had said. Going beyond that, Williams said he looked into the Secret Service agent's eyes. If she came to grief, they wouldn't have to worry about facing trial. The lawyer was sure the first burst of gunfire from her weapon would be directed their way.

Now, he could only hope his client wasn't feeling the call of martyrdom.

Burke Godfrey looked over Elspeth Kendry's head. He would begin as he usually did when addressing a large gathering. He would start by speaking to the far reaches of the gathering. The last would be first.

"Mr. Williams has it exactly right, my dear friends and neighbors. In trying times, we must all strive to face our difficulties with a sense of peace."

A smattering of amens rose from the congregation.

Even the cops, Godfrey could see, relaxed a bit.

"We are all afflicted with sorrows over the course of our lives. The proper response is to pray for the strength to overcome them. In my present situation, I need more than my own prayers, I must ask for yours, too."

"You have mine," a female voice called out. Other voices quickly called out, "Mine, too."

Godfrey raised a hand in benediction. "Thank you, sisters and brothers. I'll need all the help I can get."

The minister cast a quick glance at Elspeth, let her know that he had a thousand people in the palm of his hand. Her life was his to take, if he wanted it. But Godfrey didn't see any fear in her face; he saw she was holding something under her coat.

And he remembered Benton Williams' warning.

Moreover, Godfrey's sense of stagecraft told him he was alone on the platform now.

The lawyer, minor character that he was, had made his exit.

Godfrey didn't mind; he never liked to share the spotlight.

Lifting his head, he informed the multitudes, "My dear wife, my poor tormented Erna, has taken leave of her senses."

The crowd gasped. Godfrey didn't know where that thought had come from, but he knew how to play along with an idea that got a response he liked.

He continued, "The *torture* of her imprisonment, of being deprived of the company of her family and friends has driven her mad." Godfrey quickly overrode the current of angry murmurs. "I wouldn't have believed this, if I hadn't seen it with my own eyes."

"Testify!" a male voice demanded.

"I will, brother, I will. I visited Erna in the vile federal prison in West Virginia where she's being kept. I saw the woman I've loved for over forty years, but when I heard her speak, I knew she'd been replaced by a stranger. She confessed to me that she knew she had done wrong by taking the life of Andrew Hudson Grant, and was remorseful for her deed."

The overwhelming vocal response was a woeful moan.

But one man called out, "The hell she did!"

Elspeth didn't turn to look for the speaker, but she'd bet there would several cops who'd pinpoint the creep. He'd be taken aside, talked to, have his personal information entered into several databases. If he had any outstanding warrants, he'd be arrested.

"There's more to this story, my friends," Godfrey continued, "and this is what truly breaks my heart. Erna told me that she is going to implicate *me* in this terrible crime."

The crowd knew just how to respond to this news.

Boos, jeers and shouts of *no* resounded across the park.

The cops got tense again.

Like an eccentric conductor of a great symphony orchestra, Godfrey raised his hands and dropped them in graceful arcs. After the crescendo came not the diminuendo but the rest. Then after the quiet came the voice of sweet reason.

"Please don't blame Erna. She's suffered who knows what anguish in the time she's been locked away from us."

"Torture!" a woman called, remembering Godfrey's word.

He was pleased that the seed he'd planted had already taken root.

"That may well be, sister. I only visited that awful place for less than an hour and had my private parts grabbed for simply wanting to see my wife."

The boos and jeers were louder this time.

With them came calls of "Shame!"

Godfrey looked back at Elspeth.

It angered him that she remained stoic.

But it was not lost on him that she still held her weapon.

Time to close, he thought. Wrap things up on a high note.

"Friends ... friends and neighbors. Brothers and sisters, please. Let your hearts be filled with peace and love. Let your resolve remain strong." Inspiration came to Godfrey. The spirit was with him. "We must remember that the threat of being executed has already been lifted from Erna. Let us now work to see that she's freed and restored to us ... and to her right mind."

A wave of cheers filled the park. Here was a goal they all endorsed. Burke Godfrey was tempted to call for donations for his sake and Erna's. He thought better of the idea. The money would come on its own.

He simply offered his blessing. Happy with the way things had turned out.

Except he was denied the chance to smile triumphantly at the Secret Service woman.

She had disappeared into the crowd.

Reverend Godfrey would have been more upset had he known what Elspeth was thinking. She was going to draft a memo to SAC Crogher with a request to forward it to the Attorney General. To wit: Reverend Godfrey has a serious problem with strong women. Recommend, in the matter of an eventual criminal trial, a forceful female prosecutor.

McGill Investigations, Inc.

Carolyn had told McGill that she would be staying at the hospital around the clock, until the crisis with Kenny was over. Lars would return home for the time being to run his business. Abbie would be returning to school to keep her mind on her upcoming studies as best she could. That left Caitie. Would it be all right, Carolyn asked, if she stayed at the White House?

McGill assured both his ex-wife and his daughter that would

be fine.

Patti told Carolyn, "Caitie, Abbie, you and Lars are always welcome. At the White House, Camp David or wherever else we might be."

The president extended her hand to Caitie. McGill's younger daughter first embraced her mother fiercely, then her father and gave Lars a peck on the cheek. Then she left with Patti, finally giving in to tears.

Abbie, doing her best to keep her own emotions in check, asked McGill, "Will you give me a ride to school, Dad?"

"Of course," he said. Turning to Carolyn, he said, "I'll be back as soon as Abbie's settled in."

She took his hand and said, "We'd just worry more, the two of us together. Do what Kenny asked you to do, help Sweetie. I'll call if ... I'll call."

McGill, Carolyn and Abbie all embraced.

Abbie kissed Lars and McGill shook his hand.

On the way to Georgetown University, McGill and Abbie sat quietly holding hands. Up front, Deke and Leo didn't say a word. What McGill focused on were Kenny's words. He was going to beat his disease. He had things he wanted to do.

Back at his office, McGill had his own things to do.

The first was to return Clare Tracy's call.

Tapping out the numbers on his cell phone, he wondered what she wanted ...

How she had changed ...

And if talking to her would rekindle any old feelings.

The call was answered and he said, "Hello, Clare. This is Jim McGill."

Q Street, N.W.

Ellie Booker got lucky and found a parking space directly outside of Hugh Collier's townhouse. Better yet, it was the last open spot on the block. The sedan with the two feds in it that had followed her from Lafayette Park had nowhere to pull in — but when you were Secret Service working out of the White House, Ellie saw, you could damn well double-park wherever you pleased.

The two suits hadn't tried to be subtle while they were following her car, had all but tailgated her, and now they sat there parked illegally and stared at her. One of them, damn him, even took her picture. Ellie turned her back on them, ran up Hugh's front steps and banged on the door. It opened a moment later and she rushed inside, her jaw clenched.

"Where's the bloody fire?" Hugh asked. He leaned out to look for trouble, saw the man in the car with the camera pointed at him, ducked back inside and slammed the door. He turned to Ellie and asked, "Secret Service? McGill's men?"

Ellie nodded. "Has to be."

"Come with me," Hugh said.

He led her to a first floor office with no windows, flipped a switch on a black box that set a red light aglow. Hugh sat behind the room's small desk and Ellie took the only guest chair.

"If they're able to eavesdrop on us in here," he said, "Uncle Edbert is going to be very upset. The security measures in this glorified cubbyhole costs as much as the rest of the place combined."

He shook his head.

"What?" Ellie asked.

"I'm a terrible host," he said getting up. "What would you like to drink?"

"Poland Spring," she said.

"Yours before you know it."

He left the safe room, closing the door, and went to the kitchen. He plucked Ellie's bottled water from the fridge along with a bottle of Little Creatures for himself. Before returning to his colleague, Hugh used a key to open what looked like a breadbox. Inside was a device that looked like a tablet computer. He switched it on and saw an image of Ellie, sitting right where he left her, not peeking into any of his desk drawers. He wondered if she was too smart to do so. Did she suspect he would be watching her, privately recording their discussion for his own records? He wouldn't be surprised if she was.

He locked the breadbox and returned to the safe room.

Closing the door behind him, he handed Ellie her drink.

"Hope you can make do without a glass."

She nodded and took a long drink. Hugh liked that. He'd never had a woman as a close friend, but he was beginning to think his Ms. Booker might be the first. If it turned out she had a keen sense of humor, maybe the two of them could play a joke on his old man.

Knock on his door one day, share a big kiss when he opened it and say, "Look, Father, I'm cured!"

"What's funny?" Ellie asked, seeing his smile.

"Life, more often than not. I watched your feed of Reverend Godfrey preaching to the choir. Why don't you tell me what the camera missed?"

Ellie told him.

Hugh's eyes got big. "You've got that in digital sound?"

"Not the Secret Service agent, but Benton Williams. He told Burke Godfrey he was sure the fed would shoot them if Godfrey caused any trouble for her. He was speaking quietly, but he was holding the microphone right between Godfrey and himself."

Hugh said, "I recognized the woman the moment she stepped onstage; she was the bird I saw at McGill's offices. Even if we don't have audio of her making the threat, we see that she spoke to Williams immediately before he reported the threat to Godfrey. That will certainly be good enough for Uncle Edbert."

"And ninety-nine point nine percent of our viewing audience," Ellie added.

Hugh laughed. "That pesky point one percent is still holding out. We'll have to do something about those damn malcontents."

Ellie grinned, and that was enough for Hugh to think the joke on Dad was on.

"Given that he had an armed critic standing front row center," Hugh said, "I think the reverend acquitted himself commendably. Hinting his wife had fled from reason, that she was likely being tortured and that the only fair thing to do was to set her free."

Ellie nodded. "A ballsy speech for a guy who complained about a little jailhouse grope."

"Ah, but that was the underpinning to the claim of torture."

"I know," Ellie said, "but I think the guy is basically a wuss."

Hugh squinted at her. "You, you're part of that point one percent."

"Don't tell Uncle Edbert," Ellie told him.

They both laughed.

Hugh told Ellie about his meeting with Clare Tracy and her admission of becoming pregnant by McGill. Ellie shook her head. "No, no way."

"The lady made me pay ninety thousand dollars for that information, and I believe her."

Ellie said, "But I checked McGill out down to his Dr. Scholl's and found only his three kids with Carolyn Enquist, formerly McGill, née Roberts."

Hugh said, "Adoptions are confidential in this country, aren't they?"

"Yes ... You think McGill's got a kid out there he doesn't know about?"

Hugh posed another question. "Medical records are also confidential?"

Ellie knew right where he was going. "McGill's girlfriend got an abortion?"

"He may have held her hand all the way to the clinic. I don't know that, but research is one of your strengths, isn't it? And now you have two new possibilities to pursue."

Ellie nodded vigorously, and stopped abruptly.

"We've got work to do, but we've also got those creeps outside watching us."

"Terrible," Hugh said. "Almost like having paparazzi pursue you."

Ellie gave him a baleful look. "Don't you like your job?"

"For the time being, until I can open or buy a successful

brewery."

"And right now?"

Hugh said, "Well, I'm an extraordinarily good looking bloke and you're a sleek and stylish sheila, but I'll wager we can hire enough passable lookalikes to make our watchers' heads spin, leaving us free to go about our skulduggery."

Ellie smiled. "Will Uncle Edbert pay for that?"

"Bugger him, if he won't. We'll fudge our accounts."

They set about making their plans.

Ellie ever so glad Hugh had left the room.

Giving her all the time she needed to turn on the audio recorder in her handbag.

P Street, Georgetown

Sweetie's 1969 Malibu came stock with a 396 cubic inch V8 engine. After some friends of Leo Levy's from his NASCAR days worked their high-performance magic on the venerable piece of Detroit iron, it would outrun six-figure exotics and corner like it was on rails. Putnam, sitting beside Sweetie, kept begging her for a chance to drive it. He'd hit upon a persuasive argument: He'd pick up her gas tab.

Leo's friends hadn't worried about mileage and insisted that the Malibu be fed nothing but super premium. With the price of gas approaching four dollars a gallon, the toll was nearing the weekly grocery bill of that little old lady who lived in a shoe. A horde of insatiable kids and a super-muscle car, they both cost a small fortune to keep full.

Even so, allowing Putnam to sit in her driver's seat was, for Sweetie, nearly as intimate a concession as allowing him into her bed, but she had to admit that probably wasn't too far away either. Maybe if he offered to do her laundry. Sweetie smiled at the thought.

She might let Putnam pick up the gas bill eventually; that could be written off as a transportation expense. But there would never be any charge in either time or money for her affections.

They weren't for sale.

"You're smiling, Margaret," Putnam said as she pulled into a parking space near the offices of McGill Investigations, Inc. "You keep that up, you'll drive me crazy."

As soon as she shifted into park, Sweetie reached over, took Putnam's face in both hand and kissed him full on the lips. When she sat back he did look a bit delirious.

Needing him functional for the moment, she popped open her door and got out of the car, telling her passenger, "Come on, let's tell Jim about your phone call with the speaker."

McGill Investigations, Inc.

McGill knew all about Skype. Abbie used it to speak with friends; Caitie used it to talk with her theatrical agent, Annie Klein. McGill could appreciate that seeing the person you were talking to brought a new dimension to long distance conversation, but having been born way back in the twentieth century, he felt that seeing the other person often lessened rather than added to the intimacy of electronic communication.

He supposed that was the way earlier generations had felt when TV started to displace radio shows. Radio was the theater of the mind; television was right there in front of you, often with a cast of actors you wouldn't have chosen. No matter. The new medium had supplanted the old one.

Now, for the first time, McGill would have preferred Skype to the phone.

Clare Tracy's voice sounded to him exactly as it had when they'd both been twenty.

He knew that physical appearance was far more mutable but ...

He would have liked to see how Clare looked.

"How are you, Jim?" she said after he said hello.

The routine greeting brought his mind back to the present with a jolt.

"I've been better, Clare." All the anxiety he felt about Kenny was clear in his voice.

McGill heard the lock in the outer office door clack open. Footsteps followed. He recognized Sweetie's stride; someone was with her.

Having been silent a moment, Clare asked, "Anything I can do to help?"

"How's your bone marrow?" McGill asked.

He surprised himself, coming right out with that.

Showed, maybe, just a bit of the desperation he was feeling.

"It's fine as far as I know," Clare said. "Would you like to borrow a cup?"

She was trying to keep things light, but clearly knew the situation was serious.

"My son, Kenny, needs to find a donor fast."

"No family matches?"

"No. We have people volunteering, but I haven't heard any good news yet."

Clare asked, "What hospital is Kenny at?"

McGill realized Clare was going to volunteer to be tested.

The Lord moved in mysterious ways, he thought.

"GWU here in Washington."

"I'll be on the first flight I can find," Clare told him.

In the outer office, the phone rang. Sweetie picked up.

"If you're a match," McGill told her, "it's going to put you off your schedule for a bit."

Clare laughed. "I've never met your son, but if he's anything like his dad, I think I can make the sacrifice."

McGill wondered if having Clare drop in out of the blue might really be the miracle Kenny needed. Had he or anyone in his family done anything to deserve a godsend like that? He didn't know, but he wasn't going to miss the opportunity.

"Thank you, Clare. I can't tell you how much this means to me."

"Well … I might be one of a few people who has a pretty good idea."

That was true, McGill thought, as an old memory came rushing back, the reason he and Clare had broken up. The reason she'd left him, really.

With that painful time still in mind, Clare told him about her visit with Hugh Collier that morning and what she had told him.

"If he looked hard enough," she said, "he would have found out anyway. This way I got a hundred thousand dollars for Em's Em."

"For what?" McGill asked.

"You really don't know what I've been doing all this time?"

"Sorry, no."

So she told him about Mother's Milk, Em's Em, and her role in it.

"I was just a humble cop," he said. "That stuff is way over my head."

Clare laughed again. "Yeah, a humble cop who marries the first female president."

That brought a question to mind. "You know Patti?"

"Sure, we go back a long way."

McGill had always made a point of keeping his nose out of Patti's presidential and political activities, unless she needed a dinner date or brought a matter to him and asked for his opinion. Still, he wondered how he could have missed hearing about Clare.

"Small world, isn't it?" she asked, knowing what he was thinking.

Something she'd always been good at doing.

"Tiny," McGill said. "Call me when you know your arrival time. I'll meet you or send someone to pick you up."

"Thanks. I'll stop by St. Pat's before I come, light a candle for Kenny."

McGill had to clear his throat before he could express his gratitude and say goodbye.

He was no sooner off the phone than Sweetie knocked on the door.

"Come in," he said.

Sweetie entered. She looked at McGill, saw the cloud of emotion on his face.

"Everything okay with Kenny?" she asked.

"He just got another volunteer to be tested."

"That's great. Putnam's decided to help."

McGill nodded. "Good."

"Did you hear the call that just came in?"

"Heard the phone ring."

"It was a lawyer named Gerald Mishkin calling. He represents Harlo Geiger, the speaker's estranged wife. She's seeking a divorce."

"Really?"

"Yeah, and she wants to hire you."

K Street, N.W.

Metro Homicide Detective Big Mike Walker, a.k.a. Beemer, got a fine new suit, the nicest he ever owned, out of his new undercover assignment. That didn't make him one bit happier about it. He'd still have to give back the Bella Russo briefcase and the Mercedes S65 AMG that also came with the gig.

Having exited the car, Beemer walked alone down Lobbyist Lane. It was after dark now. There were lights on in several of the buildings he passed. Gaming the government was a 24/7 business, especially for those schemers new to their craft. The top dogs, the ones who routinely dressed the way Beemer did when he was trying to get someone to take a shot at him, they were off to cocktail parties, expense account dinners and the other diversions of those who carried water for the nation's plutocrats.

Not that Beemer thought about the larger implications.

He spoke softly, the microphone in the knot of his Italian silk tie picking up every word. "Know what I see, Meeker. I see bullet holes in this fine suit, and a damn Porky Pig pin on the lapel. The crime scene people will come along and photograph me layin' on the sidewalk like that."

Detective Marvin Meeker, watching from a distance, replied, "Don't you worry, Beemer, I'll take Porky off and put him in my pocket before anyone can take a picture."

"You're a real comfort, you sonofabitch. Just your luck you're the skinny one."

Beemer had been given the job as the decoy because Brad Attles, the last lobbyist to be killed, was a big black man. Lieutenant Bullard's idea was maybe the killer took a special dislike to large African-American lobbyists. So why not give him his preferred target?

They could pad Meeker out, Beemer had suggested. The lieutenant said anybody who had the eyesight to plug four lobbyists would detect something that clumsy. She hadn't even let Beemer carry his service weapon under his coat, said it would ruin the lines and be another giveaway. He had to carry his Glock in his briefcase.

"Just do a Cleavon Little," Meeker had told him.

"Yeah, sure. 'Scuse me while I whip dis out.' Fuck you."

"You'll be fine. You got two boys with long iron watching you."

Two snipers from the Special Tactics Branch. Damn good shots, but they could get bored like anyone else. Probably be playing cards when the bad guy finally showed up.

"I hate this shit," Beemer said.

"Don't blame you," Meeker conceded.

"And these damn shoes hurt."

The lieutenant said the shoes had to be high end to go with the suit. The pair of Edward Greens that Beemer had on went for better than a grand, but the biggest pair they'd been able to find were a size too small.

Meeker told Beemer, "Man, just curl up your toes. You don't stretch those things out too bad, I'll buy 'em off you when this is all over."

They'd told Beemer he could keep the shoes, too.

Metro Police Headquarters, Indiana Avenue, N.W.

As a show of respect to Rockelle Bullard, Welborn Yates went to police headquarters. He had been there before, but not recently and to be fair it was his turn to make the trek. Besides that, Rockelle had followed through and sent him a copy of the case files on the lobbyist murders. He'd finished reading them less than an hour earlier.

The cop working security at the entrance to the building looked old enough to be Welborn's father. He didn't seem to be particularly happy with what was probably his final assignment as a sworn police officer.

"State your business," he told Welborn.

Welborn produced his ID. "Captain Welborn Yates, United States Air Force, Office of Special Investigations, detailed to the White House. I'm here to see Lieutenant Rockelle Bullard. She's expecting me."

More often than not these days, Welborn, at Galia Mindel's direction, wore a business suit to work at the White House. Before going to police headquarters, though, he'd stopped at home to put on his military uniform. Didn't seem to impress the old cop one bit.

He muttered under his breath, "White House."

As if he didn't believe that for a minute.

"Something wrong?" Welborn asked.

"Bad feet, hemorrhoids and my teeth hurt. How 'bout you?"

Before Welborn could respond, the cop picked up a phone and called Rockelle.

They exchanged a few more words and Welborn was given a visitor's badge.

"Thanks," he said.

"Homicide's part of major cases," the cop responded. "Follow the signs."

Welborn knew that but said thanks again.

Rockelle Bullard took note of Welborn's uniform.

"Spiffy," she said, "anybody salute you?"

"Not a soul," Welborn told her.

Rockelle's office was a bit smaller than Welborn's, not nearly as well furnished and the paint on the walls was a generation older.

But it did come with a mini-fridge. To Welborn's great surprise, Rockelle took a bottle of White House ice tea out of it and handed it to him.

He accepted with a smile and sat down.

"How'd you get this?" he asked.

"On my way out of the residence, I asked this guy named Blessing if I might have one for the drive back here. He brought me two. I was going to drink that one in your hand, but seeing as you were nice enough to visit ..."

Welborn grinned and twisted the top off.

He raised the bottle in salute. "To your health, Lieutenant Bullard."

He took a large drink.

"That stuff is habit forming," Rockelle said, looking at him enviously.

"How they keep us at our desks," Welborn told her. "I'll see if I can get you some."

That earned him a smile.

"So what do you think, now that you read the files?" Rockelle said, taking the seat behind her desk. "You think maybe Putnam Shady has some murder in him, after all?"

Welborn shook his head. "No, I don't."

He didn't say so, because it wouldn't sound professional, but he was putting his faith in Margaret Sweeney. He didn't believe there was a killer alive who could deceive her at close range — and the scuttlebutt was that she and Putnam were getting very close.

Rockelle asked, "You start asking around yet, see if maybe other people have different opinions?"

"Not yet."

Rockelle nodded. "Could be touchy, if you did, him being a friend of the woman who works with the man who's married to the president."

Welborn smiled. "Almost sounds like the start of a nursery rhyme, doesn't it? But, no, that's not why. I'm not concerned about my job. The president likes me, and my fiancée's family has money."

"Must be nice," Rockelle said.

"Has its advantages. I did have questions about a couple of things. Your ballistics reports show each victim was shot with a different gun. Seems kind of strange, don't you think?"

Rockelle said, "I do think its strange, just don't know what to make of it yet."

"Could be a white guy thing," Welborn told her.

"What?" She thought he was messing with her.

"Well, there could be some Asian-Americans involved, maybe even some African-Americans. What I'm getting at is a certain stratum of affluent males, mostly white, likes to affect tough-guy personas to offset the fact that they make a lot of money without doing any heavy lifting."

"So they buy guns?" Rockelle asked.

"More of them than you might think," Welborn told her. "They even practice at firing ranges and become decent marksmen. So they can feel good about themselves. Consider the wife, the kids and the home to be protected. That's the number one reason they give for buying a weapon, protecting their homes."

"You read all this somewhere?" Rockelle asked.

"As a matter of fact," Welborn said.

He didn't add that he tried to make good use of all his down time at the White House and read extensively on matters that might be helpful to him in his job.

"Interesting thing is," he said, "a lot of these defenders of hearth and home wind up losing their weapons to burglars when they and the little lady are out of the house. Off on vacation or just out to see a movie."

"You getting around to something here?" Rockelle asked.

"I am. What we have is a series of shootings done with different weapons, all of them high end. The guns could have been bought or they could have been stolen. If they were purchased legally, we're probably out of luck. But assuming they weren't, it might be interesting to check reports of stolen weapons in the metro area over, say, the past year and see if there's any connection between the victims of theft and the victims of shooting."

Welborn drained the remainder of his bottle.

Rockelle considered the notion.

"Rich boy guns used to kill rich boy lobbyists?" Rockelle nodded. She liked the symmetry. "Yeah, there could be something to that." The obvious thought crossed her mind. "So why're you giving this to me instead of working it yourself?"

"Just being cooperative," Welborn said.

"Or," Rockelle told him, "you've got another angle you like better."

"An angle I like as much."

"What is it?" Rockelle asked.

"Your reports say you could find no manufacturer information on the pig pins."

"Them again?"

"Yeah," Welborn said, "I want to see if I can find out who made them."

"Who made them, who sold them, who bought them?"

"Exactly."

Rockelle said, "Fine. I'll take the guns, you take the pigs."

To make sure he was on good terms with the Metro homicide lieutenant, Welborn asked Rockelle if she'd like to come to his wedding that Saturday at the vice president's house.

"Am I going to be the only black person there?" Rockelle asked.

Welborn told her, "You're welcome to bring a date."

GWU Hospital

McGill and Carolyn held hands and looked through a pane of glass into the room where Kenny lay sleeping. McGill thought his son looked like a poorly rendered wax likeness of himself. Only the monitors attached to him and the slight rise and fall of his chest gave any sign that he was alive. Carolyn, who had been at the hospital the whole day, had been crying soundlessly ever since McGill arrived.

Her fingernails pressed ever deeper into the palm of his hand. The pain was almost an accusation that all this was his fault. He suffered stoically because maybe it was. Who knew?

Neither of them could enter the room because chemo as strong as what Kenny had been given knocked the hell out of the body's immune system. An infection that might ordinarily be fought off or treated was now as real a killer as the disease. For the same reason, neither Abbie nor Caitie had been allowed to enter the room.

Each girl had shown up at the hospital on her own initiative. Abbie had taken public transportation. Caitie had badgered the Secret Service into chauffeuring her. Now, the two sisters slept in each other's arms, more or less sitting upright on a sofa in a lounge at the end of the corridor.

McGill asked his ex-wife in a quiet voice, "Did Kenny tell you he's going to beat his disease?"

Carolyn nodded. "Four times. The last time he was so weak I almost didn't hear him."

McGill let go of Carolyn's hand and put his arm around her shoulder.

He said, "Let's take him at his word then."

Carolyn turned her face into McGill's chest, trying to muffle a despair that was now audible. He used his free hand to stroke the back of her head. It made no sense to him that their son had been given to them only to be taken so soon.

But he knew other parents had certainly shared the same thought.

Only to find out the reason for their grief would never be explained.

Not in this life.

There was nothing to be gained by continuing to stand vigil. McGill led Carolyn to the lounge where their daughters slept. The two of them sat on a loveseat, looking at their girls, both of their daughters breathing easily, their complexions aglow with good health, each of them a picture of a promising future.

How could anyone explain why one person's life could be so

consummately fortunate … while another's life seemed so casually disposable?

McGill was attempting to plumb those insoluble mysteries when Carolyn put a hand on his wrist and made an agonized confession.

"I had a terrible thought today." McGill looked at Carolyn but left it to her to say what the thought was. "When I saw that Patti came to be tested … I thought let it be anyone but her who can save my son. Now, what … what if she might have been the only one who could have saved Kenny? The last time I asked, they still didn't have a match."

McGill sighed. "I don't think any doctor would back you up on that, a moment of being less than charitable changing a medical outcome."

"Being jealous," Carolyn said.

"Okay," McGill allowed.

He didn't understand Carolyn's feelings. She and Lars had always seemed happy together to him. But if she —

"Now, Clare Tracy's coming, too."

McGill looked Carolyn in the eye. "How do you know that?"

"I saw her name on the to-be-tested list. Does Patti know?"

"She knows Clare called me. I'm going to tell her about Clare coming to town."

Carolyn nodded, and looked away. McGill, gently turned her chin back.

"What does it matter? I'd be happy if Galia Mindel or Celsus Crogher has what it takes to donate to Kenny."

"They don't. They've been eliminated."

That came as news to McGill, and showed him just how closely Carolyn was monitoring Kenny's situation.

"My point's still the same," McGill said, "anyone who can save Kenny is fine by me."

"But …" Carolyn looked over to Abbie and Caitie. Saw they were still asleep. "But Patti is your wife and the president of the United States. Clare was your first love and she runs Mother's

Milk. She's a mover and shaker, too. Then there's me, poor little miss in-between, a housewife, can't even save her own son. So dumb she divorces a guy other far more accomplished women would fight for. How's it going to make me feel if Patti or Clare can save Kenny when I can't?"

McGill was nearly at a loss as to how he might respond. Nearly.

"Wonderful," he said. "Thankful. Drop to your knees grateful. That's how you'll feel, and I won't even say I told you so." He nodded in their daughters' direction. "Look at Abbie and Caitie and tell me how you can feel second to anyone I've ever known."

McGill had kept his voice down but the force of his words made Carolyn draw back.

"I'm such a fool," she said.

"You're scared silly. You're exhausted. If you're a fool, too, that only complicates matters." He finished the riff with as much of a smile as he could muster.

Carolyn moved close and hugged him.

A moment later, Deke appeared. He had his cousin, Francis Nguyen, with him. The former Catholic priest, current pastor of an independent Christian parish in Massachusetts, extended his hands to McGill, inquiring if he wanted help.

McGill did and he left Carolyn in Father Nguyen's keeping. After kissing his sleeping girls, he took another look at Kenny and whispered a brief prayer.

Then he left for the White House to talk to the present Mrs. James J. McGill.

McGill's Hideaway

In Nixonian fashion, the First Couple had a blaze going in the fireplace and the AC cranked up high. They sat shoulder to shoulder on the leather sofa in the room and stared at the flames, listened to the crackle of wood combusting. Short of an imminent nuclear attack, they were not to be disturbed.

McGill, normally not one to blab a confidence, told Patti

about Carolyn's admission of feeling inadequate. Jealous, in her own word. He didn't feel good about doing it, but he had to relieve himself of the emotional burden.

Having done so, he laughed humorlessly and shook his head.

"What?" Patti asked.

"Here I am unloading my baggage on you, and you just might have one or two worries of your own, things you brought home from the office. What a great guy I am."

Patti turned McGill's face away from the flames and toward her.

She kissed him with a warmth the fire couldn't match.

"The day I can't be here for you is the day I resign," Patti said. "Carolyn can't be blamed for anything she's feeling right now. Neither can you."

McGill took her hand. "Kenny just looks so ... so much closer to leaving us than to staying. It's breaking my heart."

"Mine, too." She kissed him again. "Will you excuse me for a minute?"

"Sure."

Alone now, McGill went back to staring at the fire. The logs were all merrily alight, but the stack maintained its structural integrity. As the burn continued, though, there would be the inevitable collapse. The pile that had been neat and tidy when set alight would become a random smoking jumble.

Thinking about that, a sense of grim determination steeled McGill. Whatever happened to Kenny, he wasn't going to let the rest of his family fall into a charred heap. Someone would have to hold them all together, and that was going to be him. Abbie and Caitie would especially need him to be there for them. Carolyn, he'd help as much as he could, but Lars would have to shoulder most of that burden.

Knowing Lars was a solid guy gave him a measure of comfort. He'd step up.

By the time Patti returned a few minutes later, McGill was no less sad, but the awful feeling of dread that had filled his heart had receded. He was ready to discuss other matters.

Patti handed him one of the two glasses she'd brought with her. Other than the occasional beer, McGill wasn't much of a drinker, but now was not the time to decline the offer. He took a sip, felt warmed inside and tasted cherries. He loved cherries.

Patti saw he was pleased and said, "Kir. We'll keep a bottle handy."

McGill kissed his wife, and opened a new topic of discussion.

He told her about his time with Clare Tracy, how it ended and that Hugh Collier had interviewed Clare that morning. He told Patti how he'd spoken to Clare for the first time in almost thirty years earlier that day, and that Clare had volunteered to be tested as a potential donor.

"She's terrific," Patti said.

"Clare told me the two of you know each other. I had no idea."

Patti smiled. "Your disinterest in politics is ironic, considering the women in your life."

McGill said, "I came by it honestly. In Chicago, if a cop got ahead by virtue of City Hall connections, his people had nothing but contempt for him, except for the suckups. I never wanted to be one of those guys. I just worked hard and kept my nose clean."

"Moved to the suburbs when you had your twenty years in," Patti said.

McGill had been the chief of police in Winnetka, where he'd met his future wife.

"Best career move I ever made." He took another sip of the kir, liked it. "Collier is trying to find dirt on me."

"For his uncle, Sir Edbert Bickford, lord and master of World-Wide News, no friend of mine or this administration. He smears you, he smears me."

McGill said, "I've done my best to stay out of politics the past two years, but with Putnam Shady planning to take over the government and Bickford looking to hurt both of us, I think that's got to end."

"You're right, but we'll have to be careful how you go about it."

"That might be easier said than done."

"Why?" Patti asked.

McGill told her about Harlo Geiger wanting to hire him.

Patti gulped her drink, laughed and said, "This damn town."

McGill finished his kir and responded, "I don't think it'd be fair to have Putnam work the speaker if I don't see what Harlo can tell me."

"Aren't you supposed to keep client information confidential?"

"That's always been the weakest part of my game," McGill told her.

"Well, don't worry, if you get in trouble, I'll grant you a pardon."

McGill smiled, thinking maybe he'd ask for more kir.

Patti said, "I'm serious, Jim. We'll all do what we have to do in this situation. If you or anyone else working for me gets in trouble, you've got a get-out-of-jail-free card."

The logs in the fireplace collapsed with a thump.

And the phone rang, startling McGill.

"I thought —"

Patti told him, "I asked for this call when I went to get the drinks." She picked up the phone on the end table near her and said, "Yes?"

Whoever was on the other end of the call had enough to say that McGill saw his wife's face go through a series of reactions: eyes going wide, lips broadening in a smile, tears sheening both eyes.

"What is it?" McGill asked.

Patti concluded the call, saying, "Yes, thank you, that's wonderful news. Goodbye."

"What?" McGill repeated.

Patti told him, "I had Nick check to see what that latest results on the blood tests for potential donors were. Jim ... they've got *two* matches."

The glass fell out of McGill's hand.

He felt drained, and then bursting with energy. Daring to hope.

"Who, who are they?"

"The first is Clare."

"But she's not even here yet," McGill said.

"No, she's not. There was some sort of air traffic control problem tying up New York City. So she went to a hospital there and got the test. They transmitted the results to GWU. A six-point match."

"That's perfect, right?" McGill asked.

"Yes, Clare's on the Acela, coming to Washington right now."

McGill's eyes filled. "Who else?" he asked. "Who's the other donor?"

Patti told him in a word, "Me."

K Street, N.W.

Beemer had absolutely fucking *had it.* Curl his toes so they didn't stretch out his fancy shoes? He doubted if any of his ten toes would ever straighten out again. He wouldn't be at all surprised if half of them didn't have to be cut off. That fancy Mercedes, it was going to be just part of his settlement after he got done suing the city for maiming him.

That little stick-figure fuck of a partner of his, Meeker, he could do the next undercover. Didn't have to pad him out or anything. Somebody came along wanting to shoot, let the bastard turn sideways. He'd disappear from view and nobody in the world could —

"Pedestrian approaching."

The warning sounded in his earbud. They'd been giving him heads-ups for the past two hours. His attention had been drifting. He couldn't think of anything except how much his feet were hurting, felt like the sidewalk was the bed of a damn blast furnace.

Meeker had told him he was walking funny; he should try to get back into a normal stride. Beemer had said if he heard any more shit about anything he was going to take his gun out of his fancy briefcase and start shooting at any window that had a light on behind it.

No further criticism was forthcoming.

Beemer lifted his gaze from the next square of pavement ahead of him and saw someone coming his way. Looked like he was moving a bit stiffly himself. He was big, too, right about Beemer's height, but he was a white man, old enough to have white hair.

He was wearing a right nice suit of his own.

The cop in Beemer asked why a guy like that would be out for a stroll so late.

'Specially when he really was having trouble walking.

Beemer got a glance at what looked like a gold watch on the man's left wrist. Just the sort of thing your enterprising D.C. smash-and-grab man would love to take off an infirm old coot, even a big one. Then the kind of atavistic suspicion that had saved many a cop from an early grave kicked in and pierced the pain of Beemer's sore feet. He thought: What if this old SOB is running a game here? Pretending to be an easy mark. Seeing Beemer, who might resemble a lobbyist, if the guy's eyes weren't too good, and lulling him into a false sense of security.

Then, *bang*, another body's down, and Beemer's mama is crying.

When the old guy got within ten feet, Beemer thought fuck it, broke cover and held a hand out like he was a traffic cop.

"Hold it right there, grandpa," he said.

It took the old man a couple of halting steps to comply and he tottered for a moment like he might pitch forward on his face. Beemer didn't rush to catch him. Be a real foolish thing to stop somebody from falling and get gutshot for your trouble.

Meeker's voice sounded in Beemer's ear.

"The hell you doin', man?"

"Shut the fuck up," Beemer said.

The old guy thought Beemer was talking to him.

"I'm sorry. I didn't say anything."

For a moment Beemer saw fear in the eyes under the white hair.

"Not you, man."

"Then who?"

Getting angry again, Beemer said, "Never mind about that."

Despite facing a large, scowling black man, the fear passed from the white man's face.

"You're a cop," he said.

"Sonofabitch," Beemer said.

And that bastard Meeker laughed in his ear.

Beemer pulled the bud out of his ear. Squeezed the knot of his tie until he felt the microphone crumple. Made it clear to everyone he wasn't undercover material.

"How'd you know?" Beemer asked.

"My father was a chief of police. I've seen all sorts of cops."

That'd explain it, all right, Beemer thought.

"Let me see some ID, mister."

"Have I done something wrong … detective, is it?"

Guy really had him figured out. "As sore as my feet are, I don't need a reason."

"I see. You won't mind if I reach for my wallet then?"

"Just do it slow."

"That's the only way I do anything these days." He took his wallet from a pocket inside his suit coat, spread the coat wide so Beemer could see he wasn't carrying. The sore-footed cop appreciated that.

When Beemer saw who he had stopped he winced. He'd be lucky if the man didn't have his ass on a platter. Guys like him didn't get rousted. They didn't even get arrested unless they were driving drunk or playing footsie with a stripper in the Tidal Basin.

Handing the man's wallet back, Beemer said, "I'm sorry, sir."

"Perfectly all right. As I said, I know something of a cop's lot in life."

Beemer was happy about that. Probably be the only thing that would save his job.

Trying to take reparations a step further, he asked, "Can I give a ride somewhere?"

The old guy smiled. "I never much cared for cop cars."

"Me neither," Beemer said. "But tonight I got me a real sweet Mercedes. One a them AMG beauties."

"In that case, I'd be delighted."

Beemer smiled, thinking of Meeker and the others wondering

what the fuck he was doing, scratching their heads and calling him names.

"Where can I take you?" Beemer asked.

"George Washington University Hospital."

"You sick, sir?" Beemer cringed at the idea he'd been hassling a sick man.

"Almost unto death, Detective."

"Oh, Lord, I'm sorry about that. We'll get there quick."

"No need to hurry. I've been told I have at least another week. But I would like to get something for the pain."

"We'll make good time, just the same."

"Thank you, Detective."

Beemer was as good as his word, but the distinguished occupant of the cover car still had time to think it had been wise to leave his gun at home. He'd felt sure the police would be watching K Street by now, and he'd wanted to test that assumption.

It wouldn't be much longer before the press figured out the story … and then things would become much more difficult.

As they pulled up in front of the hospital, the old man wondered if his new young friend might be awake. It was late for a child to be up, but then cancer patients hardly kept regular hours.

CHAPTER 4

Thursday, August 18th, GWU Hospital

Kenny McGill's eyelids felt like they weighed a ton each, and were getting heavier by the second. The last time he'd managed to force them open, he saw his mother standing on the other side of the window. He'd had two thoughts at that moment. How the heck did his mother get so old so fast? He recognized her, but she didn't look at all like the picture of her he had in his mind. He'd always thought his mom looked like, maybe, the oldest girl in a college sorority. When she fixed herself up, though, when she and Lars would go someplace fancy, she looked like the prettiest girl, the sweetheart of ... whatever the name was in that corny old song.

The other thing Kenny thought, looking at his suddenly old mother, peering at him through a pane of glass, was he never expected to die in a fishbowl. People could stroll by and see how he was doing. See if he'd given up yet.

Maybe a doctor would ask, "Is he still swimming, nurse?"

"Afraid not, doctor. Looks like he's sinking to the bottom."

Kenny knew he was going down, too. Thing was, he didn't think it was such a bad idea. He felt so awful, so weak, so tired, it wouldn't be a bad idea to put an end to it all. The last he had heard, they hadn't found a donor for him yet. All he had to look forward to was another round of chemo treatment, and he was certain that would kill him. He didn't have anywhere near the strength he'd had going into the first infusion.

So why not just give in? Spare himself any more suffering.

That was what he'd thought the last time he … couldn't really say he fell asleep.

The last time he lost consciousness.

He hadn't really expected to ever open his eyes again. Hadn't seen any bright light waiting for him. Or Jesus reaching out to him. The absence of either of those hopeful signs had scared him. What if there was nothing waiting for him?

Then he felt a presence nearby. Not the Savior. Someone in his room.

Another person had joined him in his fishbowl. It was only curiosity that forced him to push his eyelids apart. At first, he saw only a blurred outline. Someone tall and green who didn't even have a face. Damn! Was that what the devil looked like? Could he really have done anything so bad he'd deserve to go to —

His anxiety activated his lachrymal glands.

Tears washed the film away from his eyes.

Now, to his great relief, he could see a doctor standing before him in full surgical garb, including a mask, a cap and gloves. But this person wasn't Dr. Jones; she was much smaller. So was Nick. This was the biggest —

Kenny noticed strands of white hair peeking out from the cap.

"Zack?" he rasped.

The figure in green bobbed his head. Then he gently laid a gloved hand on Kenny's leg. Kenny could feel the warmth right through the glove, the blanket covering him, and the pajama bottom he was wearing. In that one spot, he suddenly felt almost good again. He wanted Zack to put his other hand on him. Move them up and down every inch of him.

Zack said, "You could go now, if you want. But you don't have to. You've still got the strength to come through this. Think about all the things you want to do."

All Kenny could think about was how wonderful his leg was starting to feel.

Not just where Zack first touched it, but up and down.

And he thought of what Celsus Crogher had told him.

"It's all right to sacrifice your life. It can even be noble. But you *never* do it unless you have absolutely no other choice," the SAC had said.

Kenny now understood what Crogher had meant: He still had other choices.

A moment ago, he had thought all his other choices had vanished.

Then Zack had shown up, laid a hand on him and ...

His eyes closed again, thinking he hadn't seen Liesl Eberhardt yet.

He wasn't going to let go before he did that.

Olive Street, NW

Leo Levy couldn't have afforded the townhouse where he lived on his government salary, but he'd won five races before he'd quit the NASCAR circuit to keep his mother from having a heart attack. He'd always been real careful with his money, not cheap but not foolish. He had been told early by his daddy, an accountant, that if a man were smart he would build himself a stack of money that could start earning its own salary: that was, interest, dividends, capital appreciation and so forth.

That way, if the man ever felt like going fishing for the rest of his life, his money could keep right on working and providing him with income. His daddy told him that was how a smart man planned his life. There were, of course, things that couldn't be planned for, like Toby Gilman crashing in the last lap of a race down in South Carolina, his car flying to pieces, a tire clearing the safety fence and killing daddy.

Leo had finished second that day, hadn't even seen the accident.

He didn't know his father had died until a Baptist minister came to break the bad news. There weren't any rabbis who followed NASCAR as far as Leo knew, but the minister was compassionate enough to offer to drive him to the nearest temple if he felt the need to pray.

Sarah Levy hadn't feared for her son's safety before that awful day; she'd cheered him on, saying she was his biggest fan, even though Leo's father was the only one who came to his races. Mother said all the fumes from the fuel made her weak. Following Jacob's death, the thought of Leo ever racing again left her trembling. After learning that his mother had started to suffer heart palpitations, Leo gave up racing.

He refused to give up driving, though, or getting paid for being behind the wheel.

Looking over possible opportunities — and the state of the world — he decided that the most interesting, best paying work he was likely to find would involve driving for rich guys who might get themselves kidnapped, shot at or otherwise seriously inconvenienced.

Mother wouldn't have to know those details.

Leo signed up for four weeks of escape and evasion driver's ed at a school down in Florida. By the end of the course, he was offered the job of being the school's senior instructor. He took it with the stipulation that he could leave on two-weeks notice if he found a job that really tickled him.

With his position at the school and his résumé with NASCAR, Leo interviewed at least once a week for the next six months. In all that time, he didn't find a single man or woman he wanted to work for. It seemed to him that, maybe, every individual in the world with a net worth worthy of drawing hostile attention deserved every bit of it and more.

A few of them, if they were being chased, Leo would have pulled over, lowered the windows and unlocked the doors. Told the bad guys, "Have at him, boys."

It was his mother, knowing she had taken her son from the life he'd loved, who came up with a solution for him. A lady friend of hers had a brother-in-law who worked for the government in a law enforcement capacity he really couldn't talk about.

Leo liked the first part of what Mother said. Maybe he could be a getaway driver for spies on the run. He should have known better.

His mother asked him, "Have you heard about the White House Transportation Agency?"

Just what she would like: a nice safe job with a big name attached.

Chauffeuring politicians and other crooks to and from meetings.

"Mother," Leo began. He'd rather drive South Florida scumballs.

The pay and the weather were better.

"Leo," his mother rebutted.

"I didn't even vote for that ..." He was going to say dick, but changed it. "That guy in the White House."

"His term is almost over and someone new will be needing good drivers. Maybe that nice lady from Illinois."

Mother tossed a magazine his way. There on the cover was Patti Grant, former model and movie star and leading candidate for the Republican nomination. Woman had a killer smile, and she was engaged to the cop who solved the murder of her first husband. That was pretty cool, too. Working for people like that might be interesting.

Leo said, "Okay, Mother, I'll look into it."

He called the number his mother's friend's brother-in-law had provided.

Wound up driving for James J. McGill who'd gone into the private eye biz.

That was cool. Thank you, Mother.

The townhouse he'd bought in D.C. was a twelve-minute drive to the White House in all but the worst traffic conditions. If things got really blocked up, Leo could always turn on the Chevy's flashing lights and sound effects. He was the driver of a certified emergency vehicle with more bells and whistles than any ride James Bond had ever —

It was the Chevy's fall-back alarm, connected by Blue Tooth to Leo's clock radio, that woke him from a sound sleep. He sat upright with a jolt, recognizing the note of that alarm. It meant some sonofabitch had not only broken into his garage and bypassed its alarm — and that took some real electronic smarts — but also had gotten past the Chevy's primary security system.

If the sonofabitch kept going as fast as he'd started out, he was going to get away with a million-dollar car. Leo hit the panic button on the key fob that lay on his nightstand. This one not only created a horrible racket, it locked down both the garage and the car. Or was supposed to. Another feature allowed Leo to announce his ire to anyone caught in his garage.

"I'm coming for you, motherfucker. You best start praying."

Leo raced from his bedroom in his boxer shorts with his key fob and his Browning semi-auto in hand.

He burst through the door to the garage, heedless of whether someone might be waiting for him with a gun. Any child in the world would have been thrilled to see Daddy rushing to the rescue with blood in his eye the way Leo made his entrance. The Chevy, for all its capabilities, wasn't able to sigh in relief.

But it stood right where Leo had left it, disturbed only by a few smudges in its wax job.

The overhead door, however, was raised, not lowered and locked as he always left it. Leo killed the security system and though his ears were still filled with the ringing of the alarm and the thumping of his heart he strained to hear —

A car engine turned over. He heard that clearly.

Being careful now, he poked his head out into the alley and pulled it back quick.

Nobody had shot at him, and his mind had taken a snapshot of a car racing off.

Late model Ford. Virginia plate. Start of the alpha numeric sequence: 3ATX.

Had to be stolen. Steal one car to steal another.

Leo took a deep breath and let it out slowly.

Time to call SAC Crogher, let him know what had happened.

Hope his boys could process the Chevy before the boss needed him.

WorldWide News, Washington Bureau

Ellie Booker had her news readers go over hard copies of their scripts before they would see them on their Teleprompters. She wanted their deliveries to be letter perfect with points of emphasis stressed exactly as she had indicated them. Her Ken and Barbie, as she always thought of anchors who'd been hired for looks instead of brains, would be leading off the national broadcast for the network's *Sun-up America* news program.

They would be headlining a huge story that morning.

The serial killing of lobbyists on K Street.

Ellie had been the first to sniff out the killings on K Street because she had apprenticed in the if-it-bleeds-it-leads school of journalism and she worked harder than a migrant laborer. Every day she reviewed every death by violence for which the Metro cops opened a case file.

That chore was considered by most news organizations as something to be pawned off on a junior staffer. But Ellie knew from the start there was no story as compelling as one person taking the life of another. Even if the victims were poor, unknown to the public and not at all sympathetic, there could be an angle to grab headlines.

With headlines came ratings.

With ratings came status, i.e. power and money.

With status came respectability.

It was a simple progression; didn't take a genius to figure it out.

Ellie first thought she was on to something when she spotted the death of Erik Torkelson. The man had been an attorney and a lobbyist. Had been shot on K Street. Might have been the victim of a random armed robbery except nothing in the police report had said anything about personal possessions being taken. The man had just turned forty, left a wife and two children.

Another *senseless tragedy*, as reported and forgotten by local news outlets.

The number of homicides in the nation's capital was declining, but the previous year there were still one hundred and thirty-one of them. But how many of those victims, Ellie asked herself, had been K Street professionals?

Doing some digging, she'd found out Torkelson had been president of the student body at Vanderbilt and had graduated from Yale Law School. That didn't make him Superman; bullets wouldn't bounce off of him. But a guy like that ... the odds were better his racing yacht would be sunk by a whale than he'd get gunned down on K Street.

In the next ten weeks, two more lobbyists, Robert Waller and Mark Benjamin, were also murdered by gunfire. The intervals between the lobbyists' deaths, by Ellie's count, were filled by seven and nine other homicides. Waller and Benjamin had profiles similar to Torkelson's in terms of age, family and education.

Something big was going on, Ellie knew. She was sure other members of her craft with three-digit IQs must have figured that out, too. But the media play on the story had been a simple recitation of the unfortunate facts. Nobody had publicly connected the killings, though she was sure several people must be straining to do so.

It was only a question of who found the angle first.

Grabbed the headline.

Then last night Bruno Bettman came through for Ellie big time. Bruno worked front-door security at Metro Police headquarters. During his shift, everybody entering the building had to walk past him. Visitors had to be signed in; cops had to show their IDs, even if they were flashed perfunctorily. Most cops didn't think anything of continuing their conversations like Bruno wasn't even there. He heard all sorts of stuff.

Like yesterday when two homicide dicks named Meeker and Beemer walked by talking about how the bodies of all the dead lobbyists had been found with little pins stuck on them that looked like Porky Pig. And later when an Air Force investigator, name of Captain Welborn Yates, said he worked at the White House, came by and wanted to see homicide Lieutenant Rockelle Bullard, Meeker and Beemer's boss.

So maybe Yates and Bullard had talked about Porky, too.

Ellie almost got wet she was so excited by the news Bruno had provided.

She paid him two hundred bucks a week — itemized as a miscellaneous expense to accounting — to call her from a prepaid cell phone and feed her tidbits. She didn't let on to Bruno that he'd done anything out of the ordinary, didn't want him getting greedy.

Now that she had the Porky Pig pins linking three dead lobbyists she had something to go on the air with, and demand to know if the latest lobbyist to be killed, Brad Attles, the speaker's personal divorce lawyer, had also been pinned.

Ellie had to get her story out first thing that morning, because Attles' death had to be putting terrible pressure on her competitors to break the story soon. But they didn't have the Porky Pig angle to play. Didn't know to ask what the White House's interest might be.

Unless that fucker Bruno was on someone else's payroll, too.

No sooner had that disturbing thought occurred than her segment's director, sitting next to Ellie in the control room, told her something far more upsetting.

"The president is going on the air in five minutes. We're bumped."

"No, goddamnit!" Let the other networks get out of the way of her scoop, sure. That'd make her look even better. But —

The director had his phone in hand, was listening to someone else besides her.

He said, "New York says, yes, we're going with the president. She could have news on terrorism or we might have gone to war somewhere."

"Bullshit. We'd have had advance word on that kind of stuff."

The director started to reply, but Ellie stepped out of the control room. She was calling Hugh Collier. If he didn't support her, she'd call Sir Edbert Bickford. Get his nibs, himself, to back her play.

That or walk out and find a new place to work.

Where the men were as ballsy as she was.

Goddamn Patti Grant. What was she going to announce in the dog days of August?

That it was National Boating Safety Week?

The Oval Office

The president sat behind her desk in a dark blue Chanel business suit. A subtle string of pearls and her wedding band were her only accessories. Her hair and makeup were perfect. The lighting was flattering. Her notes lay on the desk in front of her.

She wouldn't need them though. She'd always been able to memorize her lines.

But the stack of paper was important as a prop.

Shuffling it gave her reason to pause in her delivery.

Let people think about what she'd just said.

Avoid delivering her speech with an unblinking stare.

Galia stood to the president's left, just outside of the camera's frame. She, not Patti Grant, was the one who seemed on edge. The chief of staff kept shifting her weight from one foot to the other.

Without looking at her, the president asked, "Low impact aerobics, Galia?"

The chief of staff stopped moving, let her shoulders relax. There was no turning back now. She was as much to blame for the present moment as anyone else. She had relayed Bob Merriman's idea that the only way for the president to be reelected was to run as a Democrat. Instead of being insulted, the president had laughed.

She had said, "Give Bob credit for intestinal fortitude. It takes more than a little guts to suggest something like that."

"It certainly does, Madam President," Galia said. "But —"

"But he's right? He very well may be. But Bob is forgetting one of the most basic rules of both Washington and Hollywood: You have much more leverage when people come to you than when you go to them."

And that was what the president's announcement was all about: leverage.

"Good luck, Madam President," Galia said, stepping back.

"Thank you, Galia."

A moment later, Patricia Darden Grant was speaking to the nation.

"Good morning. I asked for a few minutes of your time today to explain to you why I am leaving the Republican Party."

United States Capitol, the Speaker's Office

"Sonofabitch, did you just hear that?" Derek Geiger asked.

The television was on in the speaker's suite as the president made her unprecedented announcement. Richard Nixon had left office, resigning the presidency before he could be impeached, but no president had ever left his *party* while still in the White House.

Went to show, Patti Grant wasn't just another one of the boys.

"I did," Putnam Shady said with a grin.

"You think it's funny?" Geiger was annoyed by Putnam's smile.

"I think you'd better record what she has to say."

The speaker put his moment of pique aside and punched a button on his remote. The DVR's red light appeared as it started to record whatever the president might say next. They hadn't missed a thing because Patti Grant had paused after dropping her bomb. A pro, she didn't want people's exclamations to obscure her follow-through.

Geiger turned the TV off. He'd watch the recording later.

Anticipating further distractions, he told his secretary to hold all calls.

Turning back to Putnam, he said, "I assume you're one of us."

Putnam's job, as agreed to with Sweetie, was to worm his way into Geiger's confidence and then betray him completely. The more Putnam thought about that, the less it bothered him. Geiger's Super-K plan was the philosophical opposite of Putnam's Share America idea. One concentrated power in the hands of fewer fat cats than ever; the other dispersed power widely, democracy for anyone with a hundred bucks.

Despite his pledge, Putnam couldn't help being himself.

Channeling Bill Clinton, he said, "Define us."

"Us, goddamnit. The Republican Party. People of means. The job creators. Everyone who makes our country great."

"I'm all for greatness," Putnam said, "but, frankly, I don't vote."

"What? Not for anyone?" the speaker asked.

As someone who for years had seen the making of political sausage, Putnam had long ago become a vegetarian. Metaphorically speaking. He still liked a good steak and, as he'd told Sweetie, he'd voted for Patti Grant.

Other than that, he'd been truthful about not casting a ballot.

"How do you expect me to take that?" Geiger asked hotly.

Putnam stayed cool. "Any way you please. I thought you asked me here because you need a new divorce lawyer."

Patti Grant wasn't the only one aware of the Hatch Act's strictures against conducting political activity on government property. Moreover, Putnam thought Geiger might be dumb enough not to have learned a thing from history about having a recording system — other than a DVR — running as he talked to visitors to his office.

Putnam didn't intend to ever have to explain himself to a special prosecutor.

Geiger had the wits to understand his guest's allusion.

Playing along, wondering now if a third party might have bugged his office, he asked, "You think you're up to the job?"

"I haven't read family law since college, but I'm a quick study."

True beyond dispute, Putnam thought. His little tap dance would steer him clear of any prosecutor if his words were ever repeated, but they should reassure Geiger he could do the job. To solidify his position in both halves of the equation, he added,

"Mrs. Geiger has hired Gerald Mishkin, the top divorce lawyer in town."

That sat Mister Speaker back in his seat.

"How do you know that?"

"Jerry and I go back a ways; we talk."

"So you really do think you can help me?"

Phrased with lovely ambiguity, Putnam thought.

Maybe the speaker wasn't a total dope.

"I think we can work something out," Putnam said.

Thing Two

McGill did a double-take when Leo arrived at the White House that morning driving Patti's back-up limo. Deke didn't bat an eye. If anything, he looked amused and maybe a bit pleased.

Secret Service guys could sometimes think they deserved a presidential ride.

Entering the back seat, McGill asked Leo, "Where's the Chevy?"

"Elspeth Kendry and a dozen or so techies have it." Leo told McGill what had happened.

Deke said, "The thief got past your garage alarm and the Chevy's primary security system?"

Leo nodded glumly. "Yeah, the sumbitch. Damn, I wanted to shoot that boy. Musta been that guy I spotted yesterday."

"What?" McGill asked, surprised.

Leo told him about the suspicious tail he saw the day before. "I didn't want to bother you, what with Kenny bein' sick and all. But there was this guy I didn't like the feel of yesterday. He had a kid with him, maybe about ten or twelve."

"Sonofabitch is right," McGill said.

Circumstances were beginning to justify his expanded protection detail.

He didn't like that at all.

"Special Agent Kendry and her crew are goin' over the Chevy with every forensic trick in the book," Leo said. "That bastard left any little piece of himself behind, they'll find it. But it could take a while. Meantime, this is what SAC Crogher said is our new ride."

His mother, Leo thought, would love it, him being at the helm of an ocean liner.

He hated it. McGill did, too, but it was the least of his worries.

"Where to, boss?" Leo asked.

"The D.C. Ritz-Carlton."

Leo entered the name into the limo's GPS system.

McGill was going to pick up Clare Tracy. Dr. Divya Sahir Jones had requested that Clare be retested at GWU just for everyone's peace of mind. Clare, bless her, had consented.

"Twenty-second Street it is," Leo said, and Thing Two began to roll.

As of last night, the question of who would be Kenny's donor, Patti or Clare, had been left undecided, and when the president had told McGill the news she would be breaking to the world that morning, they left the matter to be discussed later.

Celsus hadn't attached a motorcycle escort to Thing Two, for which McGill gave thanks. He took his cell phone out of his pocket and tapped out Carolyn's mobile number. The last thing his ex-wife needed was to hear the blare of motorcycle sirens.

Carolyn answered by saying, "Kenny's still with us, Jim."

McGill felt a mountain lifted off his heart.

The Oval Office

"The simple truth is," the president told the nation, "I won't hang my hat anyplace I'm not wanted. It's become apparent to me I've worn out my welcome in the Republican Party. In working to advance what I see as the best interests of the American people, members of my former party have been my most stubborn opponents.

"Only two days ago, in a meeting with the chairman of the Republican National Committee, Reynard Dix, I was asked whether I intend to run for a second term as president. I have to admit this question took me by I surprise. I haven't accomplished everything I had hoped to by now, but this was due, in no small measure, to the obstruction of Congressional Republicans.

"When I told Mr. Dix that I did intend to run for a second term, he advised me I would face not just one opponent in the primary elections but several. The only way to look at this was that I was being rebuffed by my former party's leadership at a time when I enjoy a substantial margin of approval by my fellow Americans."

Patti paused to let the camera show her emotions.

She was disappointed, but far more angered and determined.

She flicked a glance at Galia.

Her chief of staff had provided bomb number two to throw.

"I'm sorry to say that more than policy differences and political calculations were involved in my former party's disaffection for me. I've learned that a senior member of my former party has described me as an 'accidental president.' He said I never would have been elected if I hadn't benefitted from a sympathy vote resulting from the murder of my first husband, Andrew Hudson Grant."

Patti's anger predominated now and it was easy to see. She'd felt exactly the same way when Galia had told her how Derek Geiger had characterized her.

"This assertion insults not only me but also everyone who voted for me."

The president hadn't named Geiger, but she'd fired a starting pistol to set the media racing to find out who had insulted her. Describing the character assassin as a senior Republican would make it easy to determine the speaker was the culprit. Geiger would be forced to explain himself quickly.

If he denied his culpability, so much the better. Galia would produce her source: Harlo Geiger. The chief of staff had made a call to the speaker's alienated spouse as soon as she'd heard from Bob Merriman of the Geigers' impending divorce. Striking while emotions were still high, Galia had even gotten Harlo's permission to record her assertion.

The president filled a glass with water.

She took a sip and continued.

"There's one more thing I should tell you about my meeting with RNC Chairman Dix. I promised him that I would deliver a substantial political beating to any primary opponent who ran against me. Now, having left my former party, I won't be able to do that. So I feel compelled to make a new promise."

Patti waited a beat as the camera moved in for a close-up of her face.

"In the general election, I will win by a substantial margin over any opponent, and by the grace of God I will be your president for a second term. I've yet to determine whether I will run as an independent candidate, as the leader of a new political party or in some other fashion.

"Thank you for giving me the time to speak with you. I'll be holding a press conference soon to elaborate on what I've said this morning."

The camera's red light went off and Patti was done.

She'd just laid down her challenge to the Democrats.

If they wanted her on their ticket, they'd have to draft her.

The Washington Ritz-Carlton

Clare Tracy was waiting when Thing Two pulled up to the hotel's main entrance. Deke got out of the limo fast, didn't give the doorman a chance to reach for the near side passenger door. A simple shake of his head made the hotel employee back off. It wasn't for the general public to see just how thickly armored a presidential limousine was.

With commendable panache, the doorman still gestured Clare to her ride.

With great discretion, she tipped him for his solicitude.

Deke had to make due with the bob of her head and a smile.

He helped Clare inside, closed the top secret door and took his seat up front.

Thing Two headed for GWU Hospital.

Clare sat beside McGill and beamed at him, happy to see him

again after so many years. "You always did know how to impress a girl."

McGill smiled back. "I wanted to bring the Harley, but it's in the shop."

He'd had a 1972 Fat Bob when they were in college. They rode it all over town, even in the winter if there wasn't snow or ice on the road — sometimes even if there was. But he had sold the Harley, reluctantly, when Abbie was born. It was time to be responsible. Not the time to risk a car-versus-bike traffic accident.

Clare smiled. She knew McGill was joking. She always knew.

"How are you, Jim? I mean, it's terrible the way you've ballooned up, got jowly and lost your hair. But other than that, you're all right?"

"Not bad," he said. "Sorry to learn you've gone blind."

She patted his hand. "Make sure I don't bump into anything."

For a moment they were silent, unselfconscious as they looked at each other, taking measure of how the passing years had exacted their due. From their bright expressions, it was clear they felt they had gotten away lightly.

Except for some recent worry lines on McGill's face.

"How's your son, Jim?" Clare asked.

"He's hanging in, says he's got things he wants to do."

"You have a picture?"

McGill took a studio portrait out of his wallet. Taken a year ago, the three McGill children had all been scrubbed, dressed to impress and on their best behavior.

For just a second, Clare bit her lower lip.

"They're all beautiful," she said. "Kenny's going to make some young lady very happy. I'm glad I'm able to help."

In that moment, McGill thought to tell Clare that Patti was another compatible donor, but he didn't want to do anything to spoil the mood.

He only said, "It's so good to see you again, Clare."

Portland, Oregon

Senator Roger Michaelson, Democrat and the junior senator from Oregon, knew treachery when he saw it. Worse, he felt the cold fear of knowing that Patti Grant, that evil bitch, was going to try to thwart him again. He snapped off the TV.

Michaelson was home for the August Congressional recess. Many of his peers were using the second half of the month to take their longest vacation of the year. Europe was still a favorite destination for many. Younger, more daring representatives of the people or those with ethnic ties might head to Africa or Asia. If some media busybodies wanted to stir up trouble, Michaelson would bet they could find that better than half of the legislative branch of the federal government chose to take their summertime leisure outside the country.

Unpatriotic bastards.

The revelation might be defended as a matter of personal privilege.

Politically, though, preferring a foreign holiday would be indefensible.

Especially to all those Americans who couldn't afford to go overseas.

Michaelson had stayed home. He'd even declined joining a three-day fishing trip to nearby British Columbia. Besides simply unwinding at home, he'd made a point of being seen enjoying the many natural wonders of his home state. He was putting a nice chunk of his government-funded salary back into the local economy.

He had an ulterior motive, of course.

He was about to announce his intention to run for the Democratic nomination to be president. The absolute first step in that plan was to lock up his home state. Oregon had only seven electoral votes, but just ask Al Gore what losing the place you called home could mean in a presidential election.

Roger Michaelson was not about to make that mistake. He'd been attending local picnics for firefighters, little league baseball games, all sorts of ethnic festivals and every sort of aw-shucks, Jack Armstrong All-American Boy events he could stomach.

He'd been warmly received at all of them. The only time things got the least bit awkward was when, against his better judgment, he'd allowed himself to get coaxed into participating in a pick-up game of basketball with a group of soldiers home on leave. Michaelson had been an All-Big Ten player at Northwestern. Asking him to join the game had been a natural thing to do.

But the senator was reluctant to get back on the court. He hadn't played the game since Jim McGill had given him the beating of his life the last time he played. Michaelson had left plenty of bruises on the president's henchman, but there was no question he had gotten the worse of the battle by far.

Still, his main fear when he realized he had no choice but to step onto the court for at least a few minutes was that he'd lose his temper and lash out physically at some unsuspecting soldier. He could imagine a front-page photo of him standing over some young enlisted man he'd coldcocked, and a headline "Senator Michaelson Assaults Soldier Home on Leave."

It would be far better to take a bump or two from an opposing player and shrug it off. Show he could be a good sport. People would lap that up and ask for more.

Turned out, he needn't have worried. He was twenty years older than anyone else in the game, but he was in shape, and none of his skills had deserted him. They weren't as sharp as they'd once been, but they were more than enough to overwhelm younger men who didn't play the game regularly and with a passion.

Michaelson drove past flatfooted defenders to lay the ball up and in. He'd have loved to be able to dunk just once, but he didn't have the lift anymore. He remembered reading that plyometric training could restore some of the spring to aging legs and thought he'd have to give it a try. When he didn't take the ball to the hole, he swished jumpers from twenty feet out. He changed sides for a second game so everyone could have a chance to be on the winning side.

It was the most fun he'd had since … that bastard McGill.

Still, basketball had become fun again.

Made him feel better about himself.

Gave him confidence he could become president, too. But now goddamn Patti Grant was pulling some major bullshit, quitting the goddamn GOP. Saying maybe she'd run as an independent or head a new party. That was so much crap.

It was the last possibility she'd mentioned that made Michaelson's sphincter pucker.

Run in *some other fashion*. What other fashion was there except to run as a Democrat? Have his goddamn party draft her, and the hacks in Washington would do it in a heartbeat. The only reason he'd decided to get into the race was because the potential field of Democratic candidates looked so pathetic; he was sure he could win the nomination. He also had the balls to run an all-out campaign against Patricia Darden Grant.

When she was still a Republican.

He'd longed for a rematch ever since she'd beaten him in what had been the first race for elective office for both of them, the House seat on Chicago's North Shore.

Well, fuck the party's power brokers. He wasn't going to step aside for Patti Goddamn Grant. He'd run against her in the primaries regardless of what anyone else wanted.

He'd get back at his own personal Judas, too.

There was no question in his mind who had put the join-the-Democrats bug in the president's ear: Bob Fucking Merriman. He'd been suspicious that Merriman had been up to no good ever since the prick had quit his Senate staff.

Roger Michaelson's phone rang just then.

Sonofabitch. He saw it was Merriman calling.

He grabbed the phone and said, "You soulless bastard. You did this."

"Of course, I did," Merriman agreed. "Didn't see the president's formal announcement coming, though. Now we have to go to her or risk a three-way race which we're sure to lose. But you know why I did it, don't you?"

"To get her endorsement when you run for my Senate seat."

"Well, yeah. But I meant the underlying reason."

Michaelson forced himself to take a breath. Merriman was a far more subtle political thinker than he was and they both knew it. Even so, Michaelson was good at playing catch up. He took it a step at a time.

"You knew I'd be the only one to oppose the president in the primaries."

"Right," Merriman said.

Michaelson followed his former hatchetman's trail of bread-crumbs.

"And you know I'll give her a hard race. I *will* win some states."

Merriman said, "I'm counting on it."

"Because ..." You evil sonofabitch, Michaelson thought. "Because that will make me her only possible choice for vice president."

"Exactly. What ticket could the Republicans put up that could beat Grant-Michaelson?"

The idea was staggering, but hard to argue with.

That didn't keep Michaelson from saying, "If you were here, I'd strangle you."

"That's why I called," Merriman told him. "So what do you think? Patti Grant and you in the White House. Her with just the one term left. You the natural heir. Me moving up quickly in the Senate. Has some appeal, doesn't it?"

Michaelson did like the idea of being Patti Grant's successor in the Oval Office.

If he couldn't beat her, that would be the next best thing.

Give him the chance to put her accomplishments in the shade.

Get even with Merriman, too, when the time came.

"It has some appeal," Michaelson agreed.

Captain Welborn Yates' Office

Welborn called the Warner Brothers studio in Burbank, California at 10:00 a.m. With the time difference between the east coast and the west, that turned out to be too early. The switchboard was available, but the lawyers who protected the studio's intellectual property rights were unavailable. The studio's operator went the extra mile, what with Welborn calling from the White House, and told him there was a law school student working as a summer intern who usually came in early.

"That's great," Welborn said, "let me talk with him."

He didn't need any legal advice, just someone to check old files.

"Her," the operator corrected. "Christine Peterson."

"I stand corrected. I'd love to speak with Ms. Peterson."

From the doorway to his office Kira's voice asked, "You would? Who's Ms. Peterson?"

Welborn looked at her and held a finger to his lips.

"Ms. Peterson? Yes, this is Captain Welborn Yates." He reassured her that he really was calling from the White House … and, yes, there were some similarities between the real thing and the old TV show with Martin Sheen. "I'm glad you're a fan of popular culture, Ms. Peterson … Yes, of course, Christine. What I'd like to know is whether Warner Brothers or anyone affiliated with the studio has ever filed a cease and desist notice on an outside party for infringing on the image of Porky Pig."

Welborn listened for a moment.

"Yes, I think it would be best to go back to the very beginning." He thought for a second. "If I'm underestimating the number of people who might have done that, let's start with any infringer in the Washington to New York corridor. You'll do that?"

Welborn listened again.

"I think I can help you out, no problem."

He gave her his office and mobile phone numbers and hung up.

Kira asked, "Ms. Peterson would like a picture of the president … or of you?"

"Neither. She has a yen for White House M&Ms."

Kira stepped forward. "There are really people who would

infringe on Porky Pig?"

Welborn took a photocopy of the pig pin from the material Rockelle had sent him.

"Porky or not?" he asked.

Kira looked and compared the image to her memories of the cartoon character.

"Pretty close," she said, returning the image. "Allowing for a wise guy attitude."

"The pin is the signature of the K Street killer, the guy shooting the lobbyists."

"That's a crime?"

Welborn wondered what the over/under on that question would be.

Then he said, "He took several shots at Putnam Shady."

Kira considered Putnam to be a friend.

"Sorry. But thanks for reminding me. I have to add Putnam to the wedding list."

"You've invited Margaret Sweeney?"

"Yes."

"Then he's covered."

"He should receive his own invitation."

Welborn deferred. "You know best. About that."

Kira smiled. "We're going to be married a very long time. Possibly. And we're going to have a lot more people at our wedding than we thought. Last minute or not, people are flying in from all over. I have to let Uncle Mather's people know right away so we're not caught short on anything. You've talked to your parents?"

"They'll arrive tomorrow."

Showing a hint of anxiety, she said, "I'm a little nervous about meeting them."

"They'll love you, probably more than me."

That won Welborn a kiss. Kira was on her way out when Welborn stopped her.

"Wait a minute. What's the password? I don't want to be turned away from my own wedding."

"It's actually three words. I thought of you and couldn't come up with anything more perfect."

"I love you?" Welborn asked.

Kira answered, "O lucky man!"

GWU Hospital

Carolyn had heard McGill speak of Clare Tracy, but she'd never met her before. That didn't keep Carolyn from embracing Clare and saying, "Thank you, thank you so much for coming to help Kenny."

Clare didn't just abide the hug, she returned it.

As if she knew what Carolyn was enduring, and in a way she did.

"Kenny's still in his fishbowl, that's what he calls his sterile room, but would you like to see him?" Carolyn asked.

"Very much."

Carolyn took one of Clare's arms and she, in turn, took one of McGill's. It felt like one of the most natural things in the world to him, but it still made him uneasy. He had WorldWide News snooping on him and he didn't want anyone to misinterpret anything.

Kenny was awake when they stepped in front of the window looking in on his room. He was sipping clear liquid through a straw. He looked much better than he had the day before and when he saw his parents he smiled broadly.

But his eyesight must have been a bit off, McGill thought.

Because when Kenny looked at Clare, he said, "Patti."

"I wish." Clare chuckled. "The day I look that good, I'll sit for a portrait."

Carolyn told her, "There is a resemblance. Your hair color and skin tones are quite close."

Clare turned to McGill, "You care to cast a vote?"

Before McGill could be coaxed to answer, two more visitors appeared, a woman McGill didn't know and a young girl about —

"Liesl!" Kenny called out in excitement.

The girl, McGill saw, repressed a moment of shock and painted a smile on her face. She won a great deal of favor with him for doing that, not letting his son see that he wasn't quite who he used to be.

"Hi, Kenny," she called back. "Everyone from school says hello."

Introductions were made, Liesl and Mrs. Eberhardt meeting McGill and Clare, saying hello to Carolyn. A nurse showed Liesl how to use an intercom next to the room's door so she and Kenny could talk without raising their voices and disturbing other patients. Having overheard Clare's name, the nurse asked her if she was ready to have her blood drawn to confirm the results of the test done in New York.

Clare said she was, and turned to McGill.

"Will I need to catch a cab back to the hotel?"

He shook his head. "Either I'll be here or I'll have someone drive you."

"We'll have a chance to talk later?"

"Absolutely."

She stepped close to McGill and kissed his cheek.

"Tell the president hello for me, and let her know I'll vote for her whatever party she's in." Clare departed with the nurse.

Carolyn looked at McGill. "What did that mean?"

McGill hadn't seen Patti's announcement, but he'd been privy to her decision.

He told Carolyn what Patti had done.

"Oh, my," Carolyn said. "Everything's changing so fast."

Just then another nurse approached them.

"Mrs. Enquist, Mr. McGill, if you have a moment, Dr. Jones would like to see you."

McGill and Carolyn were escorted into Dr. Jones' office. The nurse left them alone with Kenny's chief oncologist and closed the door behind them. The patient's mother and father were both on edge, expecting to hear something momentous if not downright terrifying.

Dr. Jones offered drinks, but understood when they were declined.

McGill asked, "Has something gone wrong? More so than before?"

Dr. Jones shook her head. "We had to go hard with Kenny's chemotherapy. The drugs are powerful. They have to be. Quite frankly, we don't know how Kenny managed to stay functional so long without treatment. He must normally have a remarkably strong physical constitution. We hope to make that work in our favor now, but it also means with a more typical patient we would have gotten to him before the disease had progressed so far."

"You'll still be able to treat him?" Carolyn asked with a tremor in her voice.

"Yes. Finding two compatible donors in such a short time was very fortunate. That is what gives us great hope. Have you decided who you will use for Kenny, assuming our test results confirm the ones showed by Ms. Tracy's test in New York."

McGill and Carolyn looked at each other.

Carolyn said, "It has to be your call, Jim. Patti and Clare are both here because of you."

McGill's first impulse was to say Patti, but if Clare were the donor, that would allow Patti to attend to her official and political chores without interruption. It was a tough call.

Dr. Jones could see McGill's hesitation and offered a further consideration.

"I must tell you," the doctor said, "I've never seen anything like the outpouring of generosity Kenny has received. At first, I thought it was simply a byproduct of —"

"Privilege?" McGill asked. "Power?"

Now in his third year as an occupant of the White House, he had become acclimated not only to the trappings of wealth such as he'd never imagined, but also the proximity to power, the likes of which existed under no other single roof in the world.

Nonetheless, McGill had done everything he could to keep a level head.

He was just along for the ride, an ordinary guy who had gotten very lucky.

All he'd ask for when Patti left office was to keep her love and company.

"Yes, quite frankly," Dr. Jones said. "Both of those things. But what surprised me was the genuine affection all the potential donors feel for you and the president, Mr. McGill." Turning to Carolyn, she added, "And the love the president obviously feels for your son, Mrs. Enquist."

Carolyn, it seemed, had moved past her feeling of insecurity.

"She's a wonderful person. So is Clare Tracy."

Dr. Jones steepled her fingers before her mouth for a moment as if trying to decide how to phrase what she had in mind. Finding the words, she told McGill and Carolyn. "I must tell you that Kenny's wealth of potential donors has not gone unnoticed by others in the hospital, particularly the patients on this floor, their families and their physicians."

"What do you mean?" McGill asked.

Dr. Jones replied, "In the words of one young patient, 'Can I have anybody he doesn't need?'"

"I don't understand," Carolyn said.

McGill did. "The other patients are looking for donors ... and you've found some who don't match Kenny but could help other patients?"

"Six patients in the Washington-Baltimore area," Dr. Jones said. "One right here at GWU, the little girl who asked about Kenny's surplus."

This time it was Carolyn who read between the lines.

"You mean either the president or Clare Tracy would be right for her, too?"

Dr. Jones nodded. "Just so, assuming we get the same test results on Ms. Tracy." She looked at McGill. "If the president were to donate to Kenny, do you think Ms. Tracy might donate to our other patient? Beyond that, do you think the other compatible donors would be willing to help the other children in need?"

McGill asked, "Are Carolyn and I among those potential donors?"

Dr. Jones shook her head. "No, I'm sorry."

"I'll talk with my wife and Clare," McGill told the doctor. "Maybe the two of them together." He turned to Carolyn. "Do you have any preference?"

She shook her head. "All I want is for Kenny to get well, him and as many other kids as possible."

McGill told Dr. Jones, "If you'll give me the names of the other people who can help, I'll see that they get the word."

The doctor smiled. "Thank you. Please do so as soon as you can. Kenny and the others will need their procedures soon. Within the next forty-eight hours would be best."

Carolyn took McGill's hand. He nodded.

"Is there anything else?" Carolyn asked, hoping there wasn't.

But Dr. Jones nodded.

"Kenny told us he had a visitor early this morning."

"A visitor?" McGill asked.

"Another patient," the doctor said. "Kenny said he wore surgical scrubs and a mask, but he recognized the visitor. He said the man stood at his bedside."

"But I thought Kenny couldn't have anyone but medical staff in his room," Carolyn said.

"He can't and he didn't. The nursing staff is very protective of its patients. I was assured that no unauthorized person entered Kenny's room."

"But Kenny thought someone had," McGill said.

"Yes. He thought Congressman Zachary Garner came to see him."

"Who?" Carolyn asked.

"Congressman Garner represents a district in Virginia. He's a cancer patient here at the hospital. He is like Kenny only more so. Incredibly strong and tough. He should have been confined to a bed by his pain long ago, but he takes his meds and goes about his business. For a little while longer, at least. He first met Kenny in the VIP lounge, and then he did visit Kenny's room before he started his chemo."

"And Kenny thought he was at his bedside this morning?" Carolyn said.

"Yes. The peculiar thing is, Congressman Garner was in the hospital at the time. Not on this floor but at the pharmacy … and in the chapel. Kenny said talking with the congressman made him stronger, gave him hope. And his vital signs are much improved, within the limits of his condition."

"So what do you think, doctor?" McGill asked.

The oncologist offered a small wistful smile.

"I think I have gone to school for more than half my life, I read the literature of my specialty daily, and Kenny's experience is just one more thing for which I have no answer."

WorldWide News Washington Bureau

Hugh Collier had evicted the bureau chief from his own office for the duration of his stay in town. He sat in silence, sorting through the implications of Patricia Grant's defection from the Republican party. Seated opposite him was Ellie Booker, very glad now that Hugh had taken the phone out of her hand as she was about to call Sir Edbert Bickford.

Hugh's decision to go with the president's announcement was the right one.

Lobbyists getting killed was a terrific tabloid story.

But Patti Grant bailing on the GOP was bigger news by far.

Ellie would have looked like a fool if she had somehow prevailed and WorldWide News had gone with the K Street Killer story. Hugh had grinned and told her the best boob job in the world wouldn't have saved her career. She wouldn't have gotten to do the weekend weather in Wyndham.

"Where?" Ellie asked.

"Think Podunk, Aussie style," Collier told her.

She did and shuddered … but she remained a firm believer in

recycling.

The president's story was going to blow everything else out of the water for who knew how many news cycles. It might run for as long as a week.

The pundits would be debating long and loud who had been hurt more, the president or her former party. Spinners on each side would be working overtime. If the first female president in U.S. history failed to win a second term, after what she'd just done, she'd be labeled a failure and would set back the prospects of another woman winning the White House for decades. On the other hand, if she won another term, defeating whomever the Republicans might nominate, that might be the end of the GOP as a major political party. Were that to happen, Patricia Darden Grant would be recognized as one the most significant presidents ever.

With all the mad chattering that would ensue, there would be only one way for Ellie to get the sort of attention her K Street Killer story deserved: She had to find a way to connect it to the president's decision. But how ...

Hugh saw the look come over Ellie's face.

He smiled and said, "You've just had a deliciously wicked thought."

"Maybe," she replied. She popped open her laptop, pulled up her police blotter file and scrolled through that week's entries. She didn't have to go far before finding what she wanted.

"Come on, love," Hugh said, "give me a tickle."

"You do like the K Street Killer story, right?"

She'd given him the outline before he'd shelved it.

"Yes. Most days it would be a winner."

"Well, how about this," Ellie asked. "A police report filed says this past Monday shortly before midnight a townhouse on Florida Avenue was hit by fourteen rounds of nine millimeter ammunition. The property's owner was at home, sitting in his living room, and barely managed to avoid being killed."

"Another good story," Hugh said, "for another time."

Ellie shook her head.

"The property owner is Putnam Shady."

Hugh grinned. "Sounds like a name Dickens might have conjured."

"What's important about Mr. Shady's name is I know it from my investigation of James J. McGill."

Now, Hugh's eyes brightened. "He's connected to McGill?"

"He's Margaret Sweeney's landlord. She lives in the basement apartment of his townhouse. Mr. Shady is also a lobbyist."

"That's bloody marvelous."

"I didn't put it together with the other shootings because it didn't happen on K Street."

Hugh Collier mulled that over.

"It might be unrelated," he said. With a grin he added, "But where's the fun in thinking like that?"

Ellie said, "Exactly. We owe it to the public to find out if there's a connection between the killings on K Street, the attempted murder of Putnam Shady and President Grant's decision to leave the Republican party."

Hugh agreed. "It's the only responsible thing to do." Then he added a thought that had been running through his head. "Let's see if we can't weave a thread about the accusations of Erna Godfrey being tortured into the story."

He enjoyed his wicked thoughts, too.

Metro Police Headquarters

Lieutenant Rockelle Bullard went over the two lists on her desk a second time, frowning more deeply than she had on the first reading.

Detectives Meeker and Beemer were sitting in her guest chairs and knew just how she felt. They'd had the same reaction minutes earlier when they'd been poring over and highlighting the pertinent information. Meeker was still keyed up; Beemer was just sitting back enjoying how good his feet felt in the padded oversized sneakers the lieutenant was letting him wear for the next ten days.

When Rockelle looked up, Meeker said, "Pretty damn good guess, don't you think? This friend of yours really that smart or is he getting some help?"

Rockelle thought about that. Welborn was working with James J. McGill and Margaret Sweeney, two cops who had a whole lot more experience than he did. But Rockelle, like most of official Washington, had heard the story of McGill's sick son by now. She doubted that the president's husband had much on his mind but his boy.

"He's pretty good," Rockelle said of Welborn.

"Maybe he's good at acting, too," Beemer added. "Playin' his part in a script somebody wrote for him."

That, Rockelle thought, was a more likely possibility. But hardly conclusive.

"Somebody in the federal government wants to make the Metro police, and us in particular, look good?" she asked.

"Us?" Meeker asked. "Me and Beemer ain't on nobody's federal radar, not unless Beem's been cheatin' on his taxes again."

"Fuck you, man," Beemer said. "But he does have a point, lieutenant. Wasn't us who got invited to your friend's wedding."

"Okay, okay. So should I feel like I'm being set up?"

Meeker said, "Could be Captain Yates just has a warm spot for you, cop to cop, you know. He's solid with the president, you said, so what's he gonna get out of handling this case his own self?"

"He could become *Major Yates*," Rockelle said.

Beemer said, "That girl he's marryin' as rich as he said, maybe he don't need to think about that."

"It all comes down to how much you trust the guy," Meeker concluded.

Rockelle thought about that.

"Could be a fake out," she said. "He gives me something that looks good to keep me happy and looking the wrong way. Then he goes out and breaks the case with Porky Pig."

Both detectives laughed at that.

"So what're we going to do, Lieutenant?" Meeker asked.

Rockelle sighed. "Since we'll be dealing with recent widows here, I'll do the interviews. You two just keep quiet and listen as hard as you can, in case, for the very first time, I happen to miss something."

"Which widow we visiting first?" Beemer asked.

"We'll go in the order their husbands were shot: Mrs. Erik Torkelson is our first call."

"Chevy Chase, Maryland it is," Meeker said.

Rockelle called to clear the visit with the widow and the three cops hit the road.

Welborn's idea looked like it might break the case. The first three killings, anyway. Each of the lobbyists had reported a gun being stolen from his home. Each of them had been killed with a weapon firing the same caliber of bullet as the stolen gun.

Hating coincidences the way any good cop did, they had to think the killer had used the victims' personal weapons to do them in. It now fell to Rockelle to talk to the widows and see if she could determine how the thefts occurred and who the thief — and most likely the killer — was.

If everything went well, Rockelle might be promoted to captain soon.

If it didn't, she was going to be the loud drunk at Welborn's wedding.

McGill Investigations, Inc.

McGill sat behind his desk waiting for Harlo Geiger to arrive. Waiting for Sweetie, too. There was no way he would do so much as chat with the estranged wife of the speaker without a third party in the room. If need be, he could always ask Deke to step into his office, but the special agent had a demanding enough job, being the person ultimately responsible for seeing to it that the president's husband came to no harm. Asking him to witness that nothing inappropriate happened between McGill and Geiger's wife would be pushing things.

When he'd called Sweetie from GWU Hospital, she said she would meet him at the office. He had expected she would be the first to arrive. McGill had stopped by Kenny's room after leaving Dr. Jones to say goodbye to his son.

Kenny had barely waved to him.

He was still busy talking with Liesl Eberhardt.

Kenny's behavior — his interest in a girl — buoyed McGill's sense of hope.

He heard the door to the outer office open and two sets of footsteps enter: Sweetie's, and someone wearing high heels? Harlo Geiger? If so, Sweetie had timed her arrival to a faretheewell. No big surprise there.

McGill got to his feet in anticipation of meeting his new client.

Instead of a would-be divorcée, he was greeted by his younger daughter, Caitie, with Sweetie following behind.

Caitie, he now saw, was wearing tap shoes, a development of which he'd been unaware. He asked, "You're studying dance now?"

"Annie said it would be good to broaden my repertoire of talents. I'm taking singing lessons, too." Annie Klein being Caitie's talent agent.

"Somehow your mother neglected to tell me any of this."

Caitie said, "I told her I wanted to surprise you, and then Kenny got sick."

"I don't suppose you could take up the soft shoe?" McGill asked.

"What's that?"

"Quiet dancing."

Caitie made a face. Clearly her father's idea did not appeal.

McGill looked at Sweetie. "Did she come here with you?"

The outer door to the office suite opened and Sweetie turned to see who it was.

"Putnam," she told McGill. "He was chatting with Dikki, and, no, the Secret Service brought Caitie here at her request."

Caitie rushed to forestall any paternal criticism. "Dad, I was going crazy in the White House all by myself. Mom's at the hospital with Kenny. Abbie's at school. Patti's always busy. And Blessing lets me beat him at gin. That's no fun."

McGill took in all the clues he'd seen and heard and solved the mystery of his daughter's appearance.

"So you put on your tap shoes and drove everyone crazy."

Caitie couldn't quite hide a smile.

"Can you blame me?" she asked.

"You want to go home?" he parried.

"Not by myself and not until … Kenny's better."

McGill sighed, and Putnam Shady took that as a cue to poke his head into the open doorway. He said, "I play gin, and nobody beats me, unless it's fair and square."

Caitie sized up the man and his implicit challenge. "You're that good?"

"Put myself through college playing cards. Well, cards and pool. And betting college basketball." Seeing McGill frown, he added, "But I never did drugs, drank only in moderation and worked at Saint John's charity kitchen every Thanksgiving."

Putnam's résumé met with Caitie's approval.

She turned to her father and asked, "Dad?"

Considering the parameters, McGill told Putnam, "Not at your house."

In the event of a second attempt on the lobbyist's life, McGill wanted Caitie well out of harm's way.

Putnam said, "Margaret and I have been talking about taking precautions. I've booked a suite at the Four Seasons." He told Caitie. "Room service is on me."

Caitie beamed.

McGill held up a hand to stop any further pleading.

"Sweetie?" he asked.

"They'll be fine."

McGill was still reluctant, but didn't see a better option.

"All right, Miss McGill," he told Caitie, "you've finagled things to your advantage once again. But I need to speak with Mr. Shady for a while first. Give me a hug, and then wait outside."

His daughter clickety-clacked her way over to him and, God help him, he detected that she was already starting to find some rhythm moving in her shoes.

Not wanting Caitie to put on a performance in the outer office, however, in the event she grew impatient with the length of the adults' discussion, he told her, "Go talk to Deke. Ask him what the physical requirements are for becoming a Secret Service agent."

"You mean how many pushups and stuff like that?" Caitie asked.

"Exactly."

Tapping her way toward the door, Caitie said, "Can I ask to see his Uzi?"

"Only if you're going to marry him."

That stopped Caitie for a moment.

Then she blushed.

And had the grace to dash from the room.

Baltimore-Washington Parkway

The car thief who had used the name Stephen Tully to rent the Ford he'd driven to tail Leo Levy yesterday, and later tail him to his house, ditched the car five minutes after McGill's Chevy had chased him out of Leo's garage. His pride still stung; he hadn't been that close to getting caught since he was a kid.

But, damn, he'd been even closer to pulling off the biggest heist of his career. Defeating the alarm on the garage door had been easy; picking its lock had been harder. Then he'd gotten inside and up close the Chevy didn't look all that special. Yeah, it had been detailed to a showroom finish, but it still looked like a production line product.

It was only after he'd taken a minute to stare at it that he got the first feel for its power. The thing just gave off a vibe that it could devour anything else on the road. Swallow Porsches whole. Then he noticed the tires. Nothing stock about those babies, wide and fat, looked like they could run over a spike-strip like it was confetti. The brakes on those wheels had to be brutes, too. And the engine … Jeez, he'd like to put the hammer down on that.

For the first time since he was fourteen, the thief wanted to steal a car to keep for himself. That was crazy, of course. This car had to be sold overseas. Or he could ship it out of the country. Put it in storage somewhere. Reclaim it when he had the dough to retire abroad. He thought he still had some extended family in Germany.

That'd be cool. Take the Chevy out on the autobahns, give the krautpounders a serious inferiority complex. With that daydream in mind, the thief went to work. It took him an hour and a half under the car to work past the security system: a combination of ignition cutoff, engine shut down, steering wheel and transmission locks, and a siren that could probably be heard on the far side of the planet.

Finding and getting past all those measures gave him a sense of accomplishment.

Sucked him in completely, just the way some prick figured it would.

It never occurred to him to check the goddamn suspension system.

But the moment he put a toe inside the car, music started blaring so loud it felt like his brain would liquefy. Fucking audio system must have had a dozen speakers. The thief ran from the garage with his hands covering his ears.

But not before he'd heard and recognized the song that had assaulted him.

Bobby Fuller. "I Fought the Law (and the Law Won)."

Real funny, asshole, the thief thought.

Someday, he'd come back and … ah, bullshit, he was never going to get even with this guy. It was going to be all he could do to run fast enough and far enough not to get caught. The bleakness of that assessment chilled the thief, left him feeling desperate. Wound up making him take the craziest risks of his career.

He was hurrying past an auto dealership when he saw an empty car hauler in a lot out back. The truck could be used to transport up to seven passenger cars, but now it was unloaded, empty. The dealership wasn't open yet and the thief didn't see any security guards on hand.

Almost without thinking, he ran to the lot's gate and cut the lock. He was in the car hauler's cab and had the engine turned over in what seemed like seconds.

After the painstaking ordeal of trying to beat the security system on that fucking Chevy, stealing the truck was a gimme. Driving through Georgetown and Northwest D.C. and grabbing a Porsche 911 GTS, an Audi R8, a Mercedes SLS and a Tesla Roadster and putting them on the car hauler, all before their yuppie owners had finished breakfast, hadn't been much harder.

The thief had been uncertain about taking the American car; he'd had a nice German theme going and thought it would look visually consistent to anyone who glanced at the truck. But the Tesla fit in with the sports cars he'd stolen, and he doubted one in a hundred people would be able to say it wasn't another German car.

Besides, he was sure he'd need every dollar he could lay his hands on.

He was going to have to lay low for a long time if he wanted to stay free.

He pulled the car hauler up to the front gate of Spaneas Import-Export and left it there with the motor running and better than half-a-million dollars in sports cars on board. As before, he left a plain white business card with numbers for his off-shore account and prepaid cell phone on it. But this time he had added two words printed in block letters: Chevy's next.

It wasn't, of course, but Teddy Spaneas didn't know that. The thief figured the stolen car wholesaler would give him a quicker payment with perhaps a bump in his cut, if he thought the big prize would be coming soon.

Walking toward the tourist-crowded Inner Harbor, the thief started to relax. He'd stop in at the first quiet bar he came to and have a drink. Then he'd book a flight to somewhere far away. Central America maybe.

Looking back at the morning's fiasco, he thought maybe he'd get away with it after all. He'd worn surgical gloves, had been careful under the car not to nick himself and leave any trace of blood, hadn't so much as sneezed. He just might come out of this okay.

Better than okay, what with the money he'd get for the cars he'd stolen.

Only, getting on in years a bit, he shed a few hairs on his collar every day.

One of them had fallen off his collar and onto the floor under the Chevy.

He hadn't noticed, but the Secret Service's forensic team had found it.

McGill Investigations, Inc.

"So you're saying one lobbyist's worst enemy is another lobbyist," McGill asked Putnam Shady. He had his pen and notepad out, and was paying close attention.

Putnam nodded. "Yeah, if you want to think in symbolic terms. Mostly though, just like politicians, we usually move in a pack."

"Like hyenas?" McGill asked.

"I usually say jackals," Putnam said, "but hyena works, too. The point is, anybody with legislation to move has to have the money to match the other guy's troops. Or to cow the pols and their staffs."

"Give me an example of two opposing blocs," McGill said.

"Energy companies and environmentalists. You'd think this would be a walkover for big energy. They've got more money than the rest of the country combined. But every so often the environmentalists pull some soon-to-be-extinct critter, like the snail darter, out of a hat and stop the big boys dead in their tracks. Boy, does that piss them off.

"Then there are the truck companies and railroads. Both haul freight, each wants its operations subsidized by the government. So both sides hire lobbyists, neither side wins a decisive victory and subsidies morph with the times."

McGill said, "So nauseating as it may sound, it's really in the interest of both sides' lobbyists to keep the game close. Or at least in play. One side puts the other away, the winners have worked themselves out of a job."

Putnam smiled, "Theoretically, but I've never seen or even heard of that happening."

"If lobbyists need an opposition to thrive where does the enmity come in?" Sweetie asked.

Putnam gave her a look. He wanted to reveal himself to her little by little, at times of his own choosing, but circumstances were not cooperating. Still, he knew it would be worse to evade, self-defeating to be dishonest.

"Like I was saying about big energy," he said, "nobody likes to lose. It's like sports that way. You need another team to play against, but you still want to win every game. And just like athletics there are times when somebody will take a cheap shot. I've seen fistfights break out."

McGill said, "A fistfight is a long way from gunning someone down."

"Really?" Putnam said. He looked back and forth from McGill to Sweetie. "In your careers with the cops, you never saw a fight escalate fast: fists to knives to guns?"

There was no denying that for either ex-cop.

Putnam said, "Granted, the context is different. Actual bloodshed is not as likely to happen among lawyers and MBAs as among drug dealers and loan sharks, but it's not impossible or even improbable in this case, at least the way I see things."

McGill still had trouble with the idea, but he didn't want to underestimate Putnam.

Sweetie was about to say something when it sounded as if Savion Glover had arrived in the outer office to give Caitie a tutorial in tap dancing. McGill and Sweetie went to the door to see what was happening; Putnam looked on over their shoulders.

A dance lesson was under way, Caitie keeping up respectably, but the instructor was McGill's new client, Harlo Geiger.

The White House, Vice President Wyman's Office

The vice president was on the phone with his niece, Kira. He could have walked across the building from his office in the East Wing, but being a gentleman of the old school he observed a protocol stricter than what was actually required of him. He never intruded on the president's side of the building without a specific invitation from Patricia Darden Grant.

Being a stickler on this point also gave him the privilege of declining a summons from Galia Mindel or any other functionary, keeping those minions mindful of the constitutional hierarchy. He, after all, was the man a heartbeat away from the presidency.

For a little while longer anyway.

Kira was getting a bit nervous about her wedding and the unexpectedly high number of acceptances to the last minute invitations. She was worried that the necessary preparations would not be met: seating for the ceremony, food, drink, flowers.

Maybe just a bit of uncertainty Captain Yates was the right man, her uncle wondered.

"Everything will be perfect," Mather Wyman assured his niece. "Why, I've even found room for the handful of last-minute acceptances to the invitations I sent out."

Kira groaned, "Oh, Uncle Mather, I'm so sorry. I completely forgot about your friends, and mother's. Did her people accept, too?"

"Every last one of them. It's going to be a full house."

"Wait! Do you know about the password you need to get in?"

"O lucky man! Delightful and entirely appropriate."

"Welborn told you?"

"He did ... You are sure he's the one, sweetheart?"

Since the time Kira's father had passed away so tragically in a hotel fire, Mather Wyman had filled the paternal role for his niece. A widower without his own children, it was the role he came to cherish above all others. He'd have given up all his political ambitions in a heartbeat, if it would have served Kira's best interests.

"Mattie," Kira said, using the nickname that was her privilege alone, "my only concern about Welborn is that I'm not good enough for him — though I'm careful never to let him know that."

"I doubt he'd believe you if you told him word for word."

"I love you, Mattie."

"I love you, too, Kira. I'm happy you've found someone to make you happy. Now, don't worry about a thing. Your wedding is going to be perfect."

After saying their goodbyes, the vice president's phone rang almost immediately.

Kira calling back about something she'd forgotten or ...

The president saying, "Mather, could you stop by the Oval Office?"

"Immediately, Madam President."

Department of Justice Building, Washington, D.C.

Attorney General Michael Jaworsky sat motionless as he watched the DVD play on his office television. The video had been recorded that morning in the federal prison in Hazelton, West Virginia. Rather than transmit it to Washington electronically and risk an interception and a leak, one hard copy was made and it was brought directly to Washington by a special agent of the Federal Bureau of Investigation.

As a further precaution, Erna Godfrey was removed from the Hazelton penitentiary and placed in a government safe house in rural Massachusetts.

The video began with Deputy Attorney General Linda Otani identifying herself and asking Erna Godfrey to do the same. After Erna complied with the request, the DAG recited Erna's Miranda rights and asked if she was waiving them. Erna said she was.

The DAG said, "Very well, Ms. Godfrey, please feel free to say what you wish."

Looking straight at the camera, her eyes were clear and her face was composed, but she'd been given no makeup, special grooming or civilian clothing. The deputy attorney general wanted Erna to come across as being exactly what she was, a federal prisoner in possession of all her faculties making an uncoerced statement.

"My name, as I just said, is Erna Godfrey and I'm one of the people responsible for killing Mister Andrew Hudson Grant. In fact, I'm the one most responsible. I pulled the trigger on the launcher that fired the rocket that killed him.

"I am grievously sorry for what I did. The problem with that is I'll never get to express my regret, in this life, to the person I most want to hear it. That's what happens when you kill someone. If there's any remorse in your heart, you can never express it to them.

"I have seen that Mr. Grant is with the Lord, but I have no assurance that when I leave this life that I will ever stand at the Lord's side. So maybe I'll never get to tell the man I killed how sorry I am.

"I want to make it clear to everyone that I haven't changed my feelings one bit about thinking that the taking of life that we call an abortion is an abomination. As much as my heart has broken about what I did, it breaks anew each time I think of other innocent lives being taken. On that matter, I will never change my beliefs.

"Even so, it doesn't excuse what I did. Nothing can justify that. Most of the people who participated with me in the taking of Mr. Grant's life are, like me, already in prison. But there is one who is not, my husband, Reverend Burke Godfrey.

"Just a few days ago, I talked with Burke and pleaded with him to make his peace with the Lord and with the temporal authorities. He walked out on me without saying a word. I wept for him after he left. I fear for his soul. I beg of him up to this very moment to set things right.

"What weighs on my heart even more is that I know of other men and women who have worked tirelessly to end the plague of abortions and who have gone too far in their zeal. A handful of them even share my sin. That's why I asked to make this statement today. My hope is that I can persuade some of you, if not all, to confess, to God and to the authorities for what you've done.

"Please, if not for yourselves then for the children, come forward. We are never going to win this battle as long as we countenance the violence we ourselves do. Our only hope is to lead by loving example, extending our hands to those who don't understand the horrible things they are doing, and by praying that they see the light.

"That is what I will try to do, as I hope to start a ministry within the prison system. If I succeed at all, I hope the Lord will show me mercy and someday I'll be able to apologize directly to the man I killed."

Erna turned to her right and said, "That's all."

The video ended. The attorney general sat back in his chair, thinking about the legal, not the moral, meaning of what he'd just watched. Erna Godfrey had just followed in the footsteps of Joe Valachi.

Valachi had been the first insider to acknowledge the existence of the Mafia.

Insider Erna Godfrey seemed to be saying there existed an organized element in the anti-abortion movement that believed the taking of life was justified to achieve its goals.

Moreover, she implied she knew who these people were.

But she hadn't revealed any names.

The attorney general placed a call to the White House.

Hay-Adams Hotel

Speaker Derek Geiger sat alone at the desk in the master bedroom of the RNC suite, where he'd taken shelter after being evicted by his wife. He'd been trying to tend to political duties, but memories of his personal life kept intruding on his thoughts. Not the end of his marriage but an emotional trauma from boyhood.

He'd lost his dog, Beau, to a gator. Probably would have lost his own life, too, if his father hadn't killed the predator with three shots from his .45. The boyhood trauma seemed to occupy his thoughts and dreams any time he experienced emotional turmoil. If he had made his mark in any other profession, he might have sought therapy, but having your head shrunk when you were in politics was a non-starter.

Measured against the loss of his dog, the political setbacks Geiger had suffered in his career were nothing. Even his first two divorces weren't particularly troubling. Getting free of Harlo would be more aggravating, but that, too, would pass.

What was far more of a heartache was losing Brad Attles. He'd been a true friend. Like Beau. And just like the gator had taken Beau, some predatory bastard had killed Brad.

He knew there would be people who'd criticize him for comparing the death of man to the death of a dog, but those shitheels didn't understand, and fuck them anyway.

"Mr. Speaker, we're ready now," Reynard Dix said.

Geiger looked up and saw the chairman of the Republican National Committee.

"All the candidates are here?"

"Yes, sir. The ones that could get here fast. The others are flying in."

"Well, let's go give them their marching orders."

Geiger couldn't handpick his choice as the GOP's candidate for president, but with the damn Patti Grant having left the party, he was at the top of the food chain. No, wait just a minute. As far as he knew, the vice president hadn't quit the party.

Maybe Geiger could —

No, Mather Wyman was Patti Grant's man. Wasn't he?

The speaker decided to give that question some thought. If he could prevail on Wyman to spy on the president for him — for the good of the GOP — that might give the eventual Republican candidate a big advantage.

Meanwhile, he would remind the would-be occupants of the

Oval Office, waiting in the next room, the points of party dogma to which each of them must hew, and how they would conduct themselves with the legislative — his — branch of government, should one of them actually be elected.

If anyone gave him any trouble, he'd put an end to it as surely as his father had put an end to that goddamn gator.

WorldWide News, Washington Bureau

The chattering class was having a feeding frenzy with the news about Patti Grant leaving the Republican Party. Not only was the subject wall to wall on the basic cable news stations, the broadcast networks had pre-empted their soap opera programming to cover the new reality show melodrama. Undoubtedly, Jon Stewart and his staff were already working up comedy riffs for that night's *Daily Show*.

Stewart notwithstanding, the other great thinkers were starting to repeat themselves. Nobody had had the time to think the matter through and the superficial observations were getting as annoying as the video loops most stations used to illustrate the story. In the face of that reality, and needing to find something fresh to grab big numbers for WorldWide News, Hugh Collier changed his mind.

It was time to tell the world about the K Street Killer and the attack on Putnam Shady's residence. He and Ellie still didn't know if there was any connection to the president leaving her former party, but they could always raise the question.

That would start a mad dash of news outlets trying to find out if it was true. Should that be the case, someone else might find the proof, but credit for bringing the news to light would have to be shared with WWN. If there was no proof to be found, Hugh and Ellie would have the time to shift the story in another direction, raise another question.

But in the here and now, they would get the big ratings numbers.

Jack Negron and Kerri Landers, the Ken and Barbie who would read the breaking news story, were in their anchor chairs looking like the next step in human evolution. Perfect hair, flawless skin and smiles so bright they could drive at night without headlights.

Hugh and Ellie sat next to each other in the control booth waiting for the network to come out of its top of the hour commercials and go live with the introduction of the K Street Killer. The director gave the on-air talent their initial heads-up. Stop fidgeting in their seats and patting their hair. The last commercial had just started its thirty-second run when —

The phone rang.

Ellie stared death rays at it.

The call was answered nonetheless, and the message relayed.

The producer said, "The president just entered the White House press room. No advance notice."

"That bitch!" Ellie said.

Hugh gave her an avuncular pat on the leg.

"Go with the president," Hugh told the producer. "Maybe she's announcing her resignation."

Everyone in the booth gave Hugh a look. Did he know something?

"Now, now, children," he said. "Just a joke. Patti Grant is one of the few people too rich for even Uncle Edbert to buy off."

White House Press Room

The president asked all the members of the White House press corps to take their seats. Once that was accomplished, she said, "I'll take your questions shortly, but first I want to announce a new jobs initiative my administration will be putting into effect starting, appropriately, just after Labor Day, a little more than two weeks from now.

"I'm sure most of you are familiar with the expression most favored nation. In terms of international trade, most favored trading partners are given specific advantages such as lower tariffs and larger import quotas. Borrowing from that idea, my administration will begin classifying certain companies currently doing business with the federal government as most favored enterprises.

"Let me assure everyone right now that this special designation will not be applied to any business on the basis of the political contributions it makes to anyone in government. In order to become a most favored enterprise, a business must show a continuing record of providing well-paying jobs to United States citizens and legal resident aliens.

"American workers, through their tax payments, allow the federal government to stay in business. So it's only fair the government does business with the companies that want to employ those citizens and other legal residents of this country in well-paying positions. Companies that are outsourcing jobs and offshoring operations should be and will be the last to receive government contracts. If things go the way I hope, they will receive few if any contracts at all.

"The implementation of this policy won't exclude foreign companies. If, for example, a foreign manufacturer were to open a factory in the United States and employ American workers at good wages, it most certainly could be considered a most favored enterprise.

"You might be wondering how I can do all this on my own. It's very simple, really. I will veto any spending bill sent to me that disfavors American workers. It's possible the Congress, as is its right, might override my veto. But should they do that, they would have to explain to the American people why they did so; I'm sure that would be a very difficult sales job."

The newsies were bouncing in their seats like kernels of corn about to pop.

The president held up a hand.

"We'll get to all your questions in just a minute, but I want to add that I will have several more announcements to make in the coming days. Some of them, as with the most favored enterprises policy, I will be able to implement by using the powers of my office. Others will require legislation passed by Congress. It's no certainty that the House and the Senate will see things the way I do, but at the very least I will introduce ideas to be included in the public discussion."

Patti was also laying down planks for her reelection run.

And markers to see whether the Democrats would want her.

Or if she'd start from scratch, spend a lot of Andy's money and start her own party.

Washington, D.C., Route 185

Rockelle remembered how it was that she, Meeker and Beemer happened to be on their way to visit Widow Torkelson. Welborn Yates had *read* that some overprivileged young men liked to bolster their masculinity by purchasing handguns and becoming proficient in their use. Then a lot of these white-collar heroes got their firearms stolen right out of their homes.

Yes, Welborn had made the observation, after his initial reading of the Metro crime files, that the victims of the K Street killings had been shot with different high-end weapons, and then had made the intuitive leap that maybe some pissed-off sonofabitch had killed the lobbyists with their own guns.

Turned out, that looked like a real possibility.

Maybe even a probability.

That being the case, and Rockelle being someone who had done her homework ever since kindergarten, she wondered if there was anything else in the literature that would be worth knowing. Something Welborn had forgotten to let her in on or hadn't thought to be worth mentioning.

So with soft jazz coming out of Meeker's MP3 dock, and her two subordinates under orders not to disturb her, Rockelle used her department-issued PDA to search police databases for articles whose keywords included "residential burglaries, handguns stolen."

She got better than two thousand returns.

Everybody and his dog, Rover, was a writer these days.

And the drive to Chevy Chase was only six miles.

She'd have to narrow the parameters if she hoped to come with anything useful to ask Joan Torkelson. It was important to keep things as simple as possible. You were dealing with someone in the throes of grief, keeping things dry and factual was the best way to get accurate information.

Stumble around asking vague questions, you were likely to add aggravation to agony, cause emotional upset, bring the interview to a swift close without learning anything of value.

Rockelle narrowed the focus of her search: "residential burglaries, handguns stolen, most common perpetrators."

Whodunnit, after all, was the sixty-four thousand dollar question.

The first response to the query gave her what she was looking for, in general terms.

Family members and invited guests.

They out-stole handguns from homes by a three-to-one margin over professional thieves. Made sense, if you thought about it. A burglar would certainly take a gun if he found one, but he'd usually have no advance knowledge of whether a weapon was kept on the premises or where it might be found. An insider would know the gun was there and maybe where it was kept, too.

The closer the thief was to the gun's owner, the more he'd know.

Rockelle had a thought that wasn't covered by the article. Household help. She was dealing with affluent people here. Maybe there was a housekeeper, a cook, a gardener or someone else who worked in or around the home. Might even be someone who worked in more than one of the victims' homes.

"Almost there, Lou," Meeker said. "You and your machine come up with anything?"

"Yeah," Rockelle said. "Maybe the butler did it."

McGill Investigations Inc.

Caitie McGill and Harlo Geiger finished their *pas de deux* with beaming smiles and an embrace. Harlo picked up her handbag, and Caitie introduced her father.

"Dad, this is Harlo Geiger. Ms. Geiger, this is my father, James J. McGill."

The two new acquaintances shook hands. McGill introduced Sweetie, and the two women also shook hands. Putnam Shady only smiled at Harlo. He walked over to Caitie and said to McGill, "I'll have her home by midnight."

McGill didn't think that was funny, but let it slide.

Harlo accepted that Putnam did not rate an introduction, and didn't ask for one.

The two detectives ushered their new client into McGill's office.

Harlo declined the offer of coffee, tea or water. Everyone took a seat and they got down to business.

"I'm divorcing the speaker of the House of Representatives," Harlo told McGill and Sweetie. "I'd like you to find as much dirt on him as possible. I want him to be left with a guilty conscience and little else."

Sweetie asked the first question. "Why should he feel guilty?"

McGill followed up. "What kind of dirt?"

"For breaking his marriage vows," Harlo told Sweetie. To McGill, she said, "Personal, political or potting soil. Any old kind of dirt you can name."

"Why do you think your husband cheated on you?" Sweetie asked.

Harlo bluntly told Sweetie and McGill of her husband's failure to perform.

"These things happen," McGill said.

"Have they happened to you?" Harlo asked.

Thoughts came to McGill's mind of unhappy times near the end of his marriage to Carolyn. He said, "As a matter of fact."

Harlo leaned forward. "You don't have to answer, but was it because there was someone else?"

McGill thought it was more a case of Carolyn *becoming* someone else.

At least from his point of view.

"There was no one else," he said.

"You know," Sweetie said, "your husband's not a young man. Even if he'd never failed to acquit himself before, what happened might just be the first sign of an illness. Maybe something treatable, maybe something serious, but in either case not his fault."

The idea, plainly, had never crossed Harlo's mind, and she didn't like it.

In her defense, she said with a slight whine, "I found a fax from his lawyer, Brad Attles, the one who got killed. The message said Derek was planning to divorce me. That's what a man does when he's found someone new, not what he does when he loves his wife and finds out he's sick."

Both McGill and Sweetie thought that was a fair reading.

McGill had never expected to take on divorce cases when he went into private investigations, but considering this one's relevance to the political firefight that would be the next presidential election, and his determination to protect *his* wife, he felt he had no choice. He told Harlo what the investigation would cost and she didn't bat an eye.

"When can you start?" she asked.

"As soon as you can point us in a likely direction," McGill said.

"That'll be easy," Harlo told him. She reached into her handbag and brought out a sheaf of paper held together by a bulldog clip. "Before I kicked Derek out of the house, I copied his date book for the past year. His personal date book."

McGill wondered if he and Sweetie should read it.

Or just turn it over to Galia Mindel.

White House, Welborn Yates' Office

The phone rang and Welborn picked it up on the first ring. There was always the chance the president might be calling, and it wouldn't do not to respond promptly. Whatever foolish thoughts he might be having about working in the White House, as long as he was there, he intended to do an exemplary job.

"Captain Yates," he said.

"Welborn, it's Chris."

It took him a moment to place the name; the slight Valley Girl lilt helped.

Chris Peterson, the summer intern at Warner Brothers.

"I've got your M&Ms," he told her. "Will a dozen boxes do?"

"That's great. Not that I'd eat so much candy. Well, maybe one or two boxes, but the rest I want to give to family and a couple of good friends."

"Impress them with your connections?" Welborn asked.

"Exactly. You can see movie stars in any supermarket out here, but knowing someone who works in the White House, now that's cool."

"You flatter me far too much. In my world, I'm a bit player."

"Maybe now, but I'll bet you go far."

Welborn's mother told him to always be gracious about accepting a compliment.

"Thank you, Chris. I'll try to justify your optimism. Do you have anything on Porky Pig for me?"

"Yes, quite a bit, actually. I didn't know it but Porky's been around since 1935. That's why it took this long to get back to you. Here's what I have."

She gave him a list of all the people between Washington and New York who tried to take a bite of the cartoon character's bacon without permission, at least those who rose to the notice of the studio. When she finished, Welborn made sure he had her mailing address for the cachet candy.

Looking at the twenty-six names he'd written down, he knew he'd be unable to get to more than a few of them in the next twenty-four hours. On Saturday, he would be busy marrying Kira, and then they were off to Barcelona where Welborn's father, Sir Robert Reed, had a villa. The honeymoon was scheduled to last at least one week and possibly two, depending on sun exposure, chafing and the call of duty.

Leaving a case hanging fire, even with a pro like Rockelle Bullard working it, made Welborn worry that he might bail out on Kira after three days. Four if she started showing him moves he hadn't seen yet. Five if he remembered something he hadn't shown her.

The number wouldn't matter, though, if he let Kira see he was distracted.

That wouldn't be the way to get married life off on the right foot.

He skimmed his list of copyright infringers and saw a company called Loch Raven Locketry, a manufacturer of novelty items. It made him proud that trinkets could still be made in the USA — assuming LRL hadn't been offshored to Taiwan or Vietnam.

He called the phone number he'd been given and a male voice with a distinct Mid-Atlantic accent said hell yes Loch Raven Locketry was still in business at its original location and doing quite well, thank you.

And, happily, was located in nearby Baltimore.

Kira was away from her desk when he called her. He left a message.

He was going out of town on official business.

He'd do his best to make it to the church on time.

The Oval Office

Vice President Mather Wyman had been watching from the wings as the president had made her announcement of the new most favored enterprise initiative. All of the newsies present cast glances his way, all of them thinking: What the heck is that guy doing here? Wyman was a distinctly low profile veep.

Nobody knew how much, if any, influence he had with the president.

Still, he always had a sunny disposition, conducted himself in a dignified manner and hadn't committed a gaffe of any sort in almost three years. Whenever any pollster bothered to ask, he turned in an approval rating of sixty percent, plus or minus three points. Virtually nobody worried that he'd screw up if he ever had to step up to the big job.

Which was exactly the topic the president raised as soon as the two of them were alone in her office.

"Mather, I'm going to invoke Section Three of the Twenty-fifth Amendment. I'll need you to sit in for me as acting president for a short period."

Patti Grant had long ago extended to her vice president the privilege of pouring each of them a drink whenever they were together in the Oval Office. Hearing what the president had in mind, he very nearly dropped the glasses of Hennessy X.O. cognac he held in his hands. As it was, he downed his own drink like it was a shot of rotgut.

After pausing to make sure he wasn't imagining things, the vice president offered the other glass to Patti.

She said, "You might want that one, too. Let's sit down."

Having a chair under him offered the vice president a measure of both support and comfort. But he leaned forward to look closely at Patti.

"Please tell me you're well, Madam President."

She smiled. "The White House physician couldn't be more pleased."

"Then —"

"The truth is, Mather, I'm about to become a health resource for someone else."

Patti told the vice president about Kenny McGill. Wyman raised his full glass.

"God bless you, Madam President." He sipped his drink. "And may God keep and heal young Master McGill."

"From your lips, Mather," the president said. "You don't have any reservations about stepping in for me, do you?"

The vice president chuckled. "This will give my résumé a bit of extra gloss when I run for Congress."

"Good for you. I look forward to having a friend in the House."

"No more than —" A look of wonder came across Mather Wyman's face.

Patti would have had to be blind to miss it.

"Are *you* all right, Mather?"

Without a by your leave or coasters, the vice president set both of the glasses he held on the president's desk.

"Madam President, I'm quite well, but I'd like to both tell you something I've told only one other person, and I'd like to ask a favor. If you can't grant the favor, I'll understand, but in that case I'll ask you not to reveal what I tell you to anyone else."

Patti now looked closely at Mather Wyman.

Seeing neither madness nor inebriation, she nodded.

What Mather Wyman told her, she never would have guessed.

Couldn't imagine anyone else guessing.

Thinking the matter through, she said, "Yes, Mather, if that's what you wish to do, go right ahead. It's either time or past time for it. But will it play back in Ohio?"

"I'm willing to find out," the vice president said.

Patti picked up the half-full glass.

"Here's to you, Mather." She let the remainder of the cognac slide down her throat. "There is one more thing I have to say."

"Yes?"

"I'd intended to bring this up before hearing what you had to say. I'm going to insist the level of Secret Service protection you receive as acting president be extraordinary."

The vice president took a moment to think about that.

He said, "You don't want to take any chance Derek Geiger will sit in this office."

"None whatsoever," the president told him.

Georgetown, The Four Seasons Hotel

Caitie McGill sat alone in the living room of Putnam Shady's suite. The lobbyist had beaten her in their first three hands of gin, and excused himself to use the bathroom. He had been, as promised, giving her his A-game. He probably would have won anyway, but Caitie took advantage of a rationalization: She was distracted.

That crack Dad had made to her at his office, she'd never heard anything like that from him before. The more she thought about it, the more it disturbed her. What he'd said about her being married to Deke and seeing his ... she didn't even want to finish the thought.

Okay, maybe, just of late, she had been wondering what one or two of the boys in her class might look like without their clothes on, but certainly not a grown man. That was just gross. So why would —

Then she got it. She had been pushing Dad, the way she always did. She didn't particularly want to see some fancy gun; she just wanted to see how far she could take things. What Dad had showed her, making her blush in front of everyone, was that he could push back — in ways she would never expect.

He didn't just do the normal dad thing, get mad and send her back to the White House to pout. He showed her she had better be careful how she spoke to him in public because. Or — pow! — he might embarrass the heck out of her.

He must not have gone too far, though, because Sweetie would have said something if he had. Wouldn't she? Yeah, she would.

But maybe not in front of anyone else. It was all kind of confusing.

Still, Dad had let her come to the hotel with Putnam, so he couldn't be too mad. Maybe he was just worried about Kenny. She said a short, silent prayer for her brother.

A knock at the door to the suite sounded as soon as she finished.

Putnam had ordered room service for them: a bowl of fresh fruit for him, a slice of devil's food cake for her. He hadn't given her a hard time about her choice. Just said she'd have to brush her teeth afterward; the hotel provided complimentary brushes.

That was cool.

Caitie called out, "I'll get it."

Putnam's muffled voice replied, "What?"

Caitie didn't think the Four Seasons would like its guests to shout at each other. She decided just to get the door, let the waiter bring their treats in. Only when she opened the door, she didn't see a waiter.

From her point of view — standing five-foot-one — the man at the door looked like a giant. An old giant, but real big just the same. If he hadn't smiled when he saw Caitie, she might have gulped. Maybe even screamed.

The smile gave her the courage to maintain good manners.

"May I help you, sir?"

He said, "I think you already have."

Caitie didn't understand that. The big old man turned to leave but then stopped.

He said, "You look familiar. Do you have a brother?"

Caitie thought this was getting creepy, but she nodded.

"Kenny McGill, right?"

"Who *are* you?" Caitie asked.

"A friend of Kenny's. I came to see the fellow you're —"

The big old man frowned.

"Mr. Shady is behaving properly, isn't he?"

Caitie replied, "He won our first three hands of gin, but he let me order chocolate cake from room service. Is that proper enough?"

The old guy smiled. "Yes, that will do. I won't bother you further. I'll catch up with Mr. Shady later." He touched a hand to his forehead and left.

Caitie closed the door, and locked it.

Decided Putnam could open it the next time.

Chevy Chase, Maryland

Joan Torkelson met the Metro homicide cops at her front door wearing a cheerful yellow dress and a string of pearls. Rockelle knew that was just for show. The pain in her eyes made it clear she was not bearing up well.

Nonetheless, she invited the detectives into a perfectly ordered living room and offered each of them a cup of tea. They all accepted. Rockelle had told Meeker and Beemer she would beat them into pudding if they brought up Porky Pig or cracked wise about anything at all. They would be introduced and would remain silent unless she or Mrs. Torkelson addressed them directly.

Thus far, the two detectives were behaving.

Rockelle had twice spoken to Joan Torkelson on the phone; the first time the homicide lieutenant had borne the burden of making the death notification. She had extended her condolences at that time, and did so again.

"Mrs. Torkelson, I am so sorry about the death of your husband."

Joan nodded, and asked if anyone needed more sugar for their tea.

More bereavement behavior, Rockelle thought. When your world was falling apart, you made things better wherever you could. It would be hard to lean on poor Joan, but there were questions Rockelle needed to have answered.

"Mrs. Torkelson, did you and your husband entertain much at home?"

The widow looked at Rockelle as if she'd lapsed into Chinese.

Even Meeker and Beemer, mute though they stayed, looked puzzled.

Rockelle elaborated. "Did you have social gatherings for co-workers or clients from your husband's place of employment? Did you have family over for special occasions? Were there times when neighbors dropped by and stayed for a drink or dinner?"

The point of the questions was still unclear to Joan Torkelson, but she responded to the structure they represented; it was orderly.

"Why, yes. All of those things."

"Did you happen to keep guest lists for the formal parties, notes or journal entries for the more spontaneous occasions."

"Am I that easy to classify?" the widow asked.

"I'm sorry," Rockelle said. "I don't understand."

But she did.

Joan Torkelson said, "I mean, I do all those things. I'm a bit compulsive that way."

"It would be helpful if you could give me a list of everyone who's been in your home for the past year."

"You want the service people, too."

"The household help?" Rockelle asked.

"Oh, them, too, but I meant the plumber, the electrician and the cable TV people."

Rockelle hadn't thought about those types, but hey.

"Everyone," she said.

"This could take a little while," Joan Torkelson said.

"We don't mind," Rockelle told her.

"Very well. I ..." Getting to her feet, Joan's composure slipped. She grasped for it and regained her bearing. "I'll copy the names on the machine in Erik's office."

She left the room, dabbing at her eyes with a lace trimmed handkerchief.

Meeker and Beemer were dying to talk, but Rockelle held up a hand.

She handed over her PDA with the article about family members and invited guests being the most likely culprits in residential handgun thefts. The two detectives huddled and read, understanding now where the boss was going. They handed the PDA back to Rockelle just before Joan Torkelson returned with a 9X12 manila envelope.

She'd affixed a label to it: Our guests, and the year.

Imposing order wherever she could.

As soon as she sat down, Rockelle had to shake her up again.

"I need to ask," she said, "if your husband received any threats in the days preceding his death."

The woman's chin quivered for a moment before she clamped her teeth together.

Then she shook her head.

"Were you aware of anyone your husband might have argued with recently, either at his workplace or even with your neighbors?"

"Our neighbors are good friends and wonderful people," Joan Torkelson said forcefully. "This is a *good* neighborhood."

The widow's indignant expression lasted only until she realized the unintended slight she had directed at the three black detectives from the District.

"I'm sorry, I didn't mean —"

Her face crumpled and her eyes filled with tears. She brought the handkerchief out again. Rubbed her eyes with it, unconcerned now about appearances. For a moment anyway. After one last swipe, she compressed the handkerchief tightly in her right hand.

Joan said, "I thought, at first, that Erik's death was simply an act of random brutality. There's so much violence these days there's really no point in asking why it claims anyone in particular. I just had to accept that … that it found the man I loved. But when I heard about that awful pin you found on him, that made everything very personal. I was outraged; I still am."

The three Metro homicide cops looked at each other. Meeker and Beemer were *dying* to speak, but Rockelle held up a hand.

"You know something about a pin, Mrs. Torkelson?" she asked.

Joan was no fool. She saw the response her words provoked, and came to the proper conclusion. "That was supposed to be a secret."

"We didn't release it to the media," Rockelle said. "How did you hear about it?"

"I received a call from a woman, a producer, at WorldWide News. She told me about it and asked if I knew what it meant or would care to comment. I hung up on her."

Meeker finally broke his silence. "Good for you, ma'am."

"You had every right," Beemer told her.

Emboldened now, a new light came into the widow's eyes. It was cold and merciless.

"Someone killed my Erik. My husband. My children's father. Then he calls him a *pig?* Heaven help me, I wish I could get my hands on the bastard!"

"I plan to do just that, Mrs. Torkelson," Rockelle said.

"You told me on the phone, Lieutenant, all this might have something to do with Erik's gun being stolen."

"Yes, ma'am."

"Well, if you catch this man, please let me know. I'll buy a new gun."

McGill Investigations, Inc.

Harlo Geiger had left to further her plans for a new life without the speaker of the House, and McGill put his phone down after making a call to the hospital. Sweetie just looked at him, didn't need to ask the question.

"Kenny's hanging on," McGill said. "Some of the others aren't doing so well."

"The others?" Sweetie asked.

McGill told her about some of Kenny's potential donors being matches for other children in dire need. He'd promised to make calls to see if those people would be willing to donate to someone else. He'd do that right now.

As McGill made his calls, Sweetie folded her hands and bowed her head in prayer. McGill heard a soft murmur of Latin coming from her as he made his calls. His dear friend's words of supplication to the Almighty couldn't have hurt because each person McGill called informed him that he or she had been greatly disappointed about being unable to help Kenny. All of them agreed to help the other kids.

McGill gave them Dr. Jones' phone number and told them time was of the essence.

As he finished his last call, Sweetie looked up.

McGill asked her, "What do you think, Margaret? Is Kenny going to live?"

Sweetie let her face go slack, and McGill could see what she would look like as an old woman. Her strength of spirit and clarity of purpose were still evident, but there was now a gentleness to her features the likes of which he'd never seen. She took the time to give the question the consideration it deserved.

"Yes, I think he will," she said. "In fact, from what you've told me about his desire to become a doctor, he's already seeing his future. I think he'll not only survive, he may well outshine Abbie and Caitie, and that will take some doing, believe me."

Sweetie's words all but brought McGill to tears.

Especially as he'd never told her of Kenny's plans.

Still, she knew. Margaret Mary Sweeney plainly had answers to mysteries that were far beyond McGill and other lesser mortals. He wouldn't say anything about it now, not to Sweetie or anyone else, but later, after Kenny became a famous doctor, he would ask her how she'd known something he'd never told her.

Doubtless, she'd scoff and tell him he was a foolish old man whose memory was playing tricks on him.

For the moment, McGill felt reassured enough to look at puzzles with which he was better equipped to deal. He asked Sweetie, "Do you agree with Putnam that whoever killed the lobbyists is another lobbyist?"

Sweetie's face resumed its normal appearance, all symmetry and righteous energy.

She said, "I think it's possible, but I don't know if I agree with it."

"It doesn't feel right to me," McGill said.

"Who do you like?"

"Well, not to heap abuse on a despised class, but what came to me right away was some politician did it."

"How come?" Sweetie asked.

"Think about it like this. Lobbyist A and Lobbyist B fight a pitched battle, and Lobbyist A wins. Lobbyist B looks bad, sure, but who looks even worse?"

Sweetie thought about it. "The pols Lobbyist B greased to take their side."

"Yeah. Lobbyist B isn't going to want to shoulder the blame. He'll tell everyone in the lobbying brotherhood, 'Don't bother with Senator Smith or Congressman Smythe; those guys have lost their game, can't deliver on any legislation anymore.'"

Sweetie carried the ball from there. "So rather than kill a fellow pol and risk federal time, a losing pol goes after Lobbyist A. That's a safer bet because if there's anyone more hated than politicians it's the people who buy and sell them."

"Right." The thought made McGill very glad that Patti was independently wealthy. "If a pol did the killings he'd get both the satisfaction of doing in someone who had harmed his career and maybe the pleasure of cutting off a source of funds to his political enemy."

Sweetie nodded. "As far as motives for murder go, those two are pretty good."

McGill sensed reluctance. "But you're not buying the idea yet."

"I think it's possible, but you haven't made the sale yet."

"Fair enough. I'll talk to a specialist. Maybe I can find out if the idea holds water."

"What specialist?" Sweetie asked.

McGill smiled thinly. "Galia Mindel."

"Wow, you must think you're really on to something."

"We'll see."

Sweetie told McGill she had to go make sure Putnam hadn't taken Caitie's college fund away from her. Make sure the two of them were safe and sound and still in the good graces of The Four Seasons Hotel.

McGill asked for a status report on that front.

After Sweetie left, McGill intended to call Clare Tracy, see if they could squeeze in time for a drink, ask how her re-test went, and plan something in the future when he and Patti and Clare could get together for a civilized dinner, maybe even go somewhere for a whole weekend of catching up.

Before he could make his call, the phone rang.

He lifted the receiver and said hello.

Edwina Byington said, "Hello, Mr. McGill. The president will be with you momentarily."

It wasn't even that long, and what he heard told him that another woman could read his mind. "Jim, I hope you won't mind, but I've invited Clare Tracy to dine with us tonight."

Secret Service Forensics Laboratory

Elspeth Kendry answered her cell phone and heard, "Holmes is home."

She replied, "Thank you, Watson."

"That's Special Agent Watson to you."

Elspeth chuckled. "I'll remember that. Please give my thanks to Special Agent Ky as well."

"Never heard of the guy," Deke Ky said and clicked off.

Elspeth smiled and thought, okay, that was a step in the right direction. Getting on the good side of Holmes' personal bullet catcher would be essential to performing her job. If there were ever to be a dispute between the two of them, she'd have to ask SAC Crogher to intervene on her behalf. Then all Ky would have to do would be go to Holmes and tell him the new broad was a pain in the ass.

There was no doubt in Elspeth's mind who would prevail if that happened.

Far better that she and Deke Ky should get along.

She'd first thought that he might be a hardass about things, but just now he showed he didn't take himself too seriously. She'd pulled that Watson joke out of her hat, hadn't planned it at all. It could have backfired big time if he'd had a stick up his ass about it. But he'd played along without missing a beat.

She wouldn't go all stand-up comic on him, but tossing an occasional gibe his way might be a part of her plan. Who knew, maybe they could go out for a drink sometime.

She looked through the lab window where the DNA guy, Mark, was still at work, but at least he'd moved away from his scanning electron microscope, or whatever it was he'd been peering through, and had moved to a desktop computer. To be fair, Mark was probably working as fast as he could while still doing a conscientious job.

At least she hadn't had to queue up to get her job done. When the husband of the president was involved, you jumped to the head of the line. Elspeth was coming to think she was going to like that aspect of her new job, but enjoying special treatment might make it tough to go on to any other assignment and just be a grunt again.

Well, maybe if the president won a second term and she was along for the remainder of the ride, she could retire, write a book and become a talking head on some TV show. Make a small bundle and then think of something really interesting to do.

Not that her present job was a drag. Telling other people, and reminding herself, that she was a Secret Service agent was pretty cool. The building where she was presently cooling her heels was the foremost facility anywhere for detecting forgeries. It had the world's largest library of inks, which might not sound too thrilling, except every currency on the planet was printed using … ink.

So unless you wanted every jerkoff with a grudge or a streak of greed undermining the validity of the cash in your pocket or handbag, you'd need people who knew their inks, papers and presses working day and night against counterfeiters.

Not that the service was a one-trick pony. As mentioned, the lab knew all about —

Mark walked out of the geeks-only room wearing a big smile.

Elspeth hoped that wasn't only because he liked her legs.

She was already sure of that.

"Got him," the forensics tech said.

"From just one little hair, amazing."

"Might as well have left an autographed glossy," Mark told her.

He handed a low-resolution image printed on ink-jet paper. The face squinting at her belonged to one Linley Boland, age forty-seven, born in Sparks, Nevada, owner of a sealed juvenile criminal record in nearby Reno, arrested three times, as an adult, but not charged on suspicion of grand theft auto in Las Vegas.

Elspeth wondered how that worked. Had the cops caught Linley *leaning* against stolen cars three times? Might have been something close to that. The only time Linley got busted as an adult was in Athens, Georgia. The cops there found a car that had been reported stolen in Atlanta. A mook named Conrad Jarman was asleep in the front seat; Linley was sawing lumber in the back seat. The cops took them both in.

Linley swore that he'd only been hitchhiking. The guy who'd given him a lift had pulled over and said he needed some sleep. So he'd decided to get some rest, too.

Conrad, meanwhile, asserted that he was the hitchhiker, but he was in the front seat and had a slim-jim and an ignition puller on him. He swore that carrying the tools was the price he'd had to pay to get a ride, and the asshole in the back seat had made him sleep up front.

Linley said, "Who, me?"

After the cops arrived at the station, they found out Conrad didn't have a prior criminal record but Linley had a juvenile sheet and the suspicion arrests in Nevada. The cops would have liked to pin the auto theft on Linley, but Conrad's stupidity left them with no choice but to charge him.

They weren't about to let Linley skate, though.

They charged him with trespass of a motor vehicle.

The judge gave him six months, and the state took his picture and DNA.

Elspeth looked at the photo of Linley Boland again.

"Think you're a slick fucker, huh? And now you're messing with James J. McGill's car while I'm on the job? You are not going to prosper, asshole."

Elspeth saw she'd have to be careful about voicing her thoughts. She was getting Mark excited. She thanked him, shook his hand and sent him back to his lab.

Never one to leave any stone unturned, Elspeth got on the line to the Las Vegas PD and was routed to a detective named Soren Thorgrim who was part of an auto theft task force called VIPER. Detective Thorgrim was not pleased to hear the name Linley Boland.

"That prick is still breathing air?" he asked.

"Air as opposed to what?" Elspeth replied.

"Anything that would choke him out, painfully. They used to have execution chambers that worked like that."

Elspeth wondered if the detective's harsh attitude was a carry-over from the old days in the West when the authorities used to hang horse thieves.

"You want to hear the kind of shit that bastard was part of?" Thorgrim asked.

"I do," Elspeth said.

He told her Linley Boland was part of a gang that used to steal cars right out of people's garages. That certainly sounded familiar, she thought, as Leo Levy could testify. Sometimes, Thorgrim told her, the thieves were slick enough to make the grab without anyone ever seeing them. But other times the homeowners heard noise coming from their garages and arrived in time to see the pricks stealing their vehicles.

On three separate occasions, Linley Boland was identified as the thief. Only between the time the cops were called and Boland was pulled in, somebody had called the home and made the obvious threat: *We know where you live.*

The homeowners in Boland's three arrests just could not identify him in the police lineups. Detective Thorgrim gave a cynical laugh. "We could've pointed a red arrow at his ugly mug and it wouldn't have done any good.

"The only reason we heard about the threats at all was because one family's little boy, he was about eight, told us he heard it. But then *he* retracted his statement."

"Mom and/or Dad got to him," Elspeth said.

"Yeah, sometimes this job really sucks. So make me happy and tell me you feds are going to nail Boland's ass. I'll come to the trial and eat popcorn."

Elspeth said, "If he's still breathing air, we will. But tell me, detective, is there something else about Boland that's burning you? He comes across like a sack of shit, all right, but you sound like it's something personal."

After a moment of silence, Thorgrim said, "My son is Air Force, as good a kid as any father could want. I see him in uniform, my heart almost busts with pride."

"Your son's okay, right?"

"Yeah, he's fine. But the last job this car theft ring pulled, the homeowner not only interrupted it, he brought his gun with him. The thief took off, but not before the homeowner got a good enough look at him to give us a description that matched Linley Boland. Later that night, the stolen car T-boned another vehicle, killed three young Air Force pilots: Keith Quinn, Joe Eddy and Tommy Bauer."

From the regret Elspeth heard in Detective Thorgrim's voice, she was not surprised he remembered the victims' names. Then he rocked her world with a further recollection.

"There was one survivor. A young fellow named Welborn Yates."

Ristorante Treviso, Georgetown

Hugh Collier told Ellie Booker he'd take her out to any place she cared to eat, as long as he didn't have to go home and change clothes. He was wearing a black blazer, a butterscotch polo shirt and and designer jeans pre-faded to a shade of blue that Ellie had always associated with heavenly grace. With his craggy good looks and lean, strong build, Ellie could imagine Hugh as the cover boy on a men's health magazine.

Damn shame he was gay.

Still, he was more than presentable enough to get into any place that wasn't so stuffy it demanded a suit and tie. Attired in a fashion similar to her boss, she was rarely interested in dressing up to go out to eat. Not unless dinner was followed by a night in a five-star hotel and sex that was anaerobic and possibly operatic enough to bring security people on the run.

It didn't have to be with someone who could advance her career, but recently she'd decided if the sex was strategic as well as orgasmic so much the better.

With Hugh Collier, Ellie supposed she could help her job prospects by pimping out some of her more appealing gay friends.

But that wouldn't do a damn thing to provide a sexual diversion from the intense professional frustration she was feeling.

Fucking Patti Grant.

The host at Treviso gave Hugh such a bright smile, while barely taking notice of Ellie, that she knew it wouldn't be necessary to call on one of her friends — if Hugh were in the mood for a paisan. They were given a very good table, and Ellie was sure the food and the service would be excellent.

"Wonderful choice," Hugh told her, looking around as they waited for the glasses of Prosecco he ordered.

Ellie would have preferred scotch. Maybe even a boilermaker.

Hugh took note of her dour mood.

"Be of good cheer, old girl. We'll concoct some wickedness before dessert."

Ellie gave him a deadpan look and said, "Did you just call me old girl?"

He laughed. "I did attend public school in England."

"Yeah, and what's up with that? Calling private schools public. That's somebody's idea of a joke?"

"Well, of course, it is." By now, Hugh had sussed things out. "You're feeling unsure that the powers of darkness will prevail. Ye of little faith." He studied her further. "You'd also like to find a bloke to give the old bones a rattle."

"That obvious, huh? Well, what else is there when you don't do drugs and a third drink will bring the first two up?"

Hugh put one of his hands over one of hers.

"Dear Ms. Booker, your appeal both personal and professional have been near enough to make me regret my gaiety."

"Yeah? You'll throw me one for the team?"

He laughed again. "Damn, it's a close call, but I'm afraid I have to abide with *my* team. However, I will see if I can't brighten your mood."

They were interrupted by a waiter bringing their drinks. He also presented them with a platter of Ricotta and spinach fritters, the appetizer compliments of their host. That was it for Ellie. She placed her glass of sparkling wine in front of Hugh and told the waiter to bring her a Peroni.

She also told the waiter that when she and Hugh finished their meals he was to bring the check to her, and if anyone tried to comp their meals, she'd bust his nose for him. Taken aback, the waiter dared to glance at Hugh.

He nodded. "I'd do what she says; she can be dangerous."

Ellie liked that.

"Better bring me a beer, too," he added.

She liked that even better.

The waiter departed, quickly.

Hugh told Ellie, "I doubt that Uncle Edbert would let me increase your salary again so soon, but I will do something special for you. Now, try to relax and take a bit of a longer view. Patti Grant has made news of historic import with her abandonment of the Republicans. Her most favored enterprise policy is also a bombshell. She'll upset all sorts of insider deals with that one. And my guess is she'll make several more announcements soon that will cause uproars and leave all her enemies choking on her dust."

"Including us," Ellie reminded him.

"Only if we're foolish enough to try to nip at her heels. But we'll hang back, making our own plans."

"Such as?" Ellie asked.

"We'll continue to look into the lobbyist murders. We'll pursue the torture — possibly the brainwashing — of Erna Godfrey. We'll champion the cause of keeping Reverend Godfrey out of prison. That's bound to be in the offing. I'm sure there will be any number of ways we can torment the president. Not that we have do it immediately. We're here for the long haul, and to be — pardon the word — honest, it's much more fun to plague your enemies than to coddle your toadies."

Hugh was starting to perk her up. Still ...

"What about Sir Edbert? I thought he wanted to skewer the president now."

"He does. He's a bloody-minded old bugger, but he'll take his fun where he can get it. Leave that to me."

Ellie took her glass of wine back. She raised it to Hugh.

"The long haul?"

He touched his glass to hers. "The long haul."

They drank, smiling at each other.

"Tell me," Hugh said, "if I were an ordinary bloke, what would you do to me if we were to spend the night together?"

Ellie lowered her voice and told him in great detail.

"God save this queen," Hugh muttered. He looked about the restaurant and asked, "Is there any male here, other than me, that you might fancy?"

There were two young guys at the bar. Ellie nodded their way.

"The one on the right."

"You won't mind if I —"

"Not as long as you don't give him any money."

"Pay for the hotel?"

"That's all right. Make it a five-star place."

Hugh Collier strolled over to the bar to pimp out his producer. What a guy, Ellie thought.

I-95

The black Porsche Cayman S that Kira had given Welborn as an early wedding present came equipped with hands-free calling. As he drove north on I-95, he made another call to Loch Raven Locketry in Baltimore and this time the phone was picked up by a guy with an old man's voice who said, "We're closed."

"Federal agent," Welborn replied.

"Yeah, sure."

"Honest and true."

Welborn didn't do hardass well, but he was great at sounding earnest.

"What kind of federal agent?" the old guy asked, still suspicious.

"Air Force."

"Air Force?"

Welborn said, "I know some Secret Service guys, if that makes you feel better."

The old guy laughed and asked, "What's any of this got to do with me?"

"Maybe nothing, but I was informed that your company ... are you the owner by any chance?"

"Yeah, I am. Name's Mort Greenberg."

"Captain Welborn Yates. I was told your company received a cease and desist letter regarding the production of a lapel pin that —"

"That some *meshugeh* people in California thought resembled Porky Pig. The only time I ever received a letter like that, I laughed. A bigshot lawyer wouldn't make his dry cleaning bill suing me."

"Did you tell them that?" Welborn asked, a smile in his voice.

"What I told them, it was a one-off order and we weren't going into the cartoon business so stop worrying. We'd ceased and desisted already; they didn't have to bother us."

"Do you remember who placed the order?" Welborn asked.

"*Oy!* That was more years than ... than we bother with keeping records. As soon as we get past the point of needing papers for a tax audit, *pfft*, they're gone. Sadie sees to that. She thinks we've got too much mess around here as it it, and she's right."

"Do you think Sadie might remember who the customer was?"

"Unless it was Eddie Fisher, no."

Welborn didn't want to lose a thread he thought still had possibilities, so he went with a hunch. "Mr. Greenberg, I don't know anyone with immigration, so please don't get upset, but do you hire American workers?"

"Always, nothing but. Full-time people doing the metalwork here at the shop. The art we always farm out. Got a good art school here in town, you know, the Maryland Institute College of Art, MICA they call it now. Makes me smile, an art school with a nice Hebrew name. But what's all this got to do with anything?"

Welborn said, "I was just thinking. Legal workers use legal

names. Maybe you remember the name of the person who designed or fabricated the pin. Maybe they might remember the customer."

"*Schmendrik,*" Mort Greenberg said.

"I beg your pardon," Welborn said, not being up on his Yiddish.

"I just called myself a fool. Of course, I remember who designed that pin. A bigger pain in the *tuches* you should never meet."

He gave Welborn a name and an address in Baltimore.

"This is a stroke of luck," Welborn said, "your remembering all this."

"Some people you remember so you can avoid them."

"I appreciate all your help, Mr. Greenberg."

"Yeah, yeah. I'll be sure to call the Air Force the next time I want to visit my daughter in California."

Welborn laughed and gave Mort his work number. "Give me a call. I'll let you know if Air Force One is heading that way."

"Oh, so now you're friends with the president?"

"I work at the White House, just down the hall from the Oval Office."

"Yeah, sure."

"Honest and true," Welborn told him.

Metro Police Headquarters

The homicide team looking for the K Street Killer had completed their rounds, interviewing the widows Torkelson, Waller and Benjamin. Janice Waller was another meticulous family records keeper; Myra Benjamin had one of those memories that can make people a lot of money on Jeopardy. She just sat down at her kitchen table and wrote out a list of everyone who had entered her home in the past twelve months, including her children's friends.

That was another class of people Rockelle had overlooked: kids.

After a moment's thought, though, she didn't see a child passing a gun along to his father's killer. A kid got pissed off at his old man and there was a gun in the house, he did the job himself. Even if he lived in nice suburb.

Returning to her office, Rockelle assigned Beemer the task of alphabetizing and typing up the lists of visitors to the Torkelson, Waller and Benjamin homes. Beemer didn't mind. His wife was the executive secretary to a poobah at the Smithsonian, typed so fast her fingers were a blur. Beemer had her teach him to type, and he practiced his speed — in case he ever felt his job got too dangerous and wanted a transfer to an administrative post.

Beemer was good enough to keep up with a conversation as he worked.

He said, "Y'all know we got a rat in this building."

He meant the person who tipped off WorldWide News, the outfit that called Joan Torkelson for a comment on the pig pins.

Meeker said, "We know."

Rockelle added, "I got my pick. How about you two?"

"Still working on it," Beemer said. "I got maybe two guys and a woman."

Meeker shook his head. "It's one dude for me."

Rockelle said, "Bruno Bettman."

"Mr. Chuckles at the front door, yeah, he's the one," Meeker agreed.

Beemer paused in his keyboarding and looked at his colleagues.

"One of my three, too," he said.

Beemer's others were a public information lieutenant he had never liked and who talked to media people regularly as part of his job and the other was a female patrol sergeant who had gotten her ankle broken in a street scuffle and was doing rehab duty in the building, shuffling papers.

Beemer said, "I'll be done here in a minute."

Meeker told his partner, "Those other two of yours, they're possibles, all right. But I still like Bettman better."

"I do, too," Rockelle agreed. "But we don't want to come down on somebody just because we don't like him or her. We'll check out all three very discreetly."

"Done," Beemer said. He sent his work to the lieutenant's

printer.

With Rockelle's permission, Meeker raided the office fridge, giving them all soft drinks. Diet for Rockelle and Beemer, full sugar for him. The lieutenant and Beemer envied Meeker's high-burning metabolism, but got on him about it only when they could piggyback it to some other character flaw.

Beemer gave each of them copies of the guest lists from all three widows. Meeker and Beemer had glanced at the originals compiled by the women; Rockelle had deferred reading the names until now. Beemer did neat work and looking at the result in their own work space helped the three cops to focus.

Beemer finished first, having had the advantage of reading as he input the information. Rockelle finished next. The two of them waited in patient silence for Meeker to catch up.

He lifted his eyes and saw that both of the others were thinking the same thing he was.

"One name sure do stand out, don't it?" he asked.

"Putnam Shady," Rockelle said.

Beemer said, "Yeah, but he was supposed to be the dead guys' friend."

Meeker laughed. "Yeah, we all know friends always stick together, 'specially in this town."

The two detectives turned to their boss. "Lou?" Beemer said.

"Mr. Shady had his own house shot up," she said.

"Without him getting hurt at all," Meeker pointed out.

"Wouldn't be too hard to get someone to shoot out a few windows," Beemer added.

Rockelle smiled.

"What, you don't think so, lieutenant?" Beemer asked.

"Yeah, getting someone to fire shots wouldn't be hard. What'd be tougher is to find someone to do the job and not accidentally kill the guy who hired him."

The two detectives laughed.

"Might even be accidental on purpose, if the shooter got paid up front," Meeker said.

"On the other hand," Rockelle said, "Mr. Shady strikes me as nobody's fool. What if he's playing both ends against the middle? He starts up with Torkelson, Waller and Benjamin. But he's got a line in to Speaker Geiger, too. He shoots Brad Attles to get him out of the way, and he becomes the speaker's shadow."

"Damn," Meeker said. "That'd make him one devious mother-fucker."

Georgetown, The Four Seasons Hotel

"My parents were scam artists," Putnam told Sweetie.

Caitie McGill had been taken back to the White House by Deke Ky, never mentioning a word to the special agent about his Uzi, but proudly informing him that she'd finally managed to beat Putnam at a hand of gin, and with Putnam's coaching had greatly improved her game.

Deke had managed to contain his enthusiasm.

"What are your parents' names and what kind of scam did they run?" Sweetie asked Putnam.

"Their names are Charles and Mona Shady. Their con was an idea called Equine Performance International."

Sweetie asked, "What was that supposed to be?"

Putnam and Sweetie sat in facing arm chairs. Their stock-inged feet shared a common hassock. Putnam had a flute of Veuve Clicquot in hand. Sweetie held a can of Canada Dry ginger ale.

"A surefire way to play the ponies and win," Putnam told her.

"There's no such thing. Hard to believe anyone would buy that."

"Buy it they did," Putnam said, "in vast numbers. What made the sale was my dad was probably the greatest handicapper who ever lived."

"I never heard of him."

"And that was just the way he wanted it. He deliberately kept a low profile, but he'd have had to be invisible to keep the railbirds from knowing him and passing stories of how he won like clockwork. There got to be a joke how a race track was nothing more than Dad's ATM machine. It was just a question of how much he'd withdraw on a given day."

"What made him so good?" Sweetie asked.

Putnam emptied his flute and refilled it. "It was either a gift or a curse from God."

"Had he done anything to deserve a curse?"

"Not that I saw, not until he and Mom cooked up EPI."

"So a gift then," Sweetie said. "But if he could make money at will, why would he come up with a scam?"

A sad smile formed on Putnam's face. "I got a letter from my mother, postmarked in Panama, when I was in college. She explained the whole thing to me from her point of view. She wanted me to understand why she and Dad had done the things they did."

"Why didn't she just tell you?"

"Remember I told you I was raised by a black couple?"

Putnam had told Sweetie that a little over a year ago. In the context of the conversation, she hadn't pushed for an explanation. She said, "Yeah."

"Well, when I was six the scam blew up and Mom and Dad left me in the care of our former housekeepers, Emory and Sissy Jenkins, so I wouldn't have to live on the run. But they took my baby brother, Lawton, with them."

Putnam took another sip of champagne.

He continued, "The thing about Dad was, he lived in mortal fear that his gift came with an expiration date. Mom tried to reassure him that wasn't necessarily the case. She told him Michelangelo never forgot how to paint. But then she developed her own paranoia: What if, one day, Dad just dropped dead? She didn't have his gift or any other, but they both managed to spend money almost as fast as Dad won it."

Sweetie said, "Must have made for a nice life style but hardly a secure one."

"Exactly. So the two of them decided they needed a backup plan. Something that would amount to a financial killing, set them up for life."

"Enter Equine Performance International," Sweetie said.

"Right. If there was one thing Dad knew besides the horses, it was that 99.99% of race track bettors were always looking for a system, a sure thing. So they decided to give them Dad's system.

"If ever there was a sure thing, it had to be the way Charles Shady picked his ponies. So he went on the Internet just as it was starting to take off and revealed his secret. The response was enthusiastic."

Putnam emptied the bottle into his glass. His eyes had lost a bit of focus, Sweetie thought, but he wasn't slurring his words and his narrative hadn't wandered. She continued to sip her soft drink.

"Your parents concocted something preposterous, didn't they?" she asked.

Putnam raised his glass to her. "You must've been a pretty fair cop. Still are in a private sector sort of way."

Sweetie was largely immune to flattery but she warmed to Putnam's compliment.

"I do okay," she said.

"So did my parents. Dad told the world he was really nothing more than your average bettor. His advantage was that he knew which horse in a given race, if any, had been bred by..."

Putnam raised an inquiring eyebrow.

Sweetie knew the proper reply. "Equine Performance International."

"Just so. EPI was a secret cartel of the world's greatest American, European, Arab and Asian horse breeders. They'd secretly been raking in billions of wagering dollars for decades through unwitting betting agents. Typically, EPI executives asked the agents, schmoes they picked out randomly at the track, to place a bet for them with money they provided. If the horse won, which it always did, the agent got to keep ten percent of the winnings."

Sweetie said, "Your father claimed he was one of EPI's executives and ..."

"He got greedy, didn't want to give anyone a ten percent cut.

So he started placing his own bets and writing them off to ghost agents. But he'd been found out and EPI took harsh measures against anyone who risked ruining their game. *Enforcers* were now looking for him. To provide himself with the money he'd need to run and hide, he would sell the names of a dozen EPI horses who would dominate racing in the coming year."

"How much did he want for this priceless information?" Sweetie asked.

Putnam cleared his throat, looked a bit abashed.

"Only one hundred dollars. I know, I know. It looks like I'm following in my old man's footsteps, but I swear ShareAmerica is going to be legit."

"Exactly what any good conman would say," Sweetie told him.

"You don't trust me, Margaret?"

"I do." But the look in her eyes said she'd hunt him down if he ever betrayed that trust.

"Anyway," Putnam said, "the response to Dad's public offering was so overwhelming it crashed the servers, twice, of the company processing the credit card payments. Mom, Dad and Lawton took off and I haven't seen them since."

"Your parents were scam artists," Sweetie said. "Gifted ones."

"Yeah. Psychologically, it was a perfect con: Give the little guy a chance to buy into and benefit from the sneaky game the rich guys had set up to benefit themselves. In that way, ShareAmerica is just like EPI."

Sweetie wanted to hear the rest of Putnam's story. How he was raised. How some branch of the federal criminal justice system must have leaned on him and caused him to loathe authority. She wanted to know it all.

But her phone rang.

Caitie McGill was calling.

She'd forgotten to tell Putnam about the man who'd come calling.

"Here at the hotel?" Sweetie asked, hackles rising.

"Yeah," Caitie said. "He said he'd catch up with Putnam later."

The President's Bedroom

The president had changed out of her business attire, show-ered and put on a pearl satin cap sleeve sheath. She had a buyer on her personal staff, paid out of personal funds, who bought all her clothes. The public never had definitive proof of the designers she preferred or the sizes she wore. The latter was nobody's business but hers and the former prevented anyone from using her name in word-of-mouth advertising.

Jim, bless him, never made any inquiries about the particulars of her wardrobe. He was content to tell her she looked wonderful in anything she put on. He did confess, one time, that he loved the way she looked barefoot in a pair of faded jeans and an old white oxford cloth shirt. Made him think he actually got to know her back when she was in college.

Tonight, the president and her henchman would dine with the woman Jim actually did know in college, the woman who had been James J. McGill's first great love. The woman he undoubtedly would have married if —

There was a knock at the president's bedroom door.

It wasn't the polite tap of the household staff.

It was Galia. Undoubtedly come with some matter that couldn't wait. Jim was using their bathroom, getting ready for the evening. This wasn't the first time the outside world had intruded while he was in the shower. Patti took a hand towel and placed it in the sink Jim used for shaving, their signal a third party was lurking nearby. She closed the bathroom door and admitted Galia, who knew better than to knock twice.

As urgent as her business might have been, Galia took the time to appraise the president's appearance, head to toe, and nod in approval.

"You look radiant, Madam President, as usual."

"Thank you, Galia. What's the problem now?"

The chief of staff handed the president a small padded envelope bearing the stamp: RESTRICTED. Meaning access was restricted by law. It was not as drop-dead serious as a TOP SECRET label, but unauthorized peeking could still land a snoop in jail. The DVD of Erna Godfrey's statement was inside.

"You were speaking with Vice President Wyman when the attorney general called about this, and then you made your new policy announcement."

"And then you got busy until now," the president said.

"Yes, ma'am. But I took the time to view the video before bringing it to you." Galia was authorized to take a look and she gave the president the gist of Erna Godfrey's statement. "Attorney General Jaworsky thinks Mrs. Godfrey could be the contemporary equivalent of Joe Valachi."

The president tossed the envelope on her bed.

Secure in the knowledge Jim wouldn't open it.

She'd look at it later.

"Or," the president said, "like a good mafiosa she could be playing us."

That thought had also occurred to Galia. "Thinking she could get a further commutation or even a pardon for ratting out other people with blood on their hands."

"That's not going to happen while I'm in office. Tell the attorney general to let the inmate know we're always willing to listen to any-one who can help us bring criminals to justice. But there will be no quid pro quo. None whatsoever."

Galia approved. She was about to ask whether to allow Erna to pursue her in-prison ministry. The chief of staff thought that might be worthwhile, if Erna's gospel were to be limited to a message of remorse and repentance and pursuing the resolution of disputes by peaceful means.

Before she got to say any of that, there was another knock.

This one came from the bathroom.

McGill was petitioning for his own release.

"Galia's here, Jim. Come on out, if you're decent."

The chief of staff had once barged in on McGill, intentionally, while he was in the bath, and had said he could do the same to her if the matter was sufficiently urgent. Over the past year the two of them had done their best to temper their relationship. Each of them knew the other wasn't going away. If friendship was out of the question, they were working on peaceful coexistence.

McGill entered the bedroom wearing a terrycloth robe, his hair dried and brushed.

"If you need a moment, I'll go to my dressing room," he said.

The walk-in space was big enough for a propane grill, patio furniture and a hammock. But it was half the size of the president's dressing room.

"We're done, Jim," Patti said.

McGill said, "Well, if that's the case, Galia can you spare me fifteen minutes tomorrow morning?"

Galia put on her best insincere smile and said, "Of course."

She bade the First Couple goodnight.

The president didn't ask her husband what he wanted with her chief of staff.

He didn't ask her what was in the envelope on their bed.

Baltimore, Maryland

Welborn entered the address Mort Greenberg had given him into the Porsche's GPS unit and followed the directions that would take him to the home of Eli Worthington, the pain-in-the-*tuches* artist who had designed the pig pin found on the dead lobbyists on K Street. He pulled off I-95 at Russell Street, went past Oriole Park at Camden Yards, jogged right on Paca Street, made another right at W. Mulberry Street and followed it to N. Charles Street.

Just off Charles, opposite the leafy campus of Johns Hopkins University, Welborn found the side street and the address he wanted. It was a well-kept row house, a very nice piece of property. In a choice location, within lecturing distance of a first class university. Impressive digs for a freelance artist who designed trinkets.

According to Mort Greenberg, though, that had been some time ago. Possibly, Eli Worthington had moved up in the worlds of both art and real estate. Art appreciation hadn't been an offering at the Air Force Academy, but thanks to his mother's efforts, Welborn wasn't without a cursory knowledge of Western culture.

He was familiar with the works of the Old Masters, the Impressionists, the Expressionists and even some of the guys who'd emerged from the graffiti milieu, like Basquiat and Haring. But the name Eli Worthington had never appeared on his radar.

He found a parking spot down the block and walked back to Worthington's front door. The names above the doorbell were Eli and Nell. They were rendered in calligraphy.

Artful, Welborn thought. This must be the place.

He rang the bell and waited.

And waited.

There were lace curtains on the windows, and he could see there was a light on at the rear of the first floor. But he didn't get the feeling anyone was home. He rang the bell again and quickly looked back through the window. Not a soul stirred inside the row house.

He couldn't even see any motes of dust circulating through the air.

If someone was at home and lying low, or napping to put it charitably, it probably wouldn't help his case to lean on the door-bell. Not with someone who was irascible. Probably wouldn't even be a good idea to leave his card with a note on it.

Welborn walked back to his Porsche.

He decided he'd call on Eli Worthington tomorrow, right after breakfast. Just show up, peek in his window and ring the bell if he saw someone. If the place was still empty, he'd find out where the man worked or vacationed.

Track his paint-splashed ass down.

Tonight, rather than drive back to D.C., and have to do the trip all over again tomorrow, he'd take a room in Baltimore. He'd had good luck with the Royale chain and was pleased when the Porsche's internet connection told him there was one overlooking the Inner Harbor. He set off for the address on Pratt Street. Being a smart fellow, he called his betrothed and told her where he would rest his head that night.

Being a dutiful professional, also, he asked Kira to pass the information along to Edwina Byington in case the president needed him to return to the White House.

His obligations met, he started thinking about the steak he intended to have for dinner.

The Ground Floor Bistro

Linley Boland had treated himself to a morning makeover at an upscale men's grooming parlor on Calvert Street. Going in, he may have looked like a marginal character with a day's growth of stubble, but coming out with a shave, manicure, facial massage, haircut and color he looked like newly minted money.

His clothes were a bit scruffy, but he took care of that with a trip to Nordstrom. Two blazers, one navy, one black, an assortment of pastel polo shirts, three shades of khaki slacks and black slip-ons with rubber soles that would be good for running. He bought an overnight bag for his new wardrobe and left the store wearing some of his new purchases.

He had his old clothes put in a shopping bag and dropped them in a bin at a nearby resale shop. Hoping they'd be cleaned and sold before the cops could take any interest in him.

He'd expected to hear from Teddy Spaneas by the time he greeted the world in his new look, but no such luck. Made him start to think he'd gone too far dropping off four hot cars at once at the wholesaler's lot. Maybe the cars had been okay, but the hauler had been over the top. What was a guy who trafficked in luxury autos going to do with that monster?

But, hell, if Spaneas could handle selling the Chevy that the president's husband used as his ride, he should be able to cope with ditching a truck somewhere. Shouldn't be that hard. Drive it a mile or two, leave it in a lot or rail yard and walk away.

Shouldn't have been a problem.

Boland should have heard his money had been deposited by now.

He took his prepaid cell phone out of his pocket.

Looked at the fucker and silently told it to ring.

It didn't. Just sat there in his hand like … like its battery was dead? No, bullshit. The odds of that weren't worth thinking about. Only reason he even thought of it, he was getting nervous. He wanted to be far away and know he had a big chunk of money on deposit.

He put the phone away, decided to check into a nice hotel under one of his *noms de voleur*. Thief names. A French chick up in Montreal had told him that one. He'd always liked it. He checked into the Royale, put the phone on the nightstand next to his bed and took a nap, hoping the phone would wake him up.

It didn't, and Boland's gut started to knot. He'd almost gotten caught trying to steal that beast of a Chevy. He'd gone to the trouble of stealing four sports cars and a truck to carry them. He'd dropped his grabs at the wholesaler and walked away clean.

What was he going to get out of all that? Jack shit.

So damn discouraging; he might as well have been a clock-puncher at a factory that just closed. Where the hell was the justice? Nowhere.

That prick Spaneas must've gotten popped for something else.

Put out of business.

He was probably lucky he didn't get caught dropping off his cars.

There was only one thing left for him to do. Grab another car. Just one.

He knew another wholesaler up in Wilmington, Delaware. He'd grab something nice but easy, make ten-twenty grand. Get to Florida if not Central America. See what he could make happen down there.

He grabbed his overnight bag and left the room. Went down to the hotel bistro on the ground floor. Got a table by the window, ordered a weak scotch and soda and a plate of nachos. He nibbled and sipped and watched arriving guests pull up to the hotel.

Half the bastards arrived in cabs. Be a crying shame, he ever got so desperate he had to steal a taxi. But he was beginning to wonder if it would come to that because most of the other guests arrived at the hotel in rental cars that were more of an affront to his professional standards than a clean taxi.

He had to order another drink just to hold his table.

Had the scotch content upped in this one.

Then he saw the best car to come along since he sat down, a gleaming black Porsche Cayman S. True, it retailed for only 65K at the most, and his cut was likely to be little more than ten thousand. But it was a car worth taking, and ten grand was better than nothing. He watched a young, strong-looking blonde guy get out of the car, take a ticket from the valet and head toward the hotel's front entrance.

Boland got up from his table.

The President's Bedroom

McGill wore a navy blazer, a crimson silk tie and ivory linen slacks, all by Ralph Lauren. He didn't have a personal shopper, but on his first case as a private investigator he met Lida Dalman, the general manager of the Bloomingdales store in McLean, Virginia. Facing the demands of not embarrassing the president by making his own fashion choices, he relied on Ms. Dalman for advice on how to dress for any occasion that rose above sleuthing or shooting hoops.

He'd offered to pay Ms. Dalman a consulting fee; she'd said no, he should think of her suggestions as patriotism in action. The way Patti smiled at him when he appeared dressed for dinner that night, it was clear that Lida Dalman had once again done her country proud.

"You are a handsome man, James J. McGill," Patti said.

"Rory Calhoun lookalike," McGill said.

"Come on, Rory. Our guest is on her way up."

The Private Dining Room, White House Residence

McGill was willing to eat just about anything, taking an existential view of food: Even if it didn't please him, it would keep him alive — barring *e. coli* and the like. It was anytime people offered him an unfamiliar drink that he could get his back up. When it came to alcoholic beverages, he was a fundamentalist. Beer, champagne and Irish whisky, each as the occasion demanded, were all he ever required.

When Patti presented aperitifs to Clare and McGill that night, he eyed the reddish liquid in his glass with suspicion.

"And what might this be to people who know more about their intoxicants than I do?"

Both Patti and Clare laughed. The president deferred to her guest.

Clare said, "It's a Dubonnet cocktail."

McGill nodded as if that explained everything.

"Dubonnet being the famous French anesthesiologist," he said.

The two women laughed again, and now they looked at each other, taking notice this time that the pitch and the rhythm of their laughter were eerily similar. Clare had chosen to wear a black dress with spaghetti straps, and her hair was a good six inches longer than Patti's but the two of them were of a height and, without being foolish enough to lower his gaze, McGill knew their figures were … best not thought of at the moment.

Not that McGill had consciously made the comparison before.

Being commander in chief, Patti rescued the moment from awkwardness with a bit of edification. "You're not too far off," she told her husband. "The drink was conceived for a medical reason."

Generous enough to share the moment, and curious enough to want to see just how much she had in common with their guest, Patti turned to Clare to continue the story.

She did, telling McGill, "The French, being French, decided to hold a contest to see who could get their Foreign Legionnaires in North Africa to take their quinine."

McGill put his glass down. He knew the purpose of quinine. "This stuff is *malaria* medicine?"

"Non-prescription," Clare said with a grin.

McGill smiled back, and Patti saw what the attraction between these two had been.

Nonetheless, she had the grace to smile, too.

She picked up McGill's glass, held it up to the light.

"I think it's a striking color, and other than just a pinch of quinine, it's only fortified wine with a bit of spice and a few herbs."

"Okay, okay." McGill grumbled and took the glass back. "I'll take my medicine."

With the impeccable timing of every truly great butler, Blessing arrived before McGill could put the glass to his lips. Dinner, he said, was ready to be served.

That being the case, there was no longer time for an aperitif.

The Royale Hotel, Baltimore

Welborn let himself into his room, thinking it was a good thing he'd taken a change of underwear and socks with him on his trip; his mother had always told him to be prepared for unexpected eventualities. The garments were enclosed in a ziplocked plastic bag; the ones he was currently wearing would be stored in it when he changed. No body odor would be transferred to the other items in his briefcase.

He'd have his shirt and slacks dry cleaned overnight, be presentable when he met —

Damn, he sorted through his case, took out his iPad but didn't see the photocopy of the pig pin he'd taken from the file Rockelle had given to him. He'd intended to show it to Eli Worthington. He'd also planned to Google Worthington and see if he could find a picture of him online. If the man answered his door and tried to claim he was someone else, Welborn would have none of it.

Being a thorough fellow, Welborn had also thought he might find some examples of Worthington's art online. He was hardly an art critic, but he possessed a keen eye and a relatively good mind. If the images online were the kind of art Worthington routinely did, Welborn thought he'd be able to detect if the pig pin had been done by the same hand.

Unless the pin had been done in a deliberately imitative style.

As Warner Brothers had suspected. And Worthington's usual style was cubism.

Welborn didn't consider that likely. People in any line of endeavor invariably worked within their comfort zone. He'd bet Worthington's art would bear detectable similarities to the pig pin.

If only Welborn had remembered to bring the damn pig pin photocopy with him.

He'd emptied the briefcase and it wasn't there. So where the heck had he left it, seen it last? His car. He'd looked at the photocopy just before he'd driven to Baltimore. He'd tucked it in the driver's side visor of the Porsche.

Great. He'd get it and then go to the hotel restaurant and order his steak.

Royale Hotel Parking Structure

Fuck, Boland thought. The damn Porsche was in the very first slot in the parking structure. The one closest to the exit, which was good. But also the one closest to the valet stand, which was bad. He was good at getting into cars without a key, but he wasn't as quick or smooth as someone opening a lock and disarming the security system with a remote control key fob.

Why the hell couldn't the Porsche have been parked on the next level up where he could have worked on it in relative privacy?

The only thing he could do now with a valet nearby was to walk up the ramp and pretend he was one of the cheap bastards who parked his own car and didn't bother with a valet. If he was lucky, he might actually find another car up there worth taking. Not that he was going to hold his breath on that one.

Just about every car he passed had a damn rental company

sticker on it.

Clunkers in waiting.

By comparison, the Porsche was looking better than ever. Out of the corner of his eye, as he turned the corner to the next level, he saw the valet jog out of the parking structure. No one was left to man the stand at the moment. There had to be another guy on duty, Boland thought, but maybe he was taking his break. Talking to his wife or girlfriend on the phone and not paying close attention to the time.

Before he'd even made the conscious decision, Boland sprinted back down the ramp. He knew the security features on a new Porsche: engine immobilizer, wheel locks, alarm, interior monitoring. None of that mattered one little bit if you had the car's key fob. Shielding his face with his hand so the security camera focused on the valet stand wouldn't get a look at him, he grabbed the only Porsche fob on the pegboard.

He pivoted, raising his opposite hand to keep his face covered and ran to the Porsche. He didn't look to see if the valet was about to drive another car into the structure. He didn't want that guy to get a look at him either. He pressed the door-open button, heard a satisfying *clunk* as the locks on the doors disengaged. To his great approval, the fob had a remote engine start. He pressed that button and the sound of the car's 3.4 liter engine firing was music to his ears.

He'd be gone before anybody could ever —

Slam him into the car and press a gun into the base of his skull.

An angry voice yelled in his ear, "Federal officer, asshole. You better not have scratched my car."

With his ire honestly raised, Welborn could play a passable hardass.

Having no intention of going to prison, Boland's hand darted to his own gun.

Maybe the fed would shoot him, maybe he wouldn't.

But if he got to his gun, there was no question what he'd do.

The Private Dining Room, White House Residence

Everyone enjoyed the spicy penne puttanesca with vegan tomato sauce and calamata olives. The entree was a nod to Clare, a vegetarian. Just another thing that had changed from the way McGill remembered it. He recalled Clare as a girl who liked pepperoni pizza, had shared many of them with him, doing her best to make sure she got at least half the pie.

She hadn't tried to keep up with him in washing down the pizza with beer, but she always had a couple, back in the days when brew came in pint cans. Of course, McGill now drank less than a quarter of what he'd consumed in college. Neither his brain cells nor his belt size would tolerate more. So why shouldn't Clare have moderated her diet, too?

No reason at all.

It just wasn't what he remembered.

But Patti had taken the time to find out what Clare would prefer now.

Women. God bless them.

Especially the ones he knew.

McGill chased his last bite of penne with his last sip of Sonoma County Zinfandel. Another red drink, minus the quinine, and one that he had to admit went well with pasta. Continuing the color theme, dessert was raspberry sorbet.

The dinner conversation had been kept light, a mixture of reminiscing and updating, Patti was content to ask the occasional elucidating question, learning things about her husband she'd never known. None of them too shocking, some of them quite funny.

Like McGill and Clare playing an April Fool's joke on DePaul's president, the Reverend Emmett O'Malley. They'd had a mock copy of the *Chicago Tribune* printed up and left it on his desk. The headline read "Vatican Signs Contract with Nabisco to Bake All Eucharistic Hosts in U.S." A subhead added, "Deal with Mogen David to Provide Communion Wine Pending."

Showing he was a guy who could take a joke, O'Malley admitted to the university community he bought the first headline and only caught wise when he read the second.

"We were years ahead of *The Onion*," McGill said.

"Yeah, but we were too scared to keep going," Clare told Patti.

The president understood the subtext. "You mean, no one ever found out the two of you played the prank?"

McGill and Clare looked at each other and laughed.

"What?" Patti asked McGill. "What else did you do?"

"You have to remember," he told her, "kids can be heartless in their humor."

Clare said, "Finding out who had left the phony newspaper on Reverend O'Malley's desk became a campus obsession for the remainder of that spring semester. Students and faculty were all trying to solve the mystery."

"But nobody did?" Patti asked.

McGill told her, "We felt our own pressure. You know, when you're dying to tell someone a secret."

"So Jim figured out a way to relieve that pressure and still keep our secret," Clare said.

"Give," Patti told him, "or I find a new henchman."

McGill held up his hands in placation. "Okay, but remember I said Clare and I were much meaner back then; we're much nicer people now, aren't we?" Clare nodded. "What I did was find out which of the priests on campus was Reverend O'Malley's confessor."

Patti said, "You didn't?"

Both McGill and Clare nodded.

"That *was* mean," Patti said, "telling the one man who couldn't reveal your secret."

Clare admitted, "I've sometimes felt guilty about that."

"Me, too," McGill said. "That's why when I asked Reverend O'Malley to baptize Abbie I told him it was us. Sent word to Monsignor Casey, his confessor, too."

Clare said, "You did?" She smiled. "I'm glad."

"Didn't want either of us to be on the bad side of Saint Peter when the time came."

Patti yielded on red and had champagne served as an after-dinner drink.

The three of them took their drinks standing in front of the room's fireplace.

Patti raised her glass to McGill and Clare. "To old and dear friends, may we ever hold them close."

All three touched glasses and drank. Then both women looked at McGill. It was time to make the choice that had gone unspoken all evening: Who would McGill ask to be Kenny's marrow donor?

He looked at Clare and smiled.

"You don't have to say anything, Jim," she said. "I understand."

He kissed her cheek and turned to his wife.

"I'd be forever grateful if you'd help Kenny."

Patti kissed her husband. "It would be my honor."

She looked at Clare and McGill, a gleam of mischief in her eye.

"What?" McGill asked.

"I was just thinking. It's funny, the two of you keeping that secret so long."

"Funny how?" Clare asked.

Patti said, "Well, if I wasn't able to act as Kenny's donor, I can't imagine anyone I would prefer to you, Clare, and I think Jim would feel the same way."

McGill nodded, waiting to see where his wife was going.

She asked Clare, "You've consented to act as the donor for the young girl who needs the same, well, recipe as Kenny?"

"Yes."

"Maybe I've been in politics too long," the president said, "but I just had an idea, might sound a little devious, but I think it could make both of us feel even better about what we're going to do."

McGill couldn't take the suspense.

"Come on, Patti."

She looked at her husband. "What I thought was, if Clare and I donate at the same time, we let the doctors decide whose marrow goes to which child, and they never tell anyone."

Clare's jaw fell. McGill's surprise was no less evident.

"Why do that?" he asked.

"That way," Patti said, "each of us can think, if we so choose, that we've helped *two* children not just one. It's a gift multiplier."

McGill said, "It's also a way to share credit."

"Yes, it is," Patti said.

Tears welled in Clare's eyes. She threw her arms around Patti.

McGill embraced them both.

Baltimore Central District Police Station

Welborn told the cops the moment the guy started to squirm he knew he had two choices. Put a round into the bastard's skull or put him down without killing him. Using the gun would have been the safer choice. If an SOB was willing to steal someone's car, there was no telling what he might do to avoid taking the rap. On the other hand, the bullet could easily have gone straight through the jerk's head, taking bone, blood and brain with it, and continue gore laden right into Welborn's new car.

Even if the physical detritus was removed, the vibe would still be bad and driving the Porsche would never be fun again. Killing somebody could also blunt the *joie de vivre* of getting married in little more than a day from now.

That was the way Welborn explained things afterward.

As he sat with two BPD detectives in the station on Baltimore Street.

In the hotel parking structure, he'd simply whipped his elbow around, planted it hard on the thief's ear and dropped him like the sack of shit he was. Leaving him where he fell, Welborn called 911 and waited for the local cops, taking the time to get his Air Force OSI credentials out so they'd know he was one of the good guys.

The two patrolmen, who arrived ninety-seven seconds later by Welborn's watch, saw that they had a fed involved in an altercation with a civilian. They called for detectives. The detectives, hearing the fed claim he worked out of the White House, directly for the president, called the district commander, Major Pettigrew. They found him at a rehearsal dinner for his daughter's wedding.

Leaving Welborn to think, *rehearsal dinner?*

He knew he and Kira had been forgetting something.

Then one of the uniforms called out, "Got a gun here."

The cop was looking under the opposite side of the Porsche from where the thief had hit the ground. Welborn could only conclude the gun was what the thief had been reaching for. If the asshole had been a bit quicker or he had been a little slower …

There was a depressing thought.

Detective Greer asked Welborn, "You carry a backup?"

Welborn said, "No, just my duty weapon."

Greer and his partner Beekman had wanted to take that from Welborn.

He'd told them that wasn't going to happen.

As no shots had been fired, they couldn't push the matter.

Beekman asked Welborn, "You hear the gun hit the floor when you dropped this guy?"

"I heard his head hit, but that's all. I was a bit charged up."

"Not so much you didn't just clock him," Greer said.

"No, not that much."

Beekman said, "Maybe we'll get lucky just this once and find the mope's fingerprints on the weapon."

One of the paramedics on the scene brought the guy around. Asked him how many fingers he was holding up. The answer was two, but the guy mumbled, "Can't tell."

"You know your name?"

The guy was still trying to focus his eyes, but he said, "Linley Boland."

He thought about that for second and as he did he became aware of all the hard faces looking down at him. "What'd I say?" he asked.

"Linley Boland," Beekman told him.

"What'd you ask?"

The paramedic said, "Your name."

"That's my stage name."

"You're an actor?" Greer said.

"Yeah."

"Never heard of you," Beekman said. "Anybody else hear of Linley?"

No one had. He said he did dinner theater out west. Vegas once or twice.

That got Welborn's attention. He looked closely at the man. The guy didn't like Welborn's scrutiny at all.

"Real name's …" It took him a second to remember the name on the ID he was carrying. "Stephen Tully. My head hurts something awful. What happened?

The paramedic said the guy needed to get to the emergency room fast; he might have bleeding in his brain. The detectives sent the uniforms with Stephen Tully. Told them to await word as to whether Mr. Tully would be arrested.

Greer and Beekman confirmed with the valet that Welborn had arrived at the hotel with the Porsche, had shown him his Air Force ID and asked that his car be parked where he could leave the premises without delay. The valet identified the Porsche key fob as the one Welborn had given him and told the detectives he'd put the fob up on his pegboard and it had been unattended for no longer than two minutes.

That last detail came haltingly, but the valet knew better than to lie.

With Welborn's permission the two cops opened the Porsche and found his registration card. Ownership of the vehicle and his federal standing earned him a measure of deference, but he'd still had to go to the station and give his statement.

Welborn told the cops about forgetting something in his car just after checking in and going to retrieve it. He declined to say what it was he'd forgotten. As he approached his car, he saw the man calling himself Stephen Tully attempting to steal it. He drew his weapon, grabbed Tully, put his weapon on him and announced his status as a federal officer.

Tully attempted to struggle and Welborn hit him with an elbow to the head.

Then he immediately called 911.

Major Pettigrew arrived, had Welborn repeat his story and asked, "You got a phone number for the president where she'll pick up and verify who you are?"

"I do, but I don't like to bother her. Would you settle for her husband?"

The cops all laughed at that, but the major nodded.

"Yeah, that'll do. I think I'd enjoy talking with that guy."

Welborn made the call and was greatly relieved when James J. McGill answered.

His conversation with the major lasted less than a minute but it satisfied the district commander. Welborn wished the man's daughter well on her upcoming nuptials. The order was given to place Stephen Tully under arrest on suspicion of attempted auto theft.

Tully was arraigned in night court, having regained his wits and sense of balance. Earlier, while waiting for treatment in Maryland General Hospital, his phone rang and the cops let him take the call, listening in, hoping to learn something. They heard Tully say, "Yeah, yeah. Good," and not a word of the other end of the call.

But the news couldn't have been better for Tully.

Teddy Spaneas had just told him two hundred thousand dollars had been deposited in his off-shore account, and he could expect an equal amount for McGill's Chevy.

Tully told the judge he'd been drinking, must've thought he was in the hotel where his Porsche was parked and walked into the wrong parking structure where a terrible mistake happened. The judge asked for the name of his hotel.

Putting a hand to his bandaged head, Tully said, "I'm working on that, your honor."

The judged laughed, but he didn't consider it impossible the man in front of him was telling the truth, not after what he'd seen in twenty years on the bench. And Mr. Tully had no criminal record. Even so, he set bail at twenty-five thousand dollars.

Sometimes the cops got things right. He'd seen that, too.

Tully paid the bail and was released from custody at four a.m.

The Baltimore cops never checked Stephen Tully's *stage name* to see if there was a criminal record attached to it. If they had, and the judge had taken note that Linley Boland had once done time for trespass of a motor vehicle, bail might have been bumped up to fifty thousand. If the crime lab had provided overnight delivery on fingerprint identification — it didn't — Linley Boland's prints would have been connected to the gun found at the scene of the attempted auto theft and he probably wouldn't have gotten bail at all.

And three hours later, when Elspeth Kendry tracked down Welborn Yates and told him Linley Boland had been identified as the man who had killed his friends in Las Vegas, the sonofabitch still would have been locked up.

But things hadn't worked out that way.

And Boland was gone.

Thing Two

Leo opened the door for McGill and Clare Tracy as they approached the backup presidential limo. He nodded to Clare and said, "Ma'am."

She smiled at him and stepped inside.

Before McGill could follow, Deke stepped up and told him, "We'll have your car back early tomorrow."

McGill nodded and entered the limo.

Leo said, "Thank God."

He closed the rear door. The privacy shield was up. A moment later, Thing Two was en route to the Ritz-Carlton. No motorcycle escort, just a black SUV fore and aft. McGill chose to think the Secret Service was protecting Patti's spare ride rather than him.

Clare reached out and took McGill's hand. "Thank you for a

wonderful evening."

"I just wish the circumstances were different," he said. "We shouldn't have let so much time go by."

Clare's expression turned rueful. She released McGill's hand.

"That was my fault and we both know it."

McGill shook his head. "It wasn't anybody's fault."

"That's not what I meant, Jim. I've come to terms with that. I meant afterward. Letting all the years slip away and never calling you. Never even sending a Christmas card."

"I could have reached out," he said.

"But you didn't, because I told you not to, made you promise you wouldn't. If I had known you'd be so relentless about keeping your word, I wouldn't have been so foolish."

Clare looked as if she might say something more but caught herself.

McGill was not about to let anything go unspoken between them at that point.

"Christ, Clare, what could we have to keep secret now?" he asked.

So she told him. "I heard about your divorce from Carolyn a couple of years after it happened. Someone in the alumni network, someone who knew we'd been a couple at school — don't ask me who — told me. No doubt her intent included the thought of rekindling an old flame."

"And your response was?" McGill asked.

"My response was to wonder how my middle-aged heart could still race thinking about you … and then to drag my feet until it was too late."

McGill knew exactly what she meant and sighed. "You were about to call me when you heard I was going to get married again."

Clare nodded.

Thing Two pulled up to the entrance of the Ritz-Carlton. Deke got out to keep the hotel staff away from the presidential limo. Leo opened Clare's door.

"I sure know how to screw things up, don't I?" she asked McGill.

She started to go but McGill caught her hand.

"You're going to save a child's life soon, and it very well might be Kenny's. I'll always be grateful to you for that. And the promise I made about not talking to you? Consider it honored and retired. We're not going to lose touch again."

Clare leaned over and kissed McGill's cheek.

Tears ran down her cheeks as she left the limo.

McGill knew the answer to the question Hugh Collier had declined to pay a million dollars to hear: What had happened to the child he and Clare had conceived? The answer was that Clare lost the baby to eclampsia in her twenty-fourth week of pregnancy. She hadn't been feeling ill, but a routine checkup discovered high blood pressure and protein in her urine; neither had been a part of her medical history.

Both conditions usually resolved themselves within six weeks after delivery.

It had always seemed to McGill that the very fact of Clare learning that her pregnancy might be at risk was what precipitated the horrors that followed: the bleeding, the seizures and the placental abruption — the premature separation of the placenta from the uterus.

The only attempts at comfort that could be provided were that things could have been even worse: Clare might have had a stroke or died. The very thought that he might have lost Clare had scared McGill worse than anything he'd known to that time. For Clare, sinking ever deeper into depression, the thought that she might have perished along with her child began to look like a missed opportunity.

McGill didn't fight it when his family steered him into grief counseling. Clare didn't resist seeking help, but for the first six months her participation in the process was meager. Her first major breakthrough came when she agreed with her therapist that in order to concentrate on her own healing she'd have to let go of the idea that she was responsible for McGill's pain, too.

The only way she could try to do that was by freeing him to go on and have a meaningful life with someone else. She made him promise he wouldn't interfere with either of them being healed by trying to contact her in any way.

He did so, but only because he was sure Clare would soon relent and contact him.

But she hadn't. Not until yesterday.

And now, thanks to Patti's great generosity, Clare was prepared to, might in fact be the one to, save Kenny's life. McGill thought, more than ever, that you had to have faith in a power far greater than yourself. There was no way to explain life otherwise.

He hit the intercom button.

"Take me to the hospital, Leo. I want to see my son."

All the way there, he prayed he wouldn't lose another child.

CHAPTER 5

Friday, August 19th, GWU Hospital Lounge

McGill awoke with an arm around Carolyn's shoulders. That came as a surprise. He didn't remember putting it there. He and his former wife still cared for each other, but more in the manner of the neighborhood chums they'd been growing up rather than the married couple with kids they'd been more recently. Both were comfortable with the adjustment they'd made. So the only explanation could be ...

They'd fallen asleep and reached out to comfort each without even being aware of it? Had done so in a way that once would have been completely unremarkable. The physical support helping them to fight back the dread of possibly losing their son. It was perfectly understandable. But not now that he had his eyes open.

A phone rang and McGill realized that was what had roused him. He didn't think it was his phone at first because the ring-tone wasn't sounding "Hail to the Chief," which signaled a call from Patti or "Take Me Out to the Ballgame," which he heard when any other member of his family, including Sweetie, called.

This was the trill of an old metal clapper, straight out of Ma Bell's attic. McGill gently removed his arm from around his ex-wife, found his phone and clicked the talk button. Still asleep, Carolyn snuggled closer and put an arm around his middle.

Seeing no one else nearby, McGill let it be.

"Hello," he said softly.

"I'm sorry. Did I wake you?"

Galia. She'd had her own ring-tone inserted into his phone without his knowledge.

He wasn't going to get worked up about it now.

"Yes." He saw sunlight coming in through a window. "But it's time I was up anyway."

"You said you'd like to talk with me this morning. I'm calling to ask when that might be so I can plan the rest of my schedule."

McGill looked at his watch. It was 8:01.

"Is nine o'clock okay?"

"I can do that. How much time will you need?"

"Fifteen minutes at the outside."

He knew Galia would appreciate his keeping things short.

He did have another concern, though.

"I'm going to need —"

"These are strange times, Mr. McGill. I'll do whatever I can."

Galia's interruption was preemptive rather than rude, McGill realized. She was protecting Patti, herself and even him from saying something an overzealous news organization, WorldWide News say, might take the trouble to intercept. His phone was supposed to be safe from such things, but hackers kept pushing the envelope.

"Thank you." He added, "How is the president this morning?"

He heard Galia chuckle. "In fighting trim. She's about to make news again, a televised announcement. You might care to watch."

"I will."

"Kenny is … holding his own?" she asked.

"As of late last night, yes."

Carolyn opened her eyes and sat up, as if she'd heard her son's name mentioned.

McGill continued, "I'm certain the doctors would have let Carolyn and me know if there was any change."

"I'll check to be sure," Carolyn whispered to McGill. "Be right back."

McGill nodded. He thanked Galia and told her he'd see her soon.

He turned on the TV the hospital had provided for its visitors. A talking head informed McGill the president would be arriving shortly with what sources had described as a major announcement. A live shot of the East Room, set up for a news conference, showed McGill that the Senate majority leader, John Wexford, and the House minority leader, Marlene Berman, both Democrats, were sitting to the left of the lectern where Patti would speak.

To the right were two empty chairs. McGill assumed the Republican congressional leaders had sent their regrets, insincere though they might be, and would not appear.

Patti appeared as the talking head intoned, "The President of the United States."

But what McGill noticed was the presence of Putnam Shady in the East Room.

Baltimore, Maryland

Welborn found his way back to the well-kept row house of Eli and Nell Worthington. But he was having trouble focusing on the task at hand. Elspeth Kendry had called him little more than half an hour earlier, just as he'd emerged from his morning shower, and given him the news about Linley Boland, a.k.a. Stephen Tully.

Boland had been identified as the man who had tried to steal James J. McGill's Chevy from Leo Levy's garage and the man who was suspected of stealing the car in Las Vegas that had struck and killed Welborn's friends Keith Quinn, Joe Eddy and Tommy Bauer.

The fact that an eyewitness had identified Boland as the auto thief in Las Vegas didn't mean that he'd been behind the wheel when the car had caused the deaths of Welborn's friends and the end of his career as a fighter pilot. Welborn liked to think of himself as a rationalist, someone who eschewed superstition, a guy who didn't see signs and portents in cloud formations or tea leaves, but having Boland go after both Mr. McGill's car and his Porsche ... there had to be some force greater than coincidence at work here.

A force that seemed to be mocking him. Allowing him to arrest that sonofabitch Boland only to have him make bail and disappear. Where had the bastard come up with twenty-five thousand dollars to spring himself? That would bear looking into. In fact, Elspeth was already playing nice with the FBI, arranging to have them and the Secret Service work together on tracking down Boland.

Welborn told her, "Contact the Air Force OSI and get them involved, too. This SOB probably killed three of our pilots. We have a stake in this."

To her credit, she hesitated only for moment.

"I'll get right on it. Captain Yates, I'm really sorry this guy didn't stay locked up."

"Me, too."

Elspeth had tried to reach him sooner, but the bureaucracy, after normal business hours, was stacked against her. It wasn't until Kira arrived at the White House early to make sure her desk was clear before their wedding that Elspeth found someone who both knew and was willing to reveal the number of Welborn's mobile phone.

It was going to be tough for him to push Boland off into a dark corner of his mind and get through his wedding and honeymoon without spoiling both, but he was determined to do so. He'd work the assignment that had brought him to Baltimore, too. Then ...

If he had to, he'd beg the president for permission to join the hunt for Boland.

Welborn rang the doorbell at the Worthingtons' row house.

This time he heard feet shuffling inside the dwelling. A man who looked to be at least eighty years old and no more than five feet tall opened the door. He was a natty gnome wearing black flannel pants, a crisp white shirt, a gray cashmere cardigan and a wine-colored beret. He cocked his head back to look up at Welborn through trifocal glasses.

With an expression of guarded tolerance, he said to Welborn, "Well, at least you're not a Jehovah's Witness or there'd be more of you."

Welborn introduced himself, displayed his identification and took out the photocopy of the pig pin. He handed it to Eli Worthington. The little man gave it a cursory examination and handed it back.

"I remember it. Might still have the original drawing somewhere. The artistry was adequate to the task but far too derivative. I wanted to put my own imprint on it, but that schlockmeister Greenberg said it had to bear a resemblance to its cartoon progenitor."

So Warner Brothers had reason to object, Welborn thought.

"Give Greenberg some credit, though. He did a fair job of fabricating the pin."

"Do you remember who commissioned the work?" Welborn asked.

"Of course, I remember," Worthington said testily. "The only reason I did the drawing rather than pass it along to a student was my admiration for the man. I was present when he picked up the order. I wanted to make sure he was satisfied."

"Was he satisfied?" Welborn asked.

Worthington rolled his eyes. "He loved it, had a real taste for kitsch."

"And the man's name is?"

"I don't suppose there's an artist-client confidentiality privilege."

"There is not," Welborn informed him.

"Well, there certainly ought to be."

"You might raise the issue with your congressman, sir."

"You're a polite young man, I'll give you that."

"Thank you, sir."

"And as you're an investigator, and especially as you've mentioned elected officials, I'll give you a clue rather than bore you with a name."

"Sir?" Welborn asked.

"The man you want, the fellow who commissioned that pin, was so highly regarded at the time I did my drawing for him that he was called 'The Conscience of the Congress.'"

Eli Worthington smirked and closed his door on Welborn.

That was okay. Welborn was sure he could find someone with that nickname.

Worthington wasn't such a pain in the *tuches* after all.

Park Hyatt Hotel, Washington, D.C.

Ellie Booker ditched the guy at the Ristorante Treviso as soon as Hugh Collier had departed. In order not to ruffle any male feathers, Ellie paid the bar tab both the guy and his pal had run up to that point and added two more rounds for them on top of that. The deal was more than enough to satisfy them.

"Call on us anytime you need to pull a fast one," the guy said.

That was almost enough to make Ellie think she might have had a good time with the guy, but she knew better than to take chances with a complete stranger. If he wasn't infected with some virulent STD, he might be looking to launch or extend his career as a serial killer. Things didn't have to be that dramatic, of course, but the chances were pretty good that if a woman offered herself to a guy out of the blue he'd ask her to do something his wife or girlfriend would never consider.

Ellie had someone else in mind with whom to share the comped suite at the Park Hyatt, Dr. Amos Benson. The good doctor was a psychologist who had caused a momentary stir in his professional community by advocating for a change in the point of the professional ethics concerning sexual intimacy. The prevailing standard was the therapist was not to engage in sexual relations with a former patient for at least two years after the cessation of therapy. Amos Benson had wanted that interval to be shortened to six months.

Smelling a good story — a shrink lusting after a vulnerable patient — Ellie went to interview Benson. He declined to speak with her on the record, said she was free to infer what she liked about him, but if she libeled him he'd sic his cousin on her, and his cousin not only had graduated at the top of his law school class but also ate a pound of raw beef for breakfast every morning.

Ellie found the threat both scary and ... strangely appealing.

She wrote him a check worth an hour of his time and said she had issues with vengeance herself. Once somebody got on her bad side, she just had to get even. Proportionately even as a first strike, but then she felt compelled to keep getting in little cheap shots, just to let the other person know she was still angry and never to be crossed again.

She wanted to hit back at almost everyone she'd ever known: her parents, her brother and sister, former schoolmates, people she'd worked with and that prick who delivered her morning newspaper and managed to throw it into any puddle he could find.

Then she asked him, "So, you going to get together with this person who stopped being your patient six months ago?"

"Five-and-a-half months," he said. "And I hadn't made up my mind, but now that I've met you, I think maybe not."

Ellie liked that. She usually scared guys off when she was honest.

"Sure. I'm not your patient. We're just two people talking."

He returned her check on the spot.

"We won't give anyone anything to criticize," he said.

Ellie led Amos down another path altogether. First, she got him a gig as an advice columnist for a men's magazine. That was followed by a pop-psychology book deal and speaking appearances. Within a year, he was making enough money to sell his practice.

Lying in bed with Amos at the Park Hyatt, she asked him, "You know who's making me really mad these days?"

Wondering if she had an edged metal tool under her pillow, he could only hope it wasn't him. "Who?" he asked.

"The president."

"Of the United States?"

"Her," Ellie nodded. She told Amos how the woman had been

thwarting her, unintentionally but so what?

"So she has Secret Service agents with machine guns protecting her," Amos said.

Ellie smiled. "I'm not going to *attack* her, for Christ's sake. Not physically. You've helped me get my impulse control reined in that much."

"Good."

He liked to think of Ellie as excitingly dangerous.

Not crazy dangerous.

He had an idea for her. "Would you like me to study the president for you?"

"What do you mean?" Ellie asked.

"Well, I could watch her television appearances, place her public affect in context with the issues she's discussing. Give you an educated guess what she might do next. Can't say I'd be accurate every time, but maybe I'd be close enough often enough to give you an edge in how you want to cover her."

Ellie looked at him like he'd descended into the room on a cloud.

Riding in a chariot.

A laurel wreath on his head and lightning bolts in his hand.

She said, "That's brilliant! Do it, do it, do it!"

She threw herself on him. The energy he felt pulsing through her was almost overwhelming. He wanted to ask her a question: Did the president remind Ellie of her mother? But he decided to wait until later.

The East Room, the White House

The president greeted the press corps with the smile that had once been found on magazine covers and movie screens. To call it winning would be an understatement. Beguiling was much closer to the mark. Seductive to those who liked to fantasize about being intimate with people beyond their reach. Calculated or even threatening to those whose natures were more suspicious.

"Good morning," Patti said. "I'm speaking to you again today not because I've decided to rescind my decision to leave my former party but because the freedom of being unconstrained by institutional loyalties has allowed me to move forward with priorities I had previously tabled in the hope of finding an opportune moment."

Seated off to one side of the gathered newsies, Putnam Shady began to feel nervous.

Sweetie had been the one that morning to pass the word that the president wanted to see him again. Patti had, in fact, requested that he be present at her news conference. Left to his own devices, Putnam would have found a way to duck out. He could think of no good reason — one that would play to his advantage — for the president to have extended such an invitation to him.

But Sweetie, sensing his reluctance, had assured him she would be nearby.

What was he going to say to that? Okay, but keep your car running.

Even a quick getaway had been precluded once they had arrived at the White House and were told by Galia Mindel that the president wanted to meet with Putnam privately after the newsies were sent off to file their stories. If Putnam hadn't been born in the U.S., he'd have been worried he was going to be deported.

Of course, under Patti Grant's predecessor in office, American citizenship hadn't been sufficient protection to keep some people from being renditioned to countries that were less squeamish than the United States about using enhanced interrogation to make people squeal. And Putnam had admitted to the president he planned to seize control of the country.

The room was air-conditioned but Putnam began to sweat.

He wasn't sure Sweetie could save him if Patti Grant decided to fry his ass.

The president continued, "Over the years I've been in politics, there have been many discussions about how to reform government, but all of us politicians have tiptoed around the one area that has to be reformed before any other reform can be made meaningful.

"What I'm here to discuss today is the need for immediate, substantive and lasting lobbying reform."

Putnam kept his expression impassive.

But he thought: *Oh, shit, here it comes.*

"As long as corporations and other monied interests can buy the cooperation of members of Congress, we will not be a government of, by and for the people. We will remain a government of the people who can finance election campaigns."

Majority leader Wexford and minority leader Berman squirmed in their seats.

"This is not to say that every senator and representative automatically does the bidding of every big contributor on every issue, but the natural instinct to look favorably upon those who advance one's own career will incline office holders to treat kindly, perhaps much too kindly, those benefactors and their interests.

"There is, of course, a counterpoint to being helpful. If a senator or representative displays consistent independence from those who provide campaign funds, why, they'll take their money elsewhere. It will go to primary election opponents. If that fails, it will go to general election opponents. If that fails, in the next election cycle, even more money will go to the independent-minded office holder's new opposition.

"That's to be expected. Money goes where it has purchasing power. Sooner or later, if allowed to do so, it will buy what it desires."

The newsies with audio recorders paid rapt attention.

The pencil press were scribbling furiously to keep up.

"In a short-sighted, flawed and deeply cynical decision, a partisan majority of the Supreme Court has decided that corporations are equivalent to human beings and the money they use to fund election campaigns should be without limits. We can only hope that this wrong-headed decision will be reversed when new justices take their seats.

"In the meantime, however, we must not sit by idly. If flood tides of money are allowed to inundate our political process, we must eliminate its buying power. Doing that by passing strict conflict of interest legislation is imperative to restore the faith of the American people that their government is honest, open and working in *their* best interests."

Patti glanced at and gestured toward Wexford and Berman.

"I invited the leaders of the senate and the house from both parties to join me here today. Senator Wexford and Representative Berman from the Democratic party accepted and I say thank you to them."

Turning back to the press corps, Patti continued, "I also invited Speaker Geiger and Senate Minority Leader O'Donnell to attend, but as you see, their chairs are empty. It would be natural enough for people to think that's because of my recent departure from the Republican party, and undoubtedly that's part of the reason."

Putnam felt a chill run down his spine.

He knew just what the president would say next.

"The other reason Speaker Geiger isn't here is that he has concocted a plan called Super-K. In this case, the K stands for K Street where the big lobbying firms in town have their offices. Speaker Geiger's plan is to consolidate these lobbying firms into a single vast influence machine, to funnel all their lobbying money and efforts through a front man working for him."

Jaws dropped throughout the press corps.

Even the note-takers momentarily stilled.

"Some years ago a similar scheme was hatched. It resulted in members of Congress being convicted of crimes. You would think that would be enough to deter any such future efforts. But in the absence of strict legislation that hasn't been the case. The temptation to concentrate money and power in the hands of a few or even one individual is too great.

"That's why I'm proposing today that legislation be introduced and passed which states that no senator or representative will be allowed to vote for or advocate that other members vote for any bill that favors the interests of any campaign donor. If an elected member of Congress — or the president — accepts campaign donations, there must be no quid pro quo attached or even implied.

"Any member of Congress or president who violates the legislation will be subject to expulsion or impeachment, as the case may be. In that way, we will restore the faith the American people must have in their government. I humbly ask members of both parties to draft detailed legislation, with no loopholes whatsoever, to remove any hint of a conflict of interest from any vote they may take."

In short, Patti was asking Congress to turn its world upside down.

And why in the world would they do that?

Patti said, "I ask the American people to watch closely as their representatives and senators take up my challenge to them. Those who won't advance and vote for strict conflict of interest legislation are clearly wedded to big money, will serve big money and cannot be trusted to advance either their constituents' interests or the national interest.

"Every American voter has the right to expect the candidates they vote for to serve them first. I hope to see a conflict of interest bill on my desk before the end of this year. I will sign it with the whole country watching."

Patti's expression turned hard. "If Congress does not provide me with such a bill for my signature, if it attempts to equivocate and delay, it will go into an election year having to face the American people and explain to them why the present corrupt system is what they prefer.

"Thank you for giving me this opportunity to speak to you today."

There was a moment of complete silence, and then the newsies jumped to their feet and shouted a torrent of questions.

But the president was already on her way out of the room.

And Galia Mindel had taken Putnam Shady by the arm.

The White House

Galia left Putnam with Edwina Byington just outside the Oval Office.

"The president will be with you in just a moment, Mr. Shady. Please have a seat."

Putnam did as he was bade, wondering if this elderly woman with the kind demeanor was one of those characters out of a James Bond movie who would pull an enormous gun on you the minute your back was turned. Farfetched, to be sure, but Putnam's fevered imagination was further stoked by Sweetie's absence and Galia's departure.

It was just him and the old lady.

If he got done in now, no one would ever believe she did it.

Galia would have laughed had she known of the melodrama that was being screened on Putnam's personal Odeon. On the other hand she was about to take the lead in a bit of drama she and the president had rehearsed. It would serve to underscore the president's seriousness about lobbying reform, and it would be both an affront and an outrage to the country's most flagrant influence peddlers.

The chief of staff reentered the East Room, where Press Secretary Aggie Wu had asked the assembled reporters to remain for a moment until Chief of Staff Mindel could speak with them. Galia took the microphone from the president's lectern, but did not address her audience from behind it, tempting though that idea was.

"Thank you for giving me a few more moments of your time. Prior to speaking with you this morning, the president had yet to decide whether to add a further point to her message on lobbying reform. Just now she decided that the additional point should be made, and she asked me to announce it to you.

"The president has decided that in the interest of the appearance of propriety no former member of the House or Senate should be allowed onto the floor of either chamber except on purely ceremonial occasions. Neither should they be allowed to lobby Congress for a period of ten years after they leave office. The president feels far too many former federal legislators have used their public offices as springboards to private wealth. This must come to an end as soon as possible.

"Thank you for waiting so patiently," Galia said. "Oh, and one more thing, Attorney General Jaworsky will have an announcement this afternoon on a related matter. His office's press secretary will provide details about the time and place of the announcement."

She turned her back on the storm of questions shouted at her.

The chief of staff waited until she was out of sight of the assembled media mob before she allowed herself to smile. She had no idea of whether Patricia Darden Grant would be re-elected but, God, they were going to have fun with what was left of her present term of office.

Speaker Geiger, and the Republican Party, in general would be having conniptions about the revelation of the Super-K plan. How on earth could any of them hope to win a seat in next year's election after the public had learned of their intent to sell the government and its policies to the highest bidders? The only hope was to utterly deny the whole scheme.

Of course, if they did that and actually won re-election it would be poison for them to so much as have a drink with a lobbyist. The Democrats would be able to pounce and say, "You see, it's the same old business. Nothing's changed."

Of course, the Democrats played the same game. They hustled lobbying money as hard as they could. They would hate the ban on former members lobbying their successors as much as the Republicans did. But at least some of the Democrats would see where the road to lobbying reform would lead — to publicly financed elections.

The big question for the Democrats would be what should they do now?

If they were smart, they'd beg the president to head their party's ticket. Waiting even a little while would create the possibility that

Patti Grant might continue her history of revolutionizing American politics and form her own party. She would undoubtedly poach several members of the Democrat's caucus, a handful of Republicans, and would recruit a raft of forward-thinking newcomers.

Hardly the party of political daring in recent years, the Democrats would have to act boldly soon or risk being left behind and falling into irrelevance.

Galia looked at her watch. Ten minutes until her meeting with James J. McGill.

She said a brief, silent prayer for the recovery of his son.

Then she took the seat behind her desk and simply savored the moment.

The Oval Office

The old lady didn't gun Putnam down, and he doubted anyone would poison his drink while he talked with the president, but he declined the offer of refreshment anyway. He sat in an arm chair directly opposite Patricia Darden Grant. He'd come pretty far in life for a kid whose parents had abandoned him. If only old Charles and Mona could see him now.

The president was studying him, trying to see what he was made of. Putnam was used to such examinations by now, after having lived in the same building as Margaret Sweeney for three years. She was another great one for trying to plumb the depths of his soul.

Putnam decided to break the ice.

"So, Madam President, any state secrets you'd care to share with me?"

He was glad when she smiled. It made him realize how on edge he was. A president's powers were far from absolute, but she carried one helluva lot of weight, and it really wouldn't be a good idea to get her mad at you. Annual IRS audits might become the focal points of your life.

"Not a one, Mr. Shady," Patti said. "What I do have for you is an apology."

Putnam nodded. He knew right where she was going.

"For telling the world about Super-K, after I told you about it privately."

"Yes. I'm sorry I had to do that."

Putnam said, "You had to?"

The president was honest in her reply. "In an absolute sense, of course not. As a matter of practical politics, it was a necessity."

"To destroy Speaker Geiger's plan, and if you're lucky his career."

"Exactly."

"To give yourself a big leg up on the Republicans, and the Democrats, too, if you plan to go your own way — maybe with your own shiny new political party — when you run for reelection."

Patti directed one of her brighter smiles at Putnam, and for the first time he began to appreciate the power of her personality. He thought it said a lot about James J. McGill that he didn't follow along behind this woman like a puppy with his tongue hanging out. Having somewhat less intestinal fortitude, Putnam asked if he might have a bottle of sparkling water after all. Anything to redirect the force of the president's personality.

The president relayed his request to her secretary and a bottle of Poland Spring appeared on the tray of a Navy mess specialist like he'd been waiting outside the Oval Office all along. Still, the appearance of a third party and the time it took to sip his drink gave Putnam the moment he needed to regain his balance.

"You're a very perceptive fellow, Mr. Shady," the president said.

Putnam nodded. "I'll probably need to be, after Speaker Geiger gets done smearing me in the lobbying community. Of course, seeing as they shoot lobbyists these days, now might be a good time to consider a career change."

"Jim told me about your townhouse being fired on. Do you think you're still in danger?"

Putnam laughed. "Well, there will be millions of Republicans happy to dance on my grave once the word gets out that I spoiled the speaker's grand plan. That's in addition to whoever shot at me before."

"You're relying on Margaret Sweeney for protection?"

"I was. She brought me here, but I haven't seen her lately."

The president said, "She's outside right now, no doubt chatting with Edwina."

Putnam nodded. "So she's in on whatever you have planned for me."

"She's here as a favor to me and my husband. But if you know Margaret at all, you know she would never do anything to harm you or any other innocent person."

It had been a long time since Putnam considered himself an innocent, but it was reassuring to hear Margaret wasn't going to sell him out, any more than she already had.

The president asked, "How do you know I have any plans for you, Mr. Shady?"

Putnam grinned. "Madam President, after you set a guy up, the only thing left to do is bowl him over. That's why I'm here right now."

Patti favored him with another bright smile. That was when he realized physical attractiveness could be used as an anesthetic. He was certain a left cross was about to smack him on the jaw, but he wasn't going to feel much pain because he was so happy about having this beautiful woman smile at him.

It was unfair, but he wouldn't have had it any other way.

"Mr. Shady — Putnam — I think you'll be perfectly safe with Margaret watching over you, and I don't want you to pursue a new career. I want you to continue to be a lobbyist."

"If there's any point in being one after your reforms get passed," Putnam said.

"Things will certainly be different if they do. But ..."

Here it comes, Putnam thought.

"If they don't," the president continued, "I'll want Share-America to succeed."

Putnam looked at her as if he hadn't heard her words right.

"I beg your pardon."

"I mean, Putnam, if my reforms don't succeed, I'll want the American people to be the ones to seize control of their government. And I'll want you to lead that effort."

Ever suspicious, Putnam asked, "You'll back me up? Publicly?"

The president said, "Yes and yes."

Putnam took things one step further. "Of course, doing that might be just the thing to persuade Congress to pass your reforms."

"Indeed it might, Putnam. Are you in?"

What choice did he have?

Kiss up to Derek Geiger and beg forgiveness? No, thank you.

"Madam President," Putnam said, "you've bowled me over."

The Chief of Staff's Office

The first time McGill had dropped by Galia's office, he'd gotten there before she came in, sat in her chair with his feet on her desk and brought her a box of donuts — when he knew she was on a diet. In doing all those things, he'd felt justified. Galia had been mucking around in the business of McGill Investigations, Inc. and boundaries had to be set.

This time, McGill needed Galia's help, and the shoe was on the other foot. Karma. So he thought the least he could do was be on time for their appointment, and he was. The door was open but he gave it a polite knock anyway and stepped inside.

By way of greeting, he said, "Fifteen minutes?"

"A little less with each passing second," Galia replied.

McGill nodded and took a seat.

"I was persuaded to look into the killings of the lobbyists on K Street. Given a choice, I would have left the matter to the Metro cops. That's where it belongs. But with Margaret Sweeney having an interest in Putnam Shady, and now Patti showing her own interest in him —"

"You saw her announcement on lobbying reform?" Galia asked.

"Yes. Saw your postscript, too. Which I assume was something you and Patti rehearsed beforehand."

Galia nodded. She and McGill barely got along; they competed too directly for the president's time and attention ever to be friends. But Galia had come to understand that the president's husband — her henchman, as he'd have it — had a good mind and sound instincts.

"Yes, that was planned."

McGill nodded. "In working with Margaret, Captain Yates, Putnam Shady and Lieutenant Bullard, different theories have been advanced as to who might have the biggest grudge, the best reason to resort to violence, against the lobbyists who've been killed. But I seem to be the only one who thinks the most aggrieved parties are likely to be politicians, members of the House or Senate, who've had their plans thwarted by the lobbying community. Or who are simply old fashioned enough and sufficiently affronted that they object to the so-called fourth branch of government being account-able to no one."

Galia considered McGill's point of view. She nodded.

"Your idea doesn't seem far-fetched to me. I can't stand most of those pricks. The lobbyists, I mean."

McGill smiled. "You didn't do the shootings, did you, Galia?"

She smiled back. "You'd love that, wouldn't you? Solve the case and pack me off to share a cell with Erna Godfrey."

McGill shook his head. "Just teasing. I've come to know how much Patti needs you, especially now."

Galia didn't let the implied compliment win any favor.

"What can I do for you, Mr. McGill?" she asked. She looked at her watch, too, to let him know the clock was still running.

"I'd like to know who, in your opinion, I should look at in the House or Senate as possible lobbyist-killers, assuming there's any-one who might be capable of such a thing."

Galia laughed. "Oh, most of them are capable of it. But the numbers go down, as they usually do, in finding the ones who have the courage of their convictions."

"Yeah," McGill said, "there is that. If you could give me a list by this after—"

Galia held up a hand. She picked up the pen and pad of paper lying on her desk and set to writing. Within two minutes, she'd filled the page, reread the names and underlined three of them. She handed the results to McGill. He was impressed.

More so, when Galia said, "You still have three and a half minutes left if there's anything else."

McGill seized the opportunity. "I was also cajoled into accepting Harlo Geiger as a client in the matter of her divorce against against the speaker. She's looking for any dirt, anything that might bump her settlement numbers."

Galia laughed and shook her head. "This damn town."

"Indeed," McGill said. "With my circumstances being what they are at the moment, I haven't had the time to look for any of the speaker's closeted skeletons. But with Derek Geiger being one of Patti's political enemies, the thought popped into my head you might have gone to the trouble of doing a little oppo research on the man. If you can let me borrow a cup or two, I'd be grateful."

Galia was more impressed than ever by McGill's instincts, and a little sorry she'd made her offer to help. She guarded her dirt like it was gold, which in politics it was. But she had made the offer ... and it wouldn't be a bad thing to have James J. McGill owe her one.

"Of course," she said.

Not going over the fifteen minute limit by so much as a second, Galia filled and handed over another sheet of notepaper.

Longworth House Office Building, Washington, D.C.

White House Counsel Josette Fortier appeared at Speaker Derek Geiger's corner office, not having called ahead to let either the speaker or his minions know she was coming. It would have been the polite thing to do, the politically correct thing, but Geiger hadn't bothered to reply to the president's invitation to attend her announcement earlier that morning; he'd simply left the chair reserved for him empty.

Which suited the president perfectly, but the lack of politesse on Geiger's part showed just how chippy things had gotten. Ms. Fortier, an alumna of Tulane and Duke Law School, introduced herself to Geiger's middle-aged receptionist, Olita Lind.

"Is he in, please?"

As any good lawyer did, Josette asked only questions to which she already knew the answer. Derek Geiger was in; the Secret Service was keeping a discreet eye on him. Why that was, Josette didn't ask and didn't care to learn.

Ms. Lind, a single woman dedicated, in the most moral way, to the man for whom she worked regarded the female from the White House with suspicion.

"The speaker is here, but he's very busy," she said. "What may I tell him is the nature of your business?"

"Carrying out the intent of the Constitution," Josette replied.

"I beg your pardon."

The White House counsel put it in layman's terms. "I'm here on official business."

"What *sort* of official business?" Olita asked, raising an eyebrow.

"If you're privy to all of the speaker's business, I'll be happy to tell you. If you're not cleared for the big stuff ..." Josette shrugged.

Damn haughty woman, Olita thought. She'd have liked to turn this snoot over to Cecil Dexter, the speaker's chief of staff. He was a bulldog who could handle her sort. But he was on vacation in the Greek isles.

"Let me see if the speaker can spare a minute," she said.

"That's all I'll need," Josette said. There were visitors' chairs on which she might have seated herself, but she remained standing in front of Olita's desk. The receptionist buzzed the great man's office and whispered a concise explanation of the situation. The response she received seemed to disappoint her.

"Speaker Geiger will be right out. You can sit down, you know."

"Thank you, but I'll remain on my feet."

Having achieved her goal, though, she gave ground and took

two steps back.

The office suite would have done any corporate titan proud for its square footage and minions bustling about, but Geiger crossed the space, the sea of underlings parting before him, in short order. He looked Josette Fortier up and down with such intense scrutiny that it might have been considered sexual harassment, had she worked for him. Might have gotten his face slapped had he done the same thing in a bar.

"What's your name?" Geiger asked.

Josette introduced herself, using her title.

"What do you want?" he asked in a harsh tone.

Making it plain that she was to speak in front of Ms. Lind, thus to the whole office staff, thus to the news media, thus to the world. Josette Lind found comfort in the fact that Galia Mindel must have thought of that possibility and prepared for it.

She said, "In compliance with Section Three of the Twenty-fifth Amendment to the Constitution of the United States —"

Eyes going wide, Geiger said, "Patricia Grant is making Wyman Mather acting president?"

Josette continued as if she had not been interrupted, "I am transmitting to you this written declaration." She handed an envelope to the speaker. "Vice President Mather Wyman will temporarily assume to powers and duties of office as Acting President."

"When? Why?" Geiger demanded. "For how long?"

Josette refrained from smiling. "That information will be brought to you in an addendum to this notification. Good day to you, Mr. Speaker."

The White House counsel turned and headed for the door.

"Wait a minute, goddamnit!" Geiger yelled. "I want the details."

He could want all he wanted. She didn't work for him, and never would.

When the time came to fill in the blanks, she'd send her deputy.

A graduate of Notre Dame, and a former starting linebacker for its football team.

Hart Senate Office Building

Representative Marlene Berman made it a daily practice to take a thirty-minute power walk every morning before going to work. She maintained her discipline in all but the most extreme weather conditions. On the morning her beloved husband, Henry, had his bypass surgery, she'd walked to the hospital, praying for a successful outcome as furiously as she strode. Having her prayers answered in the affirmative, Marlene later began taking a second, somewhat less vigorous walk with Henry in the evening. In between, three days a week on her lunch hour, she did strength training.

So she had no trouble at all scooting over to John Wexford's office when she got the call. The Senate majority leader greeted her at the door to his office suite with a bottle of sparkling water in hand. They repaired to his office and Marlene needed only a moment to rehydrate and catch her breath before they got to the matter at hand.

"The president called me and gave me the news she's invoking the twenty-fifth," Wexford said.

Marlene slumped in her chair, thinking about that.

"She looked fit and well to me this morning," she said.

"She is. This is about Kenny McGill."

Neither of them had been formally told about the dire situation the president's stepson was facing, but after the call for donors had gone out to the hundreds of workers at the White House, it hadn't been long before word spread throughout official Washington. It was only due to a rare exercise in restraint on the part of the news media that kept the entire world from knowing. Now that the president was making a temporary transfer of her powers to Vice President Wyman, it would become news.

Marlene Berman smiled. "She's going to be his marrow donor. Good for her."

"Very good for her," Wexford said. "As an example of family values, it's hard to beat."

"I was speaking on a personal level, John. I'd do the same for any member of my family, and even for a friend or two. But you're right: This is going to play well with the public."

"Madam President already has a winning issue in her most favored enterprise initiative. The usual business curmudgeons are up in arms, saying it will interfere with making cost-effective decisions, but the man and woman on the street love it. And a flash-poll my people just finished show her ideas on lobbying reform are winners, too."

Marlene Berman's expression turned wry.

"I wasn't planning to move on to lobbying, John, how about you?"

He chuckled. "My son-in-law is something of an engineering genius. He has ideas about building cars that are going to turn the industry upside down. He already has all the venture capital he needs to start up. He's asked me if I'd like to do something productive for a change and help keep the government off his back."

Marlene laughed. "Doesn't like burdensome regulations, does he?"

"He's planning to bring a lot of jobs home to Michigan. He just doesn't want Washington micro-managing him to death. I'm going to help him, Marlene. This will be my last term in office, but please keep that to yourself for the time being."

"I will. On the lobbying matter, I don't think you'll have trouble helping your son-in-law, even if you have to act in an advisory capacity and let someone else do the actual jawboning. Who could argue with using private capital to create jobs?"

"Yeah, but that's just me. We both have colleagues who plan to make fat paychecks doing just what Patti Grant's reforms aim to stop."

"Tough luck," Marlene said. "Getting elected to office doesn't mean you get a license to print money."

"You know that and so do I, but there will be others who will feel different — at the tops of their voices."

She nodded, and Wexford could see her running numbers in her mind.

"What's your count?" he asked.

Meaning how many Democrats in the House would support Patti Grant's reforms.

"A majority of my caucus plus ten percent," she said. "How about you?"

"Close to the same. That won't be enough to pass a bill on the first go-round, but it should be enough to get her to buy in, I think."

Buy into the notion of asking Patti Grant to run for reelection as a Democrat. Wexford and Berman both liked the prospects for their party better with the president on their side than without her. But Marlene saw one big problem.

"Roger Michaelson will never go along. He hates Patti Grant and will fight her all the way. I've heard that he intends to run for our presidential nomination."

John Wexford nodded.

"I've heard that, too. And just before the president phoned me, I got another call." He smiled. "This one was from Michaelson's former chief of staff, Bob Merriman."

Senator Wexford told Representative Berman of Merriman's scheme.

Which left her to say, "The only question to ask, then, is whether we have any other potential candidate who could beat Roger Michaelson, the Republican nominee and a woman who won sixty percent of the vote the first time she ran for the White House."

The two senior Democrats looked at each other and laughed.

They decided then and there to draft Patricia Darden Grant to be the Democratic candidate to be president of the United States. Knowing full well that acceptance would come only on the nominee's terms.

McGill Investigations, Inc.

McGill called Sweetie from his office. The list of officeholders who might take serious umbrage — gunshots — at lobbyists they thought had no business screwing with the people's business lay on his desk. He'd read through the column of names several times. Galia, no doubt showing off, had put them down in alphabetical order. Showing his detachment from politics that didn't directly involve his wife, McGill failed to recognize most of the names.

He didn't watch the political talk shows on TV and found the *Washington Post* to be too much of a company town paper. It existed to tell people more than they ever cared to know about the doings of the federal government. That, of course, was one of the country's most vexing problem. How do you keep the rascals in Washington in check without having to watch them twenty-four seven?

Heck, people wanted their cars to run smoothly, but changing the oil once every *three months* was a hassle. Keeping up with politicians — and lobbyists — every single day just wasn't on America's to-do list. Maybe that was the point of the killings, to draw people's attention to the situation.

Everyone loved true-crime stories.

As long as they weren't emotionally invested in the victims.

Sweetie answered McGill's call, "Mr. Shady's suite, Margaret the nanny speaking."

McGill laughed and said, "Better watch out for that nanny thing. They have dubious reputations in certain circles."

"Kinky," he heard Putnam say in the background.

"See," McGill said.

Sweetie said, "I'd make a comment about obedience and discipline, but that would only play into someone's fantasy life."

McGill felt sure she didn't mean him.

"Will you put the protected witness on the phone, please, Sweetie?"

"For you," he heard her tell Putnam. He came on the line and asked, "You find anything, Mr. McGill?"

"Pursuing my theory." He told Putnam about the list of names Galia had given him and asked whether Putnam agreed with the emphasis Galia placed on the three underlined names. He also wanted to know if anybody on the list stood out from Putnam's POV.

After a beat to think things over, Putnam said, "I have to agree with all the names she gave you, and the ones she stressed. Those guys really have no use for the influence community."

McGill laughed. "With a gift for euphemism like that, you could go into advertising."

"Or politics," Putnam said.

"That, too. Will I have any trouble tracking these guys down, if they're in town?"

"None, whatsoever. I have their office numbers on the Hill and their home addresses in my phone."

There was a meaningful pause on both ends of the call.

McGill broke it. "You have that information because it's at least potentially useful to you, right?"

"Right." Putnam understood McGill's point. "So if I know where they work and live, they might have taken the trouble to find out the same things about me. About us: Erik Torkelson, Bobby Waller, Mark Benjamin and me."

"It's at least a possibility."

"I'm beginning to think more highly of your theory," Putnam said.

"Bat it around with Sweetie. Maybe you'll come up with something I've overlooked. Of the three emphasized possibilities, does any one of them stand out?"

"Not that I can think of," Putnam said.

"Okay, then I'll check them out the way Galia put them down, alphabetically."

Welborn Yates' Office

Welborn was surprised to find Kira sitting behind his desk. He thought she'd be off with her mother somewhere. Having last-minute alterations done on her wedding dress, in case she had lost another half-pound. He liked her just the way she was when they met, but she had felt compelled to lose weight for the wedding. It was starting to worry him. He might have to stuff her with wedding cake.

"All's well on the nuptial front?" he asked, taking one of his guest chairs.

"Now that you're here, yes. You don't plan to run off again, do you?"

"I'll try not to."

"If you leave me standing alone in front of Father Nguyen, I'll hunt you down."

"I'll leave a trail of breadcrumbs." He leaned over his desk and kissed her. "I'll be there. I'm afraid you're stuck with me now, soon-to-be Mrs. Yates."

"Who said I'm taking your name?"

"What you call yourself in public is your business. The way I'll think of you is a settled matter."

"And the children, what will we call them?"

"Huey, Dewey and Louie."

Kira laughed. "You are so lucky I can't stay mad at you."

He'd bet she could if he tried to cut short their honeymoon. Rather than put that idea to a direct test, he told her what had happened in Baltimore. With the Porsche and Linley Boland. Also with Eli Worthington.

For once, Kira, bless her, didn't think of herself or someone trying to make off with her wedding gift to her betrothed. She focused on what mattered most. The apprehension and subsequent disappearance of Linley Boland.

Maybe she wouldn't begrudge him time away, after their honeymoon.

After all, she did just now reveal a vengeful nature.

"You had him, the bastard who hurt you and killed your friends?"

"I did, and now he's gone. But Elspeth Kendry tells me both the Secret Service and the FBI have started to look for him. I suggested the Air Force OSI be added to the mix."

Kira understood what that meant. "You want in."

"I do," Welborn said, "but as you've just reminded me I have another obligation to tend to first." Off Kira's smile, he added, "And we have to get a start on adding a class of cadets to the family."

That surprised Kira. "You want children right away?"

"I want them when the time is right. We'll both know when. But that doesn't mean we can't practice the procurement process."

Kira turned a charming shade of red as her eyes went to the doorway to see if the president or some other grandee was eavesdropping.

"Should I stop talking dirty to you?" Welborn asked.

"No, but you could lower your voice a little."

He asked softly, "Whispering makes it naughtier?"

"Yes, it does."

Welborn mimicked making a note of that point.

"As long as you're here," he told Kira, "might you tell me how I can find out the identity of a former or current member of the legislative branch who is or was called 'The Conscience of the Congress'?"

Kira said, "That would be Representative Zachary Garner, Democrat of Virginia."

Welborn beamed at his fiancée. "And how do you know that?"

"He's a friend of Uncle Mather. He gave me my first pony ride at his horse farm when I was a little girl."

"Oh." Be damn inconvenient if *he* turned out to be the K Street killer.

"Is something the matter?"

Welborn dodged answering directly and asked a question of his own.

"I need to talk with him. Do you know where I might find him?"

"Not today, I don't."

"But thereafter?"

Kira told him, "He'll be one of our wedding guests."

Q Street NW, Washington, D.C.

As far as was known, Mohammed never came to the mountain, but Sir Edbert Bickford, passing through the U.S. capital, came to his nephew Hugh's townhouse. The media mogul's assumption was that a private residence was a better bet not to be bugged than the commercial property of his local news operation — if only because Hugh and the impudent young woman working with him would make sure of it.

Ms. Booker opened the front door for Sir Edbert before he could ring the bell, but he was sure that if the weather had required him to dress warmly she wouldn't have lifted a finger to take his hat or coat. He didn't know whether to fire her or seduce her.

The dilemma tickled him. Doing the former would be foolish; attempting the latter would be futile. This one wouldn't sell herself for cash or the crown jewels. Come to that, she really wasn't his type. Possibly might be, though, if she had the embellishments she'd mentioned the last time they'd met.

"Where's my nephew?" Sir Edbert demanded, staying in character.

"I have him polishing the silver."

The knight of The Most Noble Order of the Garter goggled at Ellie Booker, until he realized she was having him on and then, impudence be damned, he couldn't keep himself from laughing.

"The revolution has come, has it?"

"Not yet," Ellie said, "but the peasants are massing."

She led him to the kitchen where Hugh sat at the table drinking beer and outlining the recent actions taken by Patricia Darden Grant. By looking at the past, Hugh was trying to divine the future. Get a jump on the damn woman for once.

"G'day, Uncle," Hugh said.

"I own this hovel, don't I?" Sir Edbert asked.

"Formerly," Hugh told him. "You sold it to me for a song one day after the housekeeper failed to dust it to your liking."

The nobleman snorted.

"Care for something to drink, Sir Edbert?" Ellie asked, opening the fridge to show him what was available. A bottle of Epic Armageddon caught his eye. He'd never tasted the stuff but he loved the name.

"That one," he said, pointing.

Ellie uncapped the bottle for him and set it on the table, neither inquiring if he'd care to have his beer in a glass nor providing a coaster. She grabbed a bottle of Schweppes tonic water for herself and sat next to Hugh. Solidarity. The toiling class was indeed mobilizing.

Sir Edbert seated himself and said, "So, the two of you, all of your efforts have come to naught. Under other circumstances, I'd have to wonder if you spent all your time and a good deal of my money shagging."

Hugh grinned. "You've found us out, Uncle. I decided to give that opposites-attract idea my best effort, and Ms. Booker was gracious enough to accommodate me."

Ellie faced her employer wearing a Mona Lisa smile.

They had Sir Edbert believing for a moment.

Until Hugh added, "I'm sorry to say that though Ellie is lovely in every regard, for me there's nothing quite as appealing as a hairy arse."

That sentiment caused the gentleman from London to spew his first sip of Epic Armageddon, which he'd been enjoying but would never touch again. Hugh and Ellie roared with laughter.

"You're fired," Sir Edbert said, "both of you."

"Father will be so pleased to learn of your decision," Hugh said.

Ellie looked at Hugh. "We can take all our research to Fox."

Sir Edbert's wattles reddened and shook. "You will do nothing of the sort," he told Ellie. Turning to Hugh, he added, "And bugger your father."

"Uncle," Hugh replied with a smile, "you've come over to my side."

The knight of the realm grabbed Ellie's bottle of water and downed half of it. He glowered at the two younger people. "Have you had all your fun for the moment?"

Hugh looked at Ellie. "Have we?"

"Are we still looking for work?"

They turned to Sir Edbert.

"No, you are not," he said.

They didn't press for a rehiring bonus.

"What have you learned?" Sir Edbert asked. "About James J. McGill."

That was, after all, the original assignment.

"There's no hint of either illegal activity or marital infidelity," Hugh said.

Ellie added, "As far as I can tell there have been only three women in his life, including the president. Each knows about the other two and they all seem to get along."

"Bloody Disney ought to make a movie," Sir Edbert grumbled. "I thought there was something unseemly about this first girlfriend of his."

Hugh said, "Clare Tracy admitted to me that McGill got her pregnant."

"Were they married?"

"No."

"Well, that's a start."

Ellie told Sir Edbert, "There's no record of a live birth with Clare Tracy and James J. McGill as the parents."

"An abortion. That's even better."

"Clare Tracy is still a practicing Catholic," Ellie said. "She receives the church's sacraments. Without being able to learn the details, I discovered that she was hospitalized for three days during her senior year at DePaul University."

"That's when she had the abortion," Sir Edbert said.

Ellie shook her head. "It was a Catholic hospital, St. Joseph's. They don't do abortions. The strong inference is Ms. Tracy suffered a miscarriage and has since relied on her faith to comfort her."

"Where was McGill during all this? Why didn't he comfort her? That would be something we could —"

Hugh shook his head. "If anyone ended things, it was her. If you talked to her you would know that."

Ellie added, "McGill remains close to his ex-wife, Carolyn, even though she initiated the divorce proceedings against him. He's not a quitter."

Sir Edbert clenched his teeth; then his eyes brightened.

"What was the cause of McGill's divorce?"

Ellie said, "The former Mrs. McGill couldn't stop worrying that her husband, then a policeman in Chicago might die a violent death. The city had a rash of such killings in the years preceding the divorce. Her fear was not irrational and the anxiety was eating her up."

Sir Edbert snorted in disgust. A man couldn't be expected to leave his career because he'd married a weak ninny. Even he couldn't make anything of that, wouldn't bother to try.

It was bloody amazing that McGill would continue to have anything to do with the woman. "So we are at a loss," he said.

Hugh shook his head.

He said, "Patricia Grant is doing her level best to turn the order of things in the United States inside out and upside down. Revolutionaries would stand back in amazement watching her."

"What she proposes to do, nephew, is put the likes of us at the back of a very long queue when all the favors are being handed out. Our power, our wealth, our very way of life will be diminished. The woman is a traitor to her class."

Ellie smiled. "They said the same of Franklin Delano Roosevelt."

"And that blighter would still be in office if he'd kept his health," Sir Edbert grumped.

Hugh said, "There are differences, Uncle. Patricia Grant is limited to one more term at the most, and we now have a twenty-four hour news cycle. Let's watch her every single minute of every hour. She's bound to make a mistake and —"

"When she does, we'll pounce!" Sir Edbert said.

Ellie added, "And if it starts to look like she's not prone to pratfalls, we can toss a banana peel or two into her path."

Sir Edbert liked that idea.

He was happy Ellie Booker hadn't left him for Fox.

McGill Investigations, Inc.

Jim McGill placed a call to the Capitol Hill office of Congressman Zachary Garner, Democrat of Virginia.

Before picking up his phone, he had done some secondary source research. He found out, among other things, that Garner had been the youngest of the twenty-one Democrats on the Judiciary Committee to vote to impeach Richard Nixon. Soon thereafter, he gained a seat on the House Committee on Ethics where for decades he gave genteel hell to members of both parties who chose to act unethically or illegally.

He never used harsh language or raised his voice when questioning a member who came before the committee, but he was relentless in batting aside equivocations. He forced attempts at obfuscation to yield to clarity. He denied the use of the passive voice. Things never just happened. He assigned personal responsibility and dared the unfortunate respondent to say otherwise.

Not many did, but more than a few fell prey to memory lapses.

One congressman from California, who was later found guilty of taking kickbacks from defense contractors and sent to prison, was overheard complaining to his defense lawyer, "Who the hell does that guy think he is, the conscience of the Congress?" To which his lawyer answered, "Apparently, he's the closest thing this place has to one."

Garner's picture ran in the next day's *Washington Post*.

The headline: *Conscience of the Congress? Apparently.*

The sobriquet stuck, though Garner never used it to refer to himself.

Political adversaries covered the accolade with sarcasm, but not to Garner's face. He stood six-foot-five and had done a good deal of manual labor on his family farm, including shoeing his own horses. He'd cast a long shadow over anyone who attempted to confront him.

And apparently, McGill thought, Garner had mystical powers that let him steal into Kenny's room without being seen and give his son the strength to rally at least momentarily. Long enough, McGill prayed, for the bone marrow transplant to work its magic.

Please, Lord, save my son, McGill prayed as the phone rang in Garner's office.

The congressman had a suite in the Longworth building, just down the hall from Derek Geiger, if proximate office numbers meant anything.

McGill had felt a jolt when he'd seen Garner's name on the list Galia had given him. Had a hard time keeping the surprise off his face. He'd felt more than a little anxiety that one of the politicians most likely to object to malefactors with gunfire had befriended his sick son.

Garner was a suspect any cop would like: A guy who had been called the Conscience of the Congress wouldn't take kindly to lobbyists taking over the government, and a guy who was dying didn't have anything to lose, except the nickname he'd never acknowledged, by taking down lobbyists in a permanent way.

McGill thought he'd better tell Sweetie about what he'd learned.

The phone in Garner's office rang for a fifth time and McGill was about to hang up when someone finally answered.

"Representative Garner's office, may I help you?"

"Is he in, please?"

"Are you a constituent, sir?"

"No, I'm not. But I would like to talk with him. It's important."

"May I have your name, please?"

"James J. McGill."

There was a brief pause. "*The* James J. McGill?"

"I'm afraid so."

"May I inquire —"

McGill was tempted to invoke Patti's name, bull his way past any underling, but he'd never gone down that path and didn't want to start even now.

He said, "I'd like Congressman Garner's help with an investigation I'm working. I think he might be able to clear up a few things for me. I really can't say more than that."

There was another, longer moment of silence.

"The congressman has told us staffers he really likes your wife's ideas for lobbying reform. He thinks quite highly of the president."

"We have that in common, then."

"Yes, sir. Let me just make a call and see if I can't work something out."

"I'd appreciate that. You know where Congressman Garner is now?"

"Yes, sir. He's on his way to a wake."

"A wake?" The man was dying and he went to a wake? McGill asked, "Whose?"

"His, sir. He planned it quite some time ago."

Number One Observatory Circle

Before he went to be the guest of honor at his own wake, Representative Zachary Garner stopped at Vice President Wyman's official residence. He'd thought he might catch up for a short time with his old friend, Mather, in his East Wing office at the White House, but calling ahead to make sure he wouldn't interrupt anything important, he'd learned the vice president was at the Queen Anne mansion that came with his job.

The helpful young woman he'd talked to at the White House had told him Mather was making sure everything was ready for the wedding of his niece, Ms. Fahey. He'd known about that, of course, had his own invitation. Darling little Kira, all grown up and getting married. Time went by so fast. It had already been... oh dear Lord, it had been twenty years since he'd lost his Vivian.

What surprised Zack Garner even more was how much faster his few remaining days seemed to fly by, and how what had been a firm grasp on his own moral compass seemed to be weakening by the minute. He supposed that was the way things went once you started shooting people. Try as he might, though, he couldn't chastise himself for what he'd done.

He loved his country more than his life. More than his soul, come to that.

He was only mildly disappointed with himself that he quickly thought of a way to use a final personal visit to an old friend to further his murderous goals. His driver stopped at the entrance to the grounds of the U.S. Naval Observatory, the parklike setting for the vice president's house. The security people talked to his driver and then took a look at him.

But he was an expected guest, a well-known public figure, and he had a gift-wrapped package on the seat next to him, a Waterford crystal bowl if they cared to take a look, but they didn't.

They took his word for it when he said, "A wedding gift for the young couple, in the event I'm not able to attend tomorrow."

No one asked him to step out of the car, frisked him or waved a magnetometer up one side of him and down the other. Security tomorrow would be a good deal more thorough. People might not have their private parts manipulated the way they did at airports these days, but the chance of smuggling a gun into the gala affair would be much smaller.

A day in advance of the nuptial, however, smuggling in a gun was just what Zack Garner did when his car was waved forward, and he went to see his old friend Mather Wyman.

Wyman greeted Zack Garner in his home office. The two men embraced, and when they stepped back the vice president had tears in his eyes. He said, "My God, Zack, I'm going to miss you. Any time I've faced an ethical question in this damn business, I've felt comforted just knowing I could pick up a phone and call you."

Garner lowered himself into an arm chair. The vice president sat opposite him.

"Wouldn't surprise me a bit," the congressman said, "if they have cell towers in hell by now. Everybody on their phones talking at the tops of their voices for all eternity."

The vice president laughed.

"If you're among the damned, Zack, there's precious little hope for the rest of us."

Garner shook his head. "You've always been an honest man, Mather."

The vice president blushed. Garner would have had to be dead already to miss it.

"You haven't been honest?" he asked, surprised.

The vice president waved his hand. "I haven't stolen any money. I never sold my vote when I was in the Ohio legislature."

"Well, there you are."

Mather Wyman sighed. "But I've been less than candid with just about everyone who ever trusted me."

Zack Garner leaned forward, peering at his old friend.

"Well, you've been damn clever about it. I don't know anyone who would take you for anything other than what you appear to be."

"You can't always tell by looking," the vice president said.

The congressman sat back. "Sorry, Mather, I'm not up to solving riddles these days."

"How are you at keeping secrets?"

Garner smiled. "Oh, I'm still capable of that."

"Then you'll be only the second person I've told my darkest secret."

The congressman was surprised that he was still able to squirm.

"Maybe you shouldn't," he said.

"Why? You won't blab, will you?"

"No, never. Well, not in my few remaining days anyway."

"Then I have nothing to worry about when I tell you I'm gay."

Zack Garner looked as if he hadn't heard his friend right.

"I'm sorry, what did you say?"

"I said I'm a gay man, always have been."

"But you —"

"I was married? Yes, I was, and I loved my wife more than any-one I've ever known. The thing is, Elvie was gay, too."

Garner's jaw dropped.

"I know," the vice president said. "The way things were, neither of us had much of a sex drive, and both of us were terrified of having our families find out. To protect ourselves, we got married. It really was a grand match in most ways. We were always a comfort to each other, as I'm sure you and Vivian were."

"Yes, of course," Garner said. "But ... but why are you telling me now?"

Mather Wyman told Zack Garner of his plan to run for Congress from his home district in Ohio as an independent and an openly gay man. He didn't mention that he'd soon be the first gay acting president. He would never betray the president's trust on that or any other matter.

Garner smiled in wonder. "That's wonderful, Mather. God, but I wish we might have had the opportunity to serve together."

"We will, old friend, at least in spirit. If I'm lucky enough to be elected and I ever need help in deciding what is the right thing to do, I'll simply ask myself: What would Zack Garner do in this situation?"

Now, tears filled the congressman's eyes. "Please excuse me for a moment, Mather."

Garner made his way to the bathroom off his friend's office.

He took his gun off his ankle and hid it there.

USDOJ Briefing Room, Washington, D.C.

Attorney General Michael Jaworsky stood at the lectern in the Department of Justice's briefing room. He hadn't waited for the newsies to get settled before appearing, as was customary. He had other business concerning both Erna and Burke Godfrey to attend to, but the president had given him this job to handle personally and he wanted to get it done as soon as possible. Standing in front of the crowd, unsmiling, looking as if he might start investigating them if they didn't get their act together quickly, he prompted the reporters and their supporting video and sound people to snap to attention.

"Thank you all for coming. The president has directed me to inform the American people that in the interest of safeguarding the democratic process in the presidential and congressional elections to be held next year and the campaigns leading to that election, the Department of Justice will subject all partisan political activity to unprecedented scrutiny."

That straightened the spines of the reporters in their chairs.

"This should in no way be construed as the president attempting to chill a full and free debate of the issues. It should not be taken as an attempt to seek personal or partisan advantage. It is none of those things."

"Then what the heck is it?" a voice at the back of the room called out.

The attorney general did not respond directly. He stuck to his script.

"The Supreme Court has held that constitutionally there can be no limits on monetary contributions to political campaigns. The court has equated corporations with people and money with speech. The only body that may say otherwise is a future Supreme Court."

Everybody in the room understood what that meant.

They'd just heard the opening salvo in the battle that would occur should Patricia Grant be re-elected and have the opportunity to nominate one or more new justices to the Supreme Court. She would choose legal minds that would undo what the current conservative court had wrought.

The very thought of how much drama that would add to the upcoming presidential debates made every newsie in the room want to jump for joy. But a sense of decorum and the feeling that the attorney general had more red meat to throw their way kept them in their seats and paying rapt attention.

"The infusion of limitless money in the electoral process creates the possibility of the side with the deepest pockets gaining an insurmountable advantage in advancing its messages, causes and candidates. Things may very well turn out to be that way."

The attorney general stared at the gathering to let them know how he felt about the possibility of money trumping all other considerations. He hated it. Being the nation's chief law enforcement official he might want to do something about it. But what?

He told them what.

"We all enjoy a long held and firmly established right to free speech in this country, but that freedom is not without limits. Those limits have also been firmly established. The most simplistic example, of course, is that you may not yell fire in a crowded theater when there is, in fact, no fire. You may not use the shield of free speech to further a criminal conspiracy. Nor may you use the Constitution as a license to commit fraud."

Michael Jaworsky took a sip of water.

He was about to assault two centuries of American political tradition.

"Relevant to the matter of fraud, this department will closely monitor all campaign advertising supporting candidates for federal office, including the presidency, the Senate and the House of Representatives, for intent to defraud the American public. That is, if the Department of Justice finds substantive misrepresentation or distortion of one candidate's views, record or character by another candidate for the purpose of winning an election and personal gain, that is an ill-gotten salary and other material benefits, we will initiate criminal proceedings against that candidate."

"Jesus Christ," a reporter shouted, "you can't outlaw lying in politics!"

Jaworsky cut off any others from taking up the cry. He had another bomb to drop.

"As most political advertising is done through mass media, that is television and radio, this department will look on broadcast outlets that air fraudulent advertisements as co-conspirators. They will be subject to both criminal prosecution and revocation of their broadcasting licenses. Politically fraudulent phone calls will be subject to wire fraud statutes."

Most of the broadcast reporters sat in stunned silence.

But a print reporter in the front row called out, "What about newspapers? You can't tell us what we can report."

The attorney general said, "Talk to your publications' general counsels. Ask them if you can print claims you either know or should know are fraudulent."

"You want us to fact check *ads?*" the same reporter asked.

"You want con artists elected to office?" Jaworsky shot back. "I don't, the president doesn't and I'm sure the American people feel the same way. Thank you all for coming."

The senior reporter present, the most respected media figure in the room, stood up. "If I might ask just a question or two, Mr. Attorney General?"

Jaworsky responded to the man's respectful manner.

"Yes?"

"Will these strictures be applied equally, regardless of party affiliation or lack thereof?"

"They will apply to *all* candidates, incumbents or challengers, running for federal office in the coming election. That includes the president."

"We should take your word for that, sir?"

"You should watch what we do. Vigorously report any inconsistencies or signs of favoritism."

"We're still allowed to do that?" a wiseguy in back called out.

"You're free to do anything but lie or be a party to a lie for personal gain."

"What if the Supreme Court overrules this new policy?"

"On what basis?" Jaworsky asked. "That politicians and would-be politicians have a license to commit fraud when no one else does? I would hate to be the justice to advance that argument to the American people. I don't think they'd buy it for a minute."

With that second barrage at the conservatives on the court, the attorney general left the room, admiring Patricia Grant's courage, hoping it would carry the day.

McGill on the Move

McGill received a call back from the helpful staffer in Representative Zachary Garner's office. He was still at the office, but he'd given her his cell phone number so he wouldn't be tied to his desk. She told him, "The congressman will be at the Praetorian Club for the next two hours or so. The wake is a private affair for friends and colleagues, but he'll leave word to have you admitted to the building and will spare you a few minutes to chat privately."

McGill said, "Thank you." Then he asked the obvious question. "Will members of the congressman's family also be attending the wake?"

There was a pause before the staffer answered. McGill got the feeling he should have known better than to ask such a question. "Mrs. Garner died several years ago and Colonel Thomas Garner, his son, was killed in Iraq in 2005. The congressman has no other family."

"I'm sorry for his losses," McGill said with sincerity.

He heard heartbreak in the staffer's voice. "We're all ... all going to miss him very much." In a more professional tone she gave him the club's address.

McGill said, "Thank you for your help."

The passing of a good man was always to be mourned, he thought, but he couldn't help but also think that Zachary Garner, nearing death, having lost his wife and son, would have no real restraints on his actions. He was looking better and better to McGill as the killer.

And Garner had become a friend to Kenny. Might stop by to see his son again.

McGill would have to see if he could prevent that.

He experienced an epiphany just then. If Garner was responsible for the four killings on K Street and the attempt on Putnam Shady's life, his body-count was higher than Erna Godfrey's, and he was the same stripe of zealot. Worse, if he wasn't done killing and Erna's repentance was sincere.

McGill feared for the future of the country if everyone with a grievance, real or imagined, felt their cause gave them license to take the lives of those on the other side of an issue.

He got up to go when there was a knock at his door and Deke poked his head in. "SAC Crogher is here to see you, if you can spare a moment."

McGill said, "Sure, if he cares to ride with us."

Crogher didn't want to ride with McGill, but he got into the back seat of the Chevy, buffering himself from the bane of his professional existence with the person of Special Agent Elspeth Kendry. Leo, of course, was at the wheel; Deke rode shotgun.

If the SAC had hoped for a private talk, McGill had thwarted him once again.

"Where to, boss?" Leo asked.

"The Praetorian Club." McGill relayed to Leo the address on Massachusetts Avenue he'd been given. "Anybody know anything about this place?"

Only Crogher did and now, to his further annoyance, he found himself answering McGill's question. "It started out as a fraternal organization. Now, it admits both men and women. Members come from the military, federal law enforcement, state and local cops and an occasional civilian. In short, anybody who's sworn an oath or acted on his own initiative to protect and maintain civil order is eligible to be nominated for membership."

McGill nodded. "So these good soldiers have substituted country for the emperor and act as its protectors."

"Yeah," Crogher said, hoping there wouldn't be any more questions but knowing there would be.

"And you know this because you're a member, SAC Crogher?"

Crogher was surprised McGill hadn't addressed him by his first name. To show everyone in the car who the boss was. Using his title displayed a measure of respect. So he tried to get over his grump and show he could be professional, too.

"I was invited, but I don't have the time."

"Thank you for your service, SAC Crogher. I wouldn't want anyone else looking out for the president," McGill said.

Crogher honestly appreciated that, but it didn't keep him from saying, "Other than you, you mean."

McGill smiled. "I mean in addition to me. Would you know anything about Congressman Zachary Garner?"

Crogher had read extensive biographies of every politician, military officer and foreign dignitary who sat down in the Oval Office for a private meeting with the president, the closed door coming between him and Holly G. He remembered the important details of all the bios. Representative Garner had been on his reading list.

"His parents raised horses for a living. He still owns the farm he inherited from them. He graduated from the University of Virginia with a degree in political science. After college, he served in the 82nd Airborne as a lieutenant. He probably would have been sent to Vietnam except he was seriously wounded fighting in the Dominican Republic."

That one brought McGill up short, until he remembered a reading assignment from a long ago history class at Saint Ignatius. "Lyndon Johnson sent troops there. It was right when Vietnam was heating up so nobody paid it much attention."

Crogher leaned forward and looked at McGill.

You just couldn't underestimate this SOB, he thought.

"That's right," Crogher said. "The old dictator who'd been around a long time got bounced. A new president was elected. The old bastard's friends bounced him. There was fighting in the streets and the U.S. ambassador down there thought the Cubans and Russians might try to take advantage of the situation. Turn the place communist. The Marines went in first; the airborne guys were right on their heels. Representative Garner got shot in the right leg. Looked like he might lose it, but he wouldn't let them cut it off. He not only survived, he regained full mobility."

"Strong, determined man," McGill said.

Crogher nodded and sketched the rest of a brief personal

portrait including the deaths of the man's wife and son. "Anything else I can tell you?" he asked.

McGill was certain there was any number of things the SAC would dearly love to tell him, but all he said was, "Sure. Tell me why we have the pleasure of your company."

Crogher looked at the subordinate doing her best not to allow either of her hips to make contact with either of the two men bracketing her. Then he spoke as if she wasn't present.

"Have you had any problems with Special Agent Kendry or her people?"

"Not at all." McGill thought about Crogher's question and his unexpected appearance. "Is anyone looking to do me harm?"

"Not yet," Crogher said

McGill said, "What's that mean? You're expecting a new threat?"

"It's inevitable that sooner or later someone's going to take a run at you."

Crogher had intended to tell McGill that privately, but now he was glad to be on record as having given him the warning in front of three witnesses. The car's driver, Levy, wasn't even one of his people; that was a good thing. He'd be considered impartial.

"But it's more likely you're going to face the renewal of a previously stated threat." Crogher looked for the words to explain himself, the reason he'd come to see McGill. He finally said, "I don't know how much the president shares with you but there's reason to think your threat profile might be rising."

McGill had heard enough to know where Crogher was going. "Erna Godfrey? She's really going to rat out her husband? That whole situation is going to blow up again." When the SAC was slow in responding, McGill asked, "What about my children? Are they going to be threatened again?"

Crogher said, "There's no sign of that; there are no new specific threats against you, but the old ones haven't been rescinded and we have to anticipate possibilities."

"Be ready for anything?"

"Exactly."

Goddamn, McGill thought. You fell in love with and married a woman who got elected president and look what could happen. It wasn't beyond his imagining that some cretin might even go after Kenny in the hospital where he was already fighting for his life.

At home, in Evanston, his kids had their own detail of local cops to keep them safe. Patti picked up the tab for that. But now with Abbie going to school at Georgetown and Caitie and Carolyn here in D.C. …

"You've already made arrangements to take care of my kids and Carolyn, haven't you, SAC Crogher?"

He nodded. "With the president's approval."

"Thank you." McGill turned to Elspeth Kendry. "The special agent here has done an excellent —" A thought popped into McGill's head. "An excellent job. In fact, I'd like her to to do something for me as soon as I go into the Praetorian Club."

Suspicion narrowed Crogher's eyes. He was certain that McGill had already subverted Deke Ky; he didn't want Elspeth Kendry to fall under the man's spell. McGill could see just what Crogher was thinking.

"Don't worry, SAC Crogher," he said. "I'm not going to mess with your chain of command."

"Yes, you are," Crogher said.

Elspeth Kendry's eyes tracked the conversation as if it were a tennis match.

"Okay, I am, but all for a good cause."

"The Secret Service is not a day labor service for your investigations, Mr. McGill," Crogher said.

"I never thought it was, but this particular job?"

Leo pulled the car to the curb in front of the Praetorian Club.

"Yes?" Crogher said.

"It comes with a presidential seal of approval," McGill said.

Celsus Crogher wanted to curse McGill aloud.

But there were all those witnesses present.

The Four Seasons Hotel, Washington, D.C.

Margaret Sweeney sat in an arm chair in the bedroom of Putnam Shady's suite at the luxury hotel. She was draped in a spare blanket taken from a closet. She didn't long for a cigarette, wouldn't have smoked if one had been available. But she wondered what the appropriate thing to do was after having sex for the first time since she was a teenager.

She might have asked Putnam, but he was still sleeping. He hadn't taken her virginity, but with the three rounds they'd gone since his meeting with the president that morning he'd doubled her sexual experience. It had all started with a simple conversation. She'd reassured him that she was truly on his side. To affirm that fact she'd taken his hands in hers and looked straight into his eyes.

Only this time they'd each seen something new. Something not to be denied.

She'd been very tentative at first and he'd been very patient. Funny, too, in a gentle way, acting as if he were the one who was new to all this, asking her for pointers. Wanting to know if he was doing things right. He'd gotten her to laugh and then relax, and nature took its course.

Nature was pretty spectacular, too. Things became more heated and vigorous. Putnam had long joked about having her spank him and while things didn't reach that specific point there were several moments when the role of the superior officer shifted between them. She had found she liked playing both parts.

She had enjoyed the whole experience. Didn't feel the least need to go to confession; didn't see anything they had done as rising to the level of a sin. Yet another divergence with the views of Mother Church for her. Good thing she'd had earlier differences of opinion or she might have felt guilty about something she thought was entirely wonderful.

In fact, she considered her intimacy with Putnam Shady as a perfect example of the Lord working in mysterious ways. If she'd never answered his apartment-for-rent ad, they would never have wound up where they were. She would never have taken the time to come to know him if they hadn't lived cheek to jowl for the last three years. He never would have found the depth of character he now had if she hadn't been there to influence him.

But what was the reason for such an unlikely pairing?

She looked within her soul for an answer, but the Lord wasn't forthcoming.

That was okay. The here and now was fine with her. She was looking forward to further sharing, both personally and physically. She only had to figure out what to do if she kept waking up before he did. Didn't seem like an appropriate time to say her rosary.

But if Putnam woke up more than a time or two and saw her staring at him he might think she was —

A knock at the door to the suite ended her reverie.

A loud, door-rattling knock.

Not the hotel staff, unless the place was on fire.

Putnam stirred and muttered, "What the hell was that?"

Sweetie realized by now it was a threat of some sort.

The knock came again, louder than before.

"Lock yourself in the bathroom," she told him. "Call hotel security."

There was no question who was in charge now, and Putnam did as he was told. Sweetie grabbed her Beretta off the night stand and still shrouded in the blanket entered the suite's living room and advanced toward the door, but avoided standing directly in line with it.

You never knew when someone might stop knocking and start shooting.

"Who's there?" she called out in her best cop voice.

"Metro police," came the response in the same tone.

"Identify yourself by name, rank and badge number," Sweetie said.

She heard the voice say, "Sonofabitch!" Then it added, "Who the hell are *you*, lady?"

"Margaret Sweeney. Formerly of the Chicago and Winnetka,

Illinois police departments. Currently a private investigator."

"You armed?" the voice outside the suite asked.

Sweetie said, "Yes," and moved to the opposite side of the door.

"Sonofabitch," the voice repeated. "We've got orders to bring in Mister Putnam Shady. Suspicion of murder."

"Still haven't told me who you are." Sweetie moved back to her original position.

"I'm Detective Marvin Meeker. I'm with my partner Detective Michael Walker."

"You know Lieutenant Rockelle Bullard?"

"*Sonofabitch*," Meeker said yet again.

A new voice said, "She's our boss, the one who sent us."

Sweetie sighed. "Okay, here's how we'll do this. I'll call Lieutenant Bullard. If she verifies sending you, Mr. Shady will call his lawyer. As soon as he arrives, I'll open the door."

Meeker said, "We're the police, lady. Here to make an arrest. We're the ones decide how this thing goes."

Sweetie replied, "Everything's been peaceful so far. Be a shame to change that."

She didn't get an argument on that point.

The Praetorian Club

The woman who served as the club's receptionist was attractive but severely groomed and her blouse and maybe even her skirt looked like it had come back from the dry cleaner with plenty of starch.

"Marine Corps?" McGill asked.

"Army. Drill sergeant. Retired."

"Bet you haven't lost a step," McGill said.

"No, sir. Not even half a step."

McGill gave his name and said he was there to see Representative Garner.

"Yes, sir. He left word. Please come with me."

McGill was impressed that the receptionist had been provided with the necessary information, made him think the Praetorian Club was on the ball about maintaining its security. He wouldn't have been surprised if the receptionist had been given a picture of him, maybe even a bio. If so, she was one of the few people he'd met who wasn't impressed after learning he was married to the president.

The receptionist led him to a wood paneled room off the entryway. It had an oil portrait of Omar Bradley hanging on one wall. McGill liked that. The man had been the last five-star general in the U.S. Army. Despite his preeminent rank, he'd been known as "the G.I.'s General" for his civility to soldiers of all ranks.

The receptionist saw McGill looking at the painting.

"You know who that is?" she asked.

The portrait's frame offered no inscribed identification of its subject.

McGill still answered the pop quiz question correctly.

"My grandfather talked about him," he explained.

The receptionist nodded. "Did you serve?"

"Not in the military. I spent most of my adult life as a cop."

Not the same thing, but good enough for the woman.

"Representative Garner will be with you shortly."

She left McGill alone. There were four leather arm chairs in which he might have seated himself. Instead, he walked over to a pair of windows looking out on Massachusetts Avenue. His Chevy was gone, but he was sure Leo had it parked with a clear view of the club's front entrance so he could pull up when he saw McGill exit the building.

Deke had wanted to enter the premises with him but McGill had said no.

So he'd be positioned somewhere outside, too, even closer than Leo.

The person McGill was most interested in was Elspeth Kendry — her and any of the agents working under her. McGill had asked Elspeth to set up a photo shoot. Specifically, he wanted pictures that could be used to identify anyone who entered or exited the

Praetorian Club while Zachary Garner was on the premises and for an hour afterward.

Elspeth hadn't had a camera with her in the Chevy, but the Secret Service kept photographic equipment nearby most if not all of the time. They shot pictures far more often than they shot bad guys. She had assured him she wouldn't have any problem laying her hands on several cameras in short order.

Celsus Crogher had known better than to debate the matter, but no doubt he was already questioning the wisdom of supplementing McGill's security detail. Out on the street, all of the pedestrian and vehicular traffic looked perfectly normal. The Secret Service when need be was adept at living up to the first half of its name.

The door to the room opened and McGill turned around.

"Representative Garner," he said.

The man was tall, McGill saw, and unbowed by either age or his disease, but what once must have been an athletic frame had been stripped of most of its mass. Garner's suit hung on him. He still managed to give McGill a smile of welcome that seemed genuine.

Garner said, "Mr. McGill, a pleasure to finally meet the president's henchman." The two men shook hands and Garner gestured McGill to a pair of facing chairs. "I'm not up to standing for prolonged periods anymore, don't know how much longer I'll be able to sit upright either."

McGill took his seat. He watched as Garner lowered himself. It was an exercise in closely considered movement, nothing taken for granted, accomplished by mental effort as much as physical strength. Having achieved his goal, Garner nodded in satisfaction. He was still mobile within limits.

"Now, what can I do for you, sir?" he asked McGill.

"I'm trying to get some insight into the thinking of a serial killer," McGill said, deciding at that moment how he would approach the conversation.

Garner's smile returned, this time showing amusement.

"And you came to me? Why?"

"Well, this particular killer is doing in lobbyists."

Garner nodded, possibly in approval, but he didn't say anything more.

McGill continued, "I've been looking into the matter, and people who know a thing or two about lobbyists tell me that the most likely culprit will turn out to be another lobbyist. Someone whose plans have been frustrated by a colleague representing opposing interests."

"That's certainly a plausible notion," Garner said.

"I considered it to be a possibility, but it didn't hold up for me."

"Why not?" the congressman asked.

"Well ... if you look at white-collar disputes in general, they can get heated, but they rarely result in bloodshed. At least compared to crimes of passion."

"Acts of marital infidelity?" Garner asked.

"Those certainly, but even relatively minor disputes such as bar fights. When disagreements are rooted in emotional contexts, that's when you get physical mayhem."

Garner said, "Losing a professional confrontation can get quite emotional, believe me."

McGill studied the congressman, as if the man had just confirmed something for him.

"I do believe that. If this situation had involved a single homicide, I could see one professional taking out his rage on another. But it doesn't work for me with serial murders."

"Why not?" Garner asked.

"Well, if a lobbyist lost one major battle, his firm might let it slide. After all, nobody's perfect. But if he followed a first loss with a second, I think he'd be out on his ear. Nobody likes to have a loser hanging around. It's bad for morale. Worse, it's bad for the big boss's career. If a two-time loser makes it three in a row, his head won't be the only one to roll."

"Very canny, Mr. McGill. I find that position hard to rebut."

"That's why I can't see a lobbyist killing more than two professional foes. He wouldn't be employed long enough to kill three or four."

"Maybe you should be looking for more than one killer."

McGill said, "That thought has occurred to me. Or maybe a killer and a copycat. But you know about Occam's Razor, I'm sure."

"The simplest explanation is likely the correct one."

"Exactly," McGill said. "Simple in this case is one killer. But not a lobbyist."

"Who does that leave?" Garner asked, his face impassive.

"My instinct all along has said it's a politician. Maybe that's because I'm from Chicago where politics can be a blood sport, but that's what I think. I think it's someone who worked hard to get elected the first time and then did his best for his constituents. I see someone who had his best efforts thwarted time and again by the water-carriers of moneyed interests. Someone who resents not only that an unaccountable fourth branch of government exists at all, but has personal grievances with the bastards for laying waste to genuine hard work to help his people and his country."

Garner steepled his hands under his chin.

Made McGill wonder what he might be praying for.

"That's entirely possible. Do you know anything about my background?" Garner asked.

"Only a few details. I've heard about your military service, how you were wounded."

"That's what I was hoping you'd know. Not about what happened to me as much as what happened to the Dominican Republic."

"I know that President Johnson sent in the troops, thinking the Cubans might take over if he didn't."

"The communists were certainly the bogeymen in those days and often justifiably so, but the situation in the D.R. was different. The dictator, Rafael Trujillo, was assassinated. Instead of being replaced by another of his ilk, a man named Juan Bosch was freely elected as president. A constitution was written that guaranteed the rights of the individual, that asserted civilian control over the military. Initiatives for land reform were begun. People who had never had a place to call their own or a voice in government were being recognized for the first time."

McGill remembered what Crogher had told him.

"But that didn't last. The other side fought back."

"They did, and the country's seven-month flirtation with democracy was over. The military, the big land holders and even the church didn't like the new government because it threatened their privileged positions. They called Juan Bosch and the new government communists. Fighting broke out, a civil war on a small scale. The U.S. military was called in and I was almost killed.

"Being a fellow with a sense of curiosity, I wanted to learn why I got shot. So I read everything I could find about the situation in the Dominican Republic. What I learned sickened me. The American government didn't support a democratically elected government; it backed one of Trujillo's puppets, a fellow named Joaquin Balaguer, in the election that followed the cease-fire. With the big money and the big guns behind him, Balaguer won. Authoritarian government was restored, positions of power were preserved and the people of the D.R. remained poor and disenfranchised."

McGill knew what Garner was getting at but he wanted to hear it in the man's own words. So he asked, "What's all that got to do with lobbyists getting killed?"

A weary smiled formed on the congressman's lips. "I could draw parallels to the growing concentration of wealth in this country and the attempts to suppress the votes of people who don't respect the perquisites of the wealthy and powerful, but my time is short, so let's boil things down to one simple question: Who do you think the lobbyists in this town would be working for back in the day in the D.R.?"

That pretty much told McGill what he wanted to know.

Part of it anyway. The rest he'd have to find out for himself.

He got to his feet and said, "Thank you for sparing me the time, Congressman."

He extended his hand to Garner. The congressman tried to rise to take it, but for the moment his strength was waning. He sank back into his chair and muttered, "Damn."

"May I give you a hand?" McGill asked.

"Yes, please."

McGill helped Garner to his feet. The effort wasn't difficult. As he'd suspected, much of the man had already wasted away. There was little more left of him than flesh, bones and an iron will.

Standing erect, Garner leaned in close to McGill and whispered, "I don't bother praying for myself anymore, but if there is a hereafter I'll do what I can to put in a good word for your son. Kenny is quite the young man."

McGill said the only thing he could think of: "Thank you."

He knew it would have been a mistake to go hard at Garner. You couldn't scare a man who was dying and had no family. Without incriminating himself, Garner's history lesson and the parallels he'd drawn between the Dominican Republic and the contemporary U.S. had been an implicit admission of ... the fact he was no longer fighting on the wrong side.

Still didn't give him the right to take people's lives.

He had the prominence to command public attention. He could have made a public but peaceful fight over the matter of government corruption. He should have —

McGill wondered if Garner's disease or his medication had affected his thinking.

Absolving him would be a neat rationalization. The way things were going there'd be no reason to perform an autopsy on the congressman, to learn if a physical defect had produced a moral one. Without such a medical determination, McGill would have a hard time extending the man a presumption of innocence.

Despite all that, it was hard not to like the man ... and now that he thought of it, to look more closely at him. Maybe Occam's Razor didn't apply in this case, after all.

Garner extended his hand to McGill and he shook it.

The receptionist entered the room and helped Garner back to his wake, which was seeming more appropriate with each passing minute.

McGill showed himself out. Leo pulled up a moment later. Deke opened the rear door of the Chevy for him. Settling into the back seat, he told Leo, "Take me to see my son."

B Street SE, Washington, D.C.

Derek Geiger had decided that it would be politically unwise to continue to stay at the presidential suite at the Hay-Adams. It might send the unintended message that he intended to run for the presidency next year when he had no such ambition. He didn't want any of his GOP colleagues who did intend to run to get that idea and start throwing darts at him. He also didn't want anyone to get the idea he was freeloading off of party resources either. That misperception wouldn't endear him to the party at large or to the good people of his district.

He was hardly an orphan of the storm; he could have afforded to pay for his own suite at the Hay-Adams or any other top hotel in the District, but having held public office for more than twenty-five years and having been speaker for five of those years, he'd come to feel entitled to the largesse of others. Having to dip into your own pocket, well, there was a word for people like that: taxpayers.

Geiger had thought of that little joke not long after his first election, but he'd never shared it with anyone. It was enough that the jest could make him smile when he needed a moment of uplift. He was sure someone would come to his aid and, sure enough, through the good offices of RNC chairman Reynard Dix he heard from the Brotherhood, a religious foundation that owned a large red brick townhouse on B Street and offered large comfortable rooms at nominal rents to public servants of good character.

Geiger was told the nicest two-room suite on the top floor had just come available. He was more than welcome to take shelter under the Brotherhood's roof. He accepted immediately, not even bothering to dicker about knocking the rent down to zero. He could have gotten some big-hearted donor back home in Florida to cough up the rent money, but he'd always been careful never to look as if he were directly profiting from his political office. Paying the small sum the Brotherhood asked of him would put him on a par with the other residents. He saw the expenditure not as rent but as an insurance premium to protect his reputation.

A conservatively dressed, well barbered young man met his car at the curb, carried his bags inside and showed him to his new quarters. The Brotherhood, praise the Lord, did not eschew the use of alcohol. A bottle of his favorite scotch and two crystal tumblers awaited him as a welcoming gift.

Geiger tried to tip the young man, but his gesture was politely declined.

"Thank you, Mr. Speaker," he said, "but if you'd like to make an offering to our ministry that would please me so much more."

Geiger said, "I'll do that very thing. Can you tell me where the collection box is?"

The young man smiled. "It's in the kitchen. It looks like a great big cookie jar. There's a slot in the top. Snacks are available in the kitchen twenty-four hours a day."

Feed your sweet tooth, feed the kitty, Geiger thought.

Smart. Who could criticize contributions to the Brotherhood?

He looked at the phone, a landline in the sitting room. "Is that direct dial or is there an operator?"

The young man understood what he was being asked. "It's direct dial, sir. All our phones are. That way our guests can be assured of their privacy."

Barring a wiretap, Geiger thought. Still, who knew he was there?

He asked, "No one has passed the word I'll be staying here?"

"No one from the Brotherhood, Mr. Speaker. If you haven't let anyone know, your presence here will be your secret, until you meet the other residents of the house. Whether they might speak of seeing you here I can't say."

That was something to consider, Geiger thought.

"You don't make space available to Democrats, do you?"

The young man had to repress a laugh. He said, "No, sir, we don't."

The speaker liked that. He was sure he could keep any members of his own party from revealing his whereabouts. Reynard Dix knew better than to talk. Not that Geiger knew secrecy would be important.

He just thought it was a good idea to keep as low a profile as possible.

Seeing as he was planning to have that treacherous bastard Putnam Shady killed.

GWU Hospital

McGill noticed first thing that Kenny now had some sort of intravenous line entering his neck. The sight would have made his heart sink if his son hadn't smiled upon seeing him and given him a thumb's-up. Such a display of courage, McGill decided, would have to be returned in kind. By force of will more than anything else, McGill offered a smile and made a fist and held it high.

Be strong.

Kenny mirrored his father and it took all the restraint McGill could muster not to show any fear. He took his notebook out and quickly wrote a message in block letters. ZACK GARNER SENDS BEST WISHES. He held it up to the window of his son's isolation room.

Kenny had to squint a bit to make out the words but once he did he raised his fist again. With any luck, McGill thought, Kenny would never learn what Garner had done. In the meanwhile, McGill would use any means available to rally his son's spirits.

The gowned and masked doctor and nurse in the room nodded to McGill and drew a curtain across the window. They were about to do something that might upset the family. That might in turn upset the patient, and nobody wanted that.

McGill turned to look at Carolyn who had been standing just behind his right shoulder. He saw the brave face she had put on crumple and tears fell from her eyes. McGill embraced her, stroking her hair, hoping to confer a sense of comfort he didn't feel. He walked his ex-wife to the lounge at the end of the corridor.

They sat side by side. Carolyn made no lamentation. There were other patients and family members on the floor to consider. Nobody needed to be reminded of the dire situations facing the patients there. She just cried silently until the energy behind her fear momentarily flagged. McGill did everything he could to keep his own emotions in check.

"What did you write?" Carolyn asked. "What did you show Kenny?"

McGill let her see the message.

"He's the man Kenny thought was in his room?" Carolyn asked.

"Yes."

"You spoke with him?"

"I did. He's dying; doesn't have much longer. What he told me was he would plead Kenny's case to Saint Peter."

That almost broke Carolyn up again, but she got a grip on herself.

"He'll do that before he explains his own life?" she asked.

"That's what he said." McGill wasn't about to tell Carolyn what Garner had done.

Carolyn nodded. She, too, would take help wherever it might be found.

"What's with the line going into Kenny's neck?" McGill asked.

Carolyn did her best to compose herself, to be informative.

"It's called a central line, a venous catheter. It's used to administer the drugs Kenny has to have before the BMT."

McGill, given his work background, had long had to decipher acronyms.

"Bone marrow transplant?"

"Yes. The central line eliminates the necessity of separate needle sticks each time Kenny gets an IV drug. They have to be very careful to keep the line clean so it doesn't become a source of infection."

"Jesus," McGill said before he could catch himself.

Carolyn took his hand, "Yeah, everything has to go just right because they're going to use that same line to infuse the donated marrow cells."

McGill took a moment to say a silent prayer.

Carolyn wasn't done giving him reasons to worry.

She said, "Jim, even if the whole procedure goes according to plan, the possible side effects of the chemo drugs include liver, lung and heart damage."

McGill squeezed his eyelids shuts but tears seeped out anyway.

Carolyn put an arm around him and whispered into his ear: "Remember, Kenny's one of the lucky ones. He has a donor. Other kids don't even get that far."

Q Street NW, Washington, D.C.

"That woman means to do us in entirely," Sir Edbert Bickford said.

The media mogul usually stayed in the best suites in the most expensive hotels, but as a boy he'd worked doing farm chores on family land. He could still rough it if he had to, not that moving into his nephew's guest room with its fifteen hundred thread count Egyptian cotton bed linens was exactly a hardship.

Sir Edbert, Hugh and Ellie were mulling the attorney general's announcement regarding the jeopardy in which broadcasters airing deceptive political ads would find themselves: being charged as criminal co-conspirators and losing their FCC licenses.

In a nutshell: going to prison and going broke.

If he weren't the target of the draconian measures, Sir Edbert would have admired the president's ruthlessness. Outside of royal and noble families who had lived in more robust times, you rarely saw a woman willing to be so merciless with her enemies.

As if she were reading his mind, Ellie Booker picked up on that very point.

"Maybe she means to do that more specifically than we think," she said.

Both Sir Edbert and Hugh looked at her, inquiring minds wanting to know.

"Meaning what?" Hugh said.

Ellie said, "Look at the spectrum of the media in this country that would ordinarily give Patricia Darden Grant the hardest time, politically and otherwise. Fox and us. Fox is having serious trouble in the UK, and the Justice Department is making rumblings of starting investigations of them here. So they're hardly in fighting trim. That leaves us."

Ellie paused to get three bottles of beer from the fridge: Little Creatures.

Her favorite. She opened them and set them out. Took a swig from her bottle.

"If Fox sinks of its own troubles, and Patti Grant does in WorldWide News, she'll not only have an easier time getting re-elected, she'll have clear sailing advancing her agenda in a second term. The hard right would have no champion to slam her ideas, her character."

Hugh said, "You're forgetting talk radio."

Ellie shook her head. "Jungle drums. A medium for true primitives. Standing alone, talk radio's power would be greatly diminished, and that's if the companies that own those stations have the nerve to maintain their hard right stances after we've been done in, as Sir Edbert has so succinctly put it."

Ellie took another pull on her beer.

"I think Patti Grant means to go after every broadcaster who dares to challenge her new edicts, but my money says she'll be gunning for us above all others. She nails WorldWide News, she's won the war. Come to that, she gets us to knuckle under, she wins."

Sir Edbert asked, "Shall we steal some tin cups and stake claims to the street corners where we'll do our begging?"

Hugh smiled. It was rare to hear Uncle make a joke — if he was joking.

Ellie said, "That or we find a way to hit the president hard before she can make her new policy accepted wisdom."

"Something tells me you're planning a counterattack right now," Hugh said.

"Mulling one over," Ellie admitted.

"Tell us," Sir Edbert ordered.

"There's not a hint of scandal in the president's life. As a young woman working in both modeling and acting she displayed a restraint mature beyond her years. She never overindulged in alcohol, never used illegal drugs. She was never sexually profligate. She didn't fritter away the large sums of money she earned. She married well the first time — to Andrew Hudson Grant — and cultivated a public image that allowed her to enter politics so successfully she's now president.

"The great tragedy of her life was Andy Grant's murder. The quick apprehension of the killers must have been some comfort, and it led to her second marriage with James J. McGill. Even when she experiences heartbreak, this woman comes out of it, if not ahead of where she was, at least equal to her previous standing."

"We know all this," Sir Edbert said. "It gets us nowhere."

Hugh took a hit of his beer and smiled. He sensed what was coming.

"Patience, Uncle. I believe Ellie is just getting started."

Ellie nodded. "I am. I believe the president has gotten a pass on critical scrutiny most if not all of her life. What were things like growing up for her? How did she get along with her parents? How did she do in school? Did she ever cheat on an exam? Did she have some sort of preferential admission to Yale? Was the only powder applied to her model's nose pancake make-up, really? Did she sleep with any producer or studio executive to get a movie part? How did she meet Andy Grant? Did he do anything crooked to make his pile of money? Is the philanthropic foundation he started being operated on the up and up? Did James J. McGill have any inside help to solve Andy Grant's murder so damn quickly? Did any traitors in the pro-life movement help him? Was everything about the arrest and trial of Erna Godfrey handled properly? Was Erna Godfrey coerced into making her recent statements implicating her husband and other unnamed pro-life figures?"

Ellie took a breath and smiled.

"Doubtless you gentlemen can come up with questions of your own."

"Were the president and McGill lovers before Andrew Grant died?" Sir Edbert said.

"Are the two of them putting any foundation funds to personal use?" Hugh added.

"Very good," Ellie said. "We'll compile an exhaustive list."

"And after we've done all our spadework?" Sir Edbert asked.

"We'll present our findings in the light that serves us best. We invent a new form of political literature: the unauthorized, pre-emptive attack biography. If the president is going to take modern media away from us, we'll go Gutenberg on her."

Sir Edbert Bickford beamed at Ellie.

Forget about marrying the girl, he thought, adopt her.

Hugh proved his mettle, too. "In concert with the book, we'll do a week-long series of television specials covering and reinforcing its claims. There are no regulations against doing book reports, are there?"

"And the book's publication and the TV specials' airings will occur in the last month before next year's presidential election, giving Patricia Grant no time to recover," Sir Edbert concluded.

He smiled at Hugh and Ellie. It was gratifying to the old man that the rising generation showed such promise. As regarded their work, that was. As to their drinking habits —

"Enough of this bloody beer," he said. "This calls for a toast. Hugh, you'd better have some decent champagne on hand."

Hugh smiled and nodded. "As it happens, Uncle, I do."

GWU Hospital Parking Lot

Welborn Yates sat in the Porsche Cayman that Kira had given to him and that Linley Boland had failed to take from him. He felt as if he should have the car detailed. True, the bastard who had killed his friends hadn't had time to enter the Porsche, but he'd laid his hands upon it. Left his fingerprints on it. That kind of soiling could not be tolerated. Having every square millimeter of the machine scoured and polished would be just the thing.

As sincere as those feelings were, they weren't the only thing that kept Welborn sitting behind the steering wheel looking up at the hospital. He was thinking about James J. McGill and his ex-wife up there on the oncology floor, their hearts being crushed by the fear that they would lose their son.

God, how could anyone bear that?

Dear God, he thought, please don't let Kira and me find that out. On the eve of his wedding, he was coming to understand what a leap of faith it took just to make a commitment to someone you loved. Seemed like it ought to be the easiest thing in the world. You loved a woman, she loved you, you got married. You lived happily ever after.

Except when you didn't. When love turned out to be mere infatuation. You found out you weren't nearly as well matched as you thought you were. Or you *were* meant for each other, but fate with its chill indifference struck one of you down. Just look at what had happened to the president's first husband. To have him killed like that, damn. Welborn would … go after the killer like he intended to go after Linley Boland.

Maybe, though, you and your true love got by just fine, and the way the ledger sheet got balanced was one of your kids got cancer. Welborn had joked with Kira, saying they could name their children after Donald Duck's nephews, but he wanted children, a son and a daughter at a minimum, if they could be that lucky. But what if that luck turned sour and —

A rap on the driver's side window lifted Welborn out of his seat.

Then he saw Leo Levy smiling down at him. He lowered the window.

Leo said, "You so in love with these new wheels of yours, son, you just can't bring yourself to leave them? You gonna sit in there all day?"

Welborn looked past Leo and saw McGill's Chevy parked

nearby.

The information he'd gotten from Edwina Byington that Mr. McGill was at the hospital visiting his son was good. Not that anyone should ever doubt Edwina.

"I need to see Mr. McGill," Welborn said. "I was just trying to decide how I could know if the time was right."

Leo's expression became serious. "That's a tough one, all right. Chances are the time won't be right. Not for a while, anyway. But if you're here on business, you just have to do like I do: your job. Being a pro is sometimes the only comfort available."

Being a pro, Welborn thought. That was comforting.

Welborn raised the window, got out of his car, locked it, armed the anti-theft system.

Leo extended his hand and told Welborn, "In case I don't see you tomorrow, my best wishes to you and Kira. You're gonna do fine, the two of you. As a wedding gift, I'll show you both how to really drive this little buggy of yours."

Welborn embraced Leo and thought that was how you got through the tough times.

You made sure you had some true friends close at hand.

He entered the hospital to see if he could be one to James J. McGill.

Salvation's Path Church, Richmond, Virginia

The Reverend Burke Godfrey found himself with a bad case of Pope envy. The Bishop of Rome was not only the leader of a billion congregants, he was also the head of state of Vatican City. He had a personal armed force, the Swiss Guard. You saw pictures of those boys in their striped outfits and ostrich-feather helmets, sometimes even armor looking like it was designed back in the Middle Ages, and you might think they were actors in some costume drama. But the red stripes on those uniforms symbolized the blood they had sworn to shed in defense of the Pope.

"I swear ... should it become necessary to sacrifice even my own life ..."

Now, there was a vow a man of God could appreciate in his followers.

The Pope was seen as both a spiritual leader *and* a temporal one. That was exactly the way Burke Godfrey thought it should be. Men like the Pope — and him — should hold sway in both spheres of existence. Mere politicians should tremble before them and follow their edicts with great haste and greater care.

The casual observer, Godfrey knew, might think the Swiss Guardsmen's weapons were limited to ceremonial swords and halberds, but on a trip to the Vatican he'd learned different. They also possessed assault rifles and pistols and were trained in close-quarters combat. They were the last weapons-bearing military unit to represent the Church Militant.

Lord, but that phrase rang in his ears: *The Church Militant.*

The things he could do as the leader of such a body. He wouldn't need to rule the whole country. There were parts of the United States he didn't even care to visit. If his word were law in only the Commonwealth of Virginia, that would be enough.

If he were in such a position of power, he certainly would not be facing —

"Reverend? Reverend Godfrey?"

The pastor of the Salvation's Path Church blinked and saw his lawyer Benton Williams sitting before him. It took him a moment to remember the man had come to discuss the legal strategy they would employ if — no, when — the FBI came to arrest him.

Williams was proposing to use his contacts in the Justice Department to negotiate the placement of a call to his office to demand Reverend Burke's surrender. Burke would then make his way to Williams' office and the two of them would proceed to the DOJ building without the media ever being aware of what was happening. They would go before a judge, request a reasonable bail amount, get it and pay it, and Godfrey would be back home before they released a statement to the press. A one-on-one inter-view would be granted to either WorldWide News or Fox and they would begin a two-pronged campaign, to get not just the evangelical right but a large portion of Middle America behind them, and to delay an actual trial until after the presidential election.

If Patricia Darden Grant were voted out of office, the new administration would, they all hoped, be more conservative and might drop the case out of hand.

In a rational corner of his mind, Burke Godfrey knew that this was the safest course.

Reason, however, didn't predominate in his thinking. He wanted to show both Patti Grant and Erna that no woman would best him. Now or ever. More than that, though, he wanted to resurrect the idea of the Church Militant. If he were able to succeed, other evangelicals would be certain to follow, and they would have to credit him with leading.

He would become to Christian conservatives what Martin Luther King, Jr. had become to the civil rights movement. Why, someday there might even be a monument to him placed on the National Mall ... not that he wanted to get shot to gain that honor.

So he told his lawyer, "We're going to do something a little different, Benton."

He was never going to surrender to Washington. Not just the churchman that he was but the Virginian in him rebelled at that notion. What he had in mind was Waco. The standoff with the Branch Davidians. Only this time his side would win. He was sure of it.

He might have felt less certain if he'd known Galia Mindel was also a student of that tragedy in Texas.

Rodman/McFee, Washington, D.C.

Barrett Rodman, senior managing partner of the lobbying firm that bore his name, was planning the fall campaign for his troops. Congress may have been in recess for the month of August, but he worked every day of that month, including Sundays, right up to the Labor Day weekend. Each of the five hundred and thirty-five members of the legislative branch of the federal government was assigned a pecking order number. So were each of their chiefs of staff. Every one of those one thousand and seventy human beings had been studied more closely than subjects in clinical drug trials. Their biographies were detailed to the extent that they could have been published in hardcover; some of them would have even made good reading for the general public. A few would have caused such outrage as to become best sellers. But for the purposes of Rodman/McFee, the information provided an intimate knowledge of which buttons to push for every name on the list, and the times when pushing those buttons would produce the quickest responses.

When the exhaustive and exhausting exercise was complete, Rodman jetted down to Saint Bart for three days and nights with two ladies who flew in from Paris and explored his every nerve ending. Each year brought a new pair of ma'amselles with new tricks to show him, and anticipating what they might get up to carried him through his Herculean labors.

Everyone in the firm knew better than to interrupt him during his August marathon. So when his phone rang he looked at the instrument without comprehension, as if the device itself were the source of treachery. Surely, his executive assistant, Horatius, would never —

The damn thing rang again. So it hadn't been some fool calling his number by mistake, letting it ring once before realizing in horror what he'd done and quickly hanging up. Rodman debated letting the phone ring again, but responding quickly to stimuli was one of his buttons. He couldn't hold back.

Grabbing the receiver, he asked in a deadman's voice, "What?"

"Mind your manners, Barrett," he was told.

There were only two people who had ever had the nerve to tell him that, and his mother was dead.

"Mister Speaker," he said. "To what do I owe the honor?"

"Much better," Derek Geiger said.

As intent as he was on his work, Barrett Rodman didn't miss a beat in keeping up with both the news and the gossip that circulated day and night through the nation's capital. Chatter was part of the intelligence that got fed into his calculations. He knew of the speaker's impending divorce; Gerald Mishkin was bearing the lance for Harlo Geiger. The speaker had yet to retain counsel. In the larger world, the president had trampled Geiger's sandcastle by revealing his Super-K plans to the public.

Rodman was glad of that. He didn't like the idea of any politician getting self-righteous about taking money from special interests. The thought of public financing of elections — and he was sure that was where Patricia Grant's proposed reforms would lead — was the stuff of nightmares. But if the lobbying community couldn't drive a stake through that vampire's heart it deserved to be drained bloodless. No, what pleased Rodman was that the death of Super-K meant he wouldn't have to kowtow to Geiger's new toady.

It had already brightened his day that Brad Attles had managed to get himself done in. He'd never liked Attles, but it was so difficult to express dislike for a black man these days without exposing yourself to opprobrium. Damnit, you should be able to dislike individuals whatever color skin they featured.

He was sure that idea was implicit in Dr. King's words.

The speaker told him, "I'm looking for Putnam Shady. Can you help me locate him?"

And right there he had the answer to why Geiger had called.

Geiger must have tabbed Putnam to replace Brad Attles, and then the brassy young SOB had betrayed the speaker and sided with the goddess of sweetness and light, the president.

Poor Putnam, Rodman thought. He'd had such high hopes for that young man, had even thought he might make a worthy successor one day. But of late he'd shown disturbing signs of developing a conscience. That, of course, was a fatal flaw in a lobbyist, the beginning of the end. If carried to extremes, it could lead to the penitent going off to join an order of contemplative monks. Rodman knew of two such cases.

Putnam was still bringing in clients, making rain for the firm, so his growing ennoblement had been tolerated. But soon his zest for enriching the firm would flag and from there it would be a swift fall. So while Geiger's own prospects of remaining a center of power looked sketchy, Rodman felt he was a better bet than Putnam.

That made betraying a productive employee a simple choice.

Without feeling a twinge of regret.

Rodman was careful to stifle any hint of having a conscience of his own.

"After having his home shot up," Rodman said, "Mister Shady decided to relocate to a local hotel, the name of which he declined to tell me or anyone else."

The boy might be going soft, Rodman thought, but he had shown no sign of losing his wits.

"You allowed that?" Geiger asked.

"As long as he does his job, that's all I care about."

Rodman waited to see if Geiger was smart enough to ask one last question, the one that would make betrayal inevitable.

Geiger was. "Do you know of any place Shady might turn up when he's not at his hideaway?"

"He'll be at the wedding of the vice president's niece tomorrow at the Naval Observatory grounds. You'll need a password to get in."

"A password?"

Rodman told him what it was. His sources of gossip were the best.

"Thank you, Barrett."

Rodman didn't say the speaker owed him one, but owe him he did.

"Always happy to be of service, Mister Speaker."

The senior managing partner put his phone down.

Pleased he felt no sense of shame or regret.

Most of his attention returned once more to his work.

A small corner of his mind focused on his upcoming *menage à trois*.

GWU Hospital

McGill and Carolyn took turns comforting each other, reassuring each other that Kenny would come through his ordeal and live a long, happy life, and at other moments they simply murmured prayers. Then Kenny's chief oncologist, Dr. Jones, appeared and she had both Abbie and Caitie with her. Seeing the three of them together almost stopped McGill's and Carolyn's hearts as they feared the worst.

Dr. Jones held up a cautioning hand.

"Please," she said, "don't let your imaginations run away with you. Nothing unexpected has happened with Kenny."

Abbie sat next to her mother; Caitie sat on McGill's lap.

The better to launch herself at any displeasing development.

McGill, knowing his daughter, wrapped his arms around her.

Dr. Jones said, "I wanted to have all of you here together because tomorrow afternoon will be Day Zero for Kenny. That's what we call the transplant day."

"The day Kenny starts getting better, right?" Caitie asked.

She still looked as if she wanted to hit someone or something.

"That is what we are working very hard to achieve. Before Kenny receives his transplant, he will be given a very high dose of chemotherapy and a radiation treatment as well. This will be very hard on him."

"But you have to do it?" Abbie asked.

"We do. The chemotherapy and radiation will destroy the diseased cells in Kenny's body. He will receive the new, healthy cells in a manner very much like a blood transfusion. Those are the mechanical aspects of the process. What we've come to think in recent years is that it's very important for the patient to go into the procedure with the most positive outlook possible. To that end, as you are such a close family, I would like all of you to visit Kenny in his room. You will have to scrub first and be masked, capped and gowned, but you will be able to stand next to Kenny and speak directly to him."

"Can we touch him?" Caitie asked.

"I'm sorry, no. Kenny's immune system is all but gone. We can't take any chances. Also, and you must be completely truthful with me now, has any of you experienced any infections lately. A cough, a fever, anything. Is your throat scratchy? Is your nose running. Are your eyes scratchy or your ears painful? If so, you may not enter the room."

The McGills all declared themselves healthy. Dr. Jones gave each of them a thorough visual scan looking for any signs of contradiction. Finding none, she nodded.

"One last caveat. The idea here is to give Kenny both hope and reason to live, to pull through whatever discomfort, whatever pain, he is going to experience. All of you have to be strong and loving. You may show neither fear nor anger."

Dr. Jones turned to Caitie.

"Kenny will pick up any negative emotion as easily as he would bad germs. Do you understand?"

Caitie blinked away tears and nodded. "I'll be good."

"All right then, please come with me."

Carolyn and Abbie entered Kenny's room first, a nurse already inside opening the door for them. McGill followed with Caitie, father and daughter walking hand in hand. They all stood on the same side of Kenny's bed so he wouldn't have to turn his head. Seen up close, they all saw the toll the disease and its treatment had taken on Kenny. His normally high color was gone, replaced by a hue of faded parchment. His hair had thinned and what remained look brittle. His muscle tone had dissolved to gelatin.

But there was a spark of humor in his eyes that was unchanged.

Untouched by what he'd experienced and the prospect of what lay ahead.

He said to his family, "Just like old times, huh?"

Caitie laughed first and the others followed.

Kenny asked Abbie how college was so far. He asked Caitie if she was missing her friends. Was his mother surviving on the hospital food? He told them that Liesl Eberhardt had to get back to Evanston for the start of school but she'd promised to email him every day. He wouldn't have access to a computer but Dr. Jones said the emails could be printed out and read to him by a nurse.

Kenny then asked his father, "How's the case with Sweetie going?"

"Making progress," McGill said. "It ought to be over soon."

Kenny smiled and gave a small nod, as if he'd expected nothing less.

Then an added measure of joy filled his eyes.

"Hey, look," he said.

The McGills turned and saw more visitors had arrived and were standing on the other side of the room's viewing window. Sweetie was there with Welborn Yates and Francis Nguyen. Standing behind them, towering over the others, was Congressman Zachary Garner.

McGill was uneasy for a moment seeing Garner, until he saw that Kenny was glad the man was there. Then he thought, whatever works. Everyone expressed their love for Kenny. Caitie told him that she and Abbie were going to throw a party for him when he got out of the hospital.

"Try to get the kind of cake and ice cream I like," he told his sister.

Caitie laughed and told him, "One or the other."

Just as she would have at any other time.

Dr. Jones appeared outside the viewing window. Even exercises in joy could be tiring for a patient like Kenny. It was time to wrap things up. Francis Nguyen whispered a word to her and she nodded. The former Catholic priest said through the intercom, "Dr. Jones has given her permission for us to say a prayer, if Kenny would like to do that."

Kenny had never met Francis Nguyen before, but he got a good feeling from him. He was quiet and peaceful, and if he was okay with everyone else …

"Sure," Kenny said.

In unison, they all joined in saying The Lord's Prayer.
Kenny said the final amen.

McGill Investigations, Inc.

McGill, Sweetie and Welborn formed a caravan, if not a motorcade, traveling from the hospital to McGill's and Sweetie's workplace. McGill had a parking place at the rear of the building; Sweetie and Welborn had the good fortune to find spaces on P Street just down the block. Once inside, they left Deke guarding the front door and McGill told him no interruptions, no visitors — the sole exception being Elspeth Kendry.

Sweetie got three bottles of Poland Spring from the office fridge and they sat around McGill's desk. Welborn looked as if he had something he was eager to share, but both he and McGill saw the seriousness written across Margaret Sweeney's face.

"You first, Sweetie," McGill told her.

She informed them of Putnam's arrest and that Putnam and his lawyer were awaiting the arraignment. Putnam had refused to say a word to the cops and his lawyer not only heaped scorn on the charge and the arrest, he threatened to sue the department and the cops involved. She expected the charge to be dropped or at worst Putnam would be RORed, released on own recognizance. If he had to post even a small bail amount, she was going to be highly displeased.

Sweetie's displeasure looked like it could leave welts.

The cops might have more than an irate defense counsel to worry about.

"The charge is suspicion of murder, right?" McGill asked.

Sweetie said, "Three charges of suspicion, the murder victims being three of his friends. They think they have enough to hold him until they find what they need to wrap up a case against him."

Uneasy now, Welborn asked, "What all do they have by way of evidence?"

"He was a guest at all three of his friends' houses over the past year, and each of those friends had a handgun stolen from his house, and each of the friends was killed by a bullet that could have come from his own gun," Sweetie said.

Welborn winced. "I'm afraid that was my doing. Finding out about the stolen guns and how they matched up with the murder weapons. I told Lieutenant Bullard."

Sweetie looked at him. It was a measure of her discontent that she overlooked the fact that Welborn had acted without malice toward Putnam, had in fact done some good police work. McGill took all that in and it made him wonder just how far Sweetie's relationship with Putnam Shady had progressed. He couldn't recall seeing her so agitated.

He pushed that thought aside. It was none of his business.

But he said, "Surely, Putnam couldn't have been the only one who'd had access to all three homes and might be considered a suspect."

"He didn't even have the opportunity to shoot Bobby Waller or Mark Benjamin. He was with me when those killings happened. But Lieutenant Bullard said he could have had an accomplice commit those crimes."

Welborn said, "She's liked Putnam from the start. I don't understand why. I told her I didn't see him doing it."

Sweetie sighed. "Some cops get a hunch and become fixated on it. She had two of her detectives, a couple of guys called Meeker and Beemer, do some checking. They found a maitre d' at one of the fancier steak houses in town who remembered Putnam and his friends having a quiet but very intense argument. He wasn't able to overhear what was said, but the dispute concluded with Putnam standing abruptly enough to knock his chair over. He threw down his napkin and walked out. Stormed out, according to the maitre d'."

McGill nodded. Under ordinary circumstances that would have been enough to make him suspicious, too.

He asked, "Why did Lieutenant Bullard feel it was necessary to pinch Putnam now before she had enough evidence for a prosecutor to make a case?"

Through compressed lips, Sweetie said, "It's his parents. They're fugitives. The feds want them on interstate fraud charges."

"The sins of the father," McGill said, "and the mother."

"They abandoned Putnam when he was six years old," Sweetie told McGill. "They're the last people he's going to use as role models."

McGill said, "You know that, but ..."

Sweetie looked as if she truly wanted to curse.

Vulgarity was crude, but it did vent steam.

She said, "But a cop would reasonably do what they did. The two things that burn me are they haven't looked for any alternative possibility, and they didn't take my word it wasn't Putnam. For all I know, they might think I was a part of it."

"We know that's not true," McGill said. "And I know Putnam didn't do the killings because —"

Welborn cut McGill off, saying, "Congressman Zachary Garner did."

Sweetie looked at Welborn. Then she asked McGill, "Is that right?"

McGill nodded. "Yeah, but now I think he had to have had help."

Deke knocked and opened the door.

"Special Agent Kendry is here," he said. "So is Harlo Geiger."

McGill went into the outer office to greet the two women. He asked Elspeth Kendry to join Sweetie and Welborn in his office. He got Harlo a can of ginger ale from the fridge and handed her a copy of the list of 24-karat dirt on the speaker that Galia Mindel had provided to him.

He said, "I hope that will do, and if you have any questions I'll do my best to answer them in a few minutes. I have to wrap up a few things with my colleagues."

Harlo had already started to read the list and her eyes got big and a smile appeared on her face. She looked up at McGill and the smile now stretched ear to ear. The speaker, McGill was certain, would soon be a man far more in touch with the financial realities of the American people.

"Thank you, Mr. McGill, thank you. I'll recommend you to all my friends."

"This was a one-time special, Ms. Geiger. I don't do matrimonial investigations."

"But other matters?"

"Possibly," McGill conceded.

He was in business, after all. But the way politics in Washington were turning into a pitched battle, he suspected the only client he might have time for was the one to whom he was married. Of course, doing the odd job for an outsider or two might be good cover.

He added, "If you don't mind waiting, I have a question for you."

"I'll be right here," she said, and went back to her reading.

McGill told Sweetie and Welborn of his conversation with Zack Garner and the story of the man's military experience, Garner's study of the policy issues that led to his war wound, and his implied conclusion that he had been fighting for the wrong side. That and equating lobbyists with lackeys of the ruling class.

"Given the chance," Welborn asked, "he was suggesting that he would have fought with the rebels?"

McGill said, "With the democratically elected government, one that proposed to make things better for the common people."

McGill also told Sweetie and Welborn about Garner saying he would go to bat for Kenny if he got the chance to meet God face to face, but there was no use trying to plead his own case.

Sweetie understood the implication.

"He could speak on Kenny's behalf because he's a young boy, an innocent who has never harmed anyone. But Garner, maybe he killed somebody in the Dominican Republic before he got shot, and he tacitly admitted to being involved in the lobbyist killings."

Elspeth refocused the conversation. "Thing is, he didn't confess to anything, did he?"

McGill shook his head. "No, he didn't. Which leads to a disturbing conclusion."

Sweetie said, "He's not done until he's dead."

Knowing his moment had come, Welborn said, "Here's something that at least points the finger at the congressman."

He told them about meeting with Eli Worthington and learning the art teacher had designed the pig pins found on the bodies of the lobbyists, and that the pins had been commissioned by Zachary Garner.

McGill, upon hearing Welborn's description of Worthington, raised an important point. "If this guy is as old as you say, we'd better get a sworn statement from him while he's still around to make that point."

They all agreed on that. Welborn took a measure of comfort that he likely had taken some of the weight off Putnam as a suspect.

Sweetie replied, "Unless the Metro cops can find some connection between Putnam and Garner, a way for Putnam to have taken possession of the pins. I'll cover that base."

Elspeth said, "If the congressman's going to die any time now, there's no way for the justice system to punish him. That means all we have to do is keep him from killing anyone else."

McGill sighed. "What I've learned about politicians since I've come to town is there are damn few of them who are lone wolves."

"So you do think Garner has accomplices," Welborn said.

McGill nodded. "The more I think about it, and having talked to the man, maybe he stole the guns and decided on the targets, but he must have had kindred spirits pull the triggers."

"Who would that be?" Elspeth asked.

McGill told her, "My guess is at least some of the people at his wake. I hope you took nice, sharp pictures, special agent."

Sweetie left after she called Putnam and learned that his lawyer had sprung him, ROR. He also told her the repairs on his townhouse had been made, completed to specifications to repel an attack similar to the previous one. That and a bit more. Sweetie told him she'd be there in fifteen minutes.

"You going to let the cops in if they get overeager again?" McGill asked.

Sweetie gave him a televangelist's — or a politician's — answer. "I'll pray on it."

Welborn left to see Kira, telling McGill, "If I don't get home soon, I'll be beyond the power of prayer to help."

That left Elspeth Kendry. McGill asked her, "If you study the pictures you took of the people entering and exiting The Praetorian Club, do you think you can tell which of them has murder in his or her heart?"

"I must have missed photo interp the day they taught that," she answered.

McGill smiled. He liked his new fed. The time came when Deke needed a little time off, he could see letting her be his close-in bodyguard.

"That being the case," McGill said, "how would you feel about keeping an eye on Congressman Garner's house, maybe snap a few more pictures, see if anyone from his wake has any after-hours business with him?

She nodded. McGill was a special case, she could see. The guy was smart.

Had clout, too. Not even SAC Crogher held any sway over him.

"Something wrong, Elspeth?" McGill asked.

She got to her feet. "No, sir, not at all. I was just thinking that working this detail is going to require a lot of outside-the-class-room thinking. It should be interesting."

"Feel free to talk with Deke," McGill said. "He can give you pointers."

McGill followed Special Agent Kendry into his outer office. Harlo Geiger was sitting there contemplating her future, humming "Girls Just Wanna Have Fun." She stopped and got to her feet when she saw McGill. Harlo spared a glance at Elspeth as she left but saw no competition or any other point of relevance.

McGill said, "Thank you for waiting, Miz Geiger."

He gestured her into his office. Left the door open, as he didn't have a chaperone.

They took their respective seats and Harlo said, "I want to give you a bonus. I've heard about your son. I'll hold a good thought for him. I can only imagine how hard it must be for you to work at a time like this. So coming up with all this information ..." She held up the list McGill had given her. "That was great work."

McGill offered a wan smile.

Doing what little he had to push the case along had been the only moments — no, there were a few others — that allowed him to take his mind off Kenny.

He certainly didn't deserve a bonus simply for thinking that tapping Galia Mindel's wealth of oppo research had been the answer to his Harlo Geiger problem.

"Whatever you care to make the tab for my services," McGill said, "I'd like you to divide it in two and make your checks payable to the scholarship fund of Saint Ignatius High School in Chicago and St. Jude Children's Research Hospital in Memphis."

Harlo took a notebook and pen out of her purse and wrote down the names, making sure she had them right. She told McGill he had a wonderful heart.

He did believe in charity, did whatever he could. But in this case there was the added benefit of having no money trail between the speaker's former wife and him.

That business disposed of, McGill asked the first question he had for Harlo.

"If you don't mind telling me, does the speaker own any handguns that he keeps in Washington?"

For a heartbeat, McGill could see that she wondered why he would ask that, but she pushed the curiosity aside. He'd come through for her; she'd come through for him.

"He used to have three: a semi-auto, a revolver and an exotic. The first two I put in his bags when I threw him out; the exotic, I think he said somebody took that right after the first of this year."

"You mean, someone burgled your home? Was anything else

taken?"

"No, no. Our house — my house — has fantastic security. Derek liked to carry that gun around with him. He said somebody took it from his briefcase while he was out. I don't know if that meant at one of his offices on the Hill or somewhere else."

"What kind of an exotic weapon was it?" McGill asked.

"It was one of those plastic guns, the kind that aren't supposed to set off metal detectors. I think it was made in Austria."

"A Glock?" McGill asked. He knew that company had long integrated polymers into the manufacture of its semi-autos.

"Not a Glock. I know that name. This was one of those jaw-breaker names with ten syllables. Derek said you had to get them handmade to order, one at a time."

"I see," McGill said. He stood up and extended his hand to Harlo. "Thank you for your help."

She leaned far over McGill's desk and kissed his cheek.

"No, thank you, Mr. McGill."

Reminding himself to be sure to wipe off Harlo's lipstick before anyone saw it, McGill used her gratitude as license to ask two more questions.

"You saw this plastic gun?"

She nodded. "Looked like your usual semi-auto, only maybe a little smaller. Matte black plastic."

"Did the speaker report it stolen?"

"He said he did." She waved a hand and left with a bounce in her step.

McGill took his seat again. He called the White House, Edwina Byington's extension.

"Is the president busy?" he asked.

"Now and for the next few hours, Mr. McGill."

He thanked her. Recalling the other moments his mind had drifted away from Kenny's ordeal, he called Clare Tracy. She said she'd love to meet him for a drink.

The Ritz-Carlton Bar

McGill and Clare sat at a corner table. Deke sat two tables away, facing out, setting a buffer, watching for anyone who thought to approach, his back to the people he was protecting. Couldn't ask for better or more discreet security. Clare took a moment to marvel at the perks her old boyfriend currently enjoyed. Paid to marry well, she thought.

She reached a hand across the table. McGill took it.

"How's Kenny doing?" she asked.

"They're throwing everything they have at him, and he keeps taking it. Won't let anything break his spirit. I don't know where he gets the strength."

"I do. He has two strong parents and a whole lot of people who love him."

McGill had to clear his throat. "Yeah. Tomorrow's the day. My guess is the girl who needs the same marrow type as Kenny will have her procedure tomorrow, too."

Clare nodded. "She will. Dr. Jones called me today, asked me to be ready."

"Sorry you had to hang out in Washington all day. Be away from your work."

"Oh, I got plenty of work done. My assistant routed all my calls here. You might not believe it, but without a word from me, everyone I talked to seemed to know why I'm here. I was told what a swell gal I am more times than I cared to hear. But apparently doing a good deed inspires people to be generous. I set a single-day record for fundraising. I was going to treat myself to a drink before I heard from you."

Clare had a Virgin Mary in front of her.

McGill had a Sam Adams.

"Probably wise for you to go alcohol free," he said.

"Doctor's orders."

"Too bad," he said. "I'd love to have seen the Ritz-Carlton's reaction if we'd ordered a pitcher of beer and a pizza."

Clare laughed. "For someone with Secret Service protection, they wouldn't have batted an eye. The beer would be cold, the mugs frosted and the pie the best you ever had."

"Wasn't that long ago I was a simple chief of police."

"Yeah, in Winnetka. Mansions along the lakefront and everybody else having to make do with mere million-dollar homes."

"True. But it's still a long way from there to here."

"Yeah, for a combination of privilege and power, you can't beat the presidency."

Clare turned away for a moment. Not exactly a subtle cue.

"What is it?" McGill asked.

Clare looked over at Deke. He was still looking the other way, but he might be listening in their direction. As the room was mostly empty, there wouldn't be much else for him to hear. Clare turned to McGill and said softly, "I wonder if I'm going to be found out."

"Regarding what?" McGill asked, keeping his voice down.

"Please do your best to understand, Jim, but I've gone behind the president's back and fiddled with her plan, the one that neither of us would know who made the donation to Kenny. When I talked with Dr. Jones, I asked her to see to it that my donation goes to the little girl who needs it. I asked her to keep that to herself. She agreed."

McGill thought he knew what Clare had been thinking, but he wanted to hear it from her. "Why did you do that?"

"Because if anything were ever to happen to Carolyn — and I pray it never does — Patti would be the next in line to be Kenny's mom, not me. She should be the one who saves him."

McGill refrained from telling Clare that a save was no sure thing.

"You're also making a statement about you and me," he said.

"Yes, I am. I love you and always will, but thanks to me things didn't work out for us. If they had, I'm sure you wouldn't let anyone else come between us."

"No, I wouldn't."

"And you won't let anyone come between you and Patti."

"No, I won't."

"So let's not blur things. Thanks to you, we got to see each other again, and I still get a chance to save a life. You can tell Patti about our secret when you're old and gray."

McGill smiled and kissed Clare's hand.

"If it hadn't been Patti —"

"I know," Clare said, "and if you personally need the transplant of any organ I can spare, just let me know."

McGill smiled. She took his hand and kissed it.

McGill's Chevy

McGill took one last glance at the Ritz-Carlton and then turned his attention to the two men sitting in the front seat of the Chevy as it headed to the White House.

"Either of you guys know anything about a plastic handgun manufactured in Austria — not a Glock — that has a multi-syllabic, presumably German name?"

Leo shrugged. "Not me, boss."

Deke was thinking, but he came up blank, too. Given his duties, though, he asked the obvious question: "Does this concern a threat to you?"

"Don't think so," McGill said.

He trusted both Deke and Leo with his life. So he didn't worry about them keeping secrets. After three years of working for him, they'd proved that anything they talked about in the car or else-where stayed between them. That couldn't have been easy for Deke; SAC Crogher undoubtedly wanted to know any stray thought that passed through McGill's mind.

He told Deke and Leo about the K Street lobbyists being killed with guns that matched the calibers of ones stolen from their homes. He added the information he'd gained from Harlo Geiger about the speaker claiming that his plastic semi-auto had been stolen.

"Speaker's hardly any old lobbyist," Leo pointed out.

"No, he's the guy who wanted to have them all roll over and do tricks for him. My thinking was the killer might want to go after bigger game. That's why I asked Harlo if her soon to be ex-husband had lost a gun."

"Did you ask if the speaker filed a police report on the weapon being stolen?" Deke asked McGill.

He said, "Yeah. Harlo said she thought he did."

"Give me a minute," he said. He took out his service Black-Berry and started searching databases not available to the general public. Maybe two minutes later, he shook his head.

"No report of the speaker filing a report on a stolen handgun with the Capitol Hill PD, the Metro PD, or any police agencies in Maryland, Virginia or his home state of Florida."

McGill thought about that. "Harlo said she put two other handguns in the speaker's luggage when she sent him packing. I don't think she'd overlook the plastic gun."

"Maybe she kept it," Leo said, "for personal reasons."

McGill considered that, too. "I didn't get the feeling she lied to me, and when she felt she'd been wronged, she turned to a divorce lawyer not to violence."

"In which case, keeping a gun belonging to her ex could be a real devious move." Leo said.

"Could," McGill conceded. "But I think the speaker still has it. Maybe he didn't report it because the weapon isn't something he should have had in the first place. Fully automatic weapons are still banned; maybe what he has is off-limits, too."

"Or maybe it's the rounds the weapon fires that are illegal," Deke said. "Illegal gun, illegal ammo."

McGill nodded. "But how would he get either of those things into the country." The answer came so fast it showed how many of political Washington's folkways he'd internalized. "A congressional junket. Speaker Geiger went overseas on some mission of *vital* importance the United States, and in a spare moment he picked up a weapon and/or ammunition that would make him the envy of all his shooting buddies."

"How would he get that stuff back into the country?" Leo asked. "Even someone like the speaker couldn't just ask the customs people to look the other way."

Deke had the answer. "He could wrap it up nice and neat and ask somebody in the State Department to put it in a diplomatic pouch for him. Tell that person it was something else."

Both McGill and Leo liked that. They watched as Deke plumbed the depths of his BlackBerry again. The special agent nodded at what he found. "Three years ago, the speaker went to Brussels to talk to NATO allies about picking up more of their own defense tab. He also visited Germany, Austria and Italy."

McGill thought about that.

"I wonder if he's ever fired the damn thing. I've heard stories of plastic guns blowing up in the shooter's hands."

Deke agreed. "I've heard the same thing from ATF people. Said the failures can be catastrophic. Frames and magazines were blown out. Bolts and springs went flying. Sharp pieces of plastic caused deep cuts. Bad stuff."

"Probably didn't hit what they were shooting at either," Leo said.

McGill was still working things through. "I thought if the speaker's weapon had been taken it might be used against him, but if he still has it, means to use it —"

"He's got somebody in mind he's not so partial to," Leo said.

Putnam Shady's name came immediately to McGill's mind.

CHAPTER 6

Saturday, August 20th, Rep. Garner's House, M Street, NW

Representative Zachary Garner woke up shortly after three A.M., needing to pee. He was surprised that he'd been able to sleep at all. He was certain the next time he lost consciousness it would be forever. The tumor in his skull was growing ever larger and more insistent. By the time the doctors had found it, there was no hope of extrication by surgery. The malignancy had become too intimate a part of him.

He hobbled to the bathroom and putting a hand on the sink managed to lower himself into a sitting position on the toilet so he would neither soil himself nor make a mess on the floor. He was pleased that his personal plumbing was still functioning well for a man of his age and in his condition.

Even his wiring was holding up for the most part. They'd warned him that the tumor might blind him, leave him deaf, render him mute, make his muscles seize up. They said there wasn't a horror in the book to which he might not succumb before yielding entirely. He'd fought back with sheer willpower, the same determination that had saved his leg so many years ago. Back then, he'd simply instructed his leg to remain vital. He'd pictured in his mind every bit of vigorous running, jumping and kicking he could remember doing, going back to the time he was a small boy.

If anything had failed him in old age it was his conscience. After Vivian had succumbed to a heart attack and Tom had been blown to bits in Iraq, he'd lost all sense of the world being a just place. If taking the people he loved was the way God went about His business, and we were made in His image, well, then it must be acceptable for us to strike people dead, too.

Even those people who had invited you into their homes and introduced you to their families. Zack Garner had had a long-standing policy of never socializing with lobbyists. So it became a point of fun for many in the fourth branch of government to invite him to all manner of soirees. Those held in hotel ballrooms and more intimate gatherings in the somewhat smaller but no less grand homes of the influence peddlers.

Over the past year, he'd shocked more than a few of them by accepting their invitations. He knew from the gossip mills which of them considered themselves to be marksmen, had even heard where they kept their weapons. At opportune moments, he'd slipped into home offices, libraries and even bedrooms and stolen weapons that had been left at hand.

There were photographs in all those homes: wives, children, parents.

Just as he still had photographs of Vivian and Tom.

Some people died and some people were left behind to grieve.

That was the nature of conflict. For decades, after his military service, he'd done his best to fight his battles within not only the law but also the rules of the House of Representatives. Far more often than not, he'd lost. Money trumped both patriotism and idealism six days a week, and on the seventh day Congress played golf and made further self-serving deals.

When his doctor had told Zack Garner his condition was terminal, he knew he couldn't afford to play within the rules any longer. He'd never even make a dent in the corruption in the time remaining. The only thing left to do was to take as many of the bastards with him as he could ... while maintaining the facade of being the man he used to be.

A good man gone bad, he had the best disguise anyone could want.

Especially if bits and pieces of him remained unsullied.

Zack Garner raised himself from the commode and washed his hands.

Pretty soon now, the tumor was going to burst his brain like a water balloon.

He'd keel over and that would be that.

Until then, though, he had plans to carry out.

He lifted a slat in the mini blinds on his bedroom window. The black sedan was still there. He knew an unmarked government car when he saw one. The boys inside it had been too conscientious about keeping it clean and shiny. They should have let a nice coat of city dust build up on it. Would have faded it right out of sight.

Didn't really matter that they were sitting out there.

If they'd wanted to bring him in, they could have done so hours ago.

They'd watch him right up to the last moment, and then it would be too late.

Fifth Avenue, Naples, Florida

The sun had just begun to illuminate the morning with long, flat rays when the big Mercedes rolled toward Linley Boland looking so much like a gift it should have been decked out with a ribbon and a bow, like one of those Christmas commercial cars.

The S-600 sedan loafed along Gulf Shore Boulevard doing maybe twenty. For a twin-turbocharged, five hundred and ten horsepower engine, that was like sleepwalking. The machine retailed for nearly a hundred and sixty thousand dollars, and Boland knew where he could pull in ten percent cash for the car within the next hour.

The coot behind the wheel looked like he'd already been embalmed, and was the last person who should be driving such a luxury rocket. Boland was the guy who should be driving it. The geezer's window was down and Boland would just bet his door was unlocked. He didn't see anyone else in the car and outside there was not a soul in sight. Not driving, not walking, not doing yard work. The Mercedes was a gimme.

Boland had been up all night, tearing at himself for fucking up the job in D.C. and then barely making bail after being busted in Baltimore. He had given serious thought to looking for a new hustle. Thing was, boosting cars was all he knew.

More than that, he loved it: the hunt, the grab, the getaway.

Only he hadn't been too good at it lately. Made him think of an aging hitter who couldn't catch up to a fastball anymore. But this was a hanging curve right over the middle of the plate. Hell, it was a ball on a tee.

Something he'd always thought of as pussy even for little kids.

Not anymore. He decided to take a swing.

He wouldn't even have to kill the geezer. Just pull the door open as the car came to a halt for the stop sign at the corner of Fifth Avenue. Toss the coot out onto his keister. Jump in and drive off while the sap was still wondering what hit him.

Making the assumption the guy would give him a stationary target was where things started to go wrong. The scofflaw fuck didn't stop; he barely slowed. Boland missed his first grab at the door handle and had to run to make a second try. By that time, the geezer had turned onto Fifth Avenue and managed to rotate his head to the left, getting a look at Boland so up close and personal he could have been Mister Magoo and still ID'ed him.

Now, the old croak had to go.

Unfortunately, that was just what he did. He hit the gas the moment Boland leaned into the car and grabbed the bastard by his wattled throat. The SOB tried to shout, but all he got out were muted squawks, sounded like a cat getting stepped on. Boland squeezed harder and the old fucker pressed down farther on the gas pedal. Goddamn Kraut super-engine shot them ahead like they were launching off an aircraft carrier.

Neither Boland nor the guy whose life he was trying to end had his eyes on the road or a hand on the wheel. They were racing blind down the fanciest shopping street in town. Unless the boys in Stuttgart had engineered an autopilot into the car, Boland didn't think there was going to be a happy ending.

That feeling was emphasized when a shriek from the back seat pierced Boland's skull like a railroad spike. Every muscle from scalp to scrote seized up and, wonder of wonders, he felt the driver's neck snap in his hands. The pressure went off the gas pedal and the car immediately slowed. Boland took the risk of looking to see who was screeching at him.

It was a little broad who looked even older than the guy he'd just killed. She must have been sleeping across the back seat and he'd missed spotting her. Fuck. When she saw him looking at her, she moved her face right up next to his and screamed even louder, as if she could kill him with her vocal chords. But that didn't stop her from pawing blindly through a purse she held on her lap.

The purse scared Boland. In a place as crazy as Florida, even grannies packed heat. If she came out with a gun … she didn't. Almost as bad, though, she held a pair of scissors with a long, pointed tip. With no hesitation at all she tried to impale Boland's hand, but he saw it coming and pulled back. The scissors went an inch deep into the dead driver's neck.

Giving the old bag the idea she had just killed the guy.

She wailed, "Mort!"

Then she clasped her hands to her chest and tipped over sideways.

As if following her lead, the old guy tilted that way, too.

Boland let him go. He grabbed the steering wheel with his left hand, used his right to shift into neutral. There might not be an autopilot in the car, but if Boland remembered the Mercedes' safety features right … He steered the car toward the curb, aiming it squarely at a huge cement planter filled with bright flowers.

The S-600 was not about to be bested by such an easily avoidable collision. Its radar activated braking system sensed the obstacle in front of it, slowed smoothly and came to a stop before it could even climb the curb. What a car.

Boland pushed himself out of the Mercedes. His legs went rubbery and he had to place a hand on the vehicle to steady himself. He looked around, saw that Fifth Avenue was still deserted. He looked at the dead couple in the car they'd given their lives to defend. He was tempted to haul their wrinkled asses out and dump them on the street. Take the damn Mercedes just for spite. But if he got caught disposing of the dearly departed, they'd have won after all. He walked away, feeling like his body was on fire and his mind might black out at any moment.

He turned right at the corner of 8th Street and was halfway down the block when he heard the first siren. A jolt of adrenaline cleared his mind and deadened his pain. He picked up his pace to a brisk walk and tried to think what evidence he might have left behind. Fingerprints, sure. Sweat, maybe. Blood, no, he didn't think so.

If he got lucky, the old broad's scissors might be blamed for the old guy's broken neck. She'd stuck him right about where he'd felt the neck give. Couldn't have stabbed old Mort more than a few seconds after he'd croaked. Cop science couldn't be that precise.

Of course, if they did catch up with him, his story would be he saw the old broad attacking the old bastard and he did what he could to try and stop it.

Who could say different?

Number One Observatory Circle

Kira Fahey arrived at the grounds of Uncle Mather's government mansion at five-thirty a.m. She was by far the earliest member of the wedding party to arrive. Security for the grounds, of course, worked around the clock. She knew most of the members of the Secret Service detail who protected her uncle by both face and name.

Since getting to know Deke Ky and coming to understand

better the jobs the special agents did, how seriously they took their work, their willingness to sacrifice their own lives to protect their "packages," she had made a point of learning who these people were. She always said hello and thanked them for their service.

The special agent who came over to look into her car and make sure no terrorist was forcing her to smuggle him inside the security perimeter was Augie Latz. She'd often thought he might have asked her out, if she hadn't been engaged to Welborn. He was always polite and professional, but there was mischief — and interest — in his eyes that he couldn't hide, and didn't try.

Kira said, "Good morning, Augie. The bride-to-be has arrived. Supporting players and a cast of thousands will follow."

Special Agent Latz completed his inspection of the car's interior and looked at Kira.

"What?" she asked. "You want to offer your best wishes but can't find the words."

The special agent shook his head.

For a moment, Kira was at a loss. This would be a hell of a time for the guy to hit on her, she thought. He was cute enough, but no way was she going to give up Welborn for him. Then it occurred to her what he wanted.

"The password?" she asked.

He nodded.

"O lucky man," she said.

Latz nodded. "Thank you, Ms. Fahey. Best wishes to you and your lucky man."

"Thank you, Augie. Please convey my thanks to all your colleagues ... and if I have to give the password, don't you dare let anyone else slip by without doing the same."

"Not a chance," the special agent said.

With a slight bow and a small grin, he waved Kira on.

Kira entered the vice president's mansion without anyone else challenging her right to be present. Since Uncle Mather would be giving her away, they agreed Kira would use his office as her dressing room. It would be big enough for her, her mother and all the bridesmaids to fuss over each other, compliment one another, weep with joy, take a nip of liquid courage and do whatever else women did in such situations ... and just in case Kira got cold feet, the back door of the office led to the rear of the house and a quick getaway.

She stepped into the bathroom off the office and hung the garment bag sheltering her wedding dress over the shower rod. She put her makeup case atop the cabinet next to the sink. She'd do her face and nails; her stylist would come in an hour before the ceremony to do her hair. Her jewelry case and shoe bag she put onto the eye level shelf of a cupboard in a corner of the room. Normally used as a storage place for towels, Uncle Mather had it cleared out for her use. She placed the overnight bag containing the clothes she would change into before she and Welborn departed the reception on the lower level of the cupboard.

A place for everything and everything in its place.

But Mother and Kira's bridesmaid friends would undoubtedly bring things that would have to be stuffed somewhere. She looked up. The cupboard had a top shelf, too, but Kira even in her three-inch heels would be unable to reach up there. Uncle Mather might not even have had it cleared out. You'd have to be a really tall man to make use of that shelf.

Which, unbeknownst to her, was the exact reason Congressman Zachary Garner had chosen to leave his gun up there.

Kira turned out the light and left the bathroom.

She lay down on the couch in Uncle Mather's office, daydreaming of the moments that lay ahead. Feeling sure nothing could go wrong with her wedding now.

B Street SE, Washington, D.C.

Speaker Derek Geiger's cell phone woke him, far earlier than he had planned. He found it with a groping hand, keyed the answer button without looking and said a groggy, "Hello."

"Did I wake you, baby?"

Harlo's voice was soft and sweet. Geiger started to get excited — until he remembered the treacherous bitch was divorcing him, had tossed his ass out onto the street.

"You damn well did," he said.

"Do you miss me?" she asked.

In his gut, he knew she was fucking with him, but he still couldn't help but hope she was reconsidering — if only to give him the chance to dump her.

"The good times," he said, hedging his bets.

"I'm afraid this isn't one of them," she said and laughed.

Then she proceeded to tell him how her investigator — the most famous private eye in Washington — had discovered all of Derek's dirty little secrets for her. The world wouldn't have to know what they were, of course, but he should be entirely agreeable when Jerry Mishkin sent over a list of her new settlement demands.

Otherwise, there might be one of those awful Washington leaks, and the whole world would learn he was the most famous pimp in town.

"Oh, and Derek, I'm going to see my doctor today, and if you've given me any sort of creeping crud from one of your bimbos, then I go on TV and tell the world."

Harlo clicked off, and Derek Geiger knew he was finished.

No matter what he did or didn't do, Harlo was going to rat him out eventually.

W Street, NW, Washington, D.C.

Welborn was little more than thirty minutes behind his betrothed in waking that morning. By six-thirty A.M., he was leaning against an immaculately washed and waxed ice blue Chevy Impala. Vintage mid-sixties was his guess. It sat outside a rehabbed townhouse whose sales price, Welborn guessed, had probably quadrupled in the past ten years. The area had been largely African American for decades but was gentrifying rapidly, in spite of the housing slump. There were still people with money to spend and many of the sharpest were picking up foreclosed real estate at bargain basement prices.

He and Kira with relatively stable government jobs had joined the number of house hunters in the past six months and had three properties in mind. They'd agreed on their order of preference among the trio and would e-mail their broker with timed bids before they left for Barcelona tomorrow.

In the course of doing their real estate search, they'd learned there was already a stratum of solidly middle-class residents living in the rising neighborhoods and those people had been busy working with small banks, using their equity to secure home improvement loans and add to the pace of the gentrification.

Welborn and Kira had liked that. It would make for cultural diversity while maintaining pride of ownership. The quality of schools, police and fire service would rise to meet the vigorous demands of families with two substantial income earners.

Among the beneficiaries of an improving quality of life was Rockelle Bullard.

Outside of whose residence, and upon whose ride, Welborn lingered.

Apparently, she was not an early riser or terribly worried anyone might make off with her beautiful old car. Welborn couldn't afford to wait all day for her to notice his presence. He was getting married that day, a matter related directly to his presence outside Lieutenant Bullard's digs.

He didn't want to do more to Rockelle's car than smudge its finish. So he stepped over to his Porsche, parked in front of the Chevy, and leaned on it just hard enough to set off its alarm, which was loud enough to wake up the whole District and large parts of the adjoining states.

In short order, Rockelle's face appeared in an upstairs window facing the street.

She was downstairs and out her front door, looking none too happy, before Welborn could count ten. The index finger of her right hand was directed his way and a pointed lecture was undoubtedly about to begin when Welborn hit the control on his key fob and killed the alarm. The sudden quiet brought Rockelle to an abrupt halt on the sidewalk in front of him. Still frowning. Not liking being tricked.

"That was your car making all the racket," she said.

Welborn nodded.

"It was close enough to make me think it was mine."

"I wouldn't mess with your car," he said.

She saw the smudge on the Chevy but didn't call him on it. Instead she said, "Around here, nobody messes with my car."

"Completely understandable." Welborn handed her a copy of Eli Worthington's pig pin design.

Rockelle looked at it and asked, "Where'd you get this?"

Welborn told her the story, including who commissioned the pig.

"Congressman Zack Garner?" she asked.

"Unh-huh. You know him?"

"Know of him. Supposed to be a gentleman, and honest."

"A rarity, no doubt." Then he told the Metro homicide lieutenant of Jim McGill's interview with the congressman, and finished with, "I spent two hours of my last night as a single man doing a computer search for any connection between Garner and Putnam Shady. Couldn't find a thing."

Rockelle gave him a long look. "You're telling me in your usual polite way, I've got me a better suspect than Mister Shady."

"I am."

"But there's more than that."

"There is."

"You're telling me, if I come to your wedding, don't bring one of my detectives as my date and don't even think of leaning on Mister Shady, whom I'm guessing will be there with Margaret Sweeney."

"A reasonable assumption."

Rockelle peered at him to see if she'd divined everything Welborn had come to say.

And saw something more. "Damn, Garner's gonna be there, too?"

"He is."

"But you sure don't want me arresting him while he's there."

"That would be awkward for everybody."

Rockelle put a hand to her face, pondering one last assumption.

"But my invitation's still good. In fact, you want me there. In case the congressman goes off the deep end. That happens, the arrest is mine. I get to collar the K Street killer."

"What are friends for?" Welborn asked.

Chief of Staff Galia Mindel's Office

McGill waited until he was sure Galia had arrived for work before he stopped by her office that morning. Galia was observant in her faith on the high holy days. Most Saturdays, she was at her White House post or traveling with the president. Her only concession to the weekend was to allow herself an extra fifteen minutes of sleep … unless there was a crisis. Then she lived in her office and the Oval Office next door.

After McGill knocked, Galia invited him in, but gave him a look nonetheless.

"I liked it better when we gave each other elbow room," she told McGill.

"Me, too. May I take a seat?"

Galia nodded. McGill sat.

"What can I do for you?" The "now" was implied.

"Before I get to that, I have to tell you Harlo Geiger was impressed by the dirt you provided on the speaker."

Galia offered a thin smile. "She ought to be. There's none better. The man didn't fool around himself, but he thought it was okay to provide women to the jerks who do."

"Yeah. There's a name for that, isn't there?"

"He didn't take money for the service. I believe that's part of the job description."

McGill said, "He got compensated in some fashion. You didn't say how, but it gets down to the same thing."

"I suppose."

"Ms. Geiger offered me a bonus. I told her to split the entire amount and donate it directly to my two favorite charities: Saint Ignatius and Saint Jude."

Galia's smile was warmer now. "Nicely done. No taint attaches to you or by implication the president. Now, if you can tell me why you're here."

"I need to get a read on Derek Geiger. He seems to have lost a handgun, unless he hasn't." McGill explained what he meant and the possible connection to the killings of the K Street lobbyists. "What I'm trying to figure out is why he'd want the kind of gun meant to slip past metal detectors and whether he really lost it or if he just told Harlo that to give himself an alibi in case he ever wants to use it. Of course, now, she might be a target."

Galia, by the expression on her face, was busy processing the information McGill had given her, but she was still able to shake her head at the idea of Geiger shooting his departing spouse.

"If not Harlo, who?" McGill asked. "Assuming he still has the weapon."

Galia focused on McGill and said, "Mather Wyman."

"The vice president?" That baffled McGill.

"Think," Galia said. "What's the president about to do?"

Donate bone marrow to Kenny, McGill thought ... and invoke the twenty-fifth amendment.

Making Mather Wyman the acting president.

If he were to die, the next in line would be Speaker Derek Geiger.

"But Patti's going to be incapacitated for only a short time," McGill said. "What good would that do Geiger? Being a seat warmer for a few hours."

For just a heartbeat, scorn showed in Galia's eyes. But it was displaced by a look of deep compassion. Leaving McGill to feel a moment of whiplash.

"What, Galia?" he asked. "What are you thinking?"

"I'm sorry. I just had a thought I regret. You and Carolyn are thinking of Kenny first and foremost. I understand that; as a mother I empathize completely. But as the chief of staff, you know whom I have to think of before all others."

"The president," McGill said.

"Exactly. When I learned she would be a donor, I did the research into whether there would be any risks for her. I informed her of what they were. Don't you have this information?"

McGill shook his head, feeling a terrible sense of guilt that it had never occurred to him to think of the risk to Patti. Or to Clare and the others who'd agreed to make separate donations. He'd been so focused on Kenny he hadn't thought of anyone else.

"What are the risks?" he asked.

"They're small but real. The usual after-effects of bone marrow donation are lower back pain, fatigue, stiffness and bleeding at the collection site. But the collection is done under general anesthesia, and that always carries a risk. Slightly more than one percent of patients experience serious complications. There can also be damage to bone, nerve or muscle tissue. There's some chance the president might be incapacitated for far longer than a few hours."

"Jesus," McGill whispered. "You told her all this?"

"I had to; she had to know."

"And she's still willing to do it."

"The president told me she would resign the presidency if necessary to help Kenny."

McGill covered his eyes with a hand.

Galia told him, "The risk is small. The overwhelming majority of donors come through the procedure with little more than some localized soreness and maybe a headache."

McGill lowered his hand.

"We can't let anything happen to Mather Wyman," he said.

"No, we can't," Galia agreed. "What we have to do is talk to SAC Crogher."

The Oval Office

Edwina Byington read the expression on McGill's face as he approached her desk and didn't even try to slow him down. She gave the president two quick buzzes of the intercom as a heads-up and said, "Good morning, Mister McGill."

McGill paused at the door to his wife's sanctum sanctorum.

"Good morning, Edwina. Barring a national crisis, no interruptions."

"Yes, sir," she said.

Leaving unstated *she'd* be the one to judge both what constituted a crisis and its scope.

McGill closed the door behind him as he entered his wife's office. He stepped behind her desk and kissed her. He looked her in the eye and kissed her again. Unintentionally scaring the hell out of her.

Patti grabbed her husband's wrist, "Is something wrong with Kenny? Dr. Jones just spoke with me not five minutes ago. She asked me to be at the hospital by three this afternoon."

McGill realized he'd thrown a fright into Patti and shook his head.

"No, no. I haven't heard anything was wrong. I didn't know you'd spoken to Dr. Jones. I just came from talking with Galia and Celsus."

The president let go of her henchman's arm. He took a seat in one of her guest chairs. That gave Patti all the time she needed to figure out what her husband had learned from her chief of staff. What he had to say to Celsus Crogher, she'd have to find out.

Patti shrugged and told McGill, "I meant what I told Galia. Kenny's life is more important to me than this job. So are you."

"Makes me feel a bit overrated."

The president laughed. "Well, as long as you don't feel a *lot* overrated, we're all right. And I don't doubt you'd a take a risk greater than one-point-three percent, if I needed your help."

"Anything up to and including one hundred percent," McGill

said.

"You've joined the Secret Service?"

"In spirit if not in fact. I don't see myself working for Celsus."

The president laughed again and said, "Speaking of SAC Crogher ..."

McGill told her of Speaker Geiger and his plastic gun. Patti's conclusion was exactly what McGill had figured out on the short walk to the Oval Office.

"Geiger wants to do in the vice president and have Putnam Shady blamed for it."

"In a nutshell, yeah. Is he up to attempting something like that?"

The president said, "A desperate politician is like a cornered animal. Survival is all, risks be damned."

An unpleasant image indeed, McGill thought. He was glad Patti had Galia, Celsus and him looking out for her. To keep her from ever getting truly desperate.

McGill said, "So, Geiger's likely feeling a sense of urgency to get the deed done and move quickly past it. He couldn't ask for a better opportunity than an event where both of his would-be victims will be present as part of a milling crowd that will be focusing its attention elsewhere"

"Welborn and Kira's wedding?" Patti asked.

"If it's going to be soon, where else?"

Patti shook her head. "Nowhere."

"Question is, do we ask the young couple to postpone their nuptials again?"

"Another question is, do we even let them know what we suspect? We could be wrong."

"Galia was the one who told me the vice president would be the likely target. How are her instincts about this kind of thing?"

"Rock solid," the president told him.

"We were invited to the ceremony, weren't we?"

McGill hadn't noticed, but thought it was a safe assumption.

"We were."

"What time are the vows scheduled to be exchanged?"

"One p.m."

"Gives us time to get to the hospital afterward. Better let Celsus know what we have in mind." Patti picked up her phone and McGill told her, "Have him tell all the troops I'll be armed."

Salvation's Path Church, Richmond, Virginia

Reverend Burke Godfrey's church stood a half-mile off of I-295. The original structure had been a small building with a modest steeple and a cracked bell. The leaded glass windows were the product of an artisan of very modest talents, and water stains caused by leaking gutters streaked the stonework like trails of rusty tears.

The Catholic archdiocese had put the property up for sale when the contributions of the parishioners failed to meet operating expenses for the tenth year running. Burke and Erna Godfrey, both of them planners and savers, snapped up the church, then named Saint Mary Magdalene, for a song. As part of the deal, they agreed to rehabilitate the church and maintain it as a house of God.

The Godfreys would honor their promise but the building itself was a secondary consideration in making their purchase. What really interested them was the land that came with the church, fifty acres of it, with a brook running through it. They envisioned a complex of buildings that would rise on the property: a huge church of modern design, able to hold three to five thousand worshippers, depending on seating configurations; an administration building where the Godfreys would manage the business affairs of their ministry; a television studio that would let them minister first to the country and eventually to the world; a retreat with twenty-five luxury suites and its own dining facilities for prominent individuals who needed a time out from the world of Mammon; a day-care center to give small children the opportunity to take their first steps toward socialization in a Christian atmosphere.

All that would be laid out while allowing for ample landscaped green spaces to permit, in clement weather, worship services to be held directly beneath the gaze of heaven. That was the Godfreys' plan and they were sure it would be glorious when it was realized.

Over the course of thirty-five years, with the help of over two hundred thousand donors from all fifty states and eighteen foreign nations, they had reached their goals and more. A former Hollywood actor who had kicked drugs and found Jesus paid for a three hundred seat amphitheater to be constructed so that Bible stories and newly written Christian plays could be acted out under the stars.

It was understandable that Reverend Burke Godfrey would be reluctant to trade in such surroundings for a cell in a federal prison. It was less obvious to the casual observer that the complex had been laid out in such a fashion that it would be easily defensible by a small, well-armed force.

Reverend Godfrey had planned for a possible attack by the minions of Satan.

Which was precisely how he viewed the administration of Patricia Darden Grant.

The only building that lay outside the defense perimeter was the original stone church, now called The Chapel, lovingly renovated and shining like a small gem.

Q Street NW, Washington, D.C.

The planned attack biography on President Patricia Darden Grant was designated as Ellie Booker's baby. She would be freed from all other duties. In addition to keeping her recently elevated salary, she would be given a half-million dollar advance on the book and sole writing credit for it; if the finished manuscript met or exceeded Sir Edbert's high expectations, Ellie would be given a second half-million dollars as a bonus.

In addition, she would have the use of Hugh Collier's Washington townhouse for the duration of the project. That was Hugh's contribution. He said on such occasions as he had need of a lover, they would repair to a hotel; otherwise he would be present but take care not to disturb Ellie. He would be available to help her if she so chose.

Sir Edbert, never one to miss an opportunity to turn an additional dollar, pound or euro, suggested that Ellie might earn additional funds by subletting her condo while she stayed at Q Street. Ellie said that was something to think about, but she decided immediately to keep her place. A girl never knew when she might need a place where she could run and hide.

Ellie was outlining the book chronologically. She'd start with Patti Darden's parents, maybe even her grandparents, if they had a compelling skeleton or two in their closet. She'd move forward and describe the state of the country at the time Patti was born. She'd continue with Patti's school years, kindergarten through college.

Rumors had been whispered in Washington just last year that Patti Darden and Jean-Louis Severin, the president of France, had been lovers during their year together at Yale. No media outlet had followed up on that at the time, but she would in her book. She'd also talk with Severin's ex-wife to renew interest in the accusation that the two presidents had a second act to their affair at last year's G8 meeting in London.

Then there were Patti's years in modeling and acting. It had to be the work of masterful publicists that she had sailed through those two occupations and emerged with a reputation that Shirley Temple couldn't have topped. Even if it were true that Patti had been honest, brave and pure, she must have pissed somebody off, made enemies who were jealous, envious or just plain malicious enough to stick out a foot and trip her. Ellie would find those people, listen to the bile they had stored for years and present it as the unvarnished truth.

As Sir Edbert had suggested, Ellie would explore Patricia Darden Grant's first marriage, look for instances of infidelity either by the president or Andy Grant. The philanthropist might have had one of the country's most beautiful women as his wife, but he also had billions of dollars to his name, and other beauties must have been available to him. Why would he limit himself to just one alluring woman when he could have had many?

That would bring Ellie to the president's entry into politics, her first race for a seat in the House. Her opponent had been Roger Michaelson, now a senator from Oregon. His reputation as the president's foremost political nemesis was known to everyone who followed American politics. He and the president despised each other.

There were even rumors that James J. McGill had once beaten Michaelson to a pulp as they played a game of one-on-one basketball.

Surely, Michaelson would —

Ellie's cell phone sounded. No musical tone for her. Just an old-fashioned *rrrring*.

She cursed herself for not silencing the thing. She'd been on a roll and now —

It rang again. She saw the caller ID. Hugh was calling.

The boss's nephew or not, she answered with a surly, "What?"

He laughed and said, "If you were a bloke, I'd break your beak for you."

"Not you and Uncle Edbert both."

Hugh said, "We'll see. Someday, we shall see. But for now I have news for you that bears on your project. Reverend Burke Godfrey would like to see you in Richmond, Virginia, at his church. He wants to offer you an exclusive story."

Ellie said, "Is he about to do something *dramatic?*"

Didn't want to say criminal when you were talking on a cell.

Never knew who might be listening in.

"That would be for you to find out, wouldn't it?"

"You really think there's a tie-in?" With her book, she left unsaid.

"Almost bound to be, isn't there?"

Meaning literary license was a wonderful thing for stretching the truth.

"You're right. He wants to see me soon?"

"Soonest," Hugh said. "Bring a videocam."

Robert F. Kennedy Department of Justice Building, Washington, D.C.

Attorney General Michael Jaworsky had his golf bag in a corner of his office behind his desk. For several years now, the Church had allowed Catholics to meet their weekly obligation of attending mass by going on Saturday evening rather than Sunday morning. But what was good enough for the Vatican didn't cut it with the AG's eighty-nine-year-old, born-in Krakow mother, Marzina. *Sunday,* she insisted, was the day all *good* Catholics went to church and partook of the symbolic re-creation of their Savior's body and blood.

As the meaning of his mother's name still reflected her spirit, warlike, the nation's chief law enforcement officer didn't argue with her even now. He accompanied her to Sunday mass, as he had for as long as he could remember. That meant if there was work to do at the office on the weekend the best he could hope for was to sneak in a few holes at the Congressional Country Club Saturday evening before it got dark.

He was working toward that goal at the moment. He'd urged Deputy Attorney General Linda Otani to make her summation of the repentance of Erna Godfrey et. al. as concise as possible. You couldn't hit a golf ball if you couldn't see it.

The DAG said, "Three of Erna Godfrey's four accomplices, Walter, Penny and Winston Delk have admitted and signed sworn statements that Reverend Burke Godfrey knew of and took part in the planning of the murder of Andrew Hudson Grant. He approved the final plan and blessed those who would carry it out."

Michael Jaworsky shook his head. "Blessed them, did he? That should play well in court. What about Lindell Ricker? He's holding out?"

"Yes, but not for long."

"He'll come around?"

Linda Otani shook her head. "He'll die first. In fact, he's going to die soon. Pancreatic cancer. More aggressive than it usually is, which I'm told is saying something. Ricker says he's being struck down because he betrayed Erna Godfrey and the Delks in the first place. Checking out without further betrayal is his idea of martyrdom. He says he got that idea from a story Margaret Sweeney told him when he was first arrested."

The AG had seen the video of that interrogation. It was as good and clean an interrogation as he'd ever seen. Couldn't blame former Sergeant Sweeney now if it came back and bit them.

Linda Otani concluded, "As I see it, sir, the only decision you have to make now is whether to wait until Ricker dies or order Burke Godfrey's arrest right now."

Being older and a bit wiser, Jaworsky saw another consideration.

"Do you think doing it one way or the other would have any effect on whether Erna Godfrey gives up the names of the other killers for the sanctity of life?"

The DAG had been in the room when the video of Erna's incrimination of her husband had been made. She'd have a better feeling for what would move the woman.

Otani said, "I think she's using the threat to reveal other names as a spur to have Reverend Godfrey do what she thinks is the right thing. She seems genuinely concerned for the fate of his soul. I think her giving up the others will be conditional on what he does."

Jaworsky accepted that judgment.

He said, "Have Burke Godfrey arrested."

That should have been it for the AG that Saturday. It was still morning. He should have had time for an entire round of golf — two, if his knees allowed him to walk that far.

The way things worked out, he wouldn't even get to take his mother to mass.

Florida Avenue NW, Washington, D.C.

Sweetie and Putnam had slept together in his bed at his townhouse but hadn't followed up sexually on the night before at The Four Seasons. Returning to the place they both called home had reimposed a sense of status quo ante. Sweetie lived downstairs; Putnam lived upstairs. She was the tenant; he was the landlord. They'd started out as acquaintances, had become friends. But at that particular place, and all others save one hotel, they had never been lovers.

Sweetie, left to her own devices, would have gone down to her one-room basement apartment and done what she'd told McGill: pray on matters that concerned her.

Putnam, wisely soft pedaling things, pointed out a flaw in that plan.

"Somebody comes calling," he said, "cops or killers, you'll have to expose yourself to hostile forces to come to my aid."

Sweetie nodded. "I didn't do much witness protection when I was a cop."

"I didn't need much, until recently."

They agreed it would be better for her to stay somewhere in Putnam's ninety percent of the building. Sweetie said she'd sleep on the couch. Putnam said she could sleep with him; he wouldn't try anything. Not only because he was a man of his word but because they both knew she could kick his backside if he got frisky.

"Your word is good enough for me," Sweetie said.

They'd cleaned up separately, slipped under the top sheet in the dark and went to sleep. Neither made a move on the other, and Sweetie got up only once to check the premises, thinking she might have heard something. Going back to bed, she looked at the silhouette of Putnam's sleeping form. He was still materialistic, self-serving and situationally ethical, but the last time she'd looked she didn't walk around under a halo either.

Each of them had made changes to accommodate the other.

She was less stiff; he was less … situationally ethical.

If they hadn't made a pact, she would have reached for him as she got back into bed.

But they had and she didn't. They waited until morning to

make up for lost time.

Lying next to each other, Putnam asked, "You think these crazy young kids will make a go of it?"

"Welborn and Kira? Yeah, I do. Each of them is strong enough not to feel threatened by the other. And I think they love each other enough to give the other the benefit of the doubt when a hard decision comes up."

"The grace not to say 'I told you so,' if the decision turns out wrong?"

Sweetie smiled. "Unless it's a question of whether they should have gone skydiving, I think so."

Putnam laughed. "Well, something like that, you wouldn't have to bother with a divorce lawyer."

"We better start getting ready," Sweetie said. "Don't want to be late to the wedding. You mind if I go first?"

"We could scrub each other's back."

"Great idea … when time isn't an issue."

Putnam said, "You go first."

Sweetie started for the bathroom, but turned and looked at Putnam.

"Did you buy a wedding gift?"

He said, "Golden handcuffs."

"You, too?"

Thing was, neither of them was kidding.

They decided to keep a pair for themselves.

Letting Sweetie hit the shower first left Putnam in bed to answer his cell phone when it rang. Putnam's boss, Barrett Rodman was calling. He said, "Putnam, I've done something terrible."

"Forgot the sequence of your numbered account?"

Rodman laughed. "You know, I've often thought of you as a son."

"I know you've called me a sonofabitch. You're not firing me, are you, Pop?"

"I do that by e-mail now."

"So you've screwed me some other way?"

Rodman told Putnam about betraying him to Derek Geiger.

"That's not the terrible thing," the senior lobbyist said. "What worries me is that I've come to regret it. I may be developing a conscience."

Putnam reassured his boss, "No worries there. You just had second thoughts because you decided I'm the better bet to come out on top. You're acting out of self-interest not moral anguish."

There was a moment of silence. Then Rodman said cheerfully, "By God, if I did have a son, I'd want him to be as smart and clear-eyed as you."

"Thanks, Pop," Putnam said. "Have a good time in Saint Bart."

There had been times he wished he could go along, but now — Sweetie appeared in the bathroom doorway wrapped in a towel.

"Your turn," she said.

SAC Celsus Crogher's Office, the White House

Elspeth Kendry sat opposite Crogher. He had his hands folded on his desk, almost like a parochial school kid. Only difference was the nuns, at least at the girls' school Elspeth had attended in Lebanon, made the students sit with their hands steepled, pointing straight up to heaven. Casting your thoughts toward salvation was a minute by minute occupation when you grew up Christian in a Muslim country.

She thought the local imams cut the school a bit of slack because the nuns in their habits weren't far from being clad in burqas, and they were subservient to the local priests, which their fellow People of the Book also considered to be the right thing to do. Elspeth, taking a contradictory view, had started smoking at twelve and flicked her butts at men of any denomination as soon as their backs were turned.

Having advanced in her education, matured in her emotions and outrun the guys she'd actually hit with butts, she was able to work both with and for men who had earned their positions honestly. She regarded SAC Crogher as one of them, but he was one weird dude. He had his hands clasped so tightly his knuckles were white, but then so was the rest of him. The guy wasn't an albino but he was as pale as you could be without crossing that line.

She felt like telling him, "It'll be all right," but didn't think that would go over big.

"What's the count up to, Kendry," he asked. "How many people other than our personnel will be armed at this wedding?"

"The current number is four, likely going to five if Speaker Geiger shows up uninvited."

"Uninvited but knowing the password."

"That's right." A thought occurred to Elspeth. "Might even be six, if Margaret Sweeney gives Putnam Shady a gun."

Crogher's eyes bulged at the idea. Pale or not, his blood pressure could spike like anyone else's. "No, goddamnit," he said. "That's going too far."

"Mr. Shady passed the word through Ms. Sweeney that Speaker Geiger might attempt to —"

"Assassinate the vice president and frame him for it. We already had the first half of that assessment from Galia Mindel," Crogher said between clenched teeth. The idea boggled his mind ... but then he thought it probably shouldn't. With what politics in this country were coming to, having the bastards shoot each other was the next logical step.

"Of course," Elspeth said, "there could be an element of denial working on Mr. Shady's part. The speaker might simply intend to do him in."

An acceptable loss, Crogher thought, if it had to be anyone.

He didn't share his assessment with Kendry, though.

Some things were best held close.

What had started out as a difficult enough day to begin with — Holly G. going to the hospital, being given general anesthesia, the entire medical team needing a quick but thorough vetting to make sure none of them harbored any ill will toward the president — had gotten progressively more difficult. Crazier to Crogher's order-loving mind.

First, McGill and Galia Mindel call him into the chief of staff's office. Telling him the speaker of the House has a lethal plastic gun and Mindel thinks he means to use it against Vice President Mather. That's bad enough, but then Holly G. lets him know she and Holmes will be attending the Yates-Fahey wedding and, by the way, Holmes will be packing. Let his boys and girls know.

After that, he gets a call from Captain Yates, the bridegroom, saying *he's* going to be carrying a weapon under his dress uniform and — *and* — he's invited a homicide lieutenant from the Metro cops to be in attendance and *she* will be packing, too. That's because they suspect a senior member of Congress might attempt to kill either the speaker or Mr. Shady. The Secret Service should make sure Representative Garner is not armed when he arrives at the wedding.

Then Margaret Sweeney, a civilian, has her call put through to him and she says Mr. Shady has learned that Speaker Geiger is definitely looking for Mr. Shady and has been given the password to get into the wedding. Please check him out for a plastic weapon, should he show up. And in the event the speaker subcontracts his hit, look for a person or persons unknown carrying either the plastic handgun or its component parts.

Oh, yeah. Since Ms. Sweeney has taken personal responsibility for safeguarding Shady, she's bringing her handgun. She's licensed and has a carry permit, of course.

Christ on a crutch! You'd think the damn NRA had planned the wedding.

The bride would probably be carrying a derringer in her garter.

Crogher would have canceled the whole thing and packed the happy couple off to a chapel in Las Vegas on a Secret Service jet ... if Holly G. would have let him.

She had faith in him and his people, she'd said when he'd called to protest.

The president had told him he would see to it that everything came out right.

The idea being, as Crogher saw it, that the Secret Service would gun down Speaker Geiger if he so much as looked at anyone cross-eyed. Thereby causing a great deal of political trouble for the late speaker's party — the one the president had just left — and anyone who might care to be its presidential nominee next year.

But he wasn't going to share that thought with anyone either.

Especially not Special Agent Kendry.

Who sat there looking like getting a last-minute manicure was her biggest worry.

"None of this bothers you, Kendry?" he asked.

"I grew up in the Middle East, sir. Things like this are routine in ruling circles. Only you don't know half as much about the players as we do."

"So your only worry is ..."

"Not the people we know who will be armed. In my view, except for the speaker, they're all trustworthy, and we'll have all of them covered. My worry, sir, is someone we *don't* know about getting a weapon in."

Crogher had thought of that.

Hearing Kendry say it, though, only made him worry more.

He asked, "How about crossfires and collateral damage, Kendry. That worry you?"

"We won't let things get that far, sir."

Couldn't ruffle her feathers, Crogher thought. Just like Holly G.

Maybe he ought to retire.

Let the damn women take over everything.

GWU Hospital

The room nurse told Kenny McGill she would be right back. She had to step out for just a minute. He nodded his acceptance of the fact. He was long past sweating the small stuff. Mom, Abbie and Caitie had been standing outside his view window a moment ago, all of them doing their best to look brave, Caitie still looking mad at a world that could put her brother in such a fix.

Then Lars showed up and gave him a wave and a smile — after he'd done a double-take. Lars hadn't seen him for a few days, so that had let Kenny know just how much he'd changed. Made him glad Liesl Eberhardt had to go back to Evanston for the start of school before the meds took most of his hair. Still, he was glad Lars had come back. He was a good guy, made Mom happy. He loved Abbie and Caitie, too.

They'd all probably gone to the chapel to say another prayer for him. He'd take all the prayers he could get. Anyone in his situation would. A priest he didn't know — introduced himself as Father Mike — had come into the room earlier. He was capped, masked and gowned like anybody else who got near him. He heard Kenny's confession and gave him a sip of water in lieu of a Communion wafer or wine. Father Mike said everyone knew the Lord could change water into wine so he shouldn't feel shortchanged.

Kenny had seen the worry in the priest's eyes and said, "Don't worry, Father, I'm going to make it."

"You're in a state of grace, Kenny. Making it is the only thing possible."

Wasn't too hard to read between those lines, Kenny thought, even in his condition. But Father Mike's words had brought him great comfort. Whatever happened, live or die, there was no way he could lose.

As if to underscore that idea, just after Father Mike left, Zack appeared outside the window to his room. For a guy who said he was dying, Zack sure looked great. In fact, Kenny thought Zack was what God would look like if He wanted to put in an appearance without scaring everyone. Tall and strong, white hair and kind eyes. He was able to take all your troubles away and make them his own because there wasn't any weight too heavy for him to carry.

Zack tapped his chest, his heart, with his right hand. Then he put his fingers to his lips and blew on them, like he was blowing Kenny a kiss. But Kenny knew it was more than affection he was sending, it was his strength, his spirit. A parting gift to someone who could use it because Zack's time was almost up. He'd come to let Kenny know and tell him to be strong. Use all the strength Zack had given him, if he needed it.

The door to the room opened and Kenny saw the nurse had come back.

"It's time, Kenny," she said.

Time for the big chemo and radiation.

Then time for the bone marrow infusion.

Then —

He looked back at his window.

Zack was gone.

But Mom, Abbie, Caitie and Lars were back.

And Dad was there now, and so was Patti.

And so were Sweetie and that Putnam guy.

Nobody's ever been luckier than me, Kenny thought.

Hart Senate Office Building

Senators John Wexford and Richard Bergen and Representatives Marlene Berman and Diego Paz, the two leading Democrats in Congress and their two top lieutenants, sat around the conference table in the senate majority leader's office suite. Each of them had a sheaf of papers in front of him or her, the products of their due diligence efforts.

The party's top pollster and his people had been hard at work the past twenty-four hours talking to people in every part of the country to see how they would feel about having Patricia Darden Grant run for president as a Democrat. The numbers all but left them dumbfounded.

"I've never seen anything like this," Dick Bergen said. "If I didn't know how good Peter Newsom is at producing reliable data, I'd ask for a do-over."

"It is enough to make you wonder if wishful thinking isn't involved here," John Wexford said. "Your thoughts, Marlene?"

"I'll defer to Diego for the moment."

Congressman Paz said, "Patti Grant has had the Latino community in the palm of her hand since that day she campaigned on Olvera Street four years ago."

They all knew what he meant. Candidate Grant had visited the heart of the Mexican-American community in Los Angeles and had listened to a class of first graders serenade her in the native tongue of their parents' homeland. Then a little boy and a little girl had stepped forward and sang "De Colores" again in perfect English.

Already bilingual, speaking fluent French, the candidate declared on the spot that Spanish was too beautiful a language for her not to know. She promised to learn it as quickly as her schedule permitted, and she followed through, speaking the language with growing proficiency, though she tended on occasion to default to the French pronunciation key, which more often than not made her audiences chuckle and the president say, "*Lo siento.*" I'm sorry. "*Lo estoy haciendo otra vez.*" I'm doing it again.

Anytime she spoke in Spanish publicly, she always made sure to provide her own translation into English, making the point that people should do whatever they could to understand one another.

Paz said, "She not only kept her promise to learn Spanish, she showed everyone how *simpatica* she is. I've even heard some teenage girls — and their boyfriends — have taken to mispronouncing words the way she does. They call it speaking espanais. Not sure how the Spanish and French feel about that, but it's catching on here. So I have no trouble believing these numbers."

Marlene Berman said, "Our party had a leg up on the Republicans in attracting Latino voters. Patti Grant took that away from us. If she runs at the top of our ticket, she'll bring that vote home. She'll bring women with her. She'll bring the senior vote. She'll bring far more white men than we'd get otherwise. The numbers are right there in front of us. I believe them.

"With Patti Grant, we'll not only retake the White House, we'll increase our margin in the Senate and retake the House of Representatives. If she goes independent, I think we'll be the junior partner in a coalition government with whatever new party the president starts."

Wexford and Bergen looked at each other and nodded.

It was time to take the big jump. There were conservative members of their party who would defect to the GOP, but that number would be more than offset by their gains.

Dick Bergen said, "How's that old curse go? 'May you live in interesting times.'"

The others laughed, each of them nervous to some degree.

Wexford picked up the receiver of the landline phone on the table. "The only thing left to do then is call Galia Mindel and ask what the president's demands are."

Galia took the call and told them exactly what the president wanted.

The only sticking point was Roger Michaelson.

She said the president would want no part of him. Now or ever.

But with so many points of agreement, they agreed to defer that issue until the president recovered from her bone marrow donation and reclaimed her powers of office.

They all wished the president and Kenny McGill well.

Salvation's Path Church, Richmond, Virginia

Ellie saw snipers on roofs in the church complex. Some of the men up there were smiling, feeling strong, no doubt. She had produced a special on America's love affair with guns. She knew from interviewing dozens of *enthusiasts* that a lot of these guys loved their firearms far more than their wives or girlfriends. Took better care of their weaponry, too. The lethal iron got gun oil far more often than the ladies got perfume.

Under other circumstances, she'd have stopped, turned around and hoped they hadn't already mined the streets around the church property. But she was there by invitation. A large placard on her dashboard identified her as being with WorldWide News. Not taking any chance that might not be enough, Ellie slowed her car to a crawl, lowered the driver's window and waved a white handkerchief.

What looked to be an old garbage-hauling truck that was blocking one of the roads leading into the church's campus made room for her. As she worked her car through the narrow space, she looked at the truck. The thing could probably hold a ton of trash, she thought. If it was filled even halfway with a fertilizer bomb, ready to be set off with a remote detonator, it could take out a hundred men trying to storm the church grounds.

Looked like Reverend Godfrey wasn't going to go easily.

As she moved past the truck, it rolled back into blocking position. Ahead, a man in green camouflage fatigues and a boonie hat held up a hand like a traffic cop. In his other hand he held an assault rifle, so Ellie stopped, wondering just how many people Godfrey might have on hand and how crazy they might be.

It made her feel only marginally better when the guy gave her a grin as he approached. Ellie hit the lock release and let him slide into the passenger seat. He put his seat belt on, like a traffic accident on a private road was his big worry. He extended a hand to her and she took it. In case she wound up becoming a hostage, she wanted to have at least one guy on her side.

"Art Dunston," he said in a smooth baritone, flashing her a big smile.

His teeth were TV perfect.

Ellie introduced herself and asked, "What newsrooms have you worked?"

He mentioned affiliates of two different networks, one in South Carolina, one in Georgia. He had a hint of the South in his voice, just enough to add some warmth.

"Sports anchor?" she asked.

"In college, yeah. That's where I learned to shoot. When I started drawing a paycheck, I did general interest stories and then moved up to the big desk. I'm pretty sure I was on my way to New York, but then I got religion and Reverend Godfrey doubled my salary to come on board with him."

Taking a chance — sometimes she just couldn't help herself — Ellie asked, "Getting religion have anything to do with the big money?"

Dunston didn't take offense, he laughed. "In the beginning, sure it did. After a while, I really saw the light. I donate a large share of my income to missionary work." He looked out the windshield. Ellie followed his gaze and saw many other *soldiers* scurrying about their duties. "But I think you'll have to agree what I'm doing here today has to be about more than a career move."

Ellie nodded. Imprisonment and death rarely made executive recruiters come calling.

"Right down there," Dunston said, pointing the way, "is the admin building. Reverend Godfrey is waiting to talk with you."

Ellie put her car in motion and asked, "He's willing to speak on camera?"

"Ms. Booker, he insists on it. If you didn't bring your own camera, we'll let you use one of ours."

"So you're more than just a soldier," Ellie said.

Dunston told her, "I'm the public information officer. Or an evangelist. Depending on your point of view and the needs of the moment."

Number One Observatory Circle

Celsus Crogher met Rockelle Bullard at the entrance to the grounds of Vice President Mather Wyman's official residence. She was the first of the weapon-carrying guests to arrive. For safety's sake a surreptitious digital picture was taken of her and transmitted to all the Secret Service agents on duty. It was a thin gesture, merely adding to the hope the good guys wouldn't wind up shooting each other.

The agents in place already had a recent photo of Holmes and had been advised it would be better for their families that they die in the line of duty rather than shoot James J. McGill, even if he had his weapon drawn and was shooting, say, the speaker of the House of Representatives. They'd let the courts sort that one out.

Likewise, photos of Putnam Shady and Margaret Sweeney had been distributed, and their deaths at the hands of a special agent would be considered tragic, possibly even career ending, but not cause to lose pension benefits or to face criminal prosecution.

Putnam Shady hadn't made the targets-to-worry-about list.

Crogher introduced himself to the Metro homicide lieutenant. She nodded and returned the favor.

"May I have the code word for entry?" he asked.

If she'd forgotten it, Crogher would express insincere regret and send her on her way.

But Rockelle said, "O happy man."

Crogher masked his disappointment and asked, "Are you armed, Lieutenant Bullard."

She nodded again. "Glock in my handbag."

"Anything else?"

"Got a nail file in there, too."

The woman was sizable, Crogher thought. Maybe had ten pounds on him. An edged weapon of any kind was nothing to be disregarded, but he was more concerned about things that went bang and boom.

"If I told you I thought everyone, including you, would be better off if you let me hold your Glock while you're here, would that make any difference to you?" Crogher asked.

Rockelle gave him a brief smile. "Somebody's messing with you, aren't they, SAC Crogher? That somebody might even be named James J. McGill."

Crogher kept his mouth shut. Rockelle understood.

Unexpressed opinions often lay at the heart of professional survival.

Rockelle said, "Tell you what. I've met Mister McGill. Don't think he's a bad sort at all, but his being the president's husband, he gets privileges your average P.I. can't dream of. Ordinary cops like me or feds like you, we just got to grin and bear it."

Crogher hadn't grinned at anything since McGill had entered

his life. But he was both surprised and pleased when Rockelle opened her purse and handed her Glock to him.

She said, "Someday I might need a favor from you, and I'm sure you'll remember how understanding I was today."

Crogher thought maybe he should ask for the nail file, too.

But he nodded. Someone did right by him, someone who understood the crap he had to take putting up with Holmes, he'd pay her back.

"One more thing," Rockelle said.

"What's that?" Crogher asked.

"There might be someone here today who killed three or more people on my streets."

"I've heard that."

"We get him, whoever gets him, he's my arrest."

Crogher wanted no part of somebody else's mess.

He put his hand out and Rockelle took it.

"A pleasure meeting you, SAC Crogher," she said.

He couldn't remember the last time *anyone* had told him that.

The Vice President's Mansion

With guests starting to arrive, SAC Crogher decided to detail Special Agent Augie Latz to watch over the bride and groom.

"Two packages?" Latz asked, using service jargon for protected people. "Who gets priority?"

The special agent knew it was a dumb question as soon as he'd asked it.

He said, "Sorry, the vice president's niece, of course. If necessary, I catch the bullet for her. Captain Yates will be armed and can take care of himself, but if I'm near him and see he's about to shoot someone I either stop him or take the shot for him, depending."

Crogher gave the special agent a long look. With Rockelle Bullard neutralized, he was looking to take another wild card out of the deck. "Right, but a half-step slow, Latz. You better be up to speed when it counts."

"Yes, sir."

The special agent hustled into the mansion where the bride and groom had their respective dressing rooms: Miz Fahey in the VP's office; Captain Yates in a lounge just up a short flight of stairs. He knocked on the office door and asked if everything was okay, if they needed any help from him.

Kira called back, "Tell Welborn I'll expect him to be in top form tonight."

A chorus of feminine giggles followed, along with a maternal voice saying, "Kira, really." Then the older woman laughed, too.

Latz strained to stay alert and not let his mind wander to thoughts of —

Vice President Wyman was coming his way from the reception hall with Captain Yates and two other guests, a great-looking older woman who, from the resemblance, had to be Yates' mother and an older guy carrying a gift-wrapped box who looked like the captain, too. Yates' father?

Vice President Wyman asked, "All's well, special agent?"

"Yes, sir."

"Might the ladies tolerate a brief interruption in their preparations?"

"I just arrived, sir. You'll have to ask them about that."

Wyman tapped on the door and said, "Eliza, Kira, might I intrude for just a minute?"

"Everyone's dressed, Mather," his sister called to him.

"Come in, Uncle Mather. Tell me if I'll make Welborn swoon."

"Don't you always?" Welborn asked.

"No peeking, no peeking!" Kira warned and the bridesmaids echoed.

The door opened a crack and a hand pulled the vice president inside.

"And that was the last anyone ever saw of the poor man," Welborn joked.

He stepped over to the Secret Service agent and extended his hand, "Captain Welborn Yates." Taking his hand, Augie said,

"Special Agent Latz."

Welborn introduced his parents, Marian Yates and Sir Robert Reed. Ms. Yates nodded. Sir Robert shifted the gift box to his left arm and shook the special agent's hand. Having been trained to notice the details of his environment, Latz spotted a gold leaf embossment on the gift box's wrapping paper: a crown and below that the letters EIIR.

Sir Robert said, "Thank you for your service today, special agent."

"You're welcome, sir."

The captain took his parents up to the lounge and closed the door. Latz was left to himself again. He started thinking … about his job this time. It was common enough for a package to introduce himself to his bullet-catcher. Let the special agent know he was a regular guy and someone worth dying for. But introducing Mom and Dad? That was a new one. And Dad, with his polished Brit accent, holding the gift box in his arm just so, making sure Latz couldn't miss the golden doodad on it. Like he was sending a message.

Special Agent Latz took his BlackBerry out of his pocket and Googled the doodad. He learned it was something called a royal cypher, for Queen Elizabeth, the second one. Why it wasn't QE2, he didn't know. But the idea of a cypher was interesting. Like it was some kind of coded message between Sir Robert and him.

Yeah, right. He kept up the melodrama and —

As long as he had his phone in his hand, he speed-dialed SAC Crogher.

"Latz, sir. I was just introduced to Sir Robert Reed and I was wondering: Did anyone look inside that gift box he's carrying?"

If it really was from the Queen of England, he kind of doubted it.

Mather Wyman beamed at his niece Kira and tears welled up in his eyes. She was beautiful even at the end of a long day of shuffling paper at the White House. Now, on the morning of her wedding, in a glorious white dress designed by someone with an actual sense of style, she was positively radiant. He couldn't have been more proud of her if she were his own daughter, as he'd long ago come to think of her.

What really touched his heart, though, was how she'd accessorized. Draped around her neck in the fashion of a scarf was a crisp white cloth with the image of her late father, Neil Fahey, on it. Mather Wyman had heard the story of the miracle behind how that image came to be. It gave him renewed hope he he might someday see … Elvie, his late wife, who looked back at him from a photo in a cameo setting pinned above Kira's heart.

"Do I look all right, Uncle Mather?" Kira asked.

The vice president took out a handkerchief to dry his eyes.

"No one has ever looked better," he said. He didn't want to muss his niece's dress or makeup so he put an arm around his sister's shoulders. "Right, Eliza?"

The bride's mother agreed completely.

As his job had taught him, Vice President Mather Wyman knew when it was time to bow out of the headliner's way. "If you'll excuse me, there's something I need to retrieve from the bathroom, and then I'll be on my way."

Unable to resist, he took his niece's hand and kissed it.

Then he went into the bathroom and closed the door. He opened the door to the towel cupboard. He wanted to collect his cigars, four Cohibas. He'd started hiding his smokes from Elvie who hadn't approved of the habit, but pretended it didn't exist, so long as he changed his clothes, showered and brushed his teeth before coming anywhere near her after smoking. Taking things one step farther, Mather always made a point of storing — hiding — his cigars where his wife would not have to see them.

It was just a game they had, but it fit in well with the bigger secrets they'd kept.

After Elvie had died, he'd kept putting his Cohibas in places no one else would find them — such as the top shelf of a towel cupboard where anyone under six feet tall would have to stand on a stool to get at them. At six-three, the vice president had no trouble making the reach.

But when he took down the small humidor he found that one of his cigars was missing. He distinctly remembered there had been four left the last time he'd taken one out to smoke. Now, there were only three. So who …

One of the ladies in the other room?

That was why he'd stopped into the bathroom. To prevent a discovery and any tomfoolery that might result from it. He did a quick mental survey. Didn't think that any woman out in his office stood taller than five-eight, far too short to reach the cigars. Unless one of them stood on his desk chair. But that seemed … not so far-fetched that he hadn't worried about someone getting at his cigars.

But if the ladies had taken a cigar, they would no doubt be making sport of it.

Pretending to smoke it and so forth. He'd seen no evidence of that.

So again, who'd been at his Cohibas? It was a small thing, but disturbing.

There was a knock at the door. Eliza asked, "Mather, will you be in there much longer?"

The vice president held the humidor in what he hoped was a discreet manner and opened the door. "Just leaving, my dear," he told his sister. "Would you mind stepping into the hallway with me for just a moment?"

Eliza agreed and the vice president said goodbye to Kira and her friends.

"Well this is mysterious, isn't it?" Eliza asked, as she closed the door to the office behind her. "What is it, Mather?"

In a quiet voice, he asked, "Has anyone else visited my office this morning?"

"You mean outside of the bridesmaids and me?"

"Yes."

"Just an old friend."

"A tall old friend?"

"Well, yes, Zack Garner is quite tall."

Special Agent Augie Latz, standing unnoticed though entirely visible outside of the office at the foot of the stairway leading to the lounge, listened in on the conversation. Heard every softly spoken word. That was part of his job. The next step was an exercise in judgment. If he were to decide the content of what he'd heard had nothing to do with a threat to any protected person or wasn't evidence of a criminal conspiracy, his job would be to forget what he'd heard.

Latz decided Garner stopping by before he'd taken up his post was at least as significant as the royal cypher. He called SAC Crogher to let him know.

"Always seems a shame to tear the paper off a neatly wrapped gift," Welborn said to his parents. "Especially when there's a royal emblem on it."

"Cypher," his father corrected. "And this package is no more than a bit of stagecraft from the lads at the embassy. Her majesty's actual gift to you and Kira awaits you at my villa in Barcelona."

"Is it a pony?" Welborn asked.

His mother laughed.

"An equine gift was considered," Sir Robert said, "but more on the order of an Arabian stallion. Something spirited you and Kira might ride when you visit your mother and me on our new property in South Carolina."

"You're moving to the U.S.?" Welborn asked his father.

"With her majesty in retirement, there's really no need to keep me on. I've been pensioned off, but it is quite a nice pension," Sir Robert said.

"And you didn't think of going back to Canada?" Welborn had learned that though his father had lived most of his life in England and had served in the British military he had been born in Toronto.

Marian Yates told her son, "We did consider British Columbia, but it was a bit chilly for me. We looked at the Caribbean, too, but with the villa in Barcelona ..." She shrugged.

"So you're going live in South Carolina. Have you filed your immigration papers, Dad? I know a few people who might help, if there's any hang-up."

Sir Robert smiled. "I believe my chances are good once I marry a U.S. citizen."

"Mother, really?"

"Really."

"When?"

"We'll let you know. It will be quite a small and private ceremony. You and Kira and maybe a few others. Now, let's get on with your wedding."

She deftly undid the gift wrapping, preserving both the paper and the royal cypher. Sir Robert removed the top of the box and took out a matte pearl white vest. He held it up in front of his son and was pleased.

"Size is spot on, I'd say."

Welborn took off his shirt and put on the vest. It fit closely but not constrictively.

"Lighter than I would have though," Welborn said. "Not bulky at all. Will it work?"

"My boy, it's the same model I'm wearing."

Welborn looked at his father, studying his suit coat closely.

"Can't tell, can you?" Sir Robert asked.

"No."

"This is the newest, finest body armor available in the world today. The Japanese like to think they have something to match it, but their vest bunches as one moves, leaves a chap looking rumpled. Not at all what a man wants on his wedding day."

Welborn slipped on and buttoned the shirt that went with his dress uniform. He checked his reflection in a full-length mirror. If anything, it looked like maybe he'd done a few extra reps on the bench press to impress Kira. The Brits were very clever with their tailoring, even the bulletproof kind.

As if reading his son's mind, Sir Robert said, "Should stop anything short of .50 caliber round. Might leave some bruising or a cracked rib or two if you get hit by a volley but —"

"Robert, please," Marian said.

"Quite right, my dear. No time to talk shop."

Welborn handed Sir Robert his Berretta. The one SAC Crogher thought he'd be carrying. There was no way he could do that without Kira noticing. Which would probably spoil the mood. Not make for a great remembrance. So Dad would have his back, and he would shelter Kira with his armored torso if worse came to worse.

"Everything's going to be just fine," Welborn told Mom and Dad.

Salvation's Path Church, Richmond, Virginia

The FBI came in force to arrest Reverend Burke Godfrey but not in numbers great enough to fight a pitched battle against men with automatic weapons in fortified positions. They'd also neglected to ask the Army to lend them a few M1-Abrams tanks to clear away the garbage trucks blocking the access roads to the church's campus. Even if they'd had military armor, they wouldn't have risked the tank crews' lives, assuming that the trucks were filled with explosives.

What the federal agents did have from the start was air superiority. The equipment on their helicopters and Nightstalker planes could see in the dark, eavesdrop on conversations and cell phone communications and provide live video feeds to decision-makers in the local command center and in Washington. The FBI's birds weren't armed, but military air assets were on call and would arrive in a matter of minutes if summoned.

The first Bureau chopper arrived with the troops on the ground and provided both video and the pilot's observations to the command center where Ed Pastorini, the FBI's Crisis Management Unit leader, would orchestrate everyone's movements. He turned to Deputy Attorney General Linda Otani who had been sent along to make sure every move the government forces made would be defensible in court — or before a Congressional hearing. AG Michael Jaworsky wasn't about to let Burke Godfrey walk or the president be crucified because any of the troops had screwed up.

"How many people are there behind the barricades?" Otani asked the chopper pilot.

The response was immediate. "Approximately one hundred uniformed personnel on the ground and on rooftops, another dozen in view in building windows."

"Uniformed?" Otani asked.

"Yes, ma'am. Military fatigues complete with body armor, Fritzes and assault rifles."

The DAG looked at Pastorini. He knew what she wanted.

"Fritz is jargon for helmet," he said. "They're geared up for combat."

"Do we know if any of these people are active duty U.S. military?"

Pastorini shook his head. "Too soon to say, but we're already taking pictures of faces. They'll be matched against the databases. Then we'll know more."

Otani asked the helicopter pilot, "Do you see any children?"

"Negative."

"Thank God for that," she said.

"There could be a building full of them," Pastorini said.

"Shit." The DAG knew he was right.

When it came to human shields, you couldn't beat kids.

Pastorini said, "Your call, ma'am. What do we do next?"

Before Linda Otani could answer, they heard the sounds of gunfire coming over the radio, and the helicopter pilot said in a flat tone, "Hostile fire. They're shooting at us."

"Get out of there," Pastorini told him.

"I'll call the attorney general," Linda Otani said.

"I'll call the Air Force for a drone," Pastorini replied.

The White House, Chief of Staff's Office

Galia Mindel sat behind her desk, her face impassive as she listened to Attorney General Michael Jaworsky relay the report he'd received from Richmond. For just a moment, she could identify with the late Alexander Haig on the morning President Reagan had been shot and Haig had impulsively said, "I'm in control here."

Both the president and the vice president were out of the White House. She was there. The temptation to make an executive decision on the spot was nearly overwhelming. But doing so, if things went wrong, would be a terrible mistake. Especially for her, but also for the president.

Exercising an abundance of caution, she said, "I'll get back to you shortly, Michael, after I've spoken with the president."

"Please do, Madam Chief of Staff. None of those shots hit the FBI helicopter, but all of them came down in populated areas. No casualties were reported, but that was strictly a matter of good fortune. If the forces inside Reverend Godfrey's compound open fire again, we'll not only have to protect our people, we'll have to evacuate the civilian population for a considerable distance."

Doing something like that, Galia knew, could cut various ways. Provoke anger against the government, Godfrey or both.

"I'll make it quick, Michael."

She called the president, reached her in Thing One just as it was arriving at Number One Observatory Circle. *Have a nice time at the wedding, Madam President,* Galia thought. She described what was happening in Richmond, and recommended a course of action.

In the months between Patricia Darden Grant's election and inauguration, she and Galia had gamed any number of scenarios that might confront the new president in her first term. Among them was the situation in Waco, Texas that Bill Clinton had confronted. Having the benefit of seeing what didn't work, a frontal assault, they opted to go another way. Galia's solution, in part, was inspired by the Israelis' approach to defending their territory: Build high concrete walls.

Only these walls would keep Godfrey's people inside instead of keeping hostile neighbors outside. Godfrey liked barricades? Great. They'd give him concrete walls thirty feet high and two feet thick. The walls would encircle his property. They would be watched around the clock, and anyone trying to slip out would be arrested.

All communication with the outside world would be cut off. Phone lines would be taken down; cell communications would be jammed. As would TV, radio and Internet access. Isolation would be complete.

If those within the wall held out long enough to exhaust their supplies of food and water, airdrops would be made. Nutritious but unseasoned packets of food would be supplied. Only one kind. Forcing the inmates to eat the same thing endlessly. Water would be the only liquid provided.

After a month or two, a dedicated TV signal would be opened, strictly for the purpose of advising Godfrey that he and anyone inside over the age of fifteen would be tried on federal charges in absentia. If they were found guilty and refused to surrender, they would serve their sentences *in situ*.

Without further communication with the outside world.

That was the plan that Galia had come up with for a situation such as the one they were facing now. It was the plan to which the president had agreed.

The president told Galia, "Do it."

Ellie Booker was the first one to see the heavy construction equipment arrive, and it chilled her. She was not only the producer of a news show, she was a news junkie. She'd seen clips of this kind of equipment at work before and it didn't take an Einstein to figure out how it would be used.

"Jesus Christ," she said, "I've got to get out of here."

Reverend Godfrey gave the WorldWide News woman a sour look. He didn't like to hear the Lord's name taken in vain. It was a sin. Almost as bad was her having the nerve to blaspheme in front of him. Worse still, watching the woman scurry around and pack up her camera and other belongings in a frantic manner scared him.

He got to his feet and went to the window to see what had frightened Ellie.

Art Dunston, his public information officer, joined him there.

"All I see are some bulldozers and such," Godfrey said. "Nothing that has a bit of firepower."

Ellie looked at the preacher like he was a backwoods bumpkin, an expression he didn't care for and to which he was about to object. But Ellie turned to Dunston and asked, "Are *you* smart enough to see what's going to happen?"

"Yes, ma'am, I believe I am." Dunston's voice carried a lot more of the South now.

Slipping into his evangelist's role, Ellie thought.

"Well, tell the reverend, will you?" she asked, getting back to her packing.

He turned to Godfrey and said, "Those men and their machines, Reverend Godfrey, they mean to lock us in."

"With bulldozers and cranes? How're they going to do that? Dig a moat?"

"Look over there at that big flatbed truck," Dunston said, pointing.

Truck? Ellie hadn't seen that. She rushed to the window ... and there it was.

Dunston continued his tutorial. "What you see over there, Reverend, is a prefabricated section of concrete wall, pretty much like the State of Israel used to wall itself off from the Palestinians living on the West Bank. What's gonna happen is the dozers will dig a footing in the earth and the cranes will lower the prefab sections of wall into place. Construction like that can go up right quick."

Dunston had it exactly right, Ellie thought, but he didn't seem at all frightened by the prospect of being imprisoned. He had a peaceful smile on his face. Looked like he didn't have a worry in the world.

Ellie said, "I'm outta here." She hurried to the door but Dunston called out to her.

"Ms. Booker?" Ellie stopped to see if he was trying to stop her at gunpoint. He wasn't, but he might as well have been. "What?" she demanded.

"Firing on that helicopter? That was done against orders. Some of our recruits don't have all the training and discipline we'd like. You go racing across the campus, someone might mistake your intentions, start shooting again. That happens, the people on the other side might not hold their fire, thinking we're trying to stop their wall from going up."

Goddamnit, Ellie thought, he was right.

"The crossfire could get intense, Ms. Booker. It'd be a terrible risk to take."

For the first time since she'd left her parents' house of horrors, Ellie Booker was brought to tears. She dropped her gear. Seeing that was a sight that made Burke Godfrey smile. He'd had it with disrespectful, disobedient women.

"It might take some time, Ms. Booker," Dunston said, "but we'll negotiate a release for you, don't you worry."

Dunston didn't see Godfrey give a small shake of his head but Ellie did.

That prick meant to hold on to her.

"What if they won't let anyone out?" Ellie said.

Dunston shrugged. He looked at Godfrey, who needed a moment to see where Dunston was going, then understood, firmed his jaw and nodded.

"Worse comes to worse, Ms. Booker," Dunston said, "we'll look to the precedent of biblical times. You know about the siege of Masada?"

Ellie did and she went pale hearing the reference.

The last Jewish stronghold in the Great Revolt against the Roman Empire was the fortress at Masada. The Romans lay siege to it and when they finally breached the walls, they found that all but seven of the defenders had chosen suicide over submission.

More than nine hundred people had died by their own hands.

Masada. The fountainhead for Jonestown, Waco … and now Richmond?

Ellie's terror made Burke Godfrey chuckle.

"Probably won't be as bad as all that, Ms. Booker," he said. "Meanwhile, why don't you just consider yourself an embed?"

Number One Observatory Circle

Hearing from Special Agent Latz that Representative Garner had already gotten past the security perimeter almost unhinged SAC Crogher, especially as Thing One with Holly G. and Holmes inside had just arrived. He gestured to an agent to open the door from which the president would exit and crouched so he might address her eye to eye.

"Madam President, there's been a breach of security. I don't know how it happened, but until it can be resolved …"

Crogher wanted to say he couldn't allow her to leave the car or even permit Thing One to remain on the premises. She would have to return to the White House until the situation was understood and brought under control. That was what his training told him should be done. That was what would have been done under any other chief executive.

Patricia Darden Grant, however, was different from her predecessors in any number of ways, both substantive and stylistic.

Unfazed, the president asked Crogher, "What's the breach?"

Crogher had to make a conscious effort not to grind his teeth.

He was going to be questioned and overruled, he just knew it.

At least Holmes had the decency to keep quiet for the moment.

"Congressman Zachary Garner has made his way onto the premises without passing by this checkpoint. As your husband can tell you, this is a matter of no small concern."

"Jim?" the president asked.

"Could be," McGill said.

Crogher was grateful for even that token agreement.

Until the president asked Holmes, "Big chance or small?"

"Small."

"Madam President," Crogher said, "that's not the question. I'm not supposed to allow for *any* chance that you might be endangered."

McGill said, "Celsus is right. I feel the same way."

SAC Crogher looked at McGill, all but stupefied. The two of them *agreed?*

Even two to one, though, they couldn't outvote the president.

She said, "Celsus, the way things have been going with Kenny McGill and the damnable politics in this town, I need to see, I need to *feel* a moment of joy, even if it belongs to someone else. I'm going to watch Kira Fahey marry Welborn Yates, and you're going to see to it that it's safe for me to do so.

"For the moment, you're going to find a secure location on these grounds for me to wait in relative comfort until you can find Congressman Garner. Then I will sit next to my husband in what I hope will be good seats and we will witness the affirmation of love and hope that is the marriage of two souls. Are we clear on all that, SAC Crogher?"

"Yes, ma'am," Crogher said.

Made him think Holly G. had been influenced by her meeting with the Queen of England last year. Sounded like a royal decree to him. Not that presidents couldn't get imperious all on their own.

What surprised him was that he didn't want to argue. The president was right. Whatever she wanted, it was his job to provide.

The president turned to McGill and said, "See what you can do to help, will you, Jim?"

Her henchman kissed her and said, "As you wish."

Five minutes later, another limousine pulled up to the security checkpoint. Crogher was no longer there, but the special agents were on high alert, having been given the word to detain Zachary Garner should he try to slip *out* of the security net. They'd also been advised that Speaker Derek Geiger, should he arrive, was to be given a going-over that included everything but a body cavity search.

If Crogher had been there, after being forced to allow the president entrance, he might have insisted on the cavity search, too.

As is was, the senior special agent at the gate, Russ Chester, nodded to Geiger when he lowered his window. "Good morning, Mister Speaker. May I have the password, please?"

"O happy man."

"That's correct, sir. Will you please step out of your vehicle?"

"Step out?"

"Please, sir. Security conditions have been stepped up."

Geiger frowned upon hearing that. "Is something wrong?"

"I can't comment, sir."

"Should I be concerned for my safety?"

Special Agent Chester had been instructed by Crogher to turn the speaker around at the gate if an opportunity that wouldn't cause an uproar presented itself. Senior man that he was, Chester didn't want to overdo it, make the scare attempt transparent.

"Mister Speaker, with our mindset, there's *always* concern."

Chester's words had the unintended effect of reassuring Geiger.

Sure, Secret Service guys were paranoid all the time. Came with the job.

"I'll risk it," he said, opening the door and stepping out. "Metal-detecting wand?"

"Full-airport frisk, I'm afraid, sir."

Geiger scowled but stood his ground.

Chester did the frisk. He stopped when he got to Geiger's waist.

"What do you have under your jacket, sir?"

"A colostomy bag."

Chester knew about those things. His grandpa had had one.

"I'll need to take a look."

"I'm afraid it needs to be emptied."

"Yes, sir. I've seen it before. Just a quick look."

Geiger showed him, his own real feces in a semi-transparent

plastic bag.

As far as Special Agent Chester was concerned, he'd gone the extra mile.

"Sorry for the inconvenience, sir. Enjoy the wedding."

Geiger nodded. No hard feelings. He got back into his car and moved on.

The man who had sold him the plastic gun in Austria had thrown in the colostomy bag at no extra charge. The gun nestled inside a sealed bubble surrounded by the wearer's actual bodily waste. The gun dealer had told Geiger the bag wasn't foolproof, but he said there were few people who would want to delve deeply into other people's shit.

Geiger thought security people shouldn't be so squeamish.

Vice President Mather Wyman found his old friend Representative Zachary Garner in a small room just under the roof of the mansion. It was a holding space for old chairs and other odds and ends of furniture awaiting transport to charitable resale stores. The room looked out a north-facing window to the triangular lawn where the wedding ceremony would be held. Garner sat in an armchair, looking out at the grounds, an unlit Cohiba in his dangling left hand.

Standing behind Garner, the vice president couldn't tell if his friend was conscious or even alive. Special Agent Latz stood to Mather Wyman's right. At the vice president's request, Latz had been reassigned to accompany him. The special agent moved to interpose himself between the two men.

Wyman put out a hand to stop him.

"Zack," the vice president said, "are you all right?"

The hand holding the cigar raised its thumb.

"Still present and accounted for, sir," Garner said. "Pull up a chair, Mather."

The vice president started to move forward, but this time Latz stopped him.

"Representative Garner, I'm Special Agent August Latz of the

Secret Service. May I see your other hand, sir?"

Garner raised his right hand just above his shoulder. Turned it sideways. It was empty.

Latz had noticed no movement to set aside a gun or other object.

"May I ask, sir, how you arrived here today?" Latz said.

"Two of your colleagues were watching my home this morning, special agent. They were kind enough to provide chauffeur service to me."

"The Secret Service brought you here?" Latz found that hard to believe.

"No, I'm sorry. I meant colleagues in a broader sense. These gentlemen were from the FBI. They arrived *before* the Secret Service showed up, I was told. I believe your immediate compañeros were told they could stand down."

Latz bit back a curse. *Fucking feebs.* Still, they must have rolled past the Secret Service agents on the gate — before he got there. Somebody was going to catch hell from Crogher. He just hoped the kill radius didn't extend to him.

"Did the FBI say why they were watching you, sir?"

"I asked, but they declined to answer."

That, Latz could understand. You didn't give away the game to a suspect.

The special agent gestured to the vice president. He would move a chair next to Garner's right side, where he could get a good look at the situation. He did so cautiously, without incident. Garner looked at Latz, gave him a wink.

He didn't like that, but he didn't see any threat.

In fact, if Garner wasn't about to breath his last, it wouldn't be long in coming.

The special agent gestured Wyman forward. The vice president took his seat.

"Would it be possible to get a sip of water, Mather?" Garner asked.

"Of course. Right away." He looked at Latz.

Who wasn't going anywhere. "I'll call for it, sir."

He moved behind Garner, taking up a position where he could jump on the man if Garner made — was able to make — a move he didn't like. He whispered into his wrist-mike, requested the water and brought SAC Crogher up to date on the situation. He was told to stay where he was; another agent would arrive to escort Wyman down to the wedding.

"Hope you don't mind about the cigar, Mather," Garner said.

"Not at all. Would you like me to light it for you?"

"I'd love it. But I don't think the nicotine would agree with my meds, and I'd really like to survive long enough to see Kira and her young man exchange their vows. I don't think I've got much more time than that left. That's why I came up here, to die out of the way. Not cause a fuss, get wheeled out discreetly."

The vice president said, "You stopped in to see Kira one last time."

"I did. Took most of my remaining strength to put on a good front. Mather, she's so lovely. That young man is getting a real treasure."

"I know. So does he."

"I hope they have a long time together, more than you or I had with our wives."

"So do I."

Garner turned to his friend with a ghostly grin. "I had to use your office bathroom again. While I was in there washing my hands, I thought to myself: I bet Mather still hides his cigars."

The vice president smiled sadly. "You know me too well."

Another Secret Service agent appeared. He brought with him a silver tray bearing a glass of water. Latz handed the glass to Garner. Took another look. Saw nothing threatening.

Garner sipped and handed the glass back. "Thank you."

"Zack, I have to go," the vice president said.

"Of course. You're giving away the bride."

Wyman put a hand on Garner's shoulder. "Is there anything else I can do for you?"

"One last request? Yes, there is something. If you can have someone locate him, I believe there's a guest present by the name of Putnam Shady. He should be with Mister McGill's friend Margaret Sweeney. Please tell Mister Shady I'd like to have a word with him before I go."

The vice president said he would. He kissed his friend's forehead in farewell.

Salvation's Path Church, Richmond, Virginia

Ellie Booker wanted out now. The thought that the inmates of the church campus might be headed for mass suicide scared her silly. A wave of lunacy like that started to build, nobody in its path was safe. At Jonestown, the people who didn't want to drink the poisoned Kool-Aid got shot. Survival was not an option. Ellie didn't intend to be the victim of a failed plea for mercy.

Leaving Reverend Godfrey's office, she exited the rear of the administration building. The structure sheltered her from the noise of the construction machinery. To her right she saw a group of ten men in uniform carrying rifles run past. They didn't notice her. She wondered if they were going to attack the wall builders. If that happened, she was sure the government people would shoot back, and she'd bet they had a damn sight more firepower.

Ellie took out her cell phone and waited a minute to see if the roar of a firefight would make a conversation impossible. But no gunfire ensued. The defenders must have been intent on seeing that none of the government paramilitaries was infiltrating the campus. Their movement had been defensive, and the government was showing restraint, not racking up a body count that might be criticized by the judiciary or the political right.

Shit. Patti Grant was playing it smart again. Burke Godfrey wanted to lock her out, fine. She'd lock his ass in. Prison, like home, was where you made it. The president's underlings would work things out so that any blood that was spilled would be on Godfrey's hands. Anybody who criticized her then, or tried to defend

Godfrey, would be guilty of the worst sin there was these days: losing politics.

With no one around to see or hear her, Ellie called Hugh Collier. She almost sobbed in relief when he answered on the first ring.

"You've got to get me out of here, Hugh," she told him.

He understood intuitively what she meant.

"You're inside the perimeter?" he asked. "On the church grounds?"

"Yes."

"Put her on speaker," a muffled voice said.

Ellie heard a click and then Sir Edbert said to her, "Ms. Booker, are there any other reporters on your side of the line?"

"Line, what line?" Ellie demanded.

"You have no TV?" he asked.

"I can get a video feed on my phone."

"Whilst you continue to talk?" Sir Edbert asked.

"Yes."

"Go to our streaming feed," Hugh told her.

Fearing what she might find, Ellie followed instructions. She saw a satellite view of the Salvation's Path campus. Around it was a telestrated line glowing in green and red.

"I've got it," she said. "The line is the wall they're building?"

A section of the green part of the line turned turned red as she watched.

Ellie started to sway. She had to put a hand against the building to steady herself.

"You've got to get me out of here," she demanded. "Call whoever's in charge out there; tell them I'm being held here against my will. I'm not one of these maniacs. I want out!"

The lack of a response made her wonder if she'd lost the signal.

"Are you there? Hugh? Sir Edbert?"

"Ellie," Hugh said, "this could be a tremendous opportunity."

"You are the only reporter in the midst of an historical event," Sir Edbert told her. "The story will be ours exclusively. Don't you see, the longer it lasts the better. We'll have more material, more human drama. We'll be able to play it out indefinitely and you'll be the star."

Ellie hissed, "They plan to commit mass suicide if they don't win."

The words had no sooner left her mouth than she realized she couldn't have handed two TV executives a better ending.

"You're not going to get me out, are you?" she asked.

There was no response, but this time she heard persistent static.

The video feed was gone, too.

The cell signal was being jammed. Neither Hugh nor Sir Edbert was going to tell any of the authorities about her plea for help. She'd bet her stash of krugerrands on that.

She saw what looked to be the same group of armed men again. This time they were running in the opposite direction. Like they were extras in a bad comedy. Only they had real weapons and she was sure it wouldn't be long before people started dying for real.

Then a loud voice speaking from directly overhead startled her.

Not God, but it might as well have been.

"This is United States Attorney General Michael Jaworsky. The Federal Bureau of Investigation and supporting elements of our armed forces are here to arrest Reverend Burke Godfrey."

The armed forces, Ellie thought. Looking up, squinting at the bright sky, she saw the silhouette of a familiar shape. A drone. That was the source of the public address speaker. She wondered if the drone had Hellfire missiles, too.

If so, mass suicide might be unnecessary.

The AG continued, "If Reverend Burke surrenders immediately, everyone else will be able to go home tonight. If he doesn't, we will complete building the wall and every adult found inside of it will be charged with obstruction of justice, at a minimum. Reverend Burke and those of you aiding him have fifteen minutes to decide."

The comic book commandos were back again. Two of them stationed themselves at the corner of the administration building.

This time they looked at her. Their expressions were unfriendly, and now they looked purposeful.

Ellie realized what task they had been given. It was neither offensive nor defensive. It was restrictive. No one would be allowed to dash to freedom. The Richmond Wall would go up as its predecessor in Berlin had and there would be no escape to the West or any other point of the compass.

A new thought entered Ellie's mind: With all the guns in this place, there had to be one she could get her hands on.

GWU Hospital

Dr. Jones, the chief oncologist on Kenny McGill's medical team, was in her office reviewing the schedule for bone marrow transplants that would be done that day when Barbara Marcos knocked on her door.

Jones looked up, surprised and a little displeased by the interruption.

Barbara both saw and understood the reaction. You didn't want to break a doctor's concentration when people's lives depended upon her.

"I'm sorry to disturb you, Doctor, but there may be a problem."

"What kind of problem?"

"I called the White House to confirm that the president would be here on time to make her donation. The first person I talked to said that he couldn't confirm anything about the president's schedule and demanded to know how I had come by the phone number I'd called. When I explained about Kenny McGill's BMT he backed off a bit and agreed to transfer me. Someone else came on and said he would see if he could get my message to the president. I told him this was a matter of life and death. He said right now it was the president's life they were worried about. Then he said, 'Oh, shit.' Like he shouldn't have let me know that. Then he broke the connection."

Dr. Jones' face fell. "My God, is there a threat to the president?"

"I don't know. But even if she's delayed for very long, what do we do?"

The doctor fought hard to keep her focus but it wasn't easy. Both the president and Clare Tracy had spoken to her in confidence. Fortunately, their desires meshed. The president wanted her bone marrow to go to Kenny McGill; Clare Tracy wanted hers to go to Annabelle Chalmers. So that worked. Both women wanted their decisions to be kept from the other. That worked, too. The president asked that her choice be kept from her husband and everyone else. Dr. Jones had agreed to that as well. Though Clare Tracy hadn't asked for the same confidence, the doctor decided to extend it to her.

Barbara Marcos said, "If the president can't make the donation in time, do we honor Ms. Tracy's request to give her donation to Annabelle?"

The second half of the question — Do we let Kenny McGill die? — went unspoken.

Before she could process all the consequences of the choice, Dr. Jones nodded.

Then she asked herself if that was really the ethical choice.

Clare Tracy's original motivation had been to try to save the life of Kenny McGill.

Would it still be her choice to donate to Annabelle if she learned the president was unable to donate to Kenny?

Could Ms. Tracy reverse herself now and let nine year old Annabelle die?

Would it be ethical to ask her to make such a terrible choice?

Dr. Jones said, "I'm going to call Artemus Nicolaides. He's the White House physician. He has to get through to the president and tell us what the situation is."

"And quickly," Barbara replied.

Number One Observatory Circle

McGill found that two front row seats on the green where the wedding ceremony would be held had been reserved for Patti and him. Welborn was talking with Francis Nguyen, the former Catholic priest who would bless the young couple's union. He spotted Sir Robert Reed, Welborn's father, whom he'd met last year at the dinner given by the Queen at Buckingham Palace. With Sir Robert was an attractive woman who looked too much like Welborn to be anyone other than his mother.

McGill nodded to the couple and went to speak with Welborn. He shook hands with Francis Nguyen and asked if he might borrow the groom for a minute.

"Of course, but don't keep him too long, if you wish the ceremony to start on time."

"No worries, Pastor," Welborn told him.

He and McGill moved off to one side of the flower-covered wedding trellis.

"What is it, Jim?" Welborn asked. He still had trouble not calling McGill sir.

"Do you know Zachary Garner by sight? I'm looking for him."

"He's the guy?" Welborn asked. "He did the K Street killings?"

"It's complicated, Welborn. Do you know him?"

The young Air Force captain nodded. "He introduced himself to me earlier. Told me how lucky I am to marry Kira. I thanked him and said that I knew."

"Have you seen him recently? I need to find him."

Welborn turned toward the gathering crowd and looked around.

So did McGill. He didn't see Garner but he noticed Sir Robert was looking his way.

"There he is, Jim," Welborn said.

McGill followed the younger man's gaze but didn't see Garner. "Where?"

"You're looking too low. Top right window in the VP's house."

McGill followed Welborn's directions, saw a figure seated behind the window but couldn't make out who it was.

"You're sure that's him?"

"Yes, sir," Welborn said, reverting to military courtesy.

The form of address reminded McGill that Welborn had a fighter pilot's vision.

McGill said, "Thank you."

"Do you need any help ... Jim?"

"Yeah, if I'm not back in time for the wedding, ask the president to grant me clemency." Welborn gave McGill a dubious look until he added, "Just kidding."

He was about to leave when Sir Robert stepped forward, "Is there any way I might be of service, Mr. McGill?"

McGill thought about that. He said, "Yes. Mingle a bit until the ceremony starts. If you hear anybody express an interest in my whereabouts or those of Congressman Garner or Putnam Shady, please direct them to the room at the top right of Vice President Wyman's house."

"Top right from this vantage point?" Sir Robert asked. "The room with ... ah, there's Representative Garner in the window. Yes, I see."

And McGill saw where Welborn got his eyesight.

Turning to Welborn, McGill said, "If you're not busy getting married and you see Putnam and Sweetie, please send them up, too. Right away."

McGill congratulated Welborn and Sir Robert on the happy occasion and left.

He wasn't sure what would happen putting everyone in the same room.

In Washington, there were three likely possibilities. Might be a happy resolution. One party or the other might walk out. Or the whole thing could blow up in their faces.

Preoccupied with his thoughts, McGill missed seeing Rockelle Bullard get up from her seat and start to follow him. Neither McGill nor Rockelle noticed Derek Geiger's arrival, but Geiger saw them head for the mansion, and then he noticed the groom and a distinguished looking gentleman watch McGill and the woman following him depart.

Newburyport, Massachusetts

Both Galia Mindel and Attorney General Michael Jaworsky made the trip to the nondescript house on the edge of the town in the northeastern corner of the state. The I-95 highway was close at hand for swift ground transport. A boat stood ready on the nearby Atlantic. The yard behind the house was large enough to land a helicopter. The federal government stood ready to evacuate Erna Godfrey by any means necessary.

Six special agents of the FBI, three male, three female, worked rotating eight-hour shifts guarding Erna. Another dozen agents formed an undercover security perimeter, watching Newburyport and scouting parks and woodlands, looking for any sign of strangers appearing in the vicinity, tourists who looked like they might have packed firearms and/or explosives in their vehicles.

No one was supposed to know where Erna had been taken once she was removed from the penitentiary in Hazelton, West Virginia, but secrets were more slippery than mercury, and once revealed could be equally toxic. Living in the age of WikiLeaks, every precaution had to be taken.

Even so, Galia and Jaworsky knew that the greatest risk would be their conversation with Erna Godfrey. Revealing what was happening at the church she had co-founded with her husband might serve their purpose or it might turn Mrs. Burke Godfrey against them. They'd know which within a matter of minutes.

The FBI agent driving them to the house from Boston said, "The subject has been notified she has visitors coming. She'll be waiting in the living room."

Jaworsky said, "What's her state of mind?"

The agent spoke softly into his radio and got a reply.

"Calm but curious is the evaluation."

"As much as we could hope for," Galia said.

The car pulled up to the house. Trees shielded it from the nearest neighbors. The front door opened as Galia and the AG approached it. An agent let them in and closed and locked the door behind them. He radioed his counterparts, advising them of the safe entry.

Erna Godfrey, wearing a tracking anklet and clothes from K-Mart, sat on a love seat. She looked at her visitors and her eyes widened. She clasped her hands tightly, as if bracing for bad news.

"Have you killed Burke?" she asked.

The visitors sat in arm chairs across from Erna.

Jaworsky placed a briefcase on his lap.

He said, "Your husband is alive, as far as we know, Mrs. Godfrey."

Galia added, "But he has placed himself in a great deal of jeopardy."

"How?" Erna asked.

Jaworsky said, "He's resisting arrest."

"Oh, Lord," Erna said. "I never thought he'd actually do it. Not after what happened to me." She paused to think about that. "Maybe I've got that wrong. It could be he's doing it because of what's happened to me."

"What is it you think he's doing, Mrs. Godfrey?" Galia asked.

"It's not a matter of thinking. If Burke won't give himself up, Ms. Mindel, I know what he's doing. He's using the church grounds as his last redoubt. He's planned for something like this for many years."

Both Galia and Jaworsky drew the inference that Erna had been privy to those plans, knew details that would help them keep Godfrey and his followers bottled up. Maybe even provide ideas on how he might be persuaded to surrender.

But all Galia asked for the moment was, "You know who we are?"

Erna laughed. "Of course, I do. We study our enemies almost as hard as we study the Good Book. The attorney general has a higher public profile than the president's chief of staff, at least in the Grant administration. You stay out of the limelight, Ms. Mindel, but there are photos of you in the public record."

Despite the lack of a direct threat, Galia felt a chill.

"We're your enemy, Mrs. Godfrey?" she asked. "Even now that

you've come to recognize that killing people isn't the way to save lives."

Erna gave the question a moment's thought.

"No, you're not the enemy — you're the opposition. Someone to be converted with prayer and reason. Someone to be shown the error of your ways."

"Someone whose ultimate fate is to be left in God's hands?" Galia asked.

"Yes, exactly."

"We can live with that. Would you like to see how your husband's plan to resist arrest is working out?" Jaworsky asked.

Erna was curious. "Yes, I would."

The attorney general opened his briefcase. He handed three eight-by-ten photographs to Erna. The first was an aerial view of the campus, its roads blocked, men with rifles on rooftops. That was just as she'd heard Burke describe how he'd start out. The second picture showed construction machinery being brought in, and she wondered what that was for. The third photo answered her question: A huge ugly wall had been put up around the beautiful grounds she and Burke had worked so long and hard to build.

She looked up at Galia and Jaworsky clearly distressed.

Galia told her, "What we're trying to do, obviously, is contain the situation without anyone being hurt. In the event that your husband and the others with him hold out long enough to run short of food and water, we will resupply them."

"They've got enough to last a very long time, Ms. Mindel."

The visitors kept straight faces but were happy to learn something they hadn't known. They were less than pleased by the idea the siege might continue up to or through the next presidential election. They'd have to work on that.

"That's unfortunate, Mrs. Godfrey," Galia said. "The more drawn out this situation becomes, the more likely it is someone will get hurt. One of your husband's followers already has taken shots at an FBI helicopter."

Erna blinked. "Was anyone hurt?"

"No, but that was only by the grace of God."

The AG handed Erna three more photos.

He said, "These pictures show where the bullets fired at the helicopter came back to earth."

One showed a shattered window in a house. Another went through a storefront window. The third went through the roof of a parked car.

Galia told Erna, "The one that hit the house went into a kitchen. A woman was in it at the time. She'd just gotten up from her kitchen table to rinse out her coffee cup. Otherwise she would have been hit."

"Did your husband plan for that, Mrs. Godfrey?" Jaworsky asked. "If that woman had died, the charge would be capital murder."

Erna looked stricken.

Before she could say anything, Galia added. "There was one loss of life."

The AG handed her a final photograph. Lying on its side on a lawn, blood pooled near its head, lay a golden Cocker Spaniel.

"The dog's name was Molly," Galia said. "The family that owned her is heartbroken."

Jaworsky added, "Quite angry, too. Angry at your husband and his people."

Galia followed. "Mrs. Godfrey, if your husband and his people hold out for long, others will get the idea they can flout the law and do the same thing. If that happens, there's no way *human* lives won't be lost. Possibly quite a lot of them."

Erna's face reflected the anguish in her soul.

Tears rolled down her cheeks.

She remembered the disfavor with which the Lord had gazed upon her.

She couldn't risk doing anything to add to that.

Erna told Galia and Jaworsky everything she knew about the militant anti-abortion movement. Then she had another thought.

"I better tell you about the tunnels Burke's people dug under church property."

Number One Observatory Circle

"Time to go," the president said. "The wedding starts in twenty minutes."

SAC Crogher said, "Yes, ma'am," even as he continued to listen to Special Agent Latz's voice in his ear. He whispered a reply into his wrist mike and then told the president, "The security breach has been resolved. The FBI brought a guest onto the grounds without our people realizing it. An interagency lapse of communication led to a false perception of a threat."

Crogher maintained a neutral tone, but there was no doubt in the president's mind whom the Treasury agent would blame.

She asked, "Do you know where my husband is?"

"Yes, ma'am. He's just joined one of my special agents and I presume is speaking with the person of interest."

Patti hated the idea of Jim missing the wedding, but she felt better that the situation would be in capable hands. It was a measure of her confidence in McGill that she didn't think to worry about his safety.

Within moments, the president was back in Thing One, having departed the observatory building where she'd been forced to cool her heels, and where the nation's Master Clock would confirm she had the time until Yates-Fahey wedding began exactly right.

A moment later the phone in the presidential limo chimed.

Artemus Nicolaides, the White House physician, was calling.

Speaker Derek Geiger didn't have to cross the lawn to talk with Sir Robert Reed. The man was working the wedding crowd, chatting up friends and family on both sides of the aisle. Geiger overheard the man introduce himself to the guests by name and say he was the father of the groom.

With the practiced ease of the longtime politician the speaker found an opportune moment to extend his hand and introduce himself. "Derek Geiger, please accept my best wishes on behalf of your son and his lovely bride."

"Thank you, sir," Sir Robert said. "That's very kind of you."

"If you don't mind my asking, did I see you talking with the president's husband a moment ago?"

"You have that exactly right."

"I was hoping to speak with him. Would you know where he's gone?"

"Actually, yes. He did mention that. He's stepped inside the vice president's lovely house. Up there in the top right corner, if you look at it from here."

Geiger did. "Up there?"

"Just so. I believe he's joining Representative Zachary Garner and a Mr. Putnam Shady. I think they mean to watch the ceremony from on high. I'm sure they'd be delighted to have your company, if you'd also enjoy the bird's-eye view."

"You know, I think I would. Good to meet you."

"The pleasure is mine, sir."

Geiger left and Sir Robert strolled back to where his son stood, awaiting his future wife. Welborn seemed more than a bit restless. To do more than get married.

"Dispatched the bloke upstairs just as Mr. McGill requested," Sir Robert said.

"I'd like to be up there," Welborn said.

"As would I, my boy, but first things first. Take my word, you don't want to put off the woman you love."

Welborn looked at the father he'd only recently met, silently agreeing that Sir Robert would know all about that. He watched his father take the seat next to his mother, the two of them looking like *they* were newlyweds. The man was right. He had better not do anything to —

A hand gently tapped his shoulder.

Welborn turned to see Elspeth Kendry.

A new acquaintance, he hadn't thought to invite her to the wedding. So …

She took his arm and led him a few paces from the guests and whispered to him.

"There's news," she said, "about Linley Boland."

"He's been arrested?" Welborn didn't know whether to feel exultant or crestfallen.

"Not yet. But there are a lot more cops looking for him now. He's suspected of murdering an elderly couple in Naples, Florida this morning. It looks like Boland was trying to carjack their Mercedes. The police there found his fingerprints on the car. The old folks were inside."

"That's terrible," Welborn said.

"Yeah, but that's not all. Boland's DNA was taken by the cops after you caught him, and late yesterday it was matched to another murder victim, a man named Achilles Mitchell who'd been shot dead in Baltimore earlier this week. Mitchell was discovered lying on a sidewalk right next to where a Bentley had been stolen."

"He's killing people to take their cars?" Welborn asked.

Elspeth said, "Looks like Mitchell was trying to grab the Bentley and Boland took it from him. You were the only one who got Boland instead of the other way around. You should feel pretty good about that."

What Welborn felt was woozy. If anything had gone wrong in that hotel parking structure, Kira might have been a widow before she ever became a bride.

"I just wanted you to know," Elspeth said, "with all the people looking for this guy, we're going to grab him soon. Don't give the prick another thought. Enjoy your honeymoon."

Welborn nodded and said, "Thank you."

Then he saw Margaret Sweeney and Putnam Shady coming his way. A moment earlier, he would have wanted to give them Jim McGill's message. Now, he asked Elspeth to do it.

She turned and looked at the window Welborn had mentioned.

"Up there?" she asked.

"Up there."

Elspeth said, "Special Agent Ky and Leo Levy were given the day off because Holmes was supposed to be spending the whole day with Holly G. I better go up there with the others."

Welborn nodded.

He'd be happy to stay right where he was.

Or so he told himself.

But he couldn't keep from looking over his shoulder at the third floor window.

And he saw something that didn't look right. Couldn't quite put his finger on what it was, and that disturbed him. He couldn't remember a time his eyesight had ever let him down. Not only was the acuity of his vision extraordinary, so was his ability to interpret what he saw, making immediate sense of it.

Calling on a resource that had been unavailable most of his life, he gestured to his father. Sir Robert excused himself from Welborn's mother and stepped over to his son. "What is it, Welborn?" He didn't like the sudden anxiety he saw on the young man's face.

"The window up there where Jim McGill and the others have gone, look just to the right of it. At the corner of the building, there's a drainpipe. The line of it isn't quite straight. There's a small irregularity, and a variation in color. Can you make out what it is?"

Sir Robert looked. "Yes, I see what you mean, but I can't make out the exact nature of what I'm seeing. My vision is still quite good, but I'm certain yours is better still. Do you think it might be just a piece of the pipe that has rusted through?"

Welborn couldn't tell, and it made him uneasy.

He took out his cell phone. It was on, set to vibrate. He handed it to his father.

"If it comes to me during the ceremony and if it's significant, I'll give you a sign. Hit number three on speed-dial. Tell Mr. McGill ... tell him to be alert and very careful."

Sir Robert nodded, taking his son's warning seriously.

But he did ask, "Who are numbers one and two on your speed dial?"

"Kira and the president."

"Good lad," Sir Robert told his son.

"So nice to see you again, Mr. McGill," Zack Garner said. "And you've brought someone with you, I see."

That was more than McGill had seen. He turned and looked to find Rockelle Bullard behind him, her high-heeled shoes held in her left hand. The better to sneak around. He was about to ask what she was doing, but a stern voice interrupted.

"Identify yourself, ma'am. Right now, please."

Augie Latz knew Holmes; every special agent working at the White House did.

But the big African-American woman was a stranger, and seeing her trailing Holmes and carrying her shoes was more than a little disturbing. Might be just an eccentric wedding guest or maybe it was someone sinister. Latz's hand went under his suit coat.

"Easy now," Rockelle said. "I'm Metro police."

"She is," McGill said.

Latz still had a concern, looking at her handbag.

"Are you armed, ma'am?"

"I was, but I turned my Glock over to SAC Crogher, at his request."

That took a bit of the edge off for Latz. "He'll confirm that?"

"Talk to him."

"You let him have your gun?" McGill asked, surprised.

"What, you didn't?" Rockelle asked.

McGill shook his head. Latz was sorry to see that. He'd heard that Holmes could be hard to work with, but this was his first personal experience with the man. The special agent had just confirmed with Crogher that the woman was who she said she was when Speaker Derek Geiger appeared in the doorway.

Christ, Latz thought, what next?

Most of the special agents he knew had absolutely nothing to do with politics; they got to see too much of it at sniffing distance to be fooled that there was anything majestic about the machinery of government. But the requirements of the job made it obligatory that they be able to recognize any politician with enough weight to make their lives miserable.

Even if the special agent hadn't recognized Geiger, Congressman Garner would have cleared things up for him.

"Mr. Speaker, how nice to see you here," he said. Then Garner added, "I don't recall seeing your name on the guest list, though."

A chill ran up Latz's spine when he heard that.

With a bleak smile, Geiger replied, "I was a last-minute addition. 'O lucky man.' That describes me, too, I suppose, to be in such company as this."

The vibe was getting edgier every second, the special agent thought. He saw the way Holmes was eyeing the speaker, like he was looking for where the man was carrying a gun. Latz was working up the nerve to ask him if he was armed when two more people arrived.

He recognized Margaret Sweeney. Her photo was part of Holmes' file.

The man with her was a stranger, though.

"Please identify yourself, sir." the special agent told Putnam Shady.

He did so and said, "I'm with her."

Sweetie said, "He's with me, and we were sent for by that guy over there, the one who's married to the president."

"Their presence was requested," McGill confirmed.

Latz felt an acute need for backup. Any move he might need to make with this crowd could backfire on him. He was about to get back to SAC Crogher when Elspeth Kendry appeared. He'd been introduced to Holmes' new security liaison shortly after she'd arrived at the White House. With a nod, they acknowledged each other, both feeling better about having a colleague present.

Before Latz could get back to asking for a show of hands for everyone who was armed, Zack Garner, at the window, said, "Oh, look, the president has taken her seat."

McGill winced.

"And, yes, here comes the bride, lovely Kira Fahey."

The president took Vice President Wyman's arm and was escorted down to the front row of seats. Wyman introduced the president to Kira's mother who was already seated. The president then greeted Sir Robert Reed. Welborn introduced his mother. Being forward enough to whisper into the president's ear, Welborn told her where McGill was. She nodded, but didn't look. The president shook hands with Francis Nguyen, and took her seat.

Mather Wyman walked back up the aisle to where Kira waited.

Welborn stepped to his mark in front of the wedding trellis. He turned to look at Kira and his breath caught in his throat. There were certainly other beautiful women in the world. Many of them. But Kira was so right for him the others might as well not have existed. Seeing her smile at him made him want to bounce in place … but he restrained himself.

As Kira began her stately march down the aisle accompanied by the vice president, someone released a covey of white doves. Instinctively, Welborn watched them rise into the sky. Doing so, he saw the group of faces in the room at the top of the vice president's mansion … and he looked once more at the irregular line on the drainpipe adjacent to the window up there.

It was starting to become recognizable. Another minute or two and Welborn was sure he would be able to identify what it was. But he and Kira would be looking at Francis Nguyen, away from the house. Unless …

Welborn stepped close to the pastor and whispered to him. Francis Nguyen thought about what he'd heard for a heartbeat and nodded. He was certainly not one to be dogmatic. When Kira arrived, Welborn shook Mather Wyman's hand and spoke quietly to his soon-to-be wife. She was also agreeable to his suggestion, thought it made perfect sense.

At the Fahey-Yates wedding, the bride and groom faced their guests. The celebrant also faced the gathering to start. Francis Nguyen told everyone, "We are here today to join Kira Fahey and Welborn Yates in the bonds of holy matrimony. The vows they will take form the basis of a happy and enduring marriage, and I invite all of you who are here with a spouse to join hands and reaffirm these vows for yourselves."

The president smiled. Jim wasn't sitting next to her, but he was always in her heart, and she knew she was always in his. She would renew their vows for the both of them.

Francis Nguyen turned to face the bride and groom.

Kira gazed at Welborn and he at her.

With just a corner of one eye cocked at the drainpipe.

Confronted with the prospect of a third divorce and a world of hurt, Derek Geiger was in no mood to see anyone get married. He had other matters to address, and with McGill and the others focused on the costume drama going on below it was a good time for him to make a brief departure. He'd need no more than a few minutes and then he'd slip —

Elspeth Kendry caught up with him in the hallway.

In a quiet voice, she asked, "Overcome by emotion, Mr. Speaker?"

Geiger didn't know the special agent, didn't like her attitude, but this was not the time to upbraid an underling.

He said, "I'm sure the ceremony will be lovely, but if I don't attend to a far less appealing obligation I won't be very good company for anyone."

"That obligation being?" Elspeth asked.

Geiger allowed himself a frown. He needed to back the woman off. He opened his coat and showed her the colostomy bag. "I need to empty and disinfect."

Elspeth took a step forward, not back. She leaned in. She sniffed.

She stood up and said, "Will you be returning to the room, sir?"

"If that's all right with you," Geiger said with frost in his voice.

The nerve of the woman ... but nerve was what her gender had in abundance.

"Yes, sir. That will be fine with me."

Returning to the viewing room, Elspeth took Latz aside. She whispered to him, "Geiger's up to something."

"Like what?"

"I don't know yet. He's coming back, but I want him to think I've lost interest. I'll be with Holmes. You shadow Geiger. Be subtle, but if you have to make a move don't worry about slamming him or anyone else to the floor."

Latz gave her a look. "Easy for you to say."

"No dispute there. But if you're not decisive ... well, my bet is Holmes is carrying and so is Margaret Sweeney. You want them to start shooting?"

Latz did not.

"You don't know me," Elspeth told him. "But I'll have your back, here and anywhere else you might need me."

"You'd better," Latz said.

In the bathroom down the hall, Geiger stared at the gun in his hand. Certainly looked like the real thing. A bit smaller than a standard semi-auto and the clip held only ten rounds. Nine millimeter rounds. Not a lot of stopping power. He wasn't really sure why he'd bought the gun. It had been more a flight of fancy than anything else. He was a powerful man; he ought to have an exotic weapon. Something more upscale than the kinds of guns every redneck with a pickup truck could buy.

Of course, not even the NRA had been able to bully Congress into making plastic guns legal. So he couldn't show it to anyone and say, "How's this for cool?"

He'd never thought he'd use it.

He hadn't thought his world would crumble either.

Then Patti Grant had left the Republican Party. Now, instead of throwing his weight behind a preferred candidate, there would be a mad scramble to fill the opening. A dozen or more candidates might vie for the nomination, and with all the mad hatters in the party these days there was no telling who might win. Quite likely it could be someone who didn't owe Derek Geiger a damn thing.

Worse than that, the bitch president, with her damn lobbying reform ideas and her revelation of his Super-K plan, had ruined his chances to create an empire of influence. He might easily lose the speakership; the majority leader in the House, that damn Brutus, was always looking for a way to knife him. If he were deposed, relegated to the back bench, it wouldn't be long before he was voted out of political life altogether.

Under other circumstances, he could have gone back to a plush private life, spent his old age in the comfort of Florida sunshine like millions of other old farts, without worrying if his 401K and Congressional pension would cover his monthly nut. He'd be affluent. Only now Harlo meant to bleed him dry.

Her mocking laughter still rang in his ears, telling him what her *famous* private eye had found, the fascinating story of how Derek Geiger liked to provide pretty women to men who could write big checks to the party, money that Geiger directed to favored candidates. In his mind, he had committed no crime. He'd never paid a woman to have sex with him. None of the men who had been granted sexual favors had paid for them.

The women who'd been given the money were told it was meant to help with the cost of living, tuition assistance and the like. Then they had been introduced to gentlemen of means at social occasions and nature had taken its course.

Except many of the young lovelies had police records for prostitution charges, and seated before a grand jury he was sure they would say they'd known exactly what had been expected of them in return for the money they received. The whores would be treated leniently in an attempt by the government to land the big fish — him.

He thought he might be able to win in court, but paying for defense lawyers would wipe out any money Harlo hadn't already clawed away from him. And how had her private eye been able to learn of Geiger's dirty little secret in a matter of days? Why he must have had the help of … the government? Certainly the executive branch. Most likely the White House chief of staff, Galia Mindel. And who could call upon that high and mighty harridan for help? James J. McGill, the most famous private eye in Washington.

And who had ratted out his Super-K plan to the president?

Putnam Shady.

And who had been a general do-gooder pain in his ass for years?

That old bastard who refused to die, Zack Garner.

All three of them were in the same room right this minute.

And he had a gun and ten rounds.

His original target had been only Putnam Shady.

But given his list of grievances and the sudden bleakness of his future, Geiger thought why think small. Why not go out in … okay, not a blaze of glory. But a burst of revenge.

Sure, why not? Politics was the art of the possible.

McGill's eyes, while not as keen as those belonging to Welborn Yates, had no problem taking in the details of the wedding three floors down and a hundred feet away. In fact, the elevation and the distance gave him a perspective on the event that he preferred to one barely more than an arm's length away. Here, he got to see the whole setting and everyone present.

Watching Vice President Wyman walk Kira down the aisle made him think of Abbie. She'd only just started college, but he knew that time would pass quickly, at least for him. Grad school would come next, but he could imagine Abbie getting married before she finished her formal education. Certainly, some smart young man would propose the idea of marriage to her before then, and McGill could well be the one walking his daughter to an altar.

There would be more time before he'd play the same role for Caitie, and he couldn't begin to guess who would capture her heart. Someone exceptional to be sure. There might be no traditional trip down the aisle for Caitie. The ceremony might be on pay-per-view TV.

Taking a deep breath and letting it go silently, he dared to think that Kenny might someday know the joy that Welborn was experiencing right now. Watching the woman he loved walking toward him, eager to join him in a lifetime of —

Before McGill could complete the thought, Galia Mindel's words came back to him.

"The president told me she would resign the presidency if necessary to help Kenny."

Patti was going to do it. *She* would be Kenny's donor. She wouldn't speak of resigning if she knew there were any chance that Clare might be Kenny's donor. Clare had told him she'd privately asked Dr. Jones to be the donor for the other child she could help. Patti must have spoken to the doctor in confidence as well. Given what each woman had asked, there could be no reason for the doctor to object.

But he'd bet both requests were held confidential.

He was the only other one who knew both halves of the equation.

McGill glanced at Zack Garner, sitting to his immediate left. He knew from experience that people could die with their eyes open. Any big city cop who'd been on the job a few years had seen that. There was still a glow of life in Garner's eyes, but the wattage was low. He could go at any time, right there in a room full of people. No one would know when death had occurred if they weren't looking right at him at the moment of passing.

If he was watching, McGill wondered if he'd be able to see Garner's soul depart.

That thought made him think of Kenny again. The possibility his son might die.

He turned back to look at the wedding, his eyes filling with tears.

Pastor Francis Nguyen turned to face Welborn Yates and asked, "Do you take this woman to be your wife, to love her in sickness and health, for better or worse, to cherish her and her alone for all the days and nights of your life?"

Welborn slid the gold wedding band on Kira's finger and said, "I do."

And with their vows exchanged, realization came to Welborn.

He knew what the object projecting from the drainpipe was. He looked up and confirmed it was the handle of a gun. He placed his left hand against his pant leg, thumb raised, index finger extended: Gun. His father couldn't miss the sign.

Welborn had to be reminded to kiss the bride.

McGill saw Welborn make a gesture, his pale hand contrasting with the dark blue of his dress uniform pant leg. It looked to McGill as if … he wiped the tears from his eyes. He blinked clear his vision the best he could. At first, he thought Welborn was making a fist. But … his top finger and thumb stood out from the rest of the hand.

He was replicating the hammer and barrel of a gun. And then the young Air Force captain turned his head and seemed to be looking right up at him.

Welborn was giving a warning about a gun, but what gun? Where was the gun?

He felt his cell phone vibrate. Answering it, Sir Robert answered both of his questions.

Before anything else could be said, Speaker Derek Geiger said loud enough for everyone in the room to hear, "I'll thank you to end your call, Mister McGill. Right now."

McGill, along with everyone else, turned to see Geiger standing behind Putnam Shady, holding a gun to the lobbyist's head.

GWU Hospital, Operating Room

Dr. Jones leaned over Clare Tracy and from behind her surgical mask asked, "Are you ready, Ms. Tracy?"

"I am," Clare said.

Sounded almost as if she'd spoken a vow, Clare thought.

If it wasn't as solemn as all that, it was at least a promise kept.

She had said she would do her best to save a child's life and here she was honoring her word. True, the child wasn't Kenny McGill, but Annabelle Chalmers was as precious to her parents as Kenny was to his. Dr. Jones had shown Clare a picture of

Annabelle shortly after Clare had arrived at the hospital. The photo had been taken before the leukemia had hit Annabelle hard. The little girl wasn't classically pretty but she had bright, mischievous eyes and a cockeyed smile that was endearing. The personality she displayed wasn't all that different from Kenny McGill's, the little Clare had seen of it.

Dr. Jones had told her, "Right now you're an anonymous donor to the Chalmers family, an angel without a name. Would you like to let them know your identity?"

"Let's see how it goes with Annabelle," Clare had said.

"As you like."

That was the one luxury of the choice Clare had made. If things didn't work out, she wouldn't have to take part in the grieving. If she had failed Kenny, there would have been no way to remain apart from it. She would have felt she had failed Jim again. The fear of that happening had played no small part in her decision.

Now, Dr. Jones said, "We'll start with the premedication, Ms. Tracy. As I mentioned to you earlier, the anesthesiologist will be using melatonin."

A small smile formed on Clare's lips. She'd been comforted when she heard that melatonin would be used. She took three milligrams every night as a sleep aid. Dr. Jones said she liked melatonin because it didn't impair psychomotor skills, recovery was more rapid, and there was a reduced incidence of post-op agitation and delirium.

Sounded good to Clare. She was feeling mellowed out already.

She said a silent prayer for Annabelle, Kenny and herself.

For Patti Grant, too. She'd also be slipping into unconsciousness soon.

Lord, let us all awake to a better world, Clare beseeched.

If nothing else, she wanted the opportunity to be Jim's friend again.

Clare Tracy moved without incident into the first of the four possible stages of anesthesia, induction. She was still able to speak at this time, but didn't. Stage two was known as the excitement stage. Following the patient's loss of consciousness, it was possible for respiration and heartbeat to become irregular. It was also possible for the patient to experience spastic body movements, holding of breath and vomiting. If there were a combination of these reactions the patient's airway could be compromised.

Without immediate, effective intervention, death might ensue.

Rapidly acting drugs were used to minimize the patient's time in stage two.

Clare passed through it without incident.

Stage three was known as surgical anesthesia. Muscles relaxed and the patient's breathing became regular. Eye movement slowed and then stopped. Surgery could begin, and it did. Clare's bone marrow was obtained and would be infused into Annabelle Chalmers. Nothing was guaranteed, but with a six-point match on the bone marrow the medical team was hopeful.

Kenny McGill was now dependent on his stepmother, the president, for his bone marrow transplant.

Number One Observatory Circle

Celsus Crogher saw Welborn Yates form a gun with his hand and had no doubt it meant trouble. Someone, somewhere nearby had a gun and meant to use it. The signal was given just after the bride and groom had each said "I do," and the pastor had given his final blessing and introduced the young couple to the world.

Nice timing, but Crogher would have intervened in the middle of the ceremony, if necessary, to protect Holly G. As he moved toward the president, Crogher saw Sir Robert Reed make a hurried phone call … He'd been the guy Yates had alerted. He was the one who knew what was happening.

The president saw SAC Crogher rushing toward her and got to her feet.

"Madam President," Crogher said, "stand close behind me and be prepared for me to take you to the ground."

At a moment like this, Patricia Darden Grant knew she was the one who had to follow orders. She snugged up close to Crogher. Waited to see what happened next.

Sir Robert didn't wait to be questioned. He discreetly gestured to the window at the top, right of the vice president's house and told Crogher, "Mr. McGill, Congressman Garner and others are in that room. I called to let Mr. McGill know that a gun has been wedged between the building and the drainpipe just outside the window. Immediately after I delivered my message, I heard a voice I believe was Speaker Geiger's tell Mr. McGill to end his call. Apparently, he did so."

As Welborn and Kira approached the president, she leaned to the side to get a better look at the window.

Crogher moved in front of her again. He told Holly G., "We're getting you out of here momentarily, Madam President."

"Do you have someone with my husband, Celsus?" she asked.

Welborn said, "Elspeth Kendry went upstairs to be with him."

"And I have Special Agent Latz with Garner," Crogher said.

"So two of your people are in the room and Derek Geiger still managed to coerce Jim into ending his phone call?"

SAC Crogher gave Holly G. a look that would have been grounds for dismissal under any other circumstances. If people had been following his security protocols ... He said, "We have to leave right now, Madam President, and these grounds will have to be cleared."

The president looked at her watch. "I have to get to the hospital. I promised Dr. Jones I would be on time. Kenny McGill is waiting for me."

Crogher nodded. "I'll oversee the situation here from Thing One."

The president reasserted control and shook her head.

"You'll run the show from here, Celsus. Send as many special agents with me as you like, but you're the one I'm trusting to make this situation turn out right."

She beckoned to Vice President Wyman who was standing

nearby.

"Mather, the moment I leave the grounds, you have the final word about what happens here and anything that follows, until I resume my office. I'm sorry to leave you in circumstances like this, but I trust your judgment completely."

"Thank you, Madam President. I won't let you down."

Turning to Crogher she said, "Mather Wyman is the acting president, you will follow his every order as closely as you do mine."

SAC Crogher nodded.

The last people the president addressed were the bride and groom. "Please accept my heartfelt congratulations and my regrets that your wedding day has been ... made memorable in ways you'd never have chosen. After everything has settled down, we'll have a party at the White House for everyone you care to invite, and Captain Yates?"

"Yes, Madam President," Welborn said.

"You and your wife are to leave for your honeymoon immediately. You will make sure you and Kira enjoy every moment of it. You will do your best to put everything that's happening here out of your mind. That's a presidential order, Captain. Do you understand?"

Welborn said, "Yes, ma'am. Permission to speak, ma'am?"

The president nodded.

"It would help me to follow your orders if —"

Patti put a hand on his arm and said, "We'll let you know what happens, Welborn."

Captain Yates snapped off a perfect salute. Kira kissed the president goodbye. Following the president's orders, they left on the double.

Moments later Patti was sitting alone in the back of Thing One on her way to George Washington University Hospital, all other traffic being stopped so that her motorcade might make the greatest possible speed.

She had a young man's life to save.

She had to pray Jim would live to see Kenny's recovery.

Number One Observatory Circle

Congressman Zachary Garner leaned over slowly and opened the window in front of him and then glanced at McGill. Speaker Derek Geiger saw the window go up and said, "If you're planning to jump, Zack, by all means go right ahead."

Garner grinned and with McGill's help got to his feet. He stood straight and towered above the speaker. "You always were a horse's ass, Derek. Mr. Shady isn't the one you should be pointing your gun at. I'm the guy who has been killing all your moneymen."

Garner took a step forward and McGill eased behind him. The congressman was big enough to block him from Geiger's view. But Elspeth Kendry had her eyes on McGill. He saw her, too, and held up a cautionary hand: do nothing. Not yet. McGill stuck his head out the window. Saw the gun right where Sir Robert said it would be.

McGill slipped it out of its hiding place. The weapon was slim and light, bore the name KelTec. The short magazine, he saw, couldn't hold many rounds. Small rounds at that, nine millimeter at best. He stuck the weapon in his coat pocket; it made no perceptible bulge.

Geiger finally noticed McGill wasn't visible.

"Mr. McGill, are you actually taking shelter behind a dying old man?"

The president's henchman stepped into view.

He saw Sweetie was looking for an angle of attack on Geiger. But she was on the wrong side of Putnam to make a direct grab for the gun. She'd never be able to deflect the barrel before Geiger could put a bullet into the lobbyist's head.

He gave Sweetie a tiny shake of his head.

Rockelle Bullard, standing just beyond Sweetie, had said she'd already turned her Glock over to Celsus. But McGill saw her slip a nail file out of her handbag. If things got to the point of using an improvised weapon, he couldn't begrudge her that.

McGill told Geiger, "You take shelter where you find it. A pol like you has to know that."

The speaker smiled. "You'd like me to point my gun at you, right? Give our friends from the Secret Service here the chance to shoot me."

"Yeah, that sounds good," McGill agreed. "Go for it."

Geiger said, "I don't think so. Being a private investigator, I suppose you carry your own gun. Did you bring it to the wedding?"

McGill opened his coat. His own weapon, a Beretta, was in a holster on his hip.

"And your associate, Ms. Sweeney, is she also armed?" Geiger took a quick look at Sweetie.

She nodded. She didn't want to shoot Geiger. She wanted to throttle him.

"The two of you then, please put your weapons on the floor, very carefully, and kick them toward the door."

McGill and Sweetie followed orders.

Geiger said, "And now the lady and gentleman of the Secret Service. I really would like to be the only one here with a gun in my hand."

Elspeth Kendry said, "Forget it."

Augie Latz nodded in agreement.

Geiger thumbed back the hammer of his gun.

Putnam Shady held his breath.

But Zack Garner laughed, a surprisingly strong guffaw.

"Something funny, Zack?" Geiger asked, his face tight. "You don't think I'll do it?"

Garner said, "Oh, I suppose you might, Derek. I was just thinking maybe I'd started a trend here in the capital, officeholders shooting lobbyists who displease them. I've bagged four myself. I even tried to shoot Mr. Shady before he saw the light. Now, if you shoot him, you'll be following in my footsteps."

But that wasn't the thought that seized Geiger's mind.

"You said you shot *four* lobbyists?" he asked.

Garner said, "That's right. There was Mr. Torkelson, Mr. Waller, Mr. Benjamin and, oh yes, your old friend Brad Attles."

The dying congressman authored a ghastly smile. "That threw a monkey wrench into your Super-K plan, didn't it?"

Derek Geiger knew he had no hope of leaving the room alive.

Now, hearing from Garner that he'd been the one to murder Brad, Geiger knew just how to end the standoff. He'd get at least two of his targets: Putnam Shady and James J. McGill. He'd shoot that bastard Garner, too, if the Secret Service people didn't react in time and get him first. Even if they did, Garner probably wouldn't outlive the day.

So, Shady first as long as he was right there.

Elspeth Kendry and Augie Latz saw in Geiger's eyes what was coming.

"Now!" Elspeth yelled.

The command was meant for Latz and her. But Putnam, McGill and Sweetie took it to heart as well. Putnam let his legs turn to Jell-O and collapsed. Geiger was unable to support Putnam's weight and the lobbyist fell to the floor, leaving the speaker to deal with four angry people hurling themselves at him.

He did what he could, extended the gun at McGill and pulled the trigger.

But Augie Latz got in the way and took the bullet, crashing into Geiger just as he pulled the trigger a second time and his plastic gun, a weapon not known for its reliability, exploded in his hand. Then he was driven to the floor under the weight of four bodies.

A razor sharp shard of plastic severed the speaker's carotid artery. He would have bled to death in short order, if the combined weight of his attackers hadn't slammed his head to the floor and severed his cervical spine first.

Special Agent Latz's eyes went wide and he gasped for breath. Geiger's first shot had penetrated the agent's body under his left arm, and besides whatever other damage it had done inside his chest cavity, it had apparently hit at least one lung. The special agent had also taken a face full of plastic shrapnel when Geiger's gun had exploded.

McGill, Sweetie and Elspeth pulled themselves off Geiger and each other.

"Elspeth, call for my EMT team and ambulance," McGill told her.

Whenever McGill and Patti went to any public event, they were always accompanied by his and hers ambulances and emergency medical teams. Patti always had a surgeon on hand, too; McGill had to make do with med techs. What Latz needed most was some kind of professional help fast.

McGill skittered on his hands and knees over to Latz to see if there was any immediate help he might offer.

Then, like a messenger from the god of war, Celsus Crogher burst into the room with his Uzi leveled, but no one to shoot.

McGill asked "You've got medical people with you?"

"Right behind me," Crogher said. He yelled for them, and then the SAC and Elspeth joined McGill in kneeling over the fallen agent. Each of them put a hand on Latz. All of them urged him to hold on.

They moved clear as soon as the EMTs arrived.

McGill got to his feet and turned to see Garner was down, too, but not bleeding. Rockelle Bullard knelt beside him. Garner's time was at hand. McGill took up station on the other side of the congressman.

Garner saw McGill and smiled.

"Almost done," he said.

Rockelle said, "Congressman, just in case you got any Lazarus in you, I have to inform you of your rights. You don't have to say a word to anybody."

Garner looked at her and managed to laugh.

"Where I'm going, nobody gets off on technicalities." He put his eyes back on McGill. "You found the gun?"

"It's in my pocket."

"It's Erik Torkelson's gun. The one I used to kill him."

Rockelle looked at McGill. He handed the gun to her.

"That and my dying declaration should do it, don't you think?"

To establish his guilt, he meant. In case that wasn't enough, he told them where they could find the other murder weapons.

McGill was now sure Zachary Garner hadn't acted alone. He hadn't had the physical strength to commit all four killings. Probably not any of them. McGill would bet that if anyone thought to check into it the forensics would show the lobbyists had been shot by someone shorter than Garner's six-foot-five. But McGill was not about to raise the notion of accomplices in front of the lieutenant from Metro homicide.

She likely thought Putnam Shady was still criminally liable in some way.

McGill looked over to where Sweetie had revived Putnam.

Physically, he seemed no worse for the wear.

Emotional scars would manifest soon.

The emergency medical team was wheeling Latz out of the room.

McGill was startled when a hand went around his wrist. He looked back and saw Garner had taken hold of him, and had one more thing to say.

"If there's a life after this one, I'm going to get whacked hard. But before I do, nothing's going to stop me from visiting Kenny. I'll tell him to be …"

Garner died before he could finish.

McGill and Rockelle looked at each other.

"Be what?" she asked McGill.

Strong, McGill thought. Brave. Indomitable.

But he said, "Good as new."

GWU Hospital

Special Agent August Latz was in surgery. One lung had been punctured. The liver had been damaged and the small intestine had been perforated. Of lesser but not inconsequential seriousness, the upper right eyelid was partially severed and the septum of the nose had been displaced. The damage to the face was cleansed, disinfected and left to be treated until the critical issues were resolved.

A team of trauma surgeons and nurses worked on the special agent with intense concentration and all due speed. They were at the top of their profession and working in Washington D.C. they got plenty of opportunities to hone their skills. So much so that after they finished a procedure they shared their opinions of what they had thought their chances of success had been going in.

The odds on Augie Latz were fifty-fifty.

Reagan National Airport

Welborn and Kira sat in a booth at the airport bar, an untouched glass of champagne in front of each of them. They were both trying to think of a toast that was appropriate to the moment. The sentiment was not quick in arriving. Sometimes even presidential orders couldn't carry the day.

They were booked to New York and from there to Madrid and Barcelona.

Kira had said she would have liked to sleep all the way to Sir Robert's villa.

"And wake up from a bad dream?" Welborn asked.

"Wake up and hope there's good news," Kira said.

Welborn's cell phone sounded. If he'd been following the spirit of the order the president had given him, he would have turned it off. But he answered immediately.

"Captain Welborn Yates," he said.

"We speak again, Captain," a female voice said

"Who is this, please?" he asked, and Kira leaned in to listen.

"Chana Lachlan. I asked you to warn Jim McGill about World-Wide news going after him, remember?"

"Quite clearly, Ms. Lachlan. How may I help you now?"

"Please tell Jim that I've heard WorldWide has a reporter inside the walls at Salvation's Path Church. Communications might be blocked for the moment, but at some point the president can expect unfavorable press coming out of there. The White House should be ready for that. I thought the president or Galia Mindel should know."

"Thank you, Ms. Lachlan. I'll let Mr. McGill know, and I'm sure everyone will be very appreciative. Goodbye."

Welborn clicked off.

Having heard every word, Kira asked, "Are you going to call?"

Welborn shook his head. "Not now, not on a cell phone. Too many ears listening in. I'm sorry Ms. Lachlan's call reached me on my cell."

"But don't you think—"

"I do. But both Mr. McGill and the president have more than enough on their minds right now. When we get to Madrid, we'll go to the embassy and send a cable."

"Then we'll go to Barcelona and pretend the rest of the world doesn't exist?"

Welborn kissed his bride. "We'll do our very best — for the next two weeks."

Salvation's Path Church, Richmond, Virginia

Nobody saw who did it. There was no video of it being done. Federal, state and local cops had kept onlookers at bay, so the suspicion was the deed had been done by a construction worker sympathetic to those now being held in the church grounds cum prison. On one of the gray slabs comprising the wall a red graffito had been sprayed.

FREE B.G.

Within twenty-four hours, signs demanding freedom for Burke Godfrey would appear from coast to coast and border to border.

GWU Hospital

Carolyn met a disheveled McGill in the lounge at the end of the hallway. Lars stood behind her with a hand on each of her shoulders. Both of them were crying, looking as if the worst had already happened.

"Oh, God," McGill said. "Please don't tell me …"

Carolyn stepped forward and put her arms around her ex-husband's waist; Lars put an arm around McGill's shoulders. McGill still felt as if he might keel over. Then Carolyn sent a jolt of electricity up his spine.

"Jim, Doctor Nicolaides was just here looking for you. It's Patti."

Patti? McGill pulled free, stepped back and looked at them.

"What about Patti?" he asked through a constricted throat.

"There was a problem with the anesthesia. Something about an irregular heartbeat."

"She's not —"

Lars said, "No, no. The president is alive. Doctor Nicolaides said the immediate crisis has passed, but the medical team has to assess …"

"Whether they can risk the president's life by going ahead with the procedure," Carolyn finished.

McGill saw the dilemma. "But Kenny's had that big blast of chemo. His own bone marrow has to be wiped out by now. He's got to have the donor marrow."

Carolyn nodded. Then she began to sob, turned and buried her face in Lars' chest.

In a monotone, McGill asked Lars, "Where are Abbie and Caitie?"

"In the hospital chapel. I … I think we'll join them."

McGill nodded. He collapsed onto a nearby seat. Covered his face with his hands.

A moment later he heard a familiar voice.

"Jim," he said, "we need you now."

McGill looked up and saw Nick, the White House physician.

Again, he feared the worst.

But Nick said, "A very important decision has to be made, and quickly. You are the only one who can make it."

McGill got to his feet.

Coming in Summer 2012

The Last Ballot Cast, the fourth Jim McGill novel

Jim McGill faces the most excruciating decision of his life, one that might cost the life of his wife, his son or both. Making matters worse, Damon Todd, the mad psychiatrist whom McGill shipped off to the CIA for safekeeping in *The President's Henchman*, has escaped and has vengeance in mind.

The country, in a presidential election year, will also be making a fateful decision. The election will be determined by the electoral votes of one small state, and possibly the last ballot cast.

This is the book Jim McGill fans can't miss. Questions of life and death will be answered. Political battles will be decided. There will be only one issue left to be determined ... and you'll need to read the book to find out what it is.

If you'd like to be added to my email list and receive updates on forthcoming books and learn of opportunities to receive free copies of e-books, please visit *www.josephflynn.com/contactme.html.*

ABOUT THE AUTHOR

Joseph Flynn is a Chicagoan, born and raised, currently living in central Illinois with his wife and daughter. He is the author of *The Concrete Inquisition, Digger, The Next President, Hot Type, Farewell Performance, Gasoline Texas, The President's Henchman, The Hangman's Companion, Round Robin, Blood Street Punx, Nailed, One False Step, Still Coming, The K Street Killer*. More titles will appear in the near future.